The Healing Nightfall

SARA FRASER

WARNER BOOKS

A *Warner* Book

First published in Great Britain in 1992
by Macdonald
Published by Warner in 1993
This edition published by Warner in 1998

A CIP catalogue for this book
is available from the British Library.

ISBN 0 7515 0149 2

Printed in England by Clays Ltd, St Ives plc

Warner Books
A Division of
Little, Brown and Company (UK)
Brettenham House
Lancaster Place
London WC2E 7EN

Introduction

In the year of 1849 the young, tragically widowed, Grainne
Shonley sought to rebuild her life. Her own beauty and courage
proved to be her curse. As she passed through the great houses
of the rich and mighty, and the savage, fetid slums where vice
and crime raged rampant, that curse brought upon her a cruel
and a desperate struggle for her very survival.

Chapter One

**The West of Ireland
November 1848**

The rain had been falling for so long without cessation that even the vast expanses of the bogs could absorb no more and black sheets of water were slowly spreading across their surfaces. Mist blanketed the bleak undulating country cutting visibility down to a few score yards and imparting an unearthly forbidding aspect to the ruined and abandoned cabins that dotted the landscape.

'God blast this bloody country!' Corporal Tommy Hunt of the Eighth Royal Irish Hussars regarded the desolation surrounding him with jaundiced eyes. His voluminous black cloak was saturated and his blue uniform soaked through to the skin, while from his brown furred busby streams of rainwater ran down his face and neck. Riding in single file behind him his three comrades were in a similar state of cold, drenched misery, and one of them grumbled aloud.

'Jasus Christ! I've got me bellyful o' this!'

'And me as well, matey!' another man voiced heartfelt agreement, and asked the NCO, 'Can't we turn back now, Tommy?'

'No we fokkin' well can't turn back,' the corporal shouted in sudden temper. 'Our orders are to patrol as far as Leap, and that's what we're going to do, so just hold your fokkin' tongue!'

The men stared sullenly and muttered beneath their breaths, but continued to follow. Some yards further on the road rose sharply and curved and Corporal Hunt's mount slipped and slithered and he cursed and savagely drove it upwards and over the apex of the small hill. Then abruptly he reined in and stared down the narrow valley ahead.

'What the fokk is that?'

'What's what?' Trooper Miles reined in beside him.

'That there?' The NCO pointed along the length of the track, and the trooper screwed up his eyes against the rain and peered hard.

'It looks to be a woman, Tommy.'

The other two troopers had now joined them, and the youngest and keenest sighted of them confirmed, 'It is that,' then questioned in puzzlement: 'But what's a bloody woman doing out here on her own, and what's she pulling that bloody cart for?'

'We'll soon find out, my buck,' the corporal said grimly, and kicked his horse into a fast trot towards the oncoming figure.

Harnessed between the shafts of the small, flat bodied, four wheeled cart, Grainne Shonley struggled painfully to drag it along the rutted track. Bending low and head down, her eyes fixed on the muddy ground, she fought to keep the wheels turning, her laboured breathing rasping in her throat and the muscles of her legs and shoulders burning and aching agonisingly. Trapped in her torment she was oblivious to the onset of the cavalrymen until they were scant yards from her, and then she heard the thudding and splashing of the hooves and she looked up in sudden alarm.

The horses skidded to a halt, the flailing stamping hooves splashing mud onto her long skirts, forcing her to come to a standstill, and she groaned inwardly as the cart's leading wheel slowly slid into the deep rut.

For some moments the soldiers sat staring down at her, their tough hard faces mirroring their puzzlement as they took in the long narrow box that rested on the cart's platform. The woman's shawl was pulled well forward to shield her face from the driving rain, and the Corporal ordered roughly, 'Pull your shawl back and let's see your face.'

Grainne did as she was bid and she saw the sudden change in the men's expressions.

8

'Jasus! She's a good looker!' one of the troopers exclaimed appreciatively.

Corporal Hunt stared at the young woman, noting the thin features, the lucent green eyes, and the black hair, and slowly nodded. 'She is that.' Then he asked, 'What's your name, girl?'

Quick resentment at the arrogance in his attitude rose up in Grainne but she knew that to show that resentment would be a mistake. In this tragic country racked by famine and rebellion, the military wielded the power. 'My name is Grainne Shonley,' she told him quietly.

'What's in that?' The corporal indicated the long narrow wooden box.

'My husband.'

The troopers' shock showed on their faces, and the corporal exclaimed, 'What are youse telling me, girl?'

'That that box is my husband's coffin. I've brought him back home to bury him here where he belongs.'

'Where did you bring him from?' the corporal asked curiously.

'From Liverpool.'

'And you've dragged this cart from where?'

'From Cork.'

'Jasus!' the man gusted. 'That's near on forty miles. How long has it taken ye?'

'This is my fourth day on the road.'

The corporal shook his head as if mystified, then asked, 'Have ye family hereabouts, wee girl?'

Grainne's thin face showed her uncertainty. 'My mother was living close to Skibereen a few months back, but until I reach her cabin I don't know if I'll find her there or not.'

She refrained from voicing the possible reasons for her mother not being at the cabin. Thousands were dying from starvation and disease, and thousands more were fleeing the land, wandering across the country in a desperate search for food and shelter.

For a few moments the corporal stared at Grainne, his features mirroring his own uncertainty. Then he frowned as if in self-disgust, and told her curtly, 'Listen wee girl, I'm not disbelieving of ye, but our orders are to search the baggage of anybody we come across.'

Bitter amusement flashed in the girl's eyes, and the man saw that and his own disgust burst from him in angry speech.

'Jasus Christ, girl, it's not me that gives these orders, I'm only the poor bowsy that has to carry 'um out! Coffins is a favourite way that the rebels has of moving muskets and powder and ball.'

'The rebellion is over and done with,' she riposted.

'Tell that to the land agents that are getting shot and murdered week after week, girl,' he retorted sharply.

She shrugged her slender shoulders and appeared uncaring as she told him quietly, 'If you must open the coffin then do so, it can't bring any harm to my husband now. But I should warn you that he died from burns, and the body will be in a sorry state.'

All four men looked at her with curious eyes, marvelling at her apparent unconcern, and as if she sensed what they were thinking she said calmly, 'I've done my grieving for my husband. That's not him lying in that coffin but only his poor remains.'

The corporal nodded brusquely. 'We'll not detain you long, girl.'

From his saddlebag he produced a short-handled hammer and cold chisel and handed them to the youngest trooper. 'Get it opened, Murphy.'

The youngster dismounted and within a very short space of time had levered the lid from the long narrow box. As he peered down into its interior he grimaced and held his nose against the foul stench that the sheet-swathed corpse emitted.

'Step aside,' the corporal ordered and kneed his mount to the side of the cart. He glanced briefly over into the coffin and told the young cavalryman, 'All right, get the lid back on and fix it firm.'

While this had been taking place Grainne had stood with her back to the cart, staring out across the mist-wreathed countryside, her face expressionless.

'Where is it exactly that you're heading, did you say?' Corporal Hunt questioned.

'I'm going into Skibereen first to arrange for my husband's burial. Then I'll go and seek my mother.'

'What's her name?'

'Mrs Theresa MacDermott, she lives up alongside Mr Donleavy's farm on the Drimoleague road.'

Corporal Hunt frowned thoughtfully, then shook his head, and told her with some sympathy, 'I don't want to alarm ye, wee girl, but don't go building your hopes that ye'll find her there now. There was a bad outbreak o' fever along that road just the last month and pretty near everyone that lived around there up and ran from it, and the ones that didn't run died.'

The girl's thin pale face was sad and resigned. 'I'll go and see anyway,' she murmured quietly. 'Can I leave now?'

The man nodded, and told her, 'I'm sorry we had to open the coffin, but orders is orders.'

Grainne positioned herself between the shafts of the cart once more and strained to move it, but the front wheel held fast in the deep rut and although she exerted all her strength the cart remained at a standstill.

The men exchanged glances, and abruptly the corporal ordered, 'Murphy, Miles, pull this cart into Skibereen for this wee girl. Me and Powell will go on along towards Leap village. When ye've taken it where she wants it to go, then come along this road and we'll meet up.'

He waved aside Grainne's thanks and went trotting on leaving the two troopers with her.

Chapter Two

Doctor Phillip Donovan's thin careworn features mirrored his absolute weariness of mind and body as he regarded the young priest sitting facing him on the other side of the dull-burning peat fire in his study. Father Murray had recently graduated from the famous Maynooth Seminary and his fresh young face glowing with robust good health caused the doctor to reflect sadly on his own prematurely-aged appearance.

Now, however, the young priest's face was troubled as he discussed the present state of his country with his host. It was the third winter of famine; once again the potato crops had failed and the sufferings of the people had intensified to an unendurable degree. Cabins, farms, entire villages and townships were being left abandoned and empty of life as those who could raise money emigrated in ever increasing numbers, and the destitute were forcibly evicted from their homes for non-payment of rent, while death reaped ever richer harvests among the starving and dispossessed hordes that roamed the land. All over Ireland trade was almost at a standstill, and the cruellest irony of all was that although markets were reported as being glutted with all types of provisions at very low prices, the masses of starving paupers lacked even the few pence necessary to buy those provisions, and people died of hunger within sight of plenty.

As the two men talked over this tragic state of affairs their conversation touched on the abortive rebellion of the 'Young Irelanders' which had taken place in the month of July earlier that year; a rebellion which had proved almost farcical in its ineptness and miserable failure.

'I'm bound to confess that I consider that those idjits of rebels only worsened our unhappy situation, Doctor Donovan,' Father Murray stated emphatically. 'For it lost us much sympathy over in England, and people there who were willing to try and help our poor suffering country turned against us as a result of it. Who is to help us now?'

'At the risk of offending you, Father, I feel constrained to say that it's my belief that only God himself could help us now, and He hasn't displayed much readiness to do so as of yet, has He?' the doctor said dryly.

Before the priest could reply the elderly housekeeper came bustling into the room and informed Doctor Donovan, 'There's a young woman at the front door who says she wants to see you, doctor.'

He frowned unhappily, and nodded to his housekeeper. 'Very well, Bridie. Tell her I'll be out directly.' He grimaced apologetically at his guest. 'I'm not able to turn the poor souls away, Father, although there's little or nothing I can do for any of them, except sometimes to ease their passing. Would you stay until I find out what she wants of me?'

'Surely I will.' The young priest was not anxious to leave the warm fireside for the cold wet trudge back to his own cottage.

By now dusk had fallen and Phillip Donovan peered short-sightedly at the shadowed figure standing on the flight of stone steps that led up to his front door.

'Who is it, and what do you want of me?' he questioned.

'It's Grainne Shonley, Doctor Donovan, who was Grainne MacDermott.'

The man started visibly in surprise as he heard the soft voice. 'Young Grainne?' he ejaculated. 'Young Grainne Shonley? What in Heaven's name do you here, child? You are supposed to be on the high seas to America.' He stepped out from the doorway towards her. 'Are you alone, child? Where's Con?'

She pointed behind her to the roadway, and the doctor peered through the murk at the cart with its burden, and understanding flooded through him. 'You poor creature,' he breathed pityingly, and taking her by the arm gently pulled her with him into the house.

'Come into the warm, child.' He raised his voice and called to his housekeeper, 'Bridie, bring a dish of tay to the study.'

13

Grainne allowed herself to be led into the room and seated at the fireside.

'This is Father Murray, Grainne. He's come to the parish recently to replace Father Mulcahy. Of course, you'll not be knowing that Father Mulcahy died, will you, child? The fever took him, God save his soul.'

Grainne acknowledged the priest's greeting, and thankfully spread her hands to the fire, feeling its warmth slowly begin to penetrate her saturated clothing and clammy chilled flesh.

The doctor forbore from questioning her until she had drunk the hot tea, and then insisted that she take a large dram of brandy. The fiery liquid caused her to cough, but still it restored a spark of vitality to her jaded spirits. After she had rested a while she began to relate what had happened to her during the past months.

She and her young newly-wed husband, Conrad Shonley, had joined the desperate flight from Ireland, planning to emigrate to America. In company with two friends, Denis Callaghan and Maggie Nolan, they had sailed to Liverpool. Shortly after their arrival in that wicked, bustling city, Maggie Nolan had died of fever and the heartbroken Denis Callaghan had returned to Ireland with her body. Grainne had heard nothing of him since.

She and her husband had eventually taken passage on an emigrant ship bound for New York, but shortly after sailing the vessel had caught fire and sunk, and hundreds of her crew and passengers had been lost. Grainne had been saved by some of the crew members, and had eventually made her way back to Liverpool seeking for her husband, not knowing if he were alive or dead. There were only a few survivors who had returned to the city, and many of these were badly injured. Grainne had found a terribly burned and disfigured man in the infirmary, and although his injuries were such that no real proof of identification could be obtained she had convinced herself that this was her husband, Conrad Shonley. She had cared for the man until his death, and now that he was dead, had brought his body back for burial in his beloved homeland.

Grainne told her story without any visible signs of emotion, relating only the bare outlines of what she had endured. She

14

did not tell them of the shameful bitter degredations she had undergone in Liverpool to enable her to survive and to ensure that the man she believed to be her husband received good treatment and care in that harsh, ruthless, cruel environment.

When she had done and had fallen silent the young priest offered, 'If you wish it, Mrs Shonley, I'll conduct the burial mass tomorrow.'

She thanked him with a brief bleak smile, then gravely asked the doctor, 'Do you have news of my mother, Doctor Donovan, or of Denis Callaghan?'

Donovan frowned unhappily, then sighed and told her, 'I'm sorry to say that I can only add to your grief, Grainne. Your mother and her children have left this district, together with that man she was living with, and God only knows where they might be now. You've but little chance of tracing them with the country being in its present state, I fear. And poor Denis is dead. He buried Maggie and within two weeks was gone himself. He was a terrible drunkard and wastrel to be sure, but he truly loved Maggie Nolan, and the heart was taken from him when he lost her. I believe that death came to him as a mercy.'

With sad eyes Phillip Donovan shook his head and said softly, 'You have returned to a country of the dead and the dying, child. I would not advise anyone to remain here for a moment longer than they are forced to. The situation now is worse than it has ever been, and I fear will deteriorate even further before there is a change for the better.'

Grainne kept her eyes fixed on the smouldering peat fire. She felt the sting of brimming tears, but swallowed hard and fought to keep control of her feelings. To give way to her emotions was a weakness that she would not readily allow herself to indulge in.

The young priest regarded her curiously, and then coughed nervously and asked her, 'Forgive my asking, Mrs Shonley, but you were saying that you could obtain no real proof of identification that the man you have brought back here with you was really your husband? I cannot help but wonder what made you so sure that it was indeed Conrad Shonley?'

The lucent, dark-shadowed green eyes looked steadily at him, and then she answered with a brutal honesty, 'In all truth, Father, I've asked myself that very question many many times.' She paused, and a look of speculation came upon her thin features, and she went on in a musing tone, 'I think that maybe I needed it to be him, Father. I needed to know what had happened to him. You'll understand that when the ship took fire it was all a panic and a terrible confusion, and I was up on the deck away from Con when it did happen, and I wasn't able to get back below to him. I kept on blaming myself for that. I kept thinking that if I had not left him down below as I did, then perhaps I could have done something to save him. Not knowing what had happened to Con near drove me mad. So when I found that poor soul in the infirmary, even though he was so badly hurt, yet at least I had him with me, and there was always the hope that he might recover from his injuries. That was better than not knowing what had become of him.'

She shivered visibly as the memories of that terror-filled night flooded over her, and for brief moments she heard again the wild shouts, the frantic screaming, the roar of flames and the terrified shrieking of children sounding above the crashing of timbers, the howling wind and the thunder of the waves.

The priest's ravening curiosity overcame his delicacy of feelings and he pressed her further. 'And what about now, Mrs Shonley? Do you still in your heart believe that the man outside is Conrad Shonley?'

'Really now, Father Murray, you go too far I think!' Doctor Donovan remonstrated sharply, and the younger man blushed shamefacedly and began to apologise, but Grainne cut his protestation short.

'No, Doctor Donovan, I want to speak of this. Really I do. It's a burden on my soul and I want rid of it.' Again she paused, and now her expression was puzzled, and when she spoke it was as if she were addressing herself and not her listeners. 'Now I find that deep down within me, I cannot fully believe that that is my husband's body lying out there upon that cart. I keep thinking of those times in the infirmary when I so wanted to believe that I had found Con once more, that I refused to allow any doubts to influence me. The poor man was so dreadfully hurt that the whole top half of his body and his head was all but destroyed, and he was covered in bandagings. He couldn't speak, he couldn't see, and I doubt now that he could hear. But I persuaded myself that he could hear me

16

speaking to him, and once or twice he made a slight movement of his arm when I asked him a question, just as if he had heard and understood me, and I so wanted him to be Con that I convinced myself that it was him.'

She fell silent, staring blankly before her, then blinked hard and looked with wide eyes at her audience as if surprised to see them sitting there. Then she shook her head sharply, as if to rid her brain of the memories that filled it.

It was the doctor who spoke to her this time. By now his own curiosity was fully aroused. 'And are you convinced still that he is indeed your husband, Grainne?'

She shook her head slowly. 'I don't know, Doctor Donovan. I just don't know.' Her breath caught in her throat, and she suddenly burst into heart-rending sobs.

Neither of the men attempted to comfort or soothe her. Both realised that the sobbing itself would prove a comfort and a healing of her mental agonies. For long minutes they sat watching her with sympathetic eyes, until at long last her cries softened and eased and with a piece of clean rag she wiped her eyes and blew her nose.

'Forgive me, Doctor Donovan, Father,' she beseeched them with some embarrassment.

Phillip Donovan smiled and told her warmly, 'Don't talk such nonsense, my dear girl. It was necessary that you should give way to your sorrow. And now you must eat some hot food, and afterwards you shall go to bed and rest.'

He refused to listen to her feeble protests and rang the bell for his housekeeper.

'Now then, Bridie, I want you to bring hot food for Mrs Shonley, and then prepare the front bedroom for her. She is to stay here as my guest this night.'

The young priest rose to his feet. 'Mrs Shonley, I'm only sorry that our acquaintance was not made under happier circumstances. I shall take charge of your husband this night, and have him taken to the chapel. He'll lie peaceful in God's house. I'll come here tomorrow morning and fetch you and the doctor for the Burial Mass.'

The men's kindness brought fresh tears to Grainne's eyes and again they had the good sense to leave her be and allow the merciful assuagement of her grief to take its natural course.

17

Chapter Three

In the dream Grainne found herself walking down a long stony track enveloped by grey swirling mist. Ahead of her four burial men clad in long black swallowtail coats, with blue caubeens on their heads, were carrying a coffin on their shoulders. She knew that she must find out who was in that coffin and heard herself shouting to the men to stop, but they ignored her and went on and on through the mist. She began to run, but it seemed that no matter how fast she moved the burial men remained at the same distance from her.

Then old Father Mulcahy suddenly appeared before her, holding out both arms as if to halt her desperate rush. She came to a standstill, horror causing her to scream.

'You shouldn't be here! You're dead! You're dead!'

'Go back, child, this is no concern of yours.' His cracked old voice sounded in her ear. ''Tis not your concern!'

The grey mist swirled around her, blotting all else from her sight, then cleared abruptly, and Grainne found herself in a graveyard, standing beside an open grave with a coffin lying on the heaped spoil of earth beside it. Ranged on the far side of the coffin the four burial men stood staring at her, and again Grainne screamed in horror as she saw that one of those men was Denis Callaghan. His toothless mouth gaped in a grin, and he pointed down at the coffin and shook his head.

'It's not himself!' he told her. 'It's not himself!'

Grainne felt herself falling forwards into the gaping grave and everything turned black, and she screamed and woke up. Panting with fear and clammy with sweat she lay in the narrow bed, her heart thudding frantically, her eyes wide and staring into the darkness of the room.

The door opened and the glow of a candle softly lit the wrinkled face of the housekeeper. Her head was covered by a ribboned night-cap tied beneath her hooked chin, and her body was thick with layers of nightgowns. The old woman came to the bedside and held the candle towards Grainne's face.

'Are you all right, Mrs Shonley? Ye've been shouting out loud enough to wake the dead.'

'It's the dead I've been seeing, Bridie!' Grainne gasped out, and the old woman hissed fearfully and crossed herself.

'May the holy saints preserve us! What is it ye're telling me, Mrs Shonley?'

'I dreamed that Father Mulcahy and Denis Callaghan were speaking to me.'

'For the love o' God, don't say such things!' the old woman pleaded. 'Father Mulcahy is in Heaven now, and that wicked scut Callaghan is either in Purgatory or in Hell, God help his soul.'

A little calmer now, Grainne pushed herself upright, her long black hair falling in a soft cloud about her face and slender shoulders.

'I swear on the Holy Bible that I saw and heard them both, just as clear as I can see and hear you, Bridie,' she insisted.

'And what did they tell ye?' The old crone glanced fearfully about her, and dropped her voice to a whisper.

Grainne could recall the vivid dream with absolute clarity. 'I was following a coffin, Bridie, and in the dream I knew that I had to find out who was inside it, so I ran after the burial men shouting to them to stop, but they wouldn't.'

'Oh swate Jasus protect us!' Bridie moaned, and again crossed herself.

Grainne was now completely engrossed in her recall and, ignoring the old woman, went on, 'Father Mulcahy tried to stop me following the burial men, and told me that it was none of my concern. And then, by the grave, I saw that Denis Callaghan was one of them, and he said, "It's not himself. It's not himself." Twice he said it, Bridie. He pointed at the coffin, and shook his head, and told me, "It's not himself".' She fell silent, and her expression was one of wonderment.

'Do you know something, Bridie, I was terrified in the

dream, and when I first woke up. But now I'm not feared at all. Not one little bit.'

She smiled into the other woman's frightened features. 'I think that Father Mulcahy and Denis were sent to bring me that message. I think that they were sent by God.'

'Sent by the Divil more likely, child!' the old woman snapped. 'You just out that dream from outta your mind now, d'ye hear me? Cast it from ye, because it's the Divil's work.'

'No, Bridie.' Grainne shook her head thoughtfully. 'No, I don't think it's that. I think it's a message. A message to tell me that my Con is still alive!'

'Holy Mary, Mother o' God!' the old woman wailed. 'Your poor mind has turned, child. I'll get the doctor directly.'

Before Grainne could move to stop her the housekeeper had run out of the room in a froth of petticoats, shrieking, 'Doctor Donovan, come quick! For the love o' God, come quick!'

When the doctor hurried into the room, with Bridie following him babbling prayers, Grainne greeted him with a smile.

'I'm all right, Doctor Donovan. I haven't gone mad.' She went on to relate her dream, and he listened gravely without interruption.

'Well, what do you think to that, Doctor Donovan?' she demanded eagerly when she had finished her story.

His eyes were pitying as he looked at her smiling face, and thought to himself: 'Bridie may well be right. The poor creature's mind could have given way from grief.'

As if she could read his thoughts Grainne suddenly sobered and said sharply, 'I haven't gone mad, Doctor. But that dream has filled me with a certainty that my darling Con still lives, and that poor soul that I brought from Liverpool is indeed a stranger.'

Phillip Donovan sighed heavily, and replied gently, 'Listen child, try to sleep again. You have been under immense strain these last months.'

'I'm not mad!' she burst out in angry protest, and he spread his hands and shrugged.

'I'm not suggesting anything of that sort, Grainne. But frankly, I myself am very very tired, and at this hour I'm not really capable of giving rational consideration to matters such

20

as this. Cannot we discuss it in the morning after we have buried your . . . ' He paused awkwardly, and after a brief moment of hesitation finished, ' . . . After the burial Mass.'

With a hint of petulance Grainne nodded. 'Very well then, Doctor. As you wish.'

He smiled with relief. 'Good, then I'll bid you a good night once more, child.'

The man and the old woman withdrew leaving Grainne to the quiet still darkness of her room. She made no attempt to go back to sleep, knowing that in her present excited state it would be futile. Instead she lay for a time reliving her dream, over and over again. Then she rose from her bed and in the darkness fumbled her way downstairs and into the kitchen.

Her wet clothing had been taken by old Bridie and placed before the kitchen fire to dry, and by the glow of the smouldering peat Grainne dressed in the still damp garments and quietly slipped out of the rear door and into the night.

The rain had eased and the pall of clouds had rifted in places letting shafts of moonlight through so that Grainne could see her way towards the Catholic chapel. The small township was still and quiet, no lights shone from the windows of the buildings, no sound of human or animal disturbed the night. As she moved through the streets Grainne saw that many of the houses and cabins were abandoned, and some were already falling into dereliction and ruin. Memories assailed her at every step and the faces of those she had known crowded in sharp visual images into her mind. One face above all others dominated those images: the face of Con Shonley, her adored husband, smiling, showing white teeth in swarthy handsome features topped by thick black curly hair.

She reached the chapel and went inside. The coffin was set on trestles before the altar, candles burning in tall-standing holders at each of its corners. The smell of incense hung heavy on the chill dank air and for a brief moment Grainne was a small child again, marvelling at the mystery and magic of this House of God. She moved to the side of the coffin and briefly rested her hands palms downward upon its pall-covered lid.

'I don't know now who you are,' she whispered. 'But in my heart I'm certain you are not my Con.' A rush of happiness caused her to smile. 'He's still alive. Somehow and somewhere

21

he still lives. I know that now. God sent a message to me to tell me that. But I've brought you here and I shall give you a Christian burial. You may not be Catholic or Irish for all I can know of you, but if somehow you can hear me, then I hope that what we shall do for you will give you easement and release your soul from Purgatory. I'm going to hold the wake for you and watch over you this night.'

She crossed herself and murmured a brief prayer for the well-being of this unknown man's soul, then seated herself on the front pew and with clasped hands and bowed head kept silent vigil through the long hours of darkness.

Chapter Four

The four burial men dressed in their long black swallow-
tailed coats and floppy blue caubeens covering their
shaggy hair stared curiously at the slender, shawled figure who
watched the gravedigger shovelling earth into the grave with no
sign of emotion upon her impassive face.

Some little distance from the grave Doctor Phillip Donovan
also stared at Grainne Shonley, but his eyes held concern
rather than curiosity. By the doctor's side Father Murray
frowned as the flurry of raindrops hit his broad-brimmed
shallow-crowned hat, and spattered down his cassock.

'We're in for another soaking unless we leave now, Doctor
Donovan.'

Phillip Donovan nodded absently. 'Go you on back to my
house, Father. Bridie will have the refreshments prepared. I'll
just wait for young Grainne.'

When the priest showed hesitancy to leave him, the doctor
urged, 'Go on now. I have to settle with the burial men anyway
before I can come.'

'All right then, but don't be too long, or I might have ate
everything, I've a terrible greed upon me,' the priest joked,
and then walked away.

Donovan signalled the burial men to him, and handed each
of them some coins. They saluted him, touching their fingers to
their foreheads.

'Thank you, doctor, sor!'

'God bless you, sor!'

'May God have mercy on that poor sowl!'

'Long life to ye, Doctor Donovan, sor!'

23

When they too had gone Phillip Donovan moved quietly to Grainne's side.

'Now then, my dear, shall we go back to the house? It's coming on to rain again,' he said gently. 'You can return here when the man has finished and made everything tidy. I've ordered a cross made, but told the carpenter to wait for your directions on the inscription.'

The young girl turned to face him, and he saw the tears brimming in her green eyes. Pity whelmed over him, and he gently pressed her arm between his fingers.

'There there now, my dear. You are still very young, and this terrible grief will someday mellow and become easier to bear. There will come a time when you will be able to think of Con with joy rather than with sorrow.'

Grainne smiled through her tears and shook her head. 'No, Doctor Donovan, you do not understand. I'm not weeping for Con, for for this poor man who suffered so, and now must lie buried among strangers in a strange land.'

Phillip Donovan frowned uneasily, but decided to say nothing at this point in time. He was greatly concerned about Grainne's mental state. Father Murray had come to him that morning to tell him how he had found Grainne keeping solitary vigil over the corpse, and how she had told him, Father Murray, that she hoped that if ever she or Con, her husband, were to someday be buried in a strange land then someone would hold wake over them.

The priest's face had been worried when he had told Phillip Donovan, 'Sure, she won't have it that this poor soul is her husband. She insisted that her man is still living. She says that God sent her a message to tell her so; that God sent that message in a dream she had last night. You'd best keep a close eye on the poor wee girl, doctor, because it's my feeling that her mind is turned by her grief and hardships. Sure now, she'll not be the first in this unhappy land to have been so affected will she? Such cases are a veritable plague these last years. There's thousands of the poor demented creatures roaming the land, is there not?'

Phillip Donovan had sadly been forced to agree with that latter statement. There were indeed thousands of people who had been so afflicted.

A heavier spatter of raindrops fell and he coaxed, 'Come now, Grainne, let's go back home.'

She came with him, and side by side they left the gravedigger to his sombre task.

At the house Father Murray was eating heartily of boiled bacon and cabbage and good fresh bread, and the smell of the food roused Grainne's appetite, and she also ate with gusto.

Phillip Donovan merely picked at his portion, and after only a few mouthfuls laid his knife and fork down. Grainne felt a sudden sense of shame at her own healthy appetite, and abruptly stopped eating herself. The doctor smiled at her, and chided gently, 'Bridie will be sorely offended if you don't finish your meal, child.'

'You must think me heartless,' she told him with embarrassment. 'Here I am just come from a burial, passing people on the road who are starving, and I'm stuffing myself like a pig.'

Father Murray looked very uncomfortable upon hearing her words, and also laid down his utensils and looked from one to the other of his companions.

'This is utter stupidity!' the doctor snapped curtly. 'Listen to me, girl.' Phillip Donovan appeared almost angry, his sallow, careworn features frowning. 'I know that you have suffered from starvation yourself. We have had three years of this famine now, and countless thousands have died as a result of it. The time has come when we must think first of our own survival and well-being. That is not being heartless, that is merely acting with good sense and prudence.

'As a doctor I have done, and am doing, all that lies in my power to help the sufferers. I know that you yourself, Grainne, have done so before you left for America, and you also, Father Murray, have given unstintingly of your help and compassion since you have arrived here in this parish.

'By good fortune at this moment we three have sufficient food to eat, although there are thousands starving throughout the land. That is not a reason or a cause for any personal guilt or shame. We do all that we can to aid our fellow creatures. We will not be able to continue to help them if we deliberately starve ourselves when we do not have to. All that course of action will bring about, is to add to the mass of suffering. It will not allay by a single jot the sum of that suffering. And as for the

25

matter of the burial, Grainne, you cannot bring back the dead by refusing to eat, can you?'

He paused and regarded each of them keenly, then picked up his knife and fork and proceeded to eat his own meal. After a few moments both Grainne and Father Murray copied his example.

When they had all done eating and were sitting drinking tea Phillip Donovan began to talk of the situation in Skibereen and the surrounding district.

'Do you know, it's a paradox, that while vast areas of our country are now enduring the worst effects of the famine, we here in Skibereen who suffered more than any other area perhaps initially, now find our own condition somewhat easier.' He grimaced sardonically. 'That is because the district has lost perhaps two thirds of its population, either by death or by emigration. Whereas four months ago I and my fellow doctors and the priests were quite literally working all the hours God could send us, now our efforts are no longer needed in anything like the same degree. The gravediggers, who only four months ago were not able to dig sufficient graves for the dead, now spend half their day in the shebeens, while the burial men grumble at the drop in their earnings.'

He vented a bitter, mirthless chuckle. 'God has removed our burden, by removing our people.' He glanced at the young priest's doubtful frown. 'Forgive me if that sounds blasphemous, Father, I do not mean it as such.'

Later when the young priest had left, Phillip Donovan asked Grainne, 'What are your plans for the future, child?'

She smiled at him. 'Why that's easy to answer, Doctor Donovan. I'm going to find my Con.'

He looked at her in dismay. 'Grainne, I don't wish to be cruel, or to hurt you in any way, but do you not think that you may be deluding yourself about Con being still alive?'

'No, I'm not. Con is alive,' she stated with utter conviction.

The man sighed unhappily. 'But you've no evidence for that, my dear. You say that God sent you a message in your dream. But perhaps you are indulging in wishful thinking? After all, you told me that you once believed the man we have just buried was Con.'

He spread his hands wide in a gesture of beseechment.

'Cannot you accept that because of your grief you are perhaps not thinking clearly at this time? After all that has happened to you in such a short space of time it's not to be wondered at that your brain might be confused and sorely upset.' He was unhappily aware that he was making a very bad choice of words and explanation, and he subsided into glum silence.

Grainne regarded him very intently for some moments, then challenged, 'Tell me truly now, Doctor Donovan, do you think that I've gone mad? That my brain has been unbalanced by what happened in Liverpool?'

He held her challenging gaze, and replied evenly, 'It's not only what happened in Liverpool that has caused you untold distress, is it, Grainne? Don't forget all that occurred here at home before you left these shores. Your husband was a rebel, and was accused of turning informer after the authorities arrested and then released him, was he not? So both of you suffered cruel and unjust persecution from the local people, did you not? A persecution that was instrumental in causing you to lose the baby you were carrying in your womb. A miscarriage can cause much harm to a woman's mental state, Grainne.

'Then, when you finally set out to begin a new life, you lost your mother because she chose to stay with a worthless scoundrel who ill-treated her. That also must have preyed upon your mind with ever increasing torment. The friends who went to England with you have both died. And worst of all, you suffered the loss of your husband, your belongings, your hopes, when the ship flamed and sank. You yourself have said how you forced yourself to believe that the man you found in the Liverpool infirmary was Con. And then he died also, and alone you physically dragged his body back from England to here.'

He leaned forward suddenly, and took both her hands in his, gripping them tightly in his intensity. 'Listen to me, my dear girl, your sufferings would have destroyed the vast majority of people utterly and completely. But because you are a woman who possesses unusual courage and spirit and intelligence, you have survived them. But I cannot believe that you have not undergone damage within your mental and physical being, which will require time to heal fully.'

He fell silent briefly, as if inviting reply. Then, when she made no answer, he went on. 'Grainne, I have known you, and Con, since you were small children. I was always fond and admiring of you both. It is for your sake now, that I ask you to allow time to heal the harm that has been wrought upon you.'

Grainne caught her lower lip between her sharp white teeth and her eyes were troubled. She did not want to upset or anger this man who had been so kind to her by arguing against him. She knew that he wished only her good.

On his part Phillip Donovan took her silence as a sign that his arguments were convincing her, and he urged, 'Grainne, I realise that you must have work to enable you to support yourself while the healing process takes place. You are of course more then welcome to remain here in my house for as long as you might wish. You could help Bridie in her duties. I could not pay you a large salary, since I am a poor man, but I could manage a few shillings a week. However, having said that, I cannot help but incline to the belief that it would be better for you to remove yourself entirely from a country which is so sorely stricken, and sadly holds so many unhappy personal memories for you.

'I have friends in England. If you are agreeable I can write to them and ask their assistance in finding you a place in some respectable household in that country. If I remember correctly did you not once work as a maid in Lady Dunsmore's service when she went across the water?'

Grainne nodded. 'Yes, I was lady's maid in her house in England for nearly four years from my fifteenth year.'

The man smiled encouragingly. 'There now, you already have valuable experience to draw upon, do you not, and there is nothing to prevent you from improving your knowledge and skills in that domestic sphere, which would enable you to eventually gain position as housekeeper in some great household, where you would then be enabled to gain a security in life. What think you to that idea?'

When Grainne made no immediate reply, Phillip Donovan told her gently, 'I shall leave you to ponder on what I have said to you, child. There is no need for you to make any hasty decision on this matter. As I have said previously, you are very welcome to remain here in my house for as long as you may desire.'

'Thank you, Doctor Donovan.' She smiled sadly. 'I would like to be alone for a time so that I may think more clearly.'

She went up to the bedroom she had used the previous night and seated herself on the narrow cot there. Beyond the dormer window the sky was dark clouded and wind-driven raindrops splashed to destruction against the small leaded panes of glass. For a while Grainne's mind was filled with memories of her husband and tears fell freely as she mourned her loss of him. Now she found that the earlier certainty of his survival that the dream had engendered within her had eroded, and again she wondered if the man she had just buried had indeed been Con Shonley.

'If only I knew for certain,' she murmured brokenly. 'Surely if he had survived he would have known by now that I also survived, and he would have come searching for me?'

Again her thoughts ranged back to those terrible weeks and months that had followed the loss of the *Florida* on which she and Con had sailed with such high hopes for the New World.

Tapscotts, the emigration agents and brokers who had chartered the ill-fated vessel, had issued lists of known survivors, but because of the very immensity of numbers of emigrants swarming across the Atlantic and the chaotic conditions of the trade, those same lists of survivors might never be fully completed. Some of the sailors who had rescued her had not bothered to inform the agents of their own survival, but had merely shipped out again. Then there was the likelihood of survivors from the *Florida* being picked up by vessels outward bound for South America, or the Far East, or Africa, in which case months and years might elapse before they would be in any position to notify the agents that they still lived. There were so many emigrant ships sailing day by day, and so many being lost at sea, that the loss of the *Florida* was now all but forgotten, except by those unfortunate enough to have sailed on her.

Grainne drew a long ragged breath, as she mournfully concluded that all she could do was to regard Con Shonley as being dead. Naturally she would never be able to be completely certain of this, and she knew that in her secret heart she would always hope and pray that someday, somehow, somewhere, she would meet him once again. But to begin to give credence to her dreams, and to refuse to accept bitter facts, would not serve her. She must go on with her life and accept her widow-hood.

'But I'll always love you, Con. Always,' she murmured brokenly, and then lay back upon the narrow cot and curling herself into a foetal position allowed her tearing anguish to flood forth unchecked.

It was many hours later that she went downstairs to tell Doctor Donovan, 'I'll be very grateful for any assistance you can give me in finding a position in England, Doctor Donovan.'

The man regarded her keenly, noting the tear-reddened eyes, and the almost submissive posture of her body, and he knew that finally she had accepted, and begun to come to terms with what had happened to her. With a sense of relief he reached out and took her hand in his.

'Time heals, child,' he told her gently. 'And although you may find it hard to believe at this present moment, yet there will eventually come a day when you will be able to take pleasure in your life once more, and to remember Con with joy for the happiness you shared together. You must be brave now, and believe with all your heart that time will heal your hurt, and soothe your grief.'

She raised her head and with steady eyes told him, 'I shall try to do that, Doctor Donovan. I shall really try. Con would not wish me to be a coward, would he?'

The man smiled kindly at her, and shook his head. 'No, child, he most certainly would not wish that.'

Chapter Five

Warwickshire, England
February 1849

Snow blanketed the earth and the strong wind lifted the fine top layers to send swirls of white flecks hissing through the freezing air. The powdery flakes settled and clung to Grainne's clothing, layering her in a frosty coverlet and painfully stinging her face and hands. The biting cold brought tears brimming in her eyes, and she blinked against their blurring as she struggled on through the drifts that in places came up to her knees. The road she travelled was lined by hedgerows and trees, but their naked branches gave no protection from the winds and shook and clattered in the gusts as though they also shivered with the cold.

Beyond the hedgerows there stretched open fields and tracts of wild heathland and for some miles now she had passed no human habitation, nor seen any living beasts. She transferred her bundle of belongings from one numbed hand to the other, then abruptly halted and laid the bundle on the snow, while she rubbed and blew on her frozen fingers to try and restore some warmth and feeling to them. In an effort to shelter her head from the wind she had drawn her shawl up over her poke-bonnet, and now she held the edges of the shawl to form a shield above her head as she stared around her for some sign of the house she sought. Against the all-pervading whiteness she sighted whispy plumes of dark smoke, and her spirits rose. Even if it was not her destination the plumes of smoke promised warmth and shelter, and taking up her bundle she hurried on.

Eventually, rounding a bend in the road she saw the red-brick of a large house set some distance from the roadway, surrounded by shrubs and leafless tress. The entrance driveway was guarded by tall wrought-iron gates and Grainne felt a rush of relief as she realised that this must be her destination, Millwood Hall.

She reached the front of the imposing building and mounted the balustraded flight of stone steps. There was a long iron shafted bell-pull to one side of the massive doors and Grainne tugged on it vigorously. Now that she was standing still the cold was rapidly penetrating her thin topcoat and she hugged her shawl close around her as her teeth began to chatter and shivers passed through her body. After what seemed a very long time the door slowly creaked open and a tall resplendent figure wearing a gold laced, dark blue tail-coat, light blue velvet breeches, white stockings and highly polished pumps appeared.

The man wore long side-whiskers and his hair was quiffed and powdered. His bulbous blue eyes stared superciliously at her snow-covered figure for several moments, then he scowled angrily.

'What does you want?'

'If you please, is this Millwood Hall? Mr Charles Herbertson's residence?' Grainne asked.

'O' course it is, and doon't you know any better than to come knocking on this bloody door? Goo round the bloody back!'

Before Grainne could open her mouth to reply the massive door slammed in her face. For a moment her fiery temper sparked, but then she realised the futility of that emotion and resignedly shuffled through the deep drifted snow to the rear of the great house. She passed through a large stable yard and through several smaller courtyards enclosed by outbuildings then found a door which appeared to lead into the house itself. She hammered on its panels with her fist. Eventually, after repeated knockings, the door opened and a grubby faced young girl wearing a floppy mobcap which was several sizes too large for her head peered out.

'Who be you?'

'My name's Grainne Shonley. I'm the new maidservant.' Grainne's teeth were now chattering hard and she desperately

32

wanted to get indoors and escape from the bitter cold.

The girl grinned in a friendly way, displaying gapped, crooked teeth, and jerked her head.

'Come on in me duck. Welcome to Misery 'all!'

Grainne followed the girl through a series of dark, stone-flagged corridors to emerge into a very large kitchen. Sitting on a chair, his plush-breeched legs stretched out in front of the range-fire, was the same footman who had directed Grainne to go around to the rear of the house.

''Ere's the new maid come, Walter,' the mob-capped girl announced.

He beckoned Grainne with a lordly air. 'Come over here, girl, and let's have a closer look at you.'

Grainne was more than happy to move closer to the heat of the fire, and pushing her shawl back to her shoulders she leaned forwards, holding her hands towards the flames.

'Tek off your bonnet, girl, and let's have a good look at you,' the footman ordered hectoringly. 'You must learn to obey your betters a bit quicker.'

Grainne straightened and turned to the man. She studied him coolly, noting that he appeared to be about her own age, with a fresh ruddy complexion, bulbous blue eyes and bovine features.

'A country bumpkin!' she thought amusedly. 'And he takes me to be the same.'

The young man frowned uneasily as he vaguely recognised that this was no timid, overawed young girl fresh from her native village. He tried to bluster.

'Youm agoing to be under my direction, girl, so you'd best learn quick that when I orders you to do summat, you must do it straight off. I arn't agoing to tell you agen to tek your bonnet off.'

Grainne smiled broadly and told the young man quietly, 'And I'm not going to tell you this twice either, my bucko. I've been in service before, I was lady's maid to Lady Dunsmore for nearly four years, so don't try codding me about how high and mighty you are. I take no orders from a footman.' She paused to watch the shocked expression spread across his features, and chuckled. 'So just be a good boy now and take me to see the housekeeper. It's Mrs Gurnock, isn't it?'

The mob-capped girl spluttered with laughter, and crowed, 'That's just put you to the right about, arn't it just, Walter! I knowed this young 'ooman had got a bit about her the minnit I laid eyes on her.'

The young man flushed angrily and opened his mouth, but before he could say anything Grainne lifted her forefinger warningly. 'Now don't you be saying things that later on you might be regretful of saying, Walter.' She smiled engagingly at him. 'Let's not start our acquaintance with harsh words and bad feelings. We might find that we can be good friends.' Her smile broadened and seeing the effect her good looks was having on him, her imp of devilment stirred and she could not resist flirting with him. 'Sure now, a fine-looking young fellow like you, it would be a pity for any girl to be enemies with.' She coaxed him now. 'Let's start as friends, shall we, Walter?'

After a couple of moments he surrendered to her charm and grinned ruefully. 'All right then, Miss Blarney Stone. Let's begin as friends.'

'Me name's Emily,' the young girl informed Grainne. 'I'm the scullery maid. And your name's Grainne, arn't that what you said it was?'

'It is.' Grainne smiled at the girl. 'Grainne Shonley.'

Walter rose to his feet. 'You'd best leave your bundle here then, and I should shake the snow off your bonnet and shawl afore we goes to Mrs Gurnock's room. She 'udden't like any mess on her carpets.'

'The old cow doon't like any mess anywheer, does her?' Emily grinned and stuck out her tongue cheekily. 'Her's as sour as last month's milk, the old bitch.'

The footman looked nervously about him, as if fearing that the words might have been overheard, then admonished the young girl, 'You wants to be careful what youm saying, Em. You knows how her sneaks about the bloody place.' He spoke directly to Grainne, dropping his voice so that it was little more than a whisper. 'Mrs Gurnock is a real Tartar. You take heed o' me, and tread very careful around her, Grainne, or she'll have your guts for garters, and that's no lie, that arn't. Come on, we'd best tek you to her now, afore she comes down here to give us stick.'

Grainne dutifully followed him through more long corridors and sumptuously furnished rooms, and now she began to appreciate just how large the house was. The walls were hung with paintings, and ancient weapons and pieces of armour, and their footsteps were muffled by the thick carpeting. The evidence of wealth surrounded her in opulent abundance and Grainne could not help but be impressed by it, and at the same time could not help but wonder where the other inhabitants of this great house were, because all was silent and deserted.

Mrs Ruth Gurnock was a small, slender-bodied woman dressed in black with a starched white cap of lace and ribbons on her iron-grey, severely bunned hair. Although she was middle-aged she was still a beautiful woman. Her pale skin smooth and unblemished, her dark eyes clear and lucent, and her teeth white and sound.

When Grainne was ushered into her room by Walter the housekeeper was seated at a rolltop desk set against the wall, writing in an open ledger that lay before her. She turned in her chair to face them and dismissed the footman. For long moments she studied Grainne intently, then said, 'Remove your bonnet, Shonley, and lay aside your shawl. Now stand upright with your arms at your side.'

Her voice was low-pitched and held an inflexion that sounded foreign to Grainne's ears. When Grainne had done as she was bidden the elder woman again studied her in silence. Then she sighed as if vexed.

'You are too beautiful, Shonley. Good looking girls always cause disturbance in a household.' She took a letter from one of the desk's pigeonholes and scanned it.

'You have been engaged as an under housemaid on the recommendation of Mr Adams of Birmingham, following an application made to him by a Doctor Phillip Donovan of Skibereen, Ireland.'

She laid the letter aside, and again fixed her dark eyes on Grainne's. 'I will speak plain, Shonley. The master, Mr Charles Herbertson, is a business colleague of Mr Adams, and to oblige him has directed me to accept you here. I myself would not have engaged you without prior interview, and therefore I shall be keeping an extra close watch on how you perform your duties. If I am not fully satisifed, then you will

35

not remain in this house, no matter what influence Mr Adams or Doctor Donovan might try to exert on your behalf.

'I am given to understand that you have been in the service of Lady Dunsmore for some four years as a lady's maid, and were therefore an upper servant. That counts for nothing with me, so do not assume any airs or graces. I do not tolerate such among my staff. Here you are a lower servant, and will be so treated.'

She paused, as if in expectation of a reply, but Grainne only nodded silent acceptance.

'At present the family is in London, and most of the staff with them. However, one of the upper housemaids, Hobdon, remains here and she will instruct you in your duties, and what is expected of you while you are under this roof. She will also show you your sleeping quarters. You will commence your duties tomorrow morning, so I suggest you use the hours until then in preparing yourself to work hard and well. You may go.'

She turned back to her ledger, and Grainne bobbed a curtsey and with her bonnet and shawl in her hands left the room. Walter was waiting at the end of the corridor, and he grinned as Grainne came up to him.

'What did I tell you? She's a real Tartar, arn't her?' he whispered.

Grainne smiled ruefully and nodded agreement.

'Come on, we'll goo and get summat to ate.' He led her back through the house to the kitchen.

Two other young women were now seated before the fire: a handsome blonde-haired girl wearing the black gown, high-bibbed white apron and long-ribboned lace cap of a house-maid, and the other, plump and rosy-cheeked, in the gingham dress and voluminous white apron and mobcap of a cook. They stared curiously at Grainne, and Walter introduced them both.

'This is Sarah Hobdon, and this is Patience Drew. And this 'ere is Grainne Shonley, the new maid.'

Both women nodded to Grainne, and she smiled and nodded in return, then seated herself on a long bench which flanked the great white-scrubbed table some two yards distant from the range. From her previous experience of domestic service Grainne knew that it was wiser to wait for the longer estab-lished members of the staff to initiate any conversation with her. The world of the servants in a great house was a jealously maintained hierarchical structure with as many, if not more, subtle gradations of social standing and privileges as those practised by their employers.

It was Patience Drew, the assistant cook, who asked Grainne, 'Have you been in service afore?'

Grainne nodded. 'Yes, I was lady's maid to Lady Dunsmore.'

'What family is that?' Patience Drew wanted to know.

'The Dunsmores of Kerry. They're a cadet branch of the Earls of Munster.'

The plump rosy features of the cook instantly showed that she was impressed.

'Are you to be lady's maid here?' It was the other young woman, the housemaid, Sarah Hobdon. Her tone contained a note of asperity, and Grainne understood the reason for that. In the servant's hierarchy the lady's maid ranked very highly, and was counted as one of the privileged and better paid upper servants, usually receiving at least twice as much salary as a housemaid. And to be a lady's maid to the aristocracy carried added kudos.

Grainne regarded the handsome blonde girl keenly, judging that she was perhaps manoeuvring to become a lady's maid herself in this household, and so was resentful that Grainne had come here, fearing that Grainne would get preference for that position should it become vacant.

'No, I've not come here as lady's maid,' Grainne said quietly. 'And truth to tell I'm not looking for any position as such. I'm engaged as an under housemaid and quite content to be so.'

For some seconds Sarah Hobdon stared suspiciously at the newcomer, then apparently deciding that Grainne was speaking the truth about her lack of ambition, suddenly smiled and told her, 'Well then, you'll be working under me, won't you?'

Grainne nodded. 'I expect so.'

The other woman was now relaxed and friendly. 'I'll show you what's what here, my wench. You'll be all right if you watches your P's and Q's.'

It was now beginning to get dark and the overhanging oil

lamps were lit. The cook produced a cold joint of mutton, loaves of fresh bread and a bowl of dripping, and sent Walter to draw jugs of beer from a large barrel kept in the brewhouse.

The servants seated themselves around the great table and fell voraciously on the food. Grainne had not eaten that day, and the taste of the food made her realise how ravenously hungry she was. Walter grinned slyly at her. ''Tis easy to see that youm newcome over from Paddy's Land, Grainne, the way youm tucking in. No wonder theer's a bloody famine over theer, if they all ates as quick as you does.'

The succulent meal in Grainne's mouth suddenly lost all its savour, and with an effort she swallowed and grimly asked the young man, 'Is that meant to be a joke?' Fiery spots of colour were burning in her cheeks as her hot temper rose dangerously near to breaking point. 'Do you know what it's like to be starving? Do you find it funny that in Ireland men, women and children are dying in their thousands like famished beasts?'

His bulbous eyes bulged with shock as he saw how angry she had so suddenly become, and he shook his quiffed head, protesting, 'No, girl, I warn't trying to make mock o' you. Truly I warn't! I was only kidding you on a bit.'

Grainne's temper abruptly subsided, and she felt suddenly very weary and depressed. She pushed her plate of food away from her, and asked Sarah Hobdon, 'Will you show me where I'm to sleep, please?'

Sarah Hobdon slowly shook her head. 'Not yet. 'Tisn't right that you should goo hungry to bed while there's food in plenty on this table. Walter's a fool, but he meant no harm by saying what he did. Did you, Walter?' She looked towards the footman, and he confirmed vigorously, 'No, I didn't mean no offence. I was only kidding.'

Sarah leaned across the table to push Grainne's plate back towards her. 'Now you just get this lot down you, girl, and as much more as you can manage to ate and drink as well. I know what it's like to be hungry, Grainne, and so does the rest on us here. Theer's as many who's known starvation here in England during these last years, as there is in Ireland. The difference is that it's better hidden here, but there's suffering, and hardships, and starvation enough to satisfy anybody who cares to look for it.'

Grainne felt ashamed of her own loss of temper as she heard the calm tones of the other woman, and inwardly was forced to acknowledge that what the other said was nothing but the truth. Poverty, hunger, disease and death knew no boundaries, and behind the glittering façade of all-rich, all-powerful England, millions of her fellow subjects lived and died in utter destitution.

'Come now, ate,' Sarah Hobdon urged again, and Grainne forced a smile, and obeyed the command.

There was little or no conversation during the remainder of the meal, and when it was done Emily cleared the platters from the table while the cook fetched more jugs of beer from the brewhouse.

Walter produced a short-stemmed clay pipe which he lit with a taper, and sat puffing out clouds of strong-smelling smoke. Sarah Hobdon refilled Grainne's tumbler and pressed her to drink. 'You get it down you, my duck, it'll do you good.'

Full stomachs and plentiful beer engendered a convivial atmosphere, and Grainne began to feel more at ease, but was very tired after her long and arduous journey from Ireland. Her new companions plied her with questions, and she answered readily enough, telling them that she was widowed, and had lost her husband in an emigrant shipwreck, but said nothing about the sufferings and degradations she had undergone.

On their part her companions told her a few things about the Herbertson family, and about their fellow servants who were now in London. She learned that Charles Herbertson was a successful businessman who had made his vast fortune speculating upon the great railways boom. His first wife had died some years previously, and he had then married Sophia, his present wife, who was much younger than her husband. There were no children of this marriage, and only one surviving son of the first marriage, Edwin Herbertson.

'What sort of people are they?' Grainne wanted to know. 'Are they kind to their servants?'

Her companions reacted uneasily to her innocent question, and appeared curiously loth to answer. Eventually it was Sarah Hobdon who told her, 'We'em not allowed to gossip about the family's doings, Grainne. If Mrs Gurnock was to come to hear that we'd been saying things about them, then we'd all be handed our sacks in double quick time.'

The others nodded confirmation, and then Sarah Hobdon deliberately changed the subject. 'Come on, Grainne, I'll sort out some clothes for you for work tomorrow, and get you settled in your room.'

The young woman took two candles set in tin holders from a sideboard and lighted them both at the fire, then handed one of them to Grainne.

She led the way through draughty dark corridors and up several flights of narrow stairs, to the topmost floor of the great house.

'Here it is then.' Sarah Hobdon opened a door and ushered Grainne into the room with her.

'Fit for a queen, arn't it?' the blonde-haired girl scoffed sarcastically, and held her candle high so that its wavering flames dimly illuminated the rafters and roof-tiles that sloped sharply downwards from the gable top.

The cramped room was almost filled with a double bed on which lay a bolster and some folded blankets and sheets. There were no windows, just a skylight in the roof, and the only other furnishings were a marble topped washstand against the wall and a piece of broken mirror on top of it, propped up against a tin basin and jug.

'You'll be sharing with Amy Davis and Rosy Bright. But they'm down in London now, so you'se got it all to yourself until they come back,' Sarah Hobdon informed her, and glanced at the bundle in which Grainne carried her pathetically few belongings.

'Tomorrow I'll sort out a box for you to keep your things in. I'll go and get you a working dress now. I'll only be a minute.'

She went out of the room, and Grainne looked at the stained walls, smelled the mustiness, shivered as the dank chill air began to penetrate her thin clothing, and her heart sank.

'Here's some stuff to be going on with. I'll find out the rest for you tomorrow.' Sarah Hobdon came back into the room carrying a checked patterned dress, and coarse grey apron and a floppy mobcap. 'These are clean, and they'll fit you all right. You get some sleep now, and mind that you blows out your candle soon. Mrs Gurnock don't like us to waste 'um. Goodnight now.'

'Goodnight.' Grainne listened to the other girl's retreating footsteps, and then sat down on the edge of the straw mattress. Above her head she heard the raindrops spattering against the tiles, and the wind whining through the warped casement of the skylight. There sounded a furtive rustling and scratching and muted squeaking behind the cracked stained plaster of the walls, and Grainne smiled mirthlessly.

'At least I've plenty of rats for company.' A desolation of absolute loneliness flooded over her. 'Why did you have to leave me, Con? Why?' she murmured sadly. Only the mournful whining of the wind answered her.

Chapter Six

'Grainne? Come on, wake up! It's well gone five o'clock!' Sarah Hobdon stood in the doorway holding a lighted candle, as Grainne sleepily sat up in her bed and pushed the coverings away from her legs.

'Come on, be quick. It's bloody freezing,' the blonde girl grumbled, her breath puffs of white mist in the candleglow.

Grainne shivered violently as she took her nightdress off and drew the thin day shift and dress over her head, then pulled her long drawers up over her slender hips to tie them with a large bow. Not for the first time she blessed the fact that her waist was wasplike enough to forgo the use of stays.

'Look sharp, Grainne,' Sarah badgered. 'Mrs Gurnock is down in the kitchen. She's gooing to be seeing how well you does your work this morning.' She grimaced sympathetically. 'Make sure you does everything spotless, my duck, because she's a hard one to please. And bring your candle down with you. You'll need it to see your work by.'

The two young women went downstairs to find Mrs Gurnock waiting for them in the kitchen. The woman was wearing a dark grey gown and white lace cap, and had a thick shawl over her shoulders to protect herself from the cold of the early morning. Around her slender waist she wore a leather belt from which dangled a huge bunch of keys.

Young Emily was on hands and knees scrubbing the stone-flagged floor, and Patience Drew was laying out cooking utensils.

The housekeeper's dark eyes regarded Grainne coldly. 'I see you're a slugabed, Shonley. Make sure this does not occur again. I expect the lower servants to be up and doing by five o'clock.' She turned to Sarah Hobdon. 'Give Shonley what's necessary.'

'Yes, Mrs Gurnock.' Sarah bobbed a curtsey and went into the corridor at the rear of the kitchen, to reappear shortly carrying carpet brooms, cinder-pail, a roll of cover-cloth and a large wooden housemaid's box. All of which she handed to Grainne.

'Now Shonley, I shall find out just how well-versed you are in your duties,' Mrs Gurnock snapped, and jerked her head. 'Follow me.'

She took a small lighted hand-lantern from the table and went from the room. Grainne followed closely behind her, cheered by the furtive wink Sarah Hobdon gave her as she left the kitchen.

The high-ceilinged corridors were dark and eerie, and Mrs Gurnock was a black silhouette, edged with the light of the lantern held before her, her footsteps alternately clicking sharply over the polished oaken floors and then muffled by carpeting. She halted and opened a pair of double doors. 'This is the breakfast parlour, Shonley. You will begin here. Next door there is the large drawing room. You will clean in there also.'

'Yes, Mrs Gurnock.' Grainne entered the room, and put down her implements, then asked the housekeeper, 'Please, may I light my candle from your lantern?'

The woman hissed impatiently. 'You should have taken a light from the kitchen.' Then she allowed Grainne to light her candle from the lantern's flame, and snapped, 'Get on with it, girl. If you waste any more time the morning will be gone.'

Grainne resented the other woman's attitude, but ruefully accepted that now she was a menial servant once more this was the type of treatment she must become accustomed to.

Mrs Gurnock took up her station just inside the door and watched in silence, as Grainne began to work. There was a set routine followed in most establishments, and Grainne decided to revert to the system she had been trained in as a young girl in the Dunsmore household. She opened all the shutters and windows, and took up the hearthrug to shake it vigorously out of the open window. Then laving her covercloth on the floor in

43

front of the firegrate she raked out the ashes and deposited them into her cinderpail, which had a wire sifter inside it, and a close-fitting lid. She shook the pail several times to sift the cinders, which she would utilise to lay the fresh fire. Then she went into the large drawing room next door and repeated the sequence of operations.

Her fingers were numbed with cold, and her breath plumed visibly around her head as she next prepared to clean the grates in both rooms. It was a task she detested because these grates were the type known as bright grates, part black iron, part burnished steel.

Sighing, she opened her housemaid's box and took out the bottle of Brunswick Black Lead. With a soft brush she applied the liquid varnish, rubbing it well into the surface until it dried. After that she took another brush and used it to polish the iron into a gleaming blackness. She cleaned the bright steelwork with emery paper, then smeared it with oil and polished it with a large piece of rotten-stone, rubbing hard backwards and forwards until the metal shone in the candlelight.

Once both grates were clean she did the same to the fire-irons and fenders and coal scuttles. By now, thankfully, the hard effort was engendering warmth through her chilled body, and with relief she finished the tedious task and, taking the big iron coal scuttles from each of the rooms, she went hurrying to the coalyard at the rear of the house to refill them.

She was panting beneath their weight when she returned to the breakfast room. Layering cinders, paper, sticks and fresh coals she lit fires in both rooms, using the brass and leather bellows to feed them air until they were well alight. She breathed a prayer of thanks that the coal was burning sweetly and not costing her valuable time to coax the flames. Then it was back to the scullery to take used tea leaves from the box kept there, which she dampened and strewed across the carpets. A thorough dusting of all the surfaces in the room followed, and a careful sweeping of the carpets, the damp leaves collecting the dust as they moved. With a soft leather and duster she then cleaned and polished the furniture, reclosed the windows, gave a final check to both rooms, then stood anxiously while Mrs Gurnock examined what she had done.

The housekeeper completed her inspection, and grudgingly accepted, 'Not as bad as I feared it might be, Shonley. Leave your things here and come with me. I will show you what other work needs to be done before your breakfast.'

Grainne trailed behind as the woman showed her the long stretches of stone-flagged service corridors.

'These must be swept and scrubbed. You will use caustic soda in the water to kill the grease. After these are done, you will polish the flooring in the entrance hall and the corridors adjoining it. When you have finished these tasks then come and report to me.'

'Yes, Mrs Gurnock.' Grainne bobbed a dutiful curtsey as the woman left her, and then sighed ruefully and went to fetch the necessary implements.

By eight o'clock that morning Grainne's body ached, her knees were sore, and her hands chapped and shrivel-skinned. She gave a final rub to the gleaming oaken floorboard and wearily got to her feet. Grimacing as she straightened and rubbing the small of her back, she collected all her cleaning implements and placed them in a small alcove near to the kitchen, then went in search of Mrs Gurnock.

She tapped the door of the housekeeper's office, and the woman came out to her. As she passed, Grainne could smell cloves and gin, and for a moment was puzzled, then realised that the mingled scents came from Mrs Gurnock's mouth.

'So, you take the drink, do you?' she thought, and stared keenly at the housekeeper's face, noting that the pale skin of the woman's cheeks and throat were slightly flushed, and that the fine dark eyes were somewhat glazed when she examined the work that Grainne had done.

Grainne repressed a grin. 'You've had a few jars this morning, by the looks of it, my lady,' she thought with a grim amusement.

The housekeeper traversed the corridors and then jerked her head at Grainne in dismissal. 'Go to your breakfast, Shonley. Hobdon will direct your work for the remainder of this day.'

'Yes, Mrs Gurnock.' Grainne was happy to obey. The hard work had given her a fierce appetite, and she hurried towards the kitchen with some eagerness.

When she arrived there she found that the other servants had already congregated around the large table on which the breakfast dishes were laid out. This morning as well as Walter, there were two other men present, both dressed in rough clothing, with clay-stained blue aprons tied around their bodies, and great clumping hob-nailed boots on their feet. Both men had broad red faces, heavily stubbled, and their hands were big and horny from hard labour.

'This is Jem, and this is Harold. They'm the gardeners.' They grinned broadly as Sarah Hobdon introduced them to Grainne, and she smiled and nodded in return.

Patience Drew distributed the meal, cutting big wedges of cold meat pie and pouring mugs of tea for each person. A willow basket heaped with chunks of bread was placed in the centre of the table, together with dishes of salted butter so that everyone could help themselves.

Ravenous as she was, Grainne concentrated on eating her wedge of pie, savouring its jellied richness, and sipped her hot tea, enjoying its refreshing heat spreading through her.

Sarah Hobdon smiled at her. 'Did Mrs Gurnock say anything to you about your work, Grainne?'

Grainne smiled ruefully. 'She just said that it wasn't as bad as she feared it might be.'

The others laughed at hearing this, and Sarah told her, 'That's high praise coming from her, my duck.'

'She said that I'm to take directions from you for the rest of today's work,' Grainne informed the upper housemaid, who nodded.

'Yes, you can work with me. We've got it easy with the family being away. No baths to fill and empty, no beds to make or bedrooms to clean. When they'm here it gets very hard at times, I can tell you.'

'Jasus, if this is easy, I'm not looking forwards to their return,' Grainne thought wryly, then asked aloud, 'When are they coming back here?'

Sarah shrugged her shapely shoulders. 'Could be any time now. Mrs Gurnock said the other day that John Croxall, he's the butler, would be coming back either today or tomorrow, to make ready for the family.' She looked at Walter the footman, and gibed, 'I'll bet you're looking forwards to seeing

46

Mr Croxall again, arn't you, Walter? You and him are very close friends, arn't you?'

The young man's bucolic features became instantly disgruntled, and he replied sourly, 'Ahr, I'm as close friends with John Croxall, as I am with the Devil.'

The rest of the servants roared with laughter, and Sarah sarcastically explained to Grainne, 'It's very hard on Walter and cruel unfair, because John Croxall's a bit of a slavedriver. He actually expects our Walter here to do some work occasionally, and Walter arn't been used to such harsh treatment, has you, Walter?'

Again the other servants laughed uproariously, and the young footman reddened and his protruding eyes bulged as he muttered angrily beneath his breath.

'Does Mr Croxall have much to do with us female servants?' Grainne asked innocently, and little Emily chortled.

'Not him, Grainne. Mrs Gurnock wun't let him near us if her can help it. Her likes to keep him all to herself.'

'Shhh!' Sarah Hobdon frowned warningly. 'If she hears about what you'se just said, you'll lose your place, my girl.'

But the twinkle in her eyes belied her frown, and the other servants grinned with pleasure.

'That's it now, breakfast's over,' Sarah Hobdon announced, and immediately the others rose to their feet and dispersed.

'Come on with me, Grainne,' the upper housemaid beckoned. 'I'll show you all round the house, so you'll know what is where.'

The tour through the big complex of corridors, rooms, outhouses, yards, gardens and stables took some time to complete, and Grainne was impressed with the opulent evidence of the wealth it represented, and mentally contrasted it with the suffering and starvation and death that she had just left behind her in her native country. She was driven to comment, 'It seems so unfair doesn't it, Sarah, when one family has all this, and there are millions knowing only want and suffering from their cradles to their graves?'

Sarah nodded, then told her in a low voice, 'I think the same thing, Grainne. But you'd best keep that opinion to yourself in this house. The master won't tolerate anybody voicing such truths. He's one o' them who wanted to set the army against

47

the Chartists, and if he even hears a whisper against the order o' things, then he goes bloody mad.'

She hesitated a moment, as if unsure that she should continue, then went on, 'Listen, my duck, this is in strictest confidence, understand?'

Grainne nodded solemnly.

Satisfied, the blonde girl continued. 'Well, as places go, this isn't too bad to be in service. We ates well, and we always gets our wages paid on the days appointed, as well as a full day off every month. There's a good many servants that I knows who envies us here. But, there's things happens here that you must turn a blind eye to, and keep a still tongue about, no matter what your own thoughts about what happens might be. Otherwise you'll get handed your sack without a character in double quick time. And the way things are in these parts now, it's very hard on the outside o' these walls for any girl to make her way. Without a character, then you might just as well give up all hopes of ever improving your lot. Times are cruel hard around these parts just now. I'll tell you true, that if I was to get handed me sack without a character from here, then I'd be feeling really desperate.'

Grainne knew that for a servant to be dismissed from his or her employment without a character reference was a very serious matter. To be dismissed without a reference meant that the chances of finding any other respectable position in domestic service became practically non-existent. Most men and women so dismissed faced a bleak future which all too often became a swift spiral downwards into a destitution so hopeless that they were forced to turn to crime, or to prostitution, merely to survive. So this type of dismissal was a very powerful threat to hold above a servant's head. From her own bitter experiences in Liverpool Grainne knew only too well how quickly a woman could fall to the depths.

'I was one of the lucky ones,' she thought thankfully. 'I managed to get out from that life before it destroyed me, and here I've got a fresh chance to make a new life for myself.'

However, the other girl's words had aroused a raging curiosity within Grainne. She accepted that all employers expected their servants to exercise discretion concerning household matters but there was something in Sarah Hobdon's tone that indicated happenings beyond mere household affairs. She could not help but ask, 'What do you mean, Sarah? What does happen here that I must turn blind eyes to, and say naught about?'

The blonde girl frowned, and shook her head. 'It doesn't matter. I shouldn't have said anything.'

Grainne was not to be so easily put off, however.

'Look, Sarah, I've a right to be warned in advance, haven't I? Otherwise I could maybe do or say the wrong thing and get into trouble through pure ignorance. Just because nobody was decent enough to tell me what I should know. And that wouldn't be fair, now would it?'

Sarah Hobdon's handsome face mirrored her own uncertainty and doubts.

'Come on, Sarah,' Grainne coaxed. 'You can trust me to say nothing about whatever you tell me.'

Abruptly the other girl's mood metamorphosed into irritable exasperation, and she snapped, 'I can't tell you anything more. It's my business and none of your'n. Now be quiet and come on, there's work to be done.'

Grainne dutifully followed, but her native shrewdness told her that whatever secret Sarah Hobdon was guarding was obviously troubling her, and that eventually the blonde-haired girl would be impelled to tell someone.

Grainne smiled self-mockingly, and mentally chided, 'And you do hope that it'll be yourself that she tells, don't you, you nosey cat!'

Chapter Seven

During the next couple of days Grainne worked mainly with Sarah Hobdon. Although the family were not in residence, the rooms were kept cleaned and fires lighted daily in all of them to prevent any dampness taking hold and spreading. As the upper housemaid Sarah Hobdon could have reserved for herself the lightest and least arduous tasks, such as dusting ornaments and cleaning furniture, and allotted to Grainne all the heavier work such as scrubbing floors, beating carpets, coal-carrying, grate-cleaning and so on. However, the blonde girl did not do this, but instead shared the heavier, dirtier work equally between them, a fact which caused Grainne to regard her with a burgeoning liking and respect.

Grainne also came to know her other fellow servants better. Walter, the footman, she found to be a stupid, lazy, but basically amiable young man, Emily and Patience, both likeable, decent, hardworking girls. But Grainne saw very little of the housekeeper. Mrs Gurnock would make periodic tours of inspection, ignoring Grainne and speaking only briefly to Sarah Hobdon. Then, would shut herself in her rooms until she emerged for the next tour of inspection.

On the afternoon of Grainne's fourth day at the Hall, she was in the linen store, a small room at the rear of the house, lined with shelves on which the household linen was kept ready for use after being laundered. There was a single small window set in the outer wall, and since the day was dull and overcast the room's interior was dark and gloomy. Grainne was stitching pillow-cases and to enable her to see the work she had a lighted candle, set in the middle of a circular iron holder of clear glass globes, filled with water. This candlelight striking through the globes was magnified and bent into more concentrated beams by this contraption, and threw a narrow shaft of intensified light onto the work-surface of the linen she held on her lap. Grainne was a fine needlewoman and, although the work was tedious and repetitive, she was content enough to sit here in the quiet peacefulness of this room, and allow her thoughts to wander where they might, while her fingers moved mechanically.

Inevitably it was Con Shonley, her husband, who dominated the images that came and went in her mind, and she relived their times of shared happiness. Immersed in her memories she was not aware of the footsteps approaching the linen store, and when its door was thrust open she looked up in surprise, then vented a cry of shock. For one brief instant she thought it was Conrad Shonley standing in the open doorway, his handsome swarthy features smiling at her. That instant passed and she saw that it was a stranger, tall and swarthily handsome, his hair and sidewhiskers long and oiled, stately in black tailcoat and trousers, highly polished shoes, starched white shirtfront and high stiff collar with a black neckcloth tied neatly around his throat.

Embarrassed by having cried out as she had, Grainne flustered, 'I'm sorry, but you shocked me.'

'Did I now? Well that's a terrible pity to shock a pretty woman like you.' The man's deep voice held a rustic burr, and there was a smile playing around his lips as he asked, 'Are you recovered from your shock now?'

Thinking he was mocking her, Grainne answered tartly, 'Indeed I am, and what might I do for you?'

The man chuckled, and shook his head slightly. 'Nothing, girl. Nothing at present, that is. But perhaps later you might be able to oblige me with some little service or other.'

Grainne now knew for certain that he was making mock of her, and her quick temper sparked. 'I don't know who you might be, but I've work to do myself, so I'll be obliged if you'll go and leave me to get on with it.'

'Whoa, take care now, John Croxall. She bites!' the man exclaimed, and hearing the name Grainne suddenly realised who he was.

51

'Ohh Jasus! You're the butler, arn't you?' She felt utterly mortified. 'You're Mr Croxall, and you've come back from London!'

He smiled and nodded. Grainne could only vent a long sigh of exasperation, and shake her head helplessly.

'If I'd known who you were, I wouldn't have spoken so sharp!' she offered in apology, knowing that this man could ensure her instant dismissal if he so wished.

He waved her words aside. 'Say no more about it. I'm glad to meet a girl with spirit.' He studied her briefly, and his eyes gleamed with appreciation for what he saw. Then he asked her. 'What's your name?'

'Grainne Shonley, Mr Croxall.'

'Grainne,' he repeated, savouring the sound it made. 'Grainne . . . I like that name, it suits you. It has beauty, does it not?'

Then, without another word, he turned and walked away.

For a few moments Grainne's chagrin persisted as she wished she had acted with more circumspection, but then she shrugged. 'Ah, what does it matter anyway in the heel of the hunt. He didn't seem angry with me when he left, did he?'

She concentrated on her sewing, but a short time later was again interrupted by the advent of Sarah Hobdon, who was accompanied by two other young women, dressed in outdoor cloaks and bonnets.

'Grainne, these are your bedfellows, Amy Davis and Rosy Bright,' Sarah Hobdon said, and Grainne rose politely to greet them.

Rosy Bright suited her name. She was a plump, rosy-cheeked, merry-eyed girl. Amy Davis was small and sallow skinned, and appeared frail although muffled in her voluminous black cloak.

Both girls examined Grainne closely, and Amy Davis told her, 'Youm beautiful, arn't you?' She spoke with the high-pitched lilt of Birmingham. 'I'll bet all the men am forever trying to lift your skirts.' There was nothing prurient in the girl's tone, merely an admiring envy.

At first grim unwelcome memories lanced into Grainne's mind, but she forced herself to smile, and answered, 'There's some have tried that, but only one has succeeded, and I was married to him.'

52

Her new acquaintances laughed, and Sarah Hobdon told Grainne, 'Leave that sewing for now. All the rest have come back from London as well, so you'd best come up to the kitchen and I'll tell you who they am.' She paused for a moment, and then added with a hint of malice, 'It won't do for you to take a fancy for another girl's beau, 'ull it?'

Grainne received the barb casually and merely smiled and shook her head. 'No, that will never do, will it?'

The large kitchen seemed packed with bodies, the full skirts of the women taking up three times the space that a man might fill, and there was a hubbub of voices.

Patience Drew and little Emily bustled around serving out jugs of beer and plates of food, and the gathering had a festive air.

'Have the Herbertsons come back as well?' Grainne asked, and Sarah Hobdon shook her ringleted head.

'No, they'll be arriving tomorrow.' A slight flush suddenly coloured her cheeks and she frowned. 'And this time Mr Edwin will be with them.'

Grainne's intuition told her what the reason was for that frown.

'Chases us maids, does he?' she asked without thinking, and Sarah Hobdon rounded upon her, hissing furiously.

'Don't you dare say such! Don't you dare!'

Surprised by the other girl's reaction, Grainne could only reply placatingly, 'All right, Sarah. I meant no harm by it!'

As Sarah Hobdon flounced away Grainne became conscious that Amy Davis's eyes were fixed upon her. When she returned her look the frail girl lifted her finger to her lips, looked meaningly after Sarah Hobdon, and gave a slight shake of her head. Understanding, Grainne smiled and nodded briefly.

Patience Drew brought the three new arrivals a large jug of porter, which they shared between them, taking turns to sip at the heavy dark drink.

'Ah, this is a drop o' good, this is.' Rosy Bright grinned with satisfaction, the foam of the porter thick on the soft down above her upper lip. Her accent was the drawling long-vowelled local dialect, and she radiated a ruddy good health. Grainne found herself liking the girl instinctively.

'Now then, Grainne, I'll show you who's who.' Rosy Bright

grinned. 'And theer's some real sour bleeders among 'um, so it's best youm forewarned. That's Mrs Tomlinson, the head cook.' This was a dour-faced, gaunt woman, standing now scowling around her at these intruders into her domain.

'That's Mr Charles's valet over theer.' He was an effeminate-looking, slender-bodied young man. Even at this distance Grainne could smell the fragrant scent he was drenched in. He wore a well-cut black tailcoat and trousers, with an abundance of frilled white linen. His hair was poetically long, with a centre parting, and he favoured curled side-whiskers and the small tufted beard beneath his lower lip known as the imperial.

As if sensing Grainne's regard he looked across at her, and tossed his pomaded head, his limp-wristed hand languidly waving a large silk handkerchief before his rouged face as if he wished to perfume the air around him against the smells of his fellow servants.

'He calls hisself Monsewer Armand, and says he comes from Paris,' Rosy informed with a giggle. 'But I knows that his real name is Albert Spicer, and he was born in Brummagem.'

Grainne giggled herself.

'Them two am the parlourmaids. Fanny Caldicot and Emma Smith, and they doon't half think they'm summat above the rest on us housemaids, I'll tell you.' Both of these young women had very long ringlets hanging down below their multi-feathered bonnets, and they wore brightly coloured, flounced carriage dresses and fashionably long paisley shawls.

'And that's Madamooselle Antoinette, Mrs Herbertson's maid. Her's a real Frog, and her arn't the full shillin'.' Rosy surreptitiously tapped her own head with her thick fingers. 'Her's a bit doolally tap. Mind you, that arn't to be wondered at. Mrs Sophia 'ud drive anybody bleedin' mad wi' her tantrums.'

Grainne stared at the Frenchwoman with interest. The woman was wearing unrelieved black, even her jewellery was jet, and a dark whispy veil almost hid her features. Yet although she was short and dumpy bodied, there was an indefinable air of elegance about her.

'She wears that veil because she's so bleedin' ugly.' Rosy Bright grinned, and when Grainne stared enquiringly at her, stated vehemently, 'It's God's truth, Grainne. Her really looks like a bloody frog, and I means the beast, not the people. That's why her keeps her face covered as much as she can.'

There was only one other man in the room, and he wore the elaborate dark and light blue livery with its plentiful gold lace. He was tall, with close-set eyes, a pasty complexion and powdered quiffed hair and long side-whiskers.

'Who is he?' Grainne nodded towards the tall, pigeon-chested footman.

Rosy sniffed disparagingly. 'That's Henry Jenkins, that is. He's a bloody Taffy. I can't abear him meself. Always trying to shove his hands up your skirts. He's supposed to be trothed to Fanny Caldicot.' She indicated the carroty-haired parlourmaid.

'More fool her, that's what I says. He knocks her about now, so when they'm wed it'll be God help the silly cow, because he'll have the right to serve her badly then, wun't he? Mind you, her's a nasty bitch, so perhaps they'm well suited.'

The entrance of Mrs Gurnock sobered the festive air. Although only small and slender, the woman radiated an aura of grim authority.

She clapped her hands and silence ensued immediately. 'There is much to be done to prepare for the family's reception tomorrow afternoon. Get changed into your working clothes and report to me in my office when you have done so.'

Obediently the newly arrived servants trooped from the room, and Grainne decided that she had better return to her sewing. Monsieur Armand was still standing to one side of the doorway as she went out, and he smiled at her, disclosing small white even teeth, then beckoned with his be-ringed fingers, to indicate he wished to speak to her.

Grainne halted uncertainly, and the valet put his head close to hers so that she could feel the warmth of his breath against her ear, and his perfumed scent filled her nostrils.

'Is not our Mrs Gurnock wonderful!' he lisped softly, his speech accented like a Frenchman's. 'If she lived in India she would be considered sacred.'

The gibe was given added drollery by the way in which he said it, and Grainne could not help but laugh. He grinned delightedly at her, and told her, 'I like you, Mamzelle, you have the sense of humour which it is rare to encounter among these Jean Boules. What is your name?'

'Grainne. Grainne Shonley.' Grainne had always had a soft spot for people who could make her laugh, and she was prepared to accept his overture of friendship.

'My name is Monsieur Armand de Villefranche,' he lisped, then closed one mascaraed eyelid in a huge wink and, in broadest Birmingham accents, told her, 'but you con call me Albert Spicer of Deritend, my duck.'

Grainne laughed again, and whispered back. 'All right then, I shall call you Albert.'

'*C'est bien!*' He shook her hand. 'But only call me Albert when we'em by ourselves. I have to guard me professional image.' He flourished his silk handkerchief and bowed low. '*Alors,* I must go or that sacred creature will come in search of me.'

He minced along the corridor in front of Grainne, trailing his scent behind him.

Chapter Eight

Grainne had spent a restless and uncomfortable night in the bed she shared with the two other young women. Rosy Bright's snores trumpeted for what seemed endless periods, and interspersed with these were the bouts of racking coughing which periodically shook Amy Davis's frail body. Grainne was lying awake when Sarah Hobdon came shouting along the corridor to rouse the under servants for work, and although feeling bleary-eyed from lack of sleep she slipped from the bed with almost a sense of relief. By the time her bedfellows had stirred and woken up Grainne was dressed and on her way downstairs.

Little Emily was sitting at the big kitchen table in company with Mrs Tomlinson, Patience Drew, and another squat, tow-headed kitchen maid, and as Grainne came back through the kitchen with her work tools, Emily grinned at her.

'How did you manage for sleep wi' them two, Grainne? We calls 'um the "Horn and Trumpet".'

'Not very well,' Grainne admitted ruefully. 'Still, I expect I'll get used to sharing the bed with them in time.'

'You got no other choice iffen youm to stay here, girl. It's either get used to it, or find another place in another household,' the cook, Mrs Tomlinson, informed her dourly.

'I know that,' Grainne answered quietly, 'and I wasn't whining about it. I was only answering the question truthfully.'

The elder woman regarded her keenly for a couple of seconds, then her gaunt features softened a little. 'Here, have a cup o' tay. It's a frosty morning, and you needs a bit o' warmth in your belly to start the day on.'

She poured some tea from the large pot into a crock tumbler and handed it to Grainne. 'Theer's a dish o' milk on the dresser theer, and some sugar if you wants it. But look sharp drinking it, otherwise I'll have Mrs Gurnock arter me for keeping you back from your work.'

Grainne gratefully drank the hot liquid down and, feeling greatly refreshed, went to her work.

Throughout the day Mrs Gurnock and John Croxall chivvied and drove the staff, allowing them only the briefest of intervals to gulp down their breakfast and midday dinner.

Directly after midday the carriage attended by the two footmen, Walter and Henry, was despatched to Birmingham to meet the train on which the Herbertsons were travelling. Grainne watched the vehicle's departure from an upstairs room and was forced to smile at the lordly arrogant air Walter and his fellow footman assumed as they mounted the rear step for the journey.

By mid-afternoon the preparations to receive the family had been completed, and Mrs Gurnock then sent the servants to wash and change into their best uniforms to be ready to greet the Herbertsons with the proper ceremony.

Grainne, Amy and Rosy took turns at the wash basin in their tiny attic, and then changed into their best black dresses and high-bibbed white aprons. While Grainne was brushing her long black hair prior to braiding and coiling it close to her head, Amy apologised nervously, 'I'm ever so sorry if I kept you awake wi' me coughin' last night, Grainne.' Her timid eyes flickered uneasily between Grainne's face and the floor. 'I knows it can be a terrible nuisance at times. But it arn't always so bad as it was last night.'

Grainne regarded the frail, undersized girl with pity. 'There's no need for you to apologise to me for it, Amy,' she told her gently. 'You can't help something like that. And I slept well enough.'

'And I did.' Rosy Bright put in bluffly, and smiling broadly told Grainne, 'Does you know, my duck, once my yed touches that pillow I'm away in the land o' nod, I am. Nothing can wake me.'

'So I gathered.' Grainne smiled with gentle irony.

58

'Come on girls, it's time you was all downstairs,' Sarah Hobdon called along the corridor.

Looking into the piece of broken mirror that was propped on the washstand Grainne arranged her long-ribboned lace cap on her glossy hair, using hair pins to fix it securely.

'Come on Amy.' She helped the younger girl to arrange her cap and pin it, then all three girls ran downstairs.

Outside the great front doors on the gravelled forecourt the gardeners, grooms and stableboys were being marshalled into line by John Croxall, while inside the entrance hall the indoor servants were being similarly mustered by Mrs Gurnock.

'Now listen carefully all of you.' Mrs Gurnock stood before the line to instruct them. 'When the family arrives you must bow or curtsey as they pass you. If any of them should do you the honour of having a word with you, then you must answer clearly and forthrightly. But do not answer boldly, or with any unseemly display of over-confidence, and particularly not any hint of undue familiarity.'

She fixed stern eyes on Monsieur Armand, who was standing nearest to the doors. He met the housekeeper's challenging stare with an indignant toss of his pomaded head and limp-wristed hands on hips. Mrs Gurnock's dark eyes radiated her scorn. She liked masculine men, and this effeminate creature offended her sense of propriety. Grainne bit her lips to keep from smiling. During her brief encounter with the valet she had found him friendly and amusing, and she was not repelled by his sexuality.

The sounds of iron clad wheels and horses' hooves crunching over the gravel gave notice that the family had arrived and, with a final warning glance along the motionless line, Mrs Gurnock went to join John Croxall on the forecourt. The carriage crunched to a halt, and the footmen sprang down to the ground and ran to open the door and lower the folding steps.

John Croxall bowed low, then advanced to the carriage and offered his arm for Mrs Sophia Herbertson to lean on as she descended. She was a woefully plain-faced young woman, whose red blotched, pasty complexion was not enhanced by the bilious green colouring of her bonnet and travelling cloak. Her expression was petulant, and she did not deign to acknowledge the respectful greetings of the butler or the housekeeper, but swept grandly up the stone steps and through the hallway, scowling at the line of bowing and curtseying servants as she went past them, the wide skirts of her crinolined gown hissing across the carpeting.

Mr Charles Herbertson followed more slowly behind her, allowing Croxall to take his hat and gloves from him in the entrance hall, but keeping his voluminous travelling cloak wrapped around his corpulent body as he slowly walked along the servant line. His eyes studied each of them briefly in passing. Grainne noted that he was tall, with sparse iron-grey hair and long side-whiskers, and had hard blue eyes.

The son, Edwin Herbertson, lounged through the open doorway, and regarded his father's back with a sneering expression. He was as tall as the older man, and almost as corpulent. His long hair hung down his fat cheeks in greasy strands, and despite his expensive black clothing and fine white linen, there was a suggestion of something unclean about his appearance. He came swaggering after his father, his eyes dwelling on the younger, prettier women, and when he came to Grainne he stopped and asked her, 'What's your name, girl?'

'It's Shonley, sir,' she told him, experiencing an acute repulsion as his small greedy eyes roamed over her face and breasts.

'She's the new under housemaid, Mr Edwin,' Mrs Gurnock informed him, following behind. 'Come over from Ireland.'

'Weally?' He used the affected impediment of speech favoured by the ultra fashionable young bloods and cavalry officers. 'I'm surpwised to see that she's such a pwetty and well-nouwished cweature. I thought that the Iwish were all starving.'

His eyes lingered for a moment or two longer on Grainne's full breasts, and then he swaggered on.

Mrs Gurnock frowned at Grainne, as if she personally resented the notice taken of her by Edwin Herbertson, then clapped her hands sharply and ordered the servants, 'Go on about your duties.'

As Grainne was walking towards the stairway at the rear of

the house, Mrs Gurnock intercepted her. 'I see Mr Edwin took note of you, Shonley.'

Her accusatory tone caused Grainne to stare curiously at her. 'I didn't invite him to do such, Mrs Gurnock,' she retorted defensively.

The housekeeper's expression was grim as she snapped, 'You see to it that you don't invite his notice in future either, my wench.'

With that cryptic instruction she turned and went in the opposite direction.

Grainne slowly walked on, remembering Sarah Hobdon's earlier reaction concerning Edwin Herbertson.

'There's something wrong here,' she thought, 'and it's something to do with Edwin Herbertson.'

She recalled the way his eyes had lingered so greedily on her own breasts, and decided, 'You'll be one of those who tries to make free with the servant girls, Mr Edwin. And judging by the way she felt about you coming back here you've probably tried it on already with Sarah. I'll wager that that's the secret she's guarding.'

Grainne had known such households before, where the male members of the employers' family regarded their female servants as objects that could be used for their sexual pleasure.

'Well, you'll not use me like that, Edwin Herbertson,' she promised grimly. 'Not you, or any other man.'

61

Chapter Nine

With the family in residence the housemaids' daily workloads greatly increased. All of the day rooms still had to be cleaned and fires lit in them early in the morning. Then portable hipbaths had to be set up in the family's various dressing rooms and filled with hot water, and a fire lit in the grate to warm the room. When the family came down to their breakfasts the housemaids turned their attentions to the bedrooms, working in pairs to make the beds, clean the rooms, empty the hip-baths, washbasins and chamberpots. The latter task was one that Grainne detested. The used chamberpots had to be covered with a cloth and carried down the back staircases to be emptied in the outdoor privvies, and then the pots themselves had to be scoured clean and wiped. The smell of Edwin Herbertson's pot in particular turned Grainne's stomach and made her feel nauseous.

The bedmaking was no easy work, each of the great beds having three mattresses. The heavy bottom mattress filled with straw was turned daily, as was the middle mattress of horsehair. Then the top mattress, filled with feathers, had to be pummelled and shaken and turned until all the compressed lumps had been dissolved and the mattress rendered puffed and airy-light.

Daily all the uncovered oaken floors were polished with beeswax, and once a week every carpet was rolled up and taken downstairs to be beaten, the deal floors beneath them were then scrubbed. The constant kneeling made the maids' knees sore and inflamed, and periodically one or other of the girls would be almost crippled with pain as the inflammation of their kneecaps became chronic.

Always they worked against the clock, because the part of their work in the family's living areas was expected to be completed by twelve o'clock midday. The afternoons and evenings brought no respite however, because Mrs Gurnock was always able to find them an abundance of other work. Sewing, washing, ironing and lending assistance wherever the housekeeper directed kept the girls busy from early morning until they went wearily to the comfortless attics to sleep.

Yet, despite the strict discipline and hard grinding of her days, Grainne paradoxically welcomed the non-stop toil. It ensured that she had little or no time to brood on the tragic happenings of her life, and although the sadness of losing Con still weighed upon her, yet with each passing day her grief eased a little more, and increasingly she was able to remember her husband with pleasure rather than pain.

Her relationships with the other servants were dictated by the rigid adherence to hierarchical structure and precedence which was enforced at Millwood Hall. The lower servants still took their meals in the kitchen, but the upper servants ate in the 'pugs parlour', the housekeeper's dining room, which adjoined Mrs Gurnock's suite of rooms. There were also strict lines of demarcation concerning the sort of task the differing ranks of servants could be called upon to perform. Grainne found it ironic that she and her fellow housemaids were expected to carry heavy buckets of water and scuttles of coal up several flights of stairs, while the two big strong footmen were only tasked to carry letters and calling cards on a silver salver.

There was therefore little social intercourse between upper and lower servants. Neither did any of the lower servants, with the exceptions of the two footmen, see much of the Herbertson family. The only occasion on which all the various members of the household were gathered together was on Sunday mornings, when all the servants and the family joined forces in the large library to hold a short prayer meeting.

With a large number of staff now resident there were inevitably squabbles and petty feuds, but Grainne kept aloof from these, and although several of the male servants had indicated their interest in her as a potential sexual partner she had not encouraged them. Although she had healthy sexual needs and desires, Grainne had to be in love with a man before she could

63

willingly fulfil those needs and desires, and at this time her heart was still held by her late husband. So, when certain of her male fellow servants had made advances towards her, she had politely but firmly declined. All but one of them had accepted with good humour. The exception was Henry Jenkins. He continued to pester Grainne, and did not seem able to accept the fact that she wanted nothing to do with him.

It was eleven days since the Herbertsons had returned to Millwood Hall and directly after the servants' midday dinner Mrs Gurnock sent Grainne to clean at the rear of the house. She was on her hands and knees scrubbing one of the stone-flagged service passages with hot water and caustic soda, when the Welsh footman came in search of her.

'Theer you be, Paddy. I was missing you. How are you, girl?'

Grainne frowned when she heard his high-pitched, singsong voice. She straightened up onto her knees, her hands resting lightly on the rim of the bucket of water. The hard work had warmed her thoroughly and her cheeks were flushed, while strands of her raven-black hair had escaped the confines of her mobcap to frame her oval face.

Henry Jenkins stared lustfully at her full breasts swelling out of the bib of the coarse apron.

'Bugger me, but youm a sweet-looking cratur, Paddy. I swear you've got the best pair o' tits that I'se seen in ages. When are you and me going to be getting together?'

Even at a distance she could smell the reek of beer and gin from his mouth, and with a flash of nervousness she realised that he was half drunk. Although he irritated her intensely, Grainne was mindful of the fact that in his present state he could easily be triggered into violence. The other girls had told her how when he had been drinking he battered Fanny Caldicot on the slightest pretext. So she tried to reply lightly.

'Now Henry, you know well that you've already got a sweet-heart. Sure now, what would Fanny say if she knew you were saying such things to me?'

He puffed out his chest, preening himself in his fine livery.

'Her knows better than to say anything at all to me, Paddy. I'm not a fellow who can be told what to do by any woman. Or anybody else for that matter. I'm a real man.'

Grainne found his posturing and bragging pathetic, and she was forced to drop her head to hide the scorn that sprang to her lips. Jenkins was as stupid as he was conceited, and he took her lowered head to be a coy encouragement. Grinning, he moved closer to her.

'If you were to become my sweetheart, Paddy, why then I'd send Fanny Caldicot packing double sharp. I can promise you that.'

Grainne shook her head. 'I don't want any man for sweetheart.'

'Now, Cariad, you don't really mean that, do you?' He was now standing directly over her. 'A pretty woman like you, who's a widow and knows what it's all about, well, you needs a man.'

She looked up at him and frowned. 'No. That's the last thing I need.'

He grinned confidently, and now his lust for her shapely body was driving him. 'You needs a good stiff prick up you, girl.' His hand moved to cup his groin. 'And once you've felt this between your legs, you'll be begging for more on it. Come on now, give us a little kiss.'

Bending, he grabbed her upper arm and pulled her upright. She pushed him away and spat out angrily, 'Get away from me, and keep away. I don't want you or any other man.'

He reacted with an angry scowl, and his voice rose. 'Don't think you can prick-tease me, you Irish slut. I know you wants a good fuckin', and I'm the boyo to give it you.'

He reached for her again, and this time she snatched up the bucket of dirty water and stepped backwards.

'Get away from me, and leave me in peace, or I'll chuck this lot over you,' she warned.

'You wouldn't fuckin' dare,' he shouted and came at her, hands seeking for her breasts.

Grainne lifted the bucket and hurled its contents straight into his face. He cried out in shock, and then bellowed with pain as he felt the stinging of the caustic soda in his eyes. Clapping his hands to his face he rubbed frantically.

'You fuckin' bastard!' he screamed at her. 'I'll fuckin' kill you for this.'

Grainne retreated another few steps, and readied herself to

strike at him with the empty bucket if he should again come at her. He pulled a handkerchief from his tailcoat pocket and wiped his eyes and face. When he could see clearly again he looked down at his soaked, water-dripping livery and hissed venomously, 'I'm agoing to give you what for, you Irish bitch.'

'Don't come near me,' Grainne warned again, and lifted the bucket threateningly.

'I'm going to smash your fuckin' face for you, you bitch!' He moved slowly forwards, fists balled, features working with his fury.

'You're smashing nobody's face, Jenkins!' The harsh shout stopped Henry Jenkins in his tracks, and fear overspread his angry scowl.

Grainne looked towards the end of the passage to see the butler, John Croxall, standing almost blocking the narrow entrance with his broad shoulders.

'Get back here to me, Jenkins,' John Croxall ordered, and when the footman hesitated, suddenly shouted, 'Get here, I say!'

Jenkins shambled back along the corridor, and Croxall watched him with a contemptuous frown on his swarthy features.

'Change your clothes, then go to my pantry and wait until I come there.'

When the man had disappeared John Croxall advanced along the passage towards Grainne, who was still standing with the bucket clenched in her hands. The butler's lips twitched in a grim fleeting smile.

'It's all right, Shonley. You may put the bucket down now. I'm not going to attack you.'

Feeling flustered Grainne put the bucket at her feet. Croxall glanced briefly at the water on the floor, then told Grainne, 'It's all right, Shonley, I'm not blaming you for this. I heard what went on, and I know that Jenkins has been pestering you since we returned here from London. He'll not do so again.'

Grainne's eyes widened slightly with surprise at his display of knowledge. But she made no reply, and after a moment or two he ordered, 'You'd best get this mess cleaned up, Shonley.'

Obediently she took her floorcloth and began to mop up the

dirty water, wringing the cloth out into the bucket. She was uncomfortably aware that he was still standing staring down at her, and she felt a burgeoning discomfiture beneath that silent scrutiny. Angry at herself for feeling that emotion, she tried to ignore him, and to forget he was there. But try as she might she remained uncomfortably aware of his presence, and it was with a sense of real relief that eventually she heard his footsteps receding into the distance.

The hours of the afternoon slowly passed, and Grainne scrubbed and mopped, and scrubbed and mopped, her only respite from the drudgery being when she went to the scullery to refill her bucket with fresh clean water and soda. Although on these trips she encountered other staff she said nothing concerning what had occurred between herself, Henry Jenkins and John Croxall.

With the coming of dusk old Ezra, the ancient, bent-bodied, odd-job man went through the house striking a big brass gong, its resonating echoes being the signal to the servants that it was their supper-time. Tired and hungry by now, Grainne greeted the signal with a sigh of thankfulness and finishing the last yard of stone flags she took her bucket and implements and hurried towards the kitchen.

When Grainne arrived there she found that the other lower servants had already congregated around the large table, on which the supper was set out: bread, cheese and assorted pickles, and jugs of beer. Hungry as she was Grainne concentrated on eating a thick wedge of bread and cheese, and drinking from her pot of beer. Then, when the first gnawing pangs of her hunger had been assuaged, she became aware that there was an air of hushed expectancy among her fellow servants. She glanced curiously around the table, to be greeted with knowing nods and winks from some of her companions. Then she met the virulent glare of Fanny Caldicot. Grainne glanced quickly around the table once again, and realised that Henry Jenkins was not present.

'Where's Henry Jenkins?' she asked Walter, who normally sat by his fellow footman.

Walter grinned but before he could make any reply Fanny Caldicot erupted furiously, 'Just hark to the hussy! Just hark to the hard-faced bitch!' Her features contorted with rage, she tried to mimic Grainne's soft brogue. 'Where's Henry Jenkins? Where's Henry Jenkins? As if you didn't know where he was, you bloody Irish cow!'

'That's enough o' that,' the cook, Mrs Tomlinson, ordered sharply from her seat at the head of the long table. 'There'll be no rowing in my kitchen, or you'll both be packing your boxes.'

For a few brief seconds Grainne could only stare uncomprehendingly at the furious carrot-haired parlourmaid. Then dawning comprehension caused her to demand, 'Has something happened to him?'

'As if you didn't know, you Irish whore!' Fanny Caldicot snarled venomously, and she suddenly came to her feet and lunged across the table towards Grainne, shrieking out, 'I'll tear the fuckin' eyes from your yed, you whore's melt!'

Mrs Tomlinson moved from her seat like lightning, grabbing the hefty young woman by her hair and dragging her backwards so that she fell over the bench to lie on her back on the floor. Her plump booted legs waved in the air as she shrieked obscenities.

The other servants erupted in howling laughter, but the cook bawled, 'Shurrup all on you or I'll fetch Mrs Gurnock down to you this minnit!'

The invocation of the housekeeper's name brought instant fearful silence, although some of the bolder spirits were hard put to muffle their glee.

The cook dragged Fanny Caldicot upright by sheer bodily strength, and hissed into her furious reddened face, 'Get back to your work, you stupid bitch!'

When the younger woman's mouth opened, the cook raised her fingers warningly before Fanny Caldicot's eyes.

'If I hears one more word from you, I'll make sure that youm packing your own box this very hour.'

The parlourmaid's face worked in savage grimaces, and tears of anger fell onto her plump red cheeks, but with a final sullen glare directed at Grainne, she tugged free of the cook's hand and slouched out of the kitchen.

'Goo on, the lot of you. Gerrout o' my kitchen.' Mrs Tomlinson drove the others out after the parlourmaid but restrained Grainne when she would have gone also.

'You wait here a bit, Shonley. I wants a word with you.'

Grainne halted and stood waiting while the cook told her kitchen helpers, 'You lot stay out theer in the passage as well, until I calls for you.'

Then she turned back to Grainne. 'I wants a word in private with you, my wench. Now Henry Jenkins has been given his sack by John Croxall for moithering you, and he's already packed and gone from this house. He's left here without a character.'

Grainne could understand now why Fanny Caldicot had felt so savagely towards her. She shook her head regretfully. 'It was no wish of mine to see Henry Jenkins dismissed like that, Mrs Tomlinson. I've never made any complaint to anyone against him.'

'I knows that, my duck.' The cook's dour features softened momentarily. 'And to my mind he deserves what he got. John Croxall told me what happened between you. And Fanny Caldicot has had a lucky escape, if her only could know it. The bugger's bin knocking her about for months now, and they'm only trothed. God only knows what he'd have treated her like if they'd been wed and he'd had the right to serve her badly. Iffen her's got any sense at all, which I doubt, then her 'ull stay here and leave him go.'

She patted Grainne's shoulder reassuringly. 'So don't you go bothering and regretting what's happened to that bloody sod, my duck. He's long deserved it.' Her voice dropped to a whisper. 'I wanted to tell you that in private, because I can't be seen to be taking sides, or favouring one above another. But I reckons you to be a good-living and hard-working girl.'

'Thank you,' Grainne told her with genuine warmth, and the cook nodded brusquely, and turned away shouting, 'Patience, Emily, Aggie, get back in here, there's work to be done.'

Chapter Ten

Charles Herbertson stood in the large drawing room with his back to the fire, his hands lifting the rear skirts of his frockcoat so that the heat could bathe his large buttocks. His fat florid face was grim, and his mood one of angry disgust as he regarded his only son and heir who was slouched with out-stretched legs on the ornate plum-velvet chaise longue.

Although it was nearly midday the younger Herbertson was still wearing a long flowing red-and-gold brocaded dressing gown, secured around his pot belly with enormously-tasselled gold cords. A fez-like smoking cap was perched on his greasy hair, which hung uncombed and lank down the sides of his puffy red face.

'Well, Edwin?' Charles Herbertson demanded. 'I am still awaiting your answer.'

The young man scowled petulantly. 'Dammit all, Pa, cannot you let the matter dwop? Must you keep on wepeating the same questions day after day?'

'I repeat the questions day after day because for once I would prefer the truth to come from your lips,' his father snapped heatedly.

'But I have told you the twuth wepeatedly, Pa. And still you appear unable to accept what I say. I weally cannot be blamed because a thieving little slut scwemed when I caught her stealing fwom my wooms. She lied when she said those things about me. And that is the twuth, Pa. I swear on my dear dead mother's gwave.'

'If the girl lied, then why is the university refusing to take you back?'

'Because the dons are pwiggish fools, who wesent young fellows like me having any high jinks. I've alweady admitted that I invited the slut back to my wooms to have a bit of fun with her. But I didn't harm her. She was fwightened for her own filthy hide when I caught her stealing. That's why she scweamed and kicked up such a damned fuss,' the young man whined pettishly.

The older man scowled with contempt. 'How did I ever produce a degraded animal like you? A snivelling cowardly weakling! A perverted drunkard who has brought nothing but shame upon my name!'

Edwin Herbertson reacted to his father's bitter verbal assault with a sullen glare, but made no answer, and after a moment his blood-shot eyes slid away from his father's face and he appeared to become completely engrossed in the huge tassels of his dressing gown, which he turned and twisted in his soft, grubby-fingered hands.

Charles Herbertson experienced an intense desire to take his son by the throat and throttle him physically. But with an immense exertion of self-control he merely snapped, 'Get out of my sight, damn you!'

The young man shambled from the room without speaking or even looking at his father.

Alone, Charles Herbertson vented a shuddering sigh, and his features sagged into a tragic defeated mask. He was a hard and callous man, ruthless in business and in the pursuit of his own interests. But his son was his Achilles heel.

After some considerable time, he drew in a deep breath, and his face assumed its customary arrogant lineaments. Moving to the side of the fireplace, he tugged on the long silken bellcord, and when the neat parlourmaid appeared in answer to the summons, he told her, 'I wish to speak with Mrs Gurnock.'

While he waited for his housekeeper's arrival, Charles Herbertson's thoughts ranged unhappily over his present dilemma. He was a man of overweening self-pride, both in his name, and in his wealth and possessions. Because of his ruthlessness in business he had made many enemies, and possessed no real friends. His only blood relative was his son Edwin. He had married his second wife, for whom he had no love and little

71

liking, purely in hopes that she would give him more sons of the type he craved, fashioned in his own image.

His lips curled contemptuously. All that the ugly bad-tempered bitch had produced after a succession of agonising and dangerous labours were stillborn female children. Charles Herbertson was beginning to doubt that she would ever succeed in giving him a living son. Naturally he had considered at times obtaining a divorce from Sophia, but here his own inordinate vanity stopped him from doing so. He could not tolerate the thought of failure in any course of action he set out to complete, and so he would continue with his marriage and continue impregnating his wife, even though it might lead to her premature death.

In the meantime there was the problem of Edwin. 'My cross to bear,' he thought bitterly. But he knew that while Edwin remained his sole blood relative, then he would never be able to bring himself to disown his only child, no matter what the young man might do to offend against God and man.

'He's blood of my blood, and that is paramount above all else. Damn and blast the fate that sent him to me!'

But if fate had served Charles Herbertson ill by sending him Edwin for a son, it had served him well in his choice of house-keeper. Ruth Gurnock had served him with a fierce and devoted loyalty for many years, and if there was any person in the world that he trusted, it was this small, slender, beautiful middle-aged woman who now came to the drawing room in answer to his summons.

He smiled bleakly at her. 'Mr Edwin will not be returning to the university, Mrs Gurnock.'

Her face mirrored instant concern, and he confirmed, 'He will be remaining here at the Hall while I and my wife are in America.'

'Do you know yet how long you might be absent, sir?' Ruth Gurnock asked quietly.

'Possibly nine months, possibly even a year. I have to remain there until my interests in that country have been placed on a sound footing.' He paused, his forehead furrowed as though he were deep in thought, and the woman waited in respectful silence.

'Now. Concerning Mr Edwin.' Charles Herbertson's

expression was one of resignation. 'I do not have to remind you, Mrs Gurnock, of the absolute trust and confidence I repose in you.'

'Indeed you do not, sir,' the woman assured fervently.

'Just so, Mrs Gurnock. Just so. You have proven your loyalty to me on so many occasions.' He smiled at her with genuine appreciation, then sobered again and went on: 'I confess openly that I am not confident as to the continuation of Mr Edwin's present seclusion and good behaviour, and if it were not for the fact that I shall have so many pressing concerns to attend to whilst I am in America, I would have insisted that he accompany me there. However, if the worst should happen, and he should yet again besmirch my good name, then I know that I can rely upon you to do your utmost endeavours to rectify whatever unfortunate situation might occur.'

'Indeed you can, sir,' she assured him vehemently.

He nodded. 'Just so, Mrs Gurnock. Just so. Well I think that to be all for now.' His manner became brisk. 'I shall be leaving for America in a few weeks. So you may begin to put the necessary preparations in train.'

'Very good, sir.' She bobbed a curtsey.

Mrs Gurnock hurried back to her office, and once inside rummaged in her desk for the bottle of gin she kept there. She drank straight from the bottle, exhaling gustily as the fiery spirit jolted through her. Then she sat down at her desk and shook her head in foreboding.

'What troubles will you bring down on your poor father's head this time, Edwin Herbertson, I wonder?'

In his sitting room, Edwin Herbertson was staring moodily out of the window at the bleak countryside. He was not happy here at Millwood Hall, and was feeling increasingly restless with every long dull day that passed with such grinding slowness. He was not the type of young man who was suited to the countryside and its way of life. He had no interest in the traditional pastimes and sports of a country gentleman. Hunting, shooting and fishing held no joys for him. Riding or other physical exercise he found far too arduous; the society of those few neighbouring families who were his social equals far too tedious; reading, or writing, or painting, too excruciatingly boring.

Edwin Herbertson's pleasures were purely of the flesh; drinking, eating, and sex in all its manifold perversity, and his appetite for the latter was unceasing. But Edwin Herbertson's sexual tastes were not the normal healthy lustful drives of the majority of men. Instead Edwin Herbertson's satisfactions were obtained through the infliction of pain and degradation upon his unfortunate sexual partners. Because of his wealth he could afford to buy women, but among the circles he moved in word of his perverted proclivity quickly spread and increasingly he was coming to discover that only the most desperate and degraded women would go with him. And Edwin Herbertson had no desire for raddled, diseased flesh; he craved young, fresh, tender bodies to vent his furies upon.

It was this craving that had led to him being sent down from his university. A young barmaid, flattered by the attentions of such a wealthy and free-spending young gentleman, had allowed herself to be inveigled into spending a night with him in his college lodgings. Edwin Herbertson's perverted cravings had driven him beyond control, and the girl's resultant screams of pain and terror had brought discovery hammering on his door. Only his lavish distribution of money to the girl and her family had saved Edwin Herbertson from prosecution. But the college authorities had insisted that he remove himself from their establishment.

Charles Herbertson, shamed and angered by his son's behaviour, had insisted that Edwin Herbertson remain beneath the family roof where he, his father, could keep a close watch upon his behaviour. Although the young man was now twenty-three years of age, he still physically feared his father and, above that, feared being disowned and disinherited. So, with a very bad grace he stayed on at Millwood Hall dragging out his days until such time that his father would again relent and release him upon the world outside.

But now, after several weeks in virtual captivity, Edwin Herbertson was finding his enforced celibacy becoming an ever-increasing torment. But he knew that soon that celibacy could be ended, because when his father went to America, then Edwin Herbertson would once more be free to indulge his desires to the full.

Standing now by his window he savoured that enticing

prospect. Physically slothful as he was, there would not even be any necessity to travel to Birmingham or to Warwick to find women. There were some attractive servant girls here at the Hall, and in his father's absence, Edwin Herbertson stood in place as their master. It would not be the first time he had taken his pleasures with a young maidservant frightened into submission.

Mentally he reviewed the faces and bodies of the young women in the Hall. 'Who shall I have?' he wondered, and experienced the pleasurable tightening in his groin as he dwelt on the unholy desires he would gratify upon and within their soft defenceless flesh.

Chapter Eleven

Three weeks had passed since the dismissal of Henry Jenkins, and only a few hours after he had left the house, Fanny Caldicot had packed her own box and gone after him, despite the advice which the other servants pressed upon her to remain at Millwood Hall.

Grainne could not help but feel a sense of guilt at times when she thought of the pair of them losing their employments, but when she voiced such thoughts the other servants told her not to be so stupid, and that Henry Jenkins had long deserved dismissal, and that it was Fanny Caldicot's choice to follow her brutal lover. And so, as the days passed, Grainne came to terms with what had occurred and ceased to blame herself for it.

Grainne found John Croxall's behaviour to be something of an enigma. He would greet her pleasantly and chat to her for short periods about a variety of subjects. Then, at other times, she would be busy at her work and look up to find him standing silently watching her. He would never appear to be discomfited by being found doing such, but would merely smile at her, and then after a little while would nod and walk away without a word being exchanged. At first Grainne found such incidents made her feel uneasy and vaguely threatened. But now she had grown accustomed to them and in an odd sort of way had begun to find his silent watching reassuring, as if he were guarding her from harm.

But inevitably the butler's interest in Grainne was noted by some of her fellows, and at times they would tease her concerning it. Grainne would only smile and take the banter in good part, but inwardly it began to disturb her, and one day she had a brief exchange with Mrs Tomlinson concerning John Croxall's behaviour.

'I can't help the fact that he does it, can I, Mrs Tomlinson? I can't tell him to ignore me, can I? After all, he's the butler, and I'm only a housemaid.'

The older woman's dour features grew thoughtful. 'Well, my duck, it's not surprising really, is it, that he should be interested in you? Youm a beautiful girl, and a clean-living 'un. You'd make a sweet armful for any man.'

Grainne frowned uneasily. 'You don't really think he's interested in me in that way, do you, Mrs Tomlinson?'

The other woman nodded gravely. 'I does. I think he's took a fancy for you, Grainne.'

Grainne sighed impatiently. 'I don't want any man to take a fancy for me. I buried my husband only months ago, and I want no other man.'

The older woman's stubbed brown teeth bared in a grin. 'You not wanting them arn't going to stop men from wanting you though, is it, me wench?'

Grainne's impatience became tinged with vexation. 'All I'm asking is that people leave me alone and let me just get on with my own life.'

The cook shook her mob-capped head. 'Youm too good-looking for men to let you alone, girl. But I'd advise you to walk very careful, or there could be trouble for you because of John Croxall.'

'Why so?' Grainne demanded curiously. 'What sort of trouble?'

The other woman winked conspiratorially. 'Jealous trouble, girl. Jealous trouble from another 'ooman.'

'What woman?' Grainne's curiosity was raging now.

Again Mrs Tomlinson's right eye closed in a ponderous wink. 'Her who carries the keys, my duck. Her who carries the keys.'

With that she refused to say anything more, and Grainne was forced to rest content with what she had been told. She knew whom the cook had been referring to. Only one woman in this household carried a bunch of keys. The housekeeper, Ruth Gurnock.

Grainne was sensible enough not to dwell too much on what

the cook had hinted at. She knew that she was not trying to entice John Croxall, and so decided that all she could do was to remain as she was: friendly, but not overly forthcoming towards the man.

What was giving her cause for more concern however was Amy Davis's state of health. Increasingly as the weeks passed Grainne found herself becoming more protective of the frail timid girl. Amy's bouts of night-time coughing were worsening, and many times Grainne had been woken by them in the night to find Amy saturated with sweat, and weeping with distress. The young girl's bodily strength also appeared to be weakening, and Grainne and Rosy Bright assumed more and more of their friend's workload to shield her from the wrath of the housekeeper who would tolerate no slackening of effort by her staff for any reason whatsoever.

It was in the early hours of the morning when Grainne was once again woken by Amy's racking cough, and she slipped from the bed to light her candle, then turned to look at the girl who lay in the middle of the bed between Grainne and Rosy. Rosy's snores were trumpeting loudly, and Grainne found herself envying the other girl's capacity to sleep through any disturbance. Amy was lying on her back, and in the candle-light Grainne could see the sheen of sweat that was drenching her friend's head and body. Amy's eyes were wide and her face was fearful.

'I'se got a bad pain in me chest!' she gasped out between racking coughs.

In an effort to ease her friend, Grainne lifted the thin frail body upright and held her close while she arranged the horse-hair pillow so that Amy could recline against it. Another burst of coughing shook the girl and she pressed a piece of rag across her mouth. When Amy took the rag away Grainne saw a large ominous stain spreading across it.

'Oh my God, it's blood, Grainne. It's blood, arn't it?' Amy appeared terrified at what she was seeing. 'It's the consumption that's took me, arn't it?'

Grainne's heart sank, but she tried to smile reassuringly. 'You can't know that for sure, honey. Maybe with you coughing so hard it's just fetched something up from your stomach.'

78

Panting wheezily Amy held the rag closer to the candle flame, screwing up her eyes to peer at the dark stain. Then she moaned piteously and sobbed out, 'It's blood, Grainne. I'se took the consumption like me sister did.'

'There now, there, don't upset yourself, honey. You can't have taken the consumption.'

Grainne cradled the younger girl in her arms, gently rocking her. But even as she mouthed words of comfort she knew in her heart of hearts that what Amy said was the truth. The girl was consumptive.

At half-past four Sarah Hobdon came along the corridor to rouse the lower servant girls. At the sound of her voice Amy tried weakly to rise from her bed, but Grainne held her back.

'No, honey, you're not well enough to get up this morning. I think that you should have the doctor fetched to examine you.'

'Oh no, I can't have that happen,' Amy protested nervously. 'Iffen he tells Mrs Gurnock that I bin took so badly, then I'll lose me place here.'

'Of course you won't.' Grainne spoke sharply. 'You've only got a bad chest cold. A few days in your bed will soon put you to rights, and then you'll be as good as new.'

Rosy Bright snorted to wakefulness, and Grainne quickly explained what had happened. Rosy was quick to side with her. 'You do what Grainne tells you, you silly cow,' she told Amy sharply. 'You stay in your bed. We'll do your work between us.'

Grainne went out into the corridor to speak with Sarah Hobdon.

'Listen Sarah, Amy's not well, her cough is very bad. Can she stay in her bed and the doctor fetched to look at her?'

The blonde girl's handsome features became doubtful as she heard Grainne's words.

'I doon't know about that, Grainne. Mrs Gurnock is very strict about the servants laying in their beds.'

'But the wee girl's took very badly,' Grainne argued in a low voice, not wishing to be overheard. 'And she's not well enough to work today. She's been coughing all night long, and has fetched blood up. She's as weak as a kitten.'

Sarah Hobdon shook her head worriedly. 'But I can't give

79

her permission to lay in her bed, Grainne. 'Tis more than me job's worth.'

'But she's ill!' Grainne could not believe what she was hearing. 'She's not able to get up.'

By now the other servant girls were coming into the corridor, their eyes curious as they found the two young women talking together in whispers.

'You lot get on downstairs,' Sarah ordered irritably. 'I'll be down directly.'

'Look, me and Rosy are going to do Amy's work for her,' Grainne explained. 'Mrs Gurnock can't complain if the work's still done, can she?'

Again Sarah shook her head worriedly. 'I can't leave Amy laying in her bed, Grainne. Mrs Gurnock won't stand for it. Iffen it was up to me, then I'd leave the poor cratur lay. But it's Mrs Gurnock!'

Grainne's concern for her sick friend caused her to say sharply, 'Be damned to Mrs Gurnock! I'll go and speak to her myself!'

'But she'll be asleep!' Sarah protested anxiously. 'And if you wakes her at this hour she'll give you stick.'

'I can stand that.' Grainne was determined. 'Now don't you dare go in there to worry Amy. Just leave her be.'

She went back into the cold attic and told Amy, 'Stay in bed until I come back.'

The girl nodded wanly, and in the pale glow of the candle her face was deathly white and huge dark circles ringed her eyes.

Grainne took up her own lighted candle and still in her nightshift went hurrying downstairs, leaving Sarah standing staring anxiously after her.

In the dark silence of the gloomy corridor outside Mrs Gurnock's bedroom door Grainne's determination momentarily wavered as she thought of the reception the housekeeper might afford her. But then the memory of Amy's clammy white face and wasted, sweat-drenched body came into her mind, and Grainne summoned her courage and rapped sharply on the panels, calling out, 'Mrs Gurnock? Mrs Gurnock? Can I speak with you please?'

She paused and listened, but there was no sound from

within. Again Grainne knocked, harder this time, and raised her voice. 'Mrs Gurnock? I need to speak with you.'

This time there sounded a faint murmuring, and then to Grainne's shock a deeper, male voice said something indistinguishable, and was overlayed by Mrs Gurnock's sharp call.

'Who is it? Who's there?'

'It's Grainne Shonley, Mrs Gurnock.'

She heard the housekeeper's angry exclamation, and after a few seconds the door opened slightly and Mrs Gurnock's dark eyes glimmered in the light from Grainne's candle.

'What is it, Shonley?' the woman questioned harshly.

'If you please, Mrs Gurnock, it's Amy Davis. She's ill and needs a doctor to be fetched to her.'

The housekeeper expelled her breath in a fierce hiss, then ordered Grainne, 'You attend to your duties, Shonley. I'll decide what Amy Davis needs. Now be off with you.'

She closed the door with a hard impact, and again Grainne heard the rumblings of a male voice, and the higher-pitched tones of the housekeeper replying. For a few moments Grainne stood unhappily outside the closed door. Then she came to a decision and again rapped smartly on the wooden panels.

'Mrs Gurnock? Mrs Gurnock?'

This time the housekeeper came through the door, slamming it to behind her. Wearing only her nightshift, with her hair loose and long, hanging almost to her hips, she looked far younger than her years in the soft glow of candlelight. She also looked very very angry.

'What the hell are you about, Shonley?' she spat out ferociously. 'Have I not told you to go to your duties?'

'Yes, Mrs Gurnock, you have. But what about Amy Davis?' Grainne asked determinedly.

'What about her?' the housekeeper demanded.

Grainne steeled herself to face the other woman's obvious anger.

'Are you going to have the doctor fetched to her? She needs to be looked at now.'

Ruth Gurnock's dark eyes widened with angry incredulity, as though she could not believe what was happening here, could not believe that her authority was being questioned.

81

'Who do you think you are talking to, Shonley?' she hissed furiously.

'I'm talking to you, Mrs Gurnock.' Grainne's own fiery temper was beginning to rise. 'Amy Davis is very very sick, and she needs a doctor to attend her, and she needs him now.'

Grainne suddenly thought of the man hidden in the housekeeper's room, and on unbidden impulse added, 'If you won't send for a doctor, then I'll needs go and find Mr Croxall, and ask him to help Amy.'

A kaleidoscope of differing emotions passed in lightning succession across the other woman's features. Fury dominated, but within that fury Grainne sensed that caution and fear of unwelcome discoveries being made were lurking and, casting all her own caution aside, Grainne challenged, 'Well, Mrs Gurnock, are you going to help Amy Davis, or shall I go and see Mr Croxall about it?'

Evident hatred glittered in the housekeeper's eyes, and her fists clenched hard. For a brief moment Grainne expected the woman to spring at her in a physical assault, and she tensed herself in readiness to meet that attack. Then the moment passed and Mrs Gurnock drew a long shuddering breath and jerked out, 'I'll come myself and see Amy Davis, Shonley. And then I shall decide what needs to be done for her.' She paused, and regarded Grainne with a hard challenging stare.

Grainne sensed that she had achieved all that she could do, and with a deliberate impassivity accepted. 'Very well, Mrs Gurnock. Many thanks.'

'All right then.' Mrs Gurnock nodded shortly. She now seemed to have brought her earlier fury under control, but the expression in her eyes boded ill for Grainne. 'Now go about your duties, Shonley!' she ordered curtly.

Grainne bobbed a curtsey, and walked away. As she returned upstairs to the attics she thought about the man in Mrs Gurnock's bedroom and, mindful of Mrs Tomlinson's previous hints, instinctively knew that it was John Croxall. To her own surprise she felt a slight chagrin.

'How could a fine, good looking man like him sleep with a woman old enough to be his mother? Admittedly she's a handsome woman for her age. But she's old!'

With an exclamation of impatience she castigated herself

angrily. 'For the love of Christ, Grainne! Why should it matter to you who sleeps with who in this house? There's no man means anything to you, is there! Least of all John Croxall!'

But despite that affirmation, there still lingered in her mind that disquieting sensation of chagrin.

In the attic Grainne quickly dressed and prepared for her work. Amy Davis voiced her worries about remaining in bed, but Grainne told her firmly, 'You'll stay where you are, honey. Mrs Gurnock is going to come up and see you, and then decide if it's needful to bring the doctor.'

At the door she halted and turned to stare anxiously at the younger girl who was lying on her back with the blanket pulled high around her small white face.

'I'll bring you some breakfast up on a tray, shall I, honey?' Grainne offered.

The girl's sunken, dark-ringed eyes were lustreless, and she gave a slight shake of her head. 'I couldn't ate anything, Grainne. I just wants to lay here quiet.'

Grainne forced a smile. 'All right then, honey, you lay there and rest easy. I'll come back up to see you just as soon as I can.'

By the time she arrived in the kitchen the rest of the under-servants had trooped away to their various tasks.

'What's up with Amy Davis then?' Mrs Tomlinson wanted to know.

Grainne frowned unhappily. 'She's been coughing so hard that she's brought up blood, Mrs Tomlinson. I'm feared she could be consumptive.'

The dour features of the cook were kindly as she regarded Grainne.

'Well, whatever it might turn out to be, girl, at least you'se got the comfort of knowing that you'se done your best for her. It took a fair bit o' courage to goo knocking up Mrs Gurnock at this hour o' the morn. But if I was you, I'd get on wi' your work a bit sharpish, because Mrs Gurnock can be very vindictive against them who upsets her in any way at all.'

The woman's right eye closed in her customary conspiratorial wink, and Grainne smiled and went to fetch her working tools.

*   *   *

Back in the housekeeper's bedroom a vicious verbal clash was developing.

'Up to your old tricks again, are you?' Mrs Gurnock challenged venomously. 'That saucy Irish bitch had the gall to tell me to my face that if I didn't fetch a doctor to Davis, then she'd go and see you and get your help. You've been chasing after her, haven't you?'

Lying naked on the bed, John Croxall eyed his mistress warily. It was thanks to her influence with Charles Herbertson that he had received his rapid promotion to butler, and Croxall knew that she could just as easily have him dismissed from that post and from this household. He was an ambitious man who regarded this present position as an essential stepping stone to what he eventually hoped to achieve in the way of financial independence. However, he was also possessed of considerable self-esteem, and he bitterly resented the tone she was now taking with him. Sullenly he muttered, 'I've been chasing nobody.'

'You bloody liar! You've been tupping that Irish bitch already haven't you, you bloody whoremonger?' Mrs Gurnock's face became livid as her furious jealousy fed upon itself.

The unjust accusation roused his own temper. 'Don't talk so fuckin' stupid! I've only treated the girl as I treat any of the other servants.'

'And that means you're forever trying to shove your hand up her skirts.' Ruth Gurnock was besotted with this man, but her constant gnawing jealousy gave her no peace.

Although he was a man of strong passions, John Croxall had never allowed himself to sexually harass women, and he despised men who did so. This last completely unfounded accusation caused him to lose his temper.

'No, I don't go round trying to shove my hands up any of the girls' skirts,' he said through gritted teeth. 'But I'll tell you this, if I was that way inclined then she's a sweet enough young morsel to tempt any man into doing so. And young's the word, arn't it, Ruth?'

'You're a bastard, John Croxall! A filthy bastard! Your prick rules your brains!'

'Does it now,' he hurled back at her. 'And if it does, then

84

arn't you glad of it whenever I comes to your bed? After all, you arn't no spring chicken anymore, are you, Ruth? You can't take your pick of the men at your age, can you? Although you're still as hot for it as any young wench could be.'

Hurt and shame momentarily overlayed the anger in her eyes.

'I've always been a decent-living woman, John Croxall. You're the only man apart from my dead husband that I've ever had carnal knowledge of.'

He smiled viciously, and repeated, 'Carnal knowledge of.' He appeared to be savouring the words as once more he rolled them from his tongue. 'Carnal knowledge of! I like that, Ruth, I really do. It's got a certain ring to it, arn't that so? Carnal knowledge of . . . '

His mouth twisted scornfully, and cruelty shone in his eyes. 'Why don't you call it by its proper term, Ruth? Why don't you say it straight out? I'm the only man who's ever fucked you apart from your dead deceased husband. I'm the only man who's ever fucked you, Ruth. And you likes to be fucked, don't you, Ruth? You can't get enough on it, can you?'

Her pale skin suffused darkly with her shamed embarrassment and tears brimmed in her fine eyes as her fury was momentarily quelled by his sneering contempt.

'Why do you use me so cruelly, John?' she pleaded pitifully. 'I love you above all else in this world. And you know that I would do anything for you? So why must you treat me this way? Why must you say such vile things to me?' She regarded him through her teary eyes, and saw that his sullen face still bore no signs of a softening of mood. This sparked her again into flashing fury.

'All you wants to do is to drink and to whore, you bastard!'

'It's you that makes me want to do that, with your nasty jealous nature, you miserable old cow!' he sprang back at her.

Ruth Gurnock tossed her head furiously, then spat out, 'Well, you'll not whore with that Irish bitch under this roof again, my buck. Out she goes this very day!'

He came upright in the bed, his muscular hairy body taut, and his expression deadly serious.

'Oh no she don't go out this very day, my lady. The girl's done nothing to deserve it. She stays.'

85

'So that you can get between her legs again?' she accused virulently.

'No, you stupid bitch!' he denied with an equal virulence. 'I've not touched the girl!'

'I've had my bellyful of your tricks, John Croxall!' Ruth Gurnock's agitation was causing her firm breasts to rise and fall rapidly beneath the thin cloth of her nightshift, and in the candlelight with her long hair falling about her handsome face she looked eminently desirable. So much so that despite his anger John Croxall's lust for her burgeoned uncontrollably.

Suddenly he lunged forwards and caught the woman's wrists. With a powerful jerk he brought her onto the bed, and despite her struggles pinned her body beneath his, one hand trapping both her arms above her head. He used his legs to bludgeon her thighs apart, and with his free hand he dragged her nightshift upwards to uncover her naked belly and breasts. Even though she was no longer a young woman her flesh was still white and smooth, her nipples erect upon her firm rounded breasts.

He crushed his mouth cruelly down upon hers, and his hand roamed greedily over her body, cupping, fondling, exploring, penetrating, almost, but not quite, hurting her.

Her breathing became ragged, and when he lifted his mouth from hers she sobbed out, 'You bastard! You rotten bastard!'

Croxall's big white teeth gleamed in a triumphant grin, and he whispered urgently.

'Had your bellyful of my tricks, has you, Ruth? That arn't what youm saying now though, is it? Youm wanting your belly filled with my tricks right now, arn't you? Here then. I'll give you what you wants.'

He roughly forced his pulsing manhood into her. Her hips jerked and heaved in frantic, futile effort to eject him from her body, but against his strength she was powerless. His small hard-rounded buttocks rammed up between her thighs in short savage thrusts, and suddenly she cried out, and her legs wrapped around him, and her lips sought avidly for his mouth.

Again he grinned, and then released her imprisoned arms, and her hooked fingers came digging into the thick muscles of his shoulders. He grunted deep in his throat, and his own breath became a harsh panting as he drove himself deeper and harder

86

and faster into her, and she moaned and wriggled and spread herself wider to engulf him, both of them lost in a mindless ecstasy of the flesh.

Long afterwards, he lay slumped upon her, his manhood still deep inside her, and raised himself to stare down into her sex-slackened features.

'Do you believe me now, Ruth? That I'm not chasing after Grainne Shonley?'

With eyes closed she nodded briefly.

'Then she can stay, can she?' he pressed.

Again, eyes still closed, she nodded briefly. Satisfied, he slumped back down upon her, his lips against the white soft skin of her throat.

Ruth Gurnock ran her fingers across his damp skin, and thought to herself, 'You're mine, John Croxall. And I intend that you shall remain mine. That Irish bitch will go, because she's a danger to me. I could lose you to her if she was to stay. So she'll go. But you won't know that it's me who has got rid of her, my darling. You won't know that, and so you'll not be able to blame me for it.'

The woman's lips curved in a smile of satisfaction, and she hugged his body tightly against her own.

Chapter Twelve

It was eleven o'clock in the morning and Grainne was beating carpets in one of the yards at the rear of the house when John Croxall came to her.

'Grainne?' She turned when he called her name, the willow carpet-paddle clutched in her hand, her cheeks rosy with exertion, curling strands of her black hair escaping from beneath her mobcap.

The man thought her very beautiful and was forced to warn himself, 'Hold hard now, John Croxall. It'll not serve your plans for the future to allow yourself to fall in love with this one.'

He realised that what he felt towards Grainne Shonley was more than simple physical desire. She had re-awakened his romanticism, and when he was in her company he found himself experiencing once more all those youthful longings and desires that he had thought were lost from his adult nature. But John Croxall was battling against letting these feelings overwhelm him. He had been one of eight children of a farm labourer, and his childhood had been spent in grinding poverty. At three years of age he had been out in the winter fields with his mother picking stones with his tiny hands, crying with the cold and hunger.

John Croxall dreaded the prospect of any return to that poverty. His affair with Ruth Gurnock had aided his swift rise, and he had no intention of allowing his errant emotions to deflect him from his planned course through life. He knew well that should he break with Ruth Gurnock before he was ready to make his move, then he would most assuredly be toppled by her from his present position, and that she would do her utmost to ensure his professional ruin. Nonetheless, at this moment he could not help but wish with all his heart that he was free to pursue this beautiful green-eyed girl before him.

He forced a smile, and told her gently, 'Mrs Gurnock has been to see your friend Davis.'

'What does she think? Has she sent for the doctor?' Grainne demanded eagerly.

His smile died on his lips, and he shook his head regretfully. 'No, she has told me that there is no necessity for the doctor to be called for. She recognises that Davis has taken the consumption.' He sighed sympathetically. 'I'm sure that what Mrs Gurnock has said is the truth, Grainne. She has had much experience in sick-nursing, and is very well versed in the symptoms of illnesses.'

'Oh God pity the poor little thing!' Grainne moaned softly. The news of this virtual death sentence hit her hard despite the fact that she had already known in her heart that there could be no other prognosis.

Seeing her distress, John Croxall could not resist stepping to her and laying his hands on her upper arms, murmured soothingly, 'There now, my dear, you mustn't upset yourself. These matters are God's will, and there's naught anybody can do to alter that, is there?'

He was acutely aware of her desirability, and as the fresh young scents of her body reached his nostrils he was driven by the urge to enfold her in his arms. Afraid that he might lose control, he abruptly released her arms and stepped backwards from her.

Another disquieting thought penetrated Grainne's distress, and she asked anxiously, 'What will happen to Amy now, Mr Croxall? Will she be let stay on here?'

He grimaced unhappily, then shrugged. 'I honestly don't know, Grainne. That is a decision to be taken by Mrs Gurnock.'

He stared uneasily at Grainne's worried face and, impelled by his feelings for her, he promised, 'Listen, my dear, you may rest assured that I'll do all I can to help Amy Davis.' He hesitated a moment, then told her, 'Look, you finish the task you're engaged upon, and then go upstairs and sit with Amy.

I'll tell Mrs Gurnock that I've sent you to be with your friend.'

Grainne looked at him with real gratitude, and found herself thinking what a good man he was.

He smiled, then gently touched her cheek with his fingers and urged, 'Go to it now. Finish this task and then go to your friend. We'll talk again presently.'

He walked away into the house and Grainne watched him go with a rapidly burgeoning warmth of appreciation and liking for him.

From a window above the yard Ruth Gurnock had watched all that had passed between the couple, and a terrible rage of jealousy shook her.

'I'll settle with you both,' she muttered aloud, and hatred for Grainne coursed through her. 'And I'll settle with you in particular, you young bitch, for trying to steal my man from me.'

The woman's first impulse was to rush downstairs and dismiss Grainne on the spot on any pretext. But then another idea suddenly occurred, and a bitter smile briefly writhed across Ruth Gurnock's mouth.

'No, that will be too easy on you, you young whore. There's more painful ways of skinning the cat than that.'

Grainne hurried to finish her task and then returned her tools to the storeroom next to the kitchen.

As she returned from there Mrs Tomlinson called her to the great iron cooking range.

'Youm going up to Amy, I take it, my duck.'

'I am,' Grainne told her, impatient to be away.

'Take that bit o' broth up to her then. It'll do the poor little cratur good. Mind and make sure that she ates it all down, it'll give her strength. I'se made it specially for her with best beef.'

Grainne was touched by this kindness on the part of the dour woman, but was not really surprised by it. Her own experiences in life had demonstrated many times how kindly natures could be hidden behind outwardly sour façades.

With a smile of thanks she lifted the big crock bowl with its richly steaming contents and, pausing only to take a spoon from the dresser drawer, she ran upstairs to the attics.

It came as a shock to Grainne to find Amy fully dressed in her outdoor cloak and bonnet, sitting upon the side of the bed, her small wooden box containing her few personal clothes and belongings at her feet.

'Amy? What are you doing out of your bed? Why are you dressed to go out?' Grainne demanded with shocked concern.

Framed by the rounded jutting wings of her black bonnet, Amy's face was pinched and white, and very fearful.

'I'm being sent away, Grainne,' she choked out, then burst into loud sobs.

Grainne put the bowl of broth on the wash-stand and seated herself at the girl's side, hugging her frail body close to comfort her.

'Who has told you that you're to be sent away, honey?'

'I have told her, Shonley.' Mrs Gurnock had come noiselessly to stand in the doorway. 'She is being sent back to her family.'

The woman's dark eyes were glittering and her pale face hard set, as if she were suppressing some rampaging emotion.

'But she's not well enough to travel!' Grainne protested indignantly.

Ruth Gurnock's mouth was a thin bitter line, as she shook her head dismissively. 'She cannot be allowed to remain here. She has taken a galloping consumption. I've seen the like of it many times before, and I consider it to be a highly contagious and dangerous disease, Shonley. I cannot allow the health of the rest of this household to be put in jeopardy.'

As she heard the housekeeper's words, Amy Davis once more burst into heart-rending sobs, and then was shaken by racking coughs. Desperately Grainne tried to soothe the girl, and then looked angrily at the housekeeper.

'It is no use you giving me black looks, Shonley!' The older woman had a contemptuous sneer on her face. 'I am only doing my duty.'

'But it's downright cruel to send her home when she's as ill as she is,' Grainne protested furiously. 'She should stay here and be cared for at least until she's strong enough to make the journey. God knows there are enough of us here able to look after the poor creature. It's wicked to send her away when she's like this. Purely wicked!'

Ruth Gurnock tutted impatiently, tongue against teeth.

'Have you considered, Shonley, that ill as she is the girl might prefer to be with her own family?'

This brought Grainne up short, and she felt very foolish as she recalled how often Amy had pined and wept with homesickness. The housekeeper's eyes glinted with triumph as she saw Grainne's discomfiture.

'Yes Shonley, you are too ready to place unwarranted blame on your betters, are you not? But then, that's an attribute of your countrymen. They are always ready to bite the hands that feed them.'

'There's precious little feeding of my countrymen being done these days, is there?' Grainne retorted angrily, and then directed that anger against herself, thinking, 'Stop letting yourself be goaded into foolishness, you damned idjit. It's only giving this one satisfaction to see you reacting so. And in all truth it's not the fault of the English people here that there's famine in Ireland. They've enough hunger of their own to be going on with at present.'

'Here, Davis.' Mrs Gurnock handed some coins to the girl, who had now quietened, and was sitting with her bonneted head leaning against Grainne's shoulder.

'That is a full quarter's wages, and since it still lacks three weeks to make up the quarter you'll agree that I've been more than generous to you.'

Amy took the pathetically few coins and stared down at them resting in the palm of her thin hand. Then she started to weep softly. Grainne was near to tears herself in sight of her friend's misery.

'There now, honey, you're going home to be with your family. You'll like that, won't you,' she tried to comfort the girl. 'You've told me so much about your Mammy and Daddy, and all your brothers and sisters and how much you miss them. You'll all be happy together again now, won't you?'

'You doon't understand, Grainne,' the girl moaned miserably. 'Theer's no room for me at home, and no money to feed me with neither. That's why I was put into service in the first place, was to ease the burden on me Mam and Dad. He's most o' the time too badly to work, and me Mam can only earn a bit. Without my bit o' money being sent to 'um, they'd have to goo into the work'us. We'll all have to goo into the work'us now, that's for sure!' She wailed loudly, and sobs shook her frail body.

Mrs Gurnock tutted impatiently and ordered sharply, 'Stop that skrawking, Davis! Now bring your box with you, I have to see you from this house. Come now!'

Although Grainne boiled inwardly at how Amy was being treated, she was sickeningly aware of her powerlessness to prevent it. To attempt to argue further with the housekeeper would achieve nothing, and would only drag out Amy Davis's torment. She lifted the box under one arm, and with her free hand drew the smaller girl up onto her feet.

'Come now, Amy. You must be brave, honey.'

She helped the weeping girl down to the rear door of the house. On the way they encountered other servants, but these passed them with averted eyes and hurried steps, as though afraid to speak to, or even acknowledge, Amy Davis. Although their reactions angered Grainne she accepted that it was a frequent phenomenon of the animal kingdom. A stricken beast was often deliberately ignored and avoided by its fellows, as if they feared it would bring its plight upon themselves.

In the rear courtyard Mrs Gurnock halted and told Grainne, 'Help Davis as far as the road, Shonley. Then report back here to me. I'll not have you wasting your time gadding about the countryside.'

Grainne stared at her disbelievingly. 'Is Amy expected to walk back to Birmingham carrying her box?' she challenged.

Mrs Gurnock shook her head. 'I'm not expecting anything of Davis, Shonley. She has been paid her due wages, and more than she is entitled to receive besides. She has money enough to hire a cart to take her back to Birmingham, should she so desire.'

'It's disgraceful so it is, expecting a sick girl to carry this box all those miles,' Grainne exclaimed angrily. 'Why can't she be taken back in the carriage?'

There was satisfaction hovering in the older woman's eyes, as if Grainne was reacting just how she wanted her to react.

'The carriage?' Mrs Gurnock sneered openly. 'Do you really believe that it is fitting for a discharged maidservant to be allowed the use of a carriage?' She shook her head in mock amazement. 'What is the world coming to when discharged

93

maidservants are considered to be entitled to ride in a carriage as if they were gentry?'

Grainne trembled with the urge to strike the other woman; to punch and kick her until she screamed for mercy, and then to punch and kick her some more.

The housekeeper suddenly realised that she had provoked Grainne almost beyond control. She experienced a flash of fear. The young woman was strong and lithe and might well be capable of inflicting serious injury upon her before help could be summoned. Abruptly Ruth Gurnock's attitude changed, and she pursed her lips pensively, then offered, 'Very well, Shonley. I am not a heartless woman. You may accompany Davis back to her home. But you will forfeit your wages for this day, and if you are not back here for your work sharp at five o'clock tomorrow morning, then you will forfeit that day's wages also.'

Grainne stood seething for a moment or two, then nodded shortly. 'I'll take Amy home, and I'll be back here before five o'clock tomorrow morning.'

Ruth Gurnock nodded curtly. 'Very well, Shonley.' Then she jerked her head in dismissal. 'I suggest that you be on your way. You have little or no time to waste. Birmingham lies some fourteen miles from here.'

Grainne told Amy Davis, 'Wait here for me, honey.'

She ran back into the house and upstairs to the attic. Snatching up her shawl she returned to the courtyard, and lifted Amy's box.

'Come on, honey. Let's be on our way.'

The day was bright and clear and Grainne blessed the absence of rain. As she passed through the great iron gates of Millwood Hall, with the sick girl leaning heavily on her left arm and the roped box in her right hand, Grainne experienced some trepidation at the thought of the long tramp which lay ahead of them. Millwood Hall was set in the sparsely populated countryside which stretched between the ancient city of Warwick and the equally ancient market village of Henley in Arden. When Grainne had come to Millwood Hall, she had travelled by train from Liverpool to Birmingham, and then had walked to the Hall via the Henley in Arden route. She decided now that this would be the road they would take.

She glanced at Amy Davis's woebegone features and her own heart ached for the girl. She tried to raise Amy's spirits, assuming a cheerfulness that she herself was far from feeling.

'It'll not take us long to get to Henley, Amy. It's only about four miles distant, and that's a real busy road there. We'll easy find a lift into Birmingham.'

'I'd sooner be going anywheer than back theer. What's going to happen to me Mam and Dad now? What's going to become of all on us?' the girl wailed miserably, and a sob jerked from her. 'It's all right for you. You've got a place still. You've got nothing to worry about, have you?'

In the face of this querulous outburst Grainne remained silent, but thought wryly, 'Oh yes, I've naught to worry about, except for getting you there, and me back again, and losing two days' wages most probably. At least you've a home and a family to be going back to. I've neither one or the other.'

'Me chest is hurting summat sore, and I'm feeling so weary,' Amy whined.

Grainne regarded her companion with mingled pity and slight exasperation, and decided that she would have to be cruel to be kind.

'Now just stop this whining,' she said firmly. 'What's happened has happened, and can't be altered. It's no use you weeping and wailing about it. We've a long way to go, and we'll not get there any easier with you keeping on like this. So just stop it now, and take a hold of yourself.'

'But I'm feeling so weary, and me chest is paining me summat awful,' Amy whined plaintively yet again. 'I'm not well enough to walk all the way to Brummagem.'

'I've already told you once haven't I, that we only need to walk as far as Henley.' Grainne forced herself to be firm. 'There'll be traffic passing through there on its way to Birmingham. There's hundreds of carts and waggons uses that road. We'll soon be riding like high-born ladies, so we will. So come on now, we've less than four miles to be walking.'

She strode on almost dragging the girl along, and steeled herself against the sobbing moans that dribbled in a continuous stream from Amy's lips. They covered another two miles, but increasingly Amy faltered and dragged upon Grainne's arm, until Grainne's resolve failed her, and she realised that she was not able to harden herself against Amy's distress. She halted, and leading Amy to the side of the roadway gently seated her on the grassy verge.

For a few minutes she sat cradling the coughing girl in her arms, racking her brains for some way out of this dilemma.

'We're going to need a horse, Amy, you're not strong enough to walk any further. But I've no money to hire one with. So it looks as if we'll have to use some of your wages to get you home.'

Amy's breath was wheezing in her throat, and she looked flushed and feverish, her sunken eyes mirroring her dread. Anxiously Grainne laid her fingers against Amy's forehead, and drew breath sharply as she felt the heat pulsing from the girl's skin.

Grainne stared about her, and saw in the distance plumes of smoke rising in the still air.

'That'll be Henley,' she thought. 'It's not so far now, maybe a couple of miles. There's sure to be livery stables there.'

'How much money have you got, Amy?' She bent over the seated girl.

When she counted the coins Grainne sighed. 'One pound and three shillings. Livery horses come dear. I doubt that there's enough there to hire one. And anyway, you'll be needing this money to live on, won't you?'

Amy started to say something, and then was shaken by a renewed bout of fierce wrenching coughs, which deposited a watery red stain upon the handkerchief she pressed to her mouth.

'Oh God help me, what can I do to get the poor creature to her home quickly? She needs to be in her bed and resting,' Grainne prayed in silent desperation. 'I can't carry her and her box all that way.'

Seconds passed and multiplied and became minutes and still Grainne stood racked by her indecision, while seated beneath her Amy coughed and moaned, and wept. Suddenly anger at her own indecision fired Grainne with a dogged determination.

'Maybe I can't carry you all the way to Birmingham, Amy,' she told the other girl. 'But I can carry you towards it, and maybe once we're on the main road we'll find a lift to help us the rest of the way.'

Twisting her shawl into a makeshift rope, Grainne tied the box against her stomach, then instructed Amy, 'Draw your skirts up a bit, and climb up onto my back, honey.'

At first Amy was reluctant, but Grainne overrode her weak protests, and eventually the girl obeyed. Grainne could not help but be thankful that the other girl was so slenderly built. Amy's weight was only that of a child.

'Right then, honey,' she jerked out when the girl was on her back, thin arms wrapped around her shoulders, thighs gripping her waist. 'Let's see how far I can pick-a-back you.'

Grainne trudged slowly along the rutted trackway. When her breathing grew laboured and her muscles cramped with weariness she would halt and let Amy down until she had recovered sufficient strength to go onwards once more; and so with a painful slowness the two girls progressed towards Henley in Arden.

The village consisted of two rows of buildings facing each other across the Birmingham to Stratford upon Avon turnpike road, and stretching for some three quarters of a mile. It was peculiar for having several privately owned madhouses sited there, which provided work as keepers and helpers for many of its inhabitants. When the dogs came rushing to bark and nip at Grainne's skirts as she traversed the long straggling main street, several people came from the buildings to see what had provoked the animals and wondered if the two girls had escaped from one of the local madhouses, because the spectacle of two young women playing pick-a-back was a bizarre sight.

Grainne was unaware of the curious eyes regarding her as she reached a water-trough in the centre of the village and let Amy down from her back.

'Let's take a drink, honey. I'm parched.'

Amy sank down against the wall of a house, while Grainne loosened and dropped the box, and then went to drink from the trough's pump, working the long handle until gouts of fresh sparkling water jetted from its leaden spout. The cold water numbed Grainne's lips and mouth, but she relished its impact, and after wetting her handkerchief she bathed her sweaty face and throat, then pumped more water for Amy to drink from cupped hands.

A tall greystone house fronted the water trough, and from its ground floor windows several faces peered out. When they had rested for a few minutes Grainne suggested, 'We'd best get on through this village, Amy.' She frowned at the long stretch of roadway along which no horses and carts or waggons were visible. 'Isn't it always the same,' she grumbled good-humouredly. 'When I didn't need a lift there were dozens of carts passing through here. And now, when we do need it, there's not a one.'

Amy tried to smile, but could only produce a wan grimace. Grainne regarded her friend anxiously. The girl was deathly pale now, her skin beaded with a clammy sweat.

'How are you feeling, honey?' she asked gently.

'I just wants to get home to me Mam and Dad, Grainne. That's all. I wants just to get home to 'um.'

Tears ran from Amy's eyes, and her voice was weak and thready.

'You will get home, honey,' Grainne promised fervently. 'I'll get you home, I promise.'

She looked about her, and saw an inn sign a little further down the street. On impulse, she told Amy, 'Stay here, honey. I'll only be a minute.'

She hurried towards the inn and entered its low-lintelled door. A buxom woman met her in the passageway. 'Yes, young 'ooman, what can I do for you?' Her eyes were suspicious as she took in Grainne's dishevelled appearance, bare head and lack of even a shawl.

'If you please, ma'm, I'd like a glass of brandy to take out to my friend?'

The woman frowned slightly. 'Have you got the money to pay for it?'

Grainne abruptly remembered her own empty pockets, and she shook her head at her own forgetfulness, and smiled.

'My friend has the money. I'll bring it to you when I bring the glass back. She's only down the road a few yards there.'

The buxom woman's frown deepened. 'You'll bring it before you gets anything from this house. And theer's no glasses goes outside here neither. What's drunk, is drunk inside here. Not down the road.'

For the first time Grainne became aware of the woman's open hostility, and she answered with some indignation, 'I'm not wanted to steal anything from you, ma'm. My friend is ill, that's why I need the drop o' brandy. And she has the money to pay for it.'

The woman was unperturbed by Grainne's indignation. 'Then your friend had best bring herself and her money inside here, hadn't her, young 'ooman?'

In the snug bar beside the passage a man was sitting looking out of the front window, and listening to the exchange between the two women. He was in his mid-thirties, expensively dressed in a dark Saxony paletot and tight-fitting fawn-coloured doeskin trousers, a high-collared silk shirt and a cravat. He wore ultra-fashionable side-laced, cloth-topped Albert boots on his feet, with an abundance of gold jewellery and chains adorning his person, and dangling across his brocaded waistcoat.

His brown hair, side-whiskers and moustache were well barbered and he smelled of expensive pomades. But a long scar stretching from his left temple down to his jaw, coupled with his hard hazel eyes imparted an air of menace to him that was at odds with his dandified attire. He smiled now as he heard Grainne tell the buxom landlady, 'Sure there's other inns in this place, where I'll maybe find a warmer welcome. I'll take my order there.'

'You must do as you please, young 'ooman,' the buxom woman grunted.

'Oh I shall.' Grainne walked out of the inn, her cheeks glowing with her indignation at the churlish treatment she had received.

The man watched her through the leaded windowpanes, and whistled softly in admiration. 'Arn't you the lovely girl now? I wouldn't mind getting to know you better.'

He could see as far as the water trough where the other girl was crouching against the nearby house wall, and he stared with interest as people came from the tall greystone house to crowd around the crouching girl. He watched as the beautiful black-haired girl hurried to the group, and then came to a quick decision, and drained his glass. He picked up his gold-knobbed walking cane from the table in front of him, from where he also lifted and put on his tall black top hat, and with his gloves in his hand swaggered elegantly out into the passage.

99

'Mrs Brummage?'

The buxom woman hurried to him. 'Yes, Captain Hunter, what is it you wants, sir?'

'Bring me a glass of your best brandy.'

'Yes, sir.' She bobbed a curtsey and would have turned away, but he held up his hand. 'A moment, Mrs Brummage.'

'Yes, sir?' She halted obediently.

The man seemed to be considering some matter. Then he told her, 'When you've brought me the brandy, tell that idle rascal of a husband of yours, to get my trap ready. I've a notion to take a little drive.'

While he waited for her to bring the glass of brandy he stood on the doorstep of the inn, staring at the small crowd by the water trough, noting that there seemed to be a dispute developing there.

'Wheer is it you say you've come from, girl?' a burly man clad in a blue frock-smock, and wearing an artisan's squared paper cap on his bullet head, demanded of Grainne.

'I've already told you that we've come from Millwood Hall.' Grainne could not understand why the woman at the inn had displayed hostility, and now the group around her were also displaying that attitude. 'Why do you ask?'

'Because I'm the parish constable, girl, and I've a right to ask whatever I wants to.' The burly man scowled, and a murmur of agreement sounded from his supporters.

'Look, my friend is ill, and I'm taking her back to her family.' Grainne had no wish to quarrel with these people, so she tried to speak in a placatory tone.

'Then why did you come along the road theer like a couple o' bloody loonies playing pick-a-back?' the constable demanded. 'Why warn't you walking like normal folk walks?'

'I've told you that as well. My friend is ill, she's not able to walk.'

'Phoo, that's a load o' bloody codswallop!' The man scoffed aggressively. 'I saw her walk to this bloody pump and stand drinking water wi' me own eyes.'

'We've the right to take a drink of water, if we need to,' Grainne snapped resentfully. 'Jesus Christ! The trough's put here for the use of travellers, isn't it? You wouldn't object to horses and cattle drinking from it, would you? So why are you making out as if me and my friend have committed a crime by drinking from it?'

'Doon't you get arsey wi' me, Paddy,' the constable threatened, 'or you'll bloody well soon wish you hadn't.'

The mood of the crowd was now beginning to become openly aggressive towards the two girls, and Grainne sensed that she had better talk softly if there was not to be bad trouble for her. She spread her hands and with honest bewilderment asked, 'I just don't understand what we've done that's so bad. All we want to do is to reach Birmingham. And we have to pass through here to get there, don't we? We only stopped to get a drink of water, and to rest a while.'

'But you arn't satisfactorily explained wheer it is you'se come from, has you, girl? Neither on you looks to be respectable serving wenches whom working for a gentry family. I knows Mrs Gurnock at Millwood Hall personal, my wench, and I knows how very particular her is about her staff being clad decent and respectable, and conducting themselves in the proper manner when they'm abroad. She 'udden't stand for wenches behaving like bloody loonies along the Queen's highway, and that's certain sure, that is.'

'Well whether you know Mrs Gurnock, or whether you don't, makes no odds to me.' Grainne was fast becoming tired of this exchange. 'My friend and myself will get on our way now.'

The constable shook his head. 'Oh no girl, you wun't leave here, until I'm satisfied that you'se got nothing to answer to, and that you'se got the rights to be walking free about the countryside.'

A glimmering of understanding, which quickly developed into a blinding light had lanced through Grainne's mind as he was speaking. She suddenly laughed in half angry, incredulous amusement, and the people around her exchanged shocked glances, and glared at her suspiciously.

'I understand now, why you're all behaving towards us in this way,' Grainne exclaimed, and shook her head in wonderment. 'You think us to be mad folks escaping from one of the loony houses in these parts, don't you?'

Again incredulous laughter bubbled from her, and she spread her hands beseechingly. 'Look, why don't you just make enquiries at the local madhouses and find out if there's been anyone escaping from them, before you start trying to stop innocent people going along the road.'

The constable's heavy features became smug. 'I'm doing just that this very minute, girl. I'se sent my assistant to goo to every suchlike establishment in this parish. And you and your mate theer 'ull stay right here until my assistant comes back to tell me what he's found out about you two.'

'And how long will that take?' Grainne demanded to know.

The man grinned in smug triumph. 'Not more than a few hours, I shouldn't think. All enquiries 'ull be completed by nightfall.'

'We can't stay here until nightfall,' Grainne protested in dismay. 'I've got to travel to Birmingham and return to Millwood Hall by five o'clock tomorrow morning.'

'You'll stay here as long as I requires you to stay, my wench,' the constable told her adamantly. 'And if needs be I'll bloody well put you both under lock and key to make sure of it.'

The small crowd applauded his statement, and Grainne's heart sank as she realised that she could hope for no help or support in this village.

At the rear of the crowd, standing behind the constable, Morgan Hunter had been listening attentively to all that had passed. Now he pushed through saying loudly, 'Here you are, my girl. Here's the brandy for your friend. I apologise for having been so long in procuring it.'

Grainne stared at the newcomer in shock and he moved between her and the constable and winked meaningfully as he pushed the glass into her hand.

'Come now, girl, let us make haste. I'm having my horse and trap made ready.'

He turned to face the constable and, with a deprecating nod towards Grainne said, 'I do declare Mr Wakefield, that these girls grow more stupid by the year, do they not? Why she had not the sense to inform you that I had arranged to meet them both here, I just cannot understand.'

The constable frowned doubtfully. 'Does you know 'um personal then, Captain Hunter?'

The other man chuckled and mock-chided. 'Not in the

biblical sense, my dear fellow, and not in the social sense either, I hasten to add. But know them as servants at Millwood Hall, yes I most certainly do.'

The constable began to look distinctly uncomfortable, and Hunter grinned warmly at him, and told him in a congratulatory way, 'I must say, Mr Wakefield, I'd not wish to be a wrongdoer in these parts, with a constable of your calibre being in office. You're damned quick to action, are you not?' His tone was admiring. 'It's so comforting to know that you're here, Mr Wakefield. I could have done with a few men like yourself in my regiment. I declare we'd have beaten the Sikhs in half the time it took if I'd had others like you under my command.'

The heavy, stolid features of the other man beamed with gratification at the compliment. 'I'm only doing my duty, Captain Hunter,' he stated smugly.

'And doing it with exceptional efficiency, Mr Wakefield,' Morgan Hunter declared solemnly. Then he dropped his voice low and said, sotto voce, 'Look, be a good fellow and clear these gawkers away, will you? I want to take these poor girls on to Birmingham, and have no wish to be made a peepshow because I'm acting with Christian charity.'

His hand moved secretively to that of the constable and coins passed between them.

Wakefield grinned and saluted. 'You can leave it to me, Captain Hunter, sir.'

'I am confident as to that, Mr Wakefield.' Morgan Hunter smiled, and as the constable began to disperse the small crowd of onlookers, who voiced their reluctance to move away from this free show, he walked to where Grainne was bending over Amy Davis crouching against the wall of the nearest house.

'What's the matter with the girl?' he asked Grainne.

'She's taken the consumption,' she told him, and remained bending, one arm around Amy Davis's shoulders, the other hand holding the glass of brandy to the girl's lips. 'Come now, Amy, try and take a little of this. It will do you good,' she coaxed gently.

Amy's lips opened and she sipped the drink, then coughed, her head jerking forwards, almost knocking the glass from Grainne's hand.

'Did you say that you were going to Birmingham?' Morgan Hunter asked.

Grainne nodded, her eyes still fixed anxiously on Amy's clammy-sheened, grey-white face.

'Try to take a little more, honey,' she continued to coax the girl, and slowly Amy Davis managed to take sips of the drink until she finished it.

'That's a good girl.' Grainne smiled, and told her, 'You can rest for a wee while longer, honey, and then we'll go on.'

She straightened, and for the first time gave her full attention to the man before her. His eyes mirrored his liking for what he saw. But he only smiled and offered, 'I'll take you both to Birmingham. I've a pony and trap waiting at the inn there.'

Grainne briefly studied him. His appearance was that of a wealthy, dandified gentleman, and his manner and accents also added to that impression. But despite her comparative youth, Grainne had seen and experienced a great deal, and there was something about this man which made her wary. It was not solely the piratical scar which traversed his face which gave her cause for caution. There was that in his eyes which she had seen before in the eyes of certain other men; men who had been reckless, lawless, and ruthless.

As if he could read her mind, his lips twitched in a brief smile, and he told her, 'You and your friend have naught to fear from me, my dear girl. It's perfectly obvious that the poor creature is in a sad way, and in no fit state to walk any distance. I have to go to Birmingham on personal business, and there is ample room for you both in my trap.'

He paused to see what effect his words were having, and noting that the wariness still remained in Grainne's eyes, shrugged dismissively. 'However, if you would prefer not to accompany me, I'll not trouble you further. Good day to you.'

He nodded brusquely, and turning began to walk away.

Grainne glanced down at Amy Davis. The girl was too weak and ill to be kept on the road for a moment longer than needful. Although Grainne's instincts were warning her against having anything more to do with this stranger, she knew that she could not be so selfish as to deprive Amy of a chance to be carried all the way to her home. Forcing back her own forebodings she called after the retreating figure, 'No, please, sir, wait a moment.'

He slowed, then halted and turned to face her, his features impassive.

Grainne nodded. 'If you please, sir, we would both be very grateful for your taking us to Birmingham.'

He nodded carelessly. 'Bring your friend around to the back of the inn there. And make haste, I've no more time to waste here.'

The horse and trap of Morgan Hunter was as glossy and expensive looking as the man himself and sitting beside him on the raised seat in the well of the vehicle Grainne could not help but be somewhat self conscious of her own shabby working gown, and general dishevelment.

Amy Davis was curled up on a rug on the floor directly behind the driving seat, and was sleeping.

The road surface was well maintained and the horse fresh and strong and so they made good time. Well before nightfall the thick smoke pall hanging above the city of Birmingham came into view, and the chimneys and close packed buildings of that bustling, busy city were a dark mass on the horizon.

Morgan Hunter had not spoken to either of the girls since setting out from Henley in Arden, and Grainne had been content to sit in silence, and became immersed in reverie. When at last the man did speak to her, she did not comprehend initially what he had said.

'I'm sorry,' she flustered. 'I was day-dreaming. What was that you said?'

He grinned, showing good teeth, and Grainne thought that he was really quite an attractive looking man, despite his terrible puckered scar.

'I asked you if you knew Birmingham at all?'

'No.' She shook her head. 'I was only there the once. I came by the locomotive from Liverpool, and then walked through to Millwood Hall. Do you know it well?'

He nodded. 'Well enough. Where is it your friend lives?'

'In the part called Bordesley,' Grainne informed him. 'But I don't know where exactly.'

Again he nodded. 'Well, let her sleep until we reach Bordesley, then we can find out where her home lies.'

After a slight pause, he told her, 'My name is Morgan Hunter. Captain Morgan Hunter. What name do you go by?'

'Grainne Shonley,' she told him, and with unconscious irony added, 'Mrs Grainne Shonley.'

'Where's your husband?'

'Well,' Grainne momentarily hesitated, finding it difficult to explain her feelings about Con to a stranger. 'Well, he went missing in a shipwreck, and I've had to assume him to be dead.'

Morgan Hunter with apparent casualness persisted in his questions until he had drawn from Grainne the full story of her ill-fated attempt to emigrate to America.

'And you, sir, are you married?' she finally asked in return, and he shook his head and smiled grimly.

'Not anymore.'

He did not volunteer any more information concerning that subject, and Grainne was loth to press him.

The journey continued on in silence, but now that silence was a companionable one, and Grainne felt considerably more relaxed in this man's company than she had done previously.

The countryside and hamlets now gave way to the raw new suburbs that the city was thrusting out in all directions: long terraces of shoddy jerry-built brick houses, depressing in their monotonous similarity. Further into the city the air changed in texture, became harsh and sulphurous to the taste, and the sky darkened beneath the palls of thick oily smoke that rose from the hundreds of chimneys.

'They call this place the City of a Thousand Trades, Mrs Shonley,' Morgan Hunter told her, and grimaced with distaste. 'I call it a filth-hole.'

They were now deep within the older warrens of narrow streets. On all sides stunted, shabby, pallid-featured people hurried to and fro. Traffic of all types rumbled and trundled in continuous streams. And the heat and clanging and clattering of workshops, and foundries, rolling mills, die-stamps and turning lathes battered at Grainne's senses. Open sewers ran down the middle of the roadways giving off poisonous stenches, and the walls and roofs of the buildings were thick with the grimes and greases of industrial process and waste. Pigs grunted and rummaged through the filth of the streets, mangy dogs and starving cats fought for rotting scraps of offal, and the air was filled with the sounds of metal hammering metal. This city was a city of metal, and every conceivable article manufactured from that commodity was being manufactured here among the myriads of workshops and factories that gave employment and sustenance to a quarter of a million people: people who lacked pure water supply, sewerage, clean air, decent living space, but who toiled and sweated like beasts of burden all the days of their short and brutish lives in order merely to survive.

Machines, artefacts, steam engines; buttons, buckles, cloak-pins and snuff boxes; plated goods for the dining table; guns, jewellery, medals and coins; brasswork of every description; copying machines, pneumatic apparatus, grates, fire-irons, gaslight burners, nails and steel pens. Japanned and enamelled and painted articles of all types; swords and cutlasses and daggers; cut crystals, and cottons and leatherware; the lists went on and on. Heavy or light, gigantic or tiny, intricate or simple, ornate or plain, there seemed to be nothing that this city could not manufacture.

Grainne stared around her, smelling the acrid rancid air, seeing the ragged, scald-headed, barefooted children, and their stunted, dirty, worn-featured elders swarming in the tumble-down, fetid dwelling places, and she remembered the slums of Liverpool, and marvelled yet again at the bitter paradox that where wealth was produced in such abundance, such depths of poverty and degradation should prevail.

'This is Bordesley,' Morgan Hunter stated. 'You had best wake your friend and ask her where her home is.'

Grainne turned and leaned over the girl, shaking her gently into wakefulness. Amy stirred, yawned and stretched, then smiled up at Grainne.

'We're in Bordesley, honey,' Grainne told her. 'Captain Hunter wants to know exactly where your home is.'

Amy's features crumpled, and she moaned dolefully. 'I was dreaming, Grainne. I was dreaming that we was in a lovely place. I'd forgot where I was going.'

She seemed as if she were about to break down into tears,

and Grainne said firmly, 'Come now, Amy. Sit up and look about you. We need to know where you live.'

The small pinched face was miserable as the girl surveyed the scene. Already a knot of curious onlookers were beginning to cluster about the smart equipage, and the glowering expressions on some of the men's stubbled, brutal features were making Grainne nervous.

'Quick now, Amy. Tell us the way to go,' she urged sharply.

'This is the High Street,' the girl informed with a sullen air. 'We needs to go through Adderley Street theer.' She pointed to a turning a little further on. 'Then up past the new gas works into Trinity Lane. Me Mam and Dad lives in Maguires Court theer.'

Maguires Court was reached by a covered entry set in a terrace of slum housing. Its narrow confines contained a dozen wretched tenements crammed around a great midden heap, the stench from which caused Grainne's stomach to heave as she helped her friend up the dark covered entryway. Despite the chill of the approaching night tiny half-naked children were playing around the steaming midden heap, and splashing with bare feet in the runnels of liquid filth that exuded from its base.

Grainne experienced a terrible sadness that she must leave her friend in such a place, but still did her best to appear cheerful and confident, as she told Amy Davis, 'Listen Amy, when you're better then you'll be able to find another place as housemaid. Maybe that won't be so long in coming.'

The other girl shook her head, and stated with a hopeless resignation, 'I'll never leave here again, Grainne. I'm come back to die, and both you and me knows that.'

She came to a standstill, causing Grainne to halt as well, and to Grainne's surprise the small white face was calm and the thready voice even. 'You goo on back to the carriage now, Grainne. I don't want you to come into me house. I'm not feared of dying here now. All of a sudden it doon't seem to matter anymore what becomes of me. I wants you to know that you'se bin a real good friend to me, Grainne. And I shall pray for you.'

Grainne's throat tightened unbearably, and tears stung her eyes. The other girl kissed her cheek, and then pushed her bodily towards the entry with a strength that belied her frailty.

'Goo on now. I wants you to leave me. God bless you Grainne!'

Grainne realised that the girl really meant what she said, and so, with tears falling down her cheeks, she kissed Amy and turned and ran back through the entry to where the trap waited in the roadway.

Morgan Hunter regarded her with sympathetic eyes and, as soon as she had climbed up onto the seat beside him, whipped his horse onwards. He allowed her to weep herself out, and then said softly, 'When we get away from this place, we'll stop and take some refreshment.'

She dried her eyes and looked at him in surprise. 'But I thought that you had business to attend to in the city, Captain Hunter.'

He shook his head, without looking at her, keeping his gaze concentrated on the dense traffic that they were immersed in.

'It's not important. I can come here another day.'

'But I've no wish to cause you any further trouble,' she protested. 'I want to tell you how grateful I am for all your kindness to Amy and me, Captain Hunter. I can only thank you a hundred times for it. But you have already done too much for me.'

'It's been my pleasure, Mrs Shonley,' he assured her, and then did look at her, and smiled. 'And because it's been my pleasure, then kindly allow me to take you back to Millwood Hall. I could not rest easy this night if I thought that you were having to walk all that way. Besides, the state the country is in, a woman is not safe to walk our highways any more. Particularly at night.'

Although Grainne felt uncomfortable about taking further advantage of his kindness, still she could not help but admit to herself that it was a tremendous relief for her to know that she would not have to make the long and arduous tramp back to Millwood Hall. Also, she accepted that there were indeed many dangers on the road for a woman travelling on foot, and alone.

After the noise and filth of the city the peace and sweet air of the countryside was a balm to Grainne's strained nerves. She breathed deeply of the cold freshness, relishing the cleansing from her lungs of the foul vapours of Birmingham.

They stopped briefly at a wayside inn, and ate bread and ham and cheese, and drank good rich ale, and then resumed their journey through the darkness which had now fallen over the land.

'Here, wrap this around you, or you'll catch cold.' Morgan Hunter handed her a blanket from the locker beneath the seat, and Grainne took it gratefully, and sat enveloped in its warm woollen folds, feeling sad about Amy Davis yet strangely content to be here in company with this man, who gave her such a feeling of security, despite her not knowing anything about him, other than the name he had given her.

They talked at intervals as the long miles passed, and Morgan Hunter asked her many details about her life at Millwood Hall, and about the Hall itself, and its routines of work, and the Herbertson family. Grainne answered readily enough, and only vaguely wondered how he could find such dull subjects to be of such apparently absorbing interest.

At the great iron gates of Millwood Hall, Morgan Hunter reined in the horse.

'You will be safe enough walking up the drive, Mrs Shonley.' She concurred readily, and after she had dismounted began to thank him again for all his kindness.

He shook his head and held his fingers up to his lips, invoking her silence.

'Haven't I already said to you, Mrs Shonley, that it was my pleasure to help you and your friend? Your company this day has meant more to me than you would ever believe. However, I think it best if you do not mention my name if anyone asks who aided you and your unfortunate friend. I would rather remain anonymous.'

'Very well.' She nodded, puzzled.

'If you have ever any need for my help in any way whatsoever, then leave a message for me with Mrs Brummage at the inn in Henley.' He grinned and for a moment resembled a mischievous boy. 'I trust you remember who she is, my dear. The fat unpleasant one. And now I really must leave you, but before I do so there's one thing more.'

Abruptly he leaned down from the seat and kissed Grainne

110

on her mouth. Then he whispered, 'Some day we'll meet again, Mrs Shonley. That is as certain as that the sun will rise tomorrow.'

He drove away to be swallowed by the darkness, leaving Grainne with the sensation of his lips still tingling upon her own.

Chapter Thirteen

During the days that followed Amy's departure no one mentioned her name, or enquired of Grainne how she herself had managed to get to Birmingham and back so quickly. It was as if the girl had never existed, and Grainne accepted that with a large number of servants coming and going in a household, then it was very definitely a case of being out of sight, out of mind.

The sole reference made to Amy's abrupt departure was Sarah Hobdon stating that because they were now a housemaid short then she, Grainne, and Rosy Bright would have to share the extra work between them.

Grainne missed Amy's company, for she had become fond of the younger girl. But she knew that there was no point in pining for her lost friend, and she tried to put the matter from her mind. Rosy Bright with her unfailing good humour did much to cheer Grainne and to fill the gap that Amy had left in her life. She often thought of Morgan Hunter, and remembered him with liking for the kindness he had shown to her. Also, she was honest enough to admit to herself, she thought of him often because she had found him an attractive man, and she wondered if she would indeed meet him again, and hoped that someday she would do so.

It was the first Sunday morning in April and at a quarter to eight o'clock old Ezra went through the house beating his gong to summon the servants to the ritual Sabbath day prayers.

Up in the attics the maids hurriedly changed from their soiled working dresses, canvas aprons and mobcaps into their formal, tightly fitting black gowns, starched white aprons and long-ribboned lace caps.

The buxom Rosy Bright struggled into her stays and begged Grainne, 'Lace me up, Grainne, there's a duck.'

Grainne chuckled. She had noted how just lately the other girl had suddenly begun to put on extra weight.

'Jasus, Rosy, you'll have to cut down on your eating and drinking you know. Or you'll not find stays big enough to wrap around yourself,' she advised jokingly.

Rosy giggled. 'It arn't ateing and drinking that's swelling me belly so.'

'Oh my God!' Grainne breathed with concern. 'You're not, are you?'

Rosy beamed and nodded with total unconcern. 'Of course I am. I'd have thought you'd of noticed how far gone I was before now, girl.'

'Who's the father?' Grainne asked. 'Does he work here?'

'No.' Rosy shook her head. 'He's a soldier. Come on Grainne, make haste and pull me tight, or we'll be late, and then that miserable cow Gurnock 'ull give us a roasting.'

'But what if it hurts the baby, lacing you tight?' Grainne demurred doubtfully. 'What will its father say if you hurt it by lacing?'

'It doesn't matter a fuck what he might say,' the other girl spat out vehemently. 'The bastard's bin sent to India, arn't he? So he won't have the trouble on it. We warn't even trothed, was we? The fucker promised to wed me, but once he'd got what he was after he soon scarpered and joined the bleedin' army.'

She paused, then grinned cheerily as another thought struck her. 'Mind you, once I'se birthed it, it won't really be a trouble to me neither. Me Mam 'ull keep it for me.'

Grainne shook her head bemusedly. 'Won't she mind doing that for you?'

'Bugger me, no!' Rosy's plump homely features were wreathed in smiles. 'Her's already got eight of her own, and two more o' mine, and one from me sister to see to, so another 'un arn't going to make much of a difference, is it? She wun't notice that it's theer when her's got a drop or two of "mother's ruin" down her neck. And that's often enough that is, wi' me Mam. She does like her drop o' drink and no mistake.'

'And your Daddy, what does he think about it?' Grainne was driven to ask.

Rosy laughed uproariously and spluttered. 'I arn't bin able to ask him anything about what he thinks just lately, Grainne. I'll needs take a shovel and dig the bugger up if I wants to talk to him. And if I did that then there's no guarantee that he'd be able to give me any answer. Not the state he'll be in by now, seeing as how he's bin dead and buried these four years, and good riddance to bad rubbish that is!'

The girl's mirth was infectious, and Grainne could not hold back her own laughter.

'Will you lot get a move on!' Sarah Hobdon came shouting along the corridor. 'You'd oughter be downstairs by now.'

Quickly Grainne tugged the laces on Rosy's stays, as the other girl drew in her swollen stomach, and held her breath until her face turned cherry red. Then both girls finished changing and with a final check in the broken glass went from the attic.

In a fluttering of streaming cap-ribbons, and a rustling of wide skirts and starched aprons, the maids hastened down to the big library on the ground floor. It was a long, high-beamed sombre room, its walls lined from floor to ceiling with shelves of costly leather-bound books which no one of the family ever read, and which the servants were forbidden to open.

Under Mrs Gurnock's stern gaze the servants ranged themselves in strict hierarchical order, upper servants to the front, lower servants behind them, outdoor servants at the rear. Butler, valet and lady's maid in their black clothes and frilled linen. The cook and her assistants in pristine white. The footman and coachman resplendent in best livery and powdered hair. The maids in fresh starched caps and aprons and black bombazine gowns. Grooms and stableboys in long-sleeved waistcoats, polka-dot cravats and polished knee-length leather gaiters. Gardeners and garden boys in their 'Sunday best' ill-fitting serge jackets and moleskin trousers, great clumping boots, their weather-beaten faces red and sweaty from the uncomfortable constrictions of their high collars and neck-stocks.

The family entered with a slow stately pace, all three wearing deepest mourning in honour of the dead Saviour. Mrs Sophia Herbertson's features were hidden behind the heaviest of black veils, which caused prurient knowing glances to be exchanged between the female servants. Their woefully plain mistress was obviously suffering from a recrudescence of her facial rash, which arrived in concert with each succeeding pregnancy.

The male servants bowed low and the female servants curtseyed deeply, and remained in their submissive postures until the family had arranged themselves at the end of the room, where three great high-seated armchairs resembling the thrones of royalty had been placed to receive them.

An ancient polished oaken lectern in the shape of an eagle with vast outstretched wings was standing a little in advance and to the side of the three armchairs. A huge leather-bound Bible had been placed ready upon it, already opened to the day's text. Mrs Gurnock stood facing the servants at the far side of the lectern, hands clasped before her, her fine dark eyes ranging over the serried faces searching for any signs of levity or inattention.

Mr Charles Herbertson and his wife took their seats, and Edwin Herbertson went to stand behind the lectern, staring glumly downwards at the floor. The servants straightened and waited in respectful silence. One of the garden boys coughed, and Mrs Gurnock's glare savaged him so that his eyes bulged and his face purpled as he fought to hold back further eruptions.

Charles Herbertson scowled at the servants and in his deep voice began to berate them.

'I have noticed of late that there has been an excessive consumption of strong drink in this household. This practice will cease herewith. I pay you to work hard and well, and to serve me and mine. Not to swill and gorge yourselves like pigs. I know that some of you have been raised in filth and ignorance, and have witnessed your own families behaving little better than animals, but while you are under my roof and in my employ you will conduct yourselves as I require you so to do. Be warned, that if I come to know of anyone among you who gets drunk in the future, then that one will be instantly dismissed from my service without a character. I would therefore advise you all to listen well to this morning's text, and take it into your hearts.'

He nodded curtly towards his son. 'You may read the lesson, Edwin.'

With a sullen hangdog air Edwin Herbertson stood at the lectern peering down at the open pages of the great Bible. His face, framed by lank tendrils of hair, was puffy and unhealthily flushed. Sweat sheened his skin and his eyes were badly bloodshot. When he lifted his hands to place them at each side of the lectern they were visibly shaking.

Grainne stared at the young man with acute distaste. It was common gossip among the servants that Edwin Herbertson constantly drank himself into stupors, and judging by his appearance this morning his drinking bout of the previous night must have been of mammoth proportions. Her eyes flickered to Charles Herbertson's scowling features, and she wondered if his strictures against strong drink, although directed against his servants, had really been an attempt to humiliate his own son.

Edwin Herbertson coughed and grimaced as if his mouth had filled with a vile taste, and his father's scowl deepened. Then in a hoarse, tremulous voice the young man began to read: 'Isiah. Chapter Twenty-eight.

'Woe to the cwown of pwide, to the dwunkards of Ephwaim, whose glowious beauty is a fading flower, which are on the head of the fat valleys of them that are overcome with wine . . . '

As she witnessed this farcical display of rampant hypocrisy Grainne was simultaneously swept by angry resentment, coupled with the wild urge to laugh, and she was forced to bow her head and bite her lips. Edwin Herbertson's voice went shakily on and it was many seconds before Grainne had regained sufficient control for her to risk looking at him once more and take cognisance of the words he spoke.

' . . . for stwength to them that turn the battle to the gate. But they also have erred thwough wine, and thwough stwong dwink are out of the way. The pwiest and the pwophet have erred thwough stwong dwink, they are swallowed up of wine, they are out of the way thwough stwong dwink . . . '

Grainne thought that she was going to explode, and when beside her she heard Rosy Bright suddenly erupt in a fit of strangled giggles, she could no longer restrain her own urge to laugh and she turned away, lifting her apron to cover her face. Her movement seemed to trigger a chain reaction through the ranks of the servants, and in lightning succession one after another of them burst into laughter, desperately trying to smother the sounds, but unable to stop themselves.

Behind the lectern Edwin Herbertson's face suffused darkly, and his expression grew murderous. Hatred was in the furious glare he directed at his scowling father. The older man's lips twisted in a contemptuous sneer, and Edwin Herbertson abruptly hurled the lectern, sending it crashing onto the floor, and went barging out of the library, buffeting aside those servants who impeded his way.

Charles Herbertson rose to his feet and beckoned imperiously to his wife. 'Come, Madam.'

Dutifully she rose and walked before him to the door.

Charles Herbertson regarded the servants with a stony glare, and they quailed beneath it, only two or three still tried vainly to bite back their sniggers.

'You will sorely rue this day that you have made a mockery of the Holy Bible, and of my family,' Charles Herbertson growled, and ordered Mrs Gurnock, 'Get these cretinous heathens back to their work, Mrs Gurnock, and then come to my study.'

Her pale face was worried as she bobbed a curtsey.

Charles Herbertson stalked out of the library, and no one dared to meet his angry eyes. As soon as he had disappeared the housekeeper hissed furiously, 'You heard what the master said, get back to your work. And it will be God help anybody I find slacking this day. I'll promise you that.'

She kept her dark eyes fixed on Grainne as she uttered this threat, and Grainne felt uneasy. That unease deepened when, as the maids were going back up to the attics, Sarah Hobdon whispered, 'I think Mrs Gurnock is blaming you for what happened, Grainne. You'd best take care and not let her catch you doing anything she can pick flies out of, or you'll be out of the gates this very day. I've seen the miserable bitch do it before now.'

Grainne could not repress a sensation of trepidation at the prospect of being discharged. She had seen the bedraggled women and girls in the streets of Birmingham, and had no desire to become one of them. But she made no reply, knowing the futility of protesting her innocence of any desire to

117

cause offence to her employers, or to make mock of the Bible.

In the study Ruth Gurnock nervously faced her employer. To her relief he spoke quietly to her, displaying no sign of anger directed at her.

'I do not hold you to blame for that disgraceful happening in the library, Mrs Gurnock. You cannot be censured for what occurred there.'

'Thank you, sir. Believe me I am cruelly mortified by it and I shall punish those responsible, you may be sure of that, sir. I'll make them sorry that they ever dared to make mock of the family.' She spoke vehemently, words tumbling from her lips, her normally pale translucent skin mottled by livid patches of colour.

He gestured her to silence, then told her, 'I have decided to leave for America this very week. I will take Croxall with me, and my valet and Mrs Sophia's maid. Croxall is to go to Liverpool tonight and arrange the hotel accommodation for our arrival there. I shall travel there tomorrow.'

He paused ruminatively for some seconds, then continued in a reflective tone, 'When I am gone, then you will discharge all the servants. They are to be paid any wages due them, minus the cost of the wear of their uniforms. Also each is to be fined the sum of two shillings as a just and rightful punishment for their display of insolence towards my family. And everyone of them will of course be discharged without a character. I can only hope that such a course of action will teach them the wicked error of their ways. Perhaps as a result they may show more respect for their betters in the future.'

'Yes, sir,' Ruth Gurnock replied dutifully. 'I'm sure that they will.' Then she asked tentatively, 'If you please, sir, there is one concern I would like to draw to your attention.'

He nodded permission and, bobbing a grateful curtsey, Ruth Gurnock went on: 'Well, sir, Mr Edwin is remaining here at the Hall, is he not? And I shall need help to care for him properly, sir, and to keep the house running efficiently until I can engage new staff and train them to my satisfaction.'

He steepled his fingers and touched their tips to his lips, bending his head as if in thought. Then he slowly nodded.

'Very well, Mrs Gurnock. Retain only those servants that

are essential to your needs, until such time as you have engaged and trained replacements for them, then discharge those you have retained also.'

Ruth Gurnock was in thoughtful mood as she returned to her office. The intention of Charles Herbertson to take John Croxall with him to America had come as a shock to her. She had thought that only the valet and the lady's maid would accompany the couple. But now, given pause for reflection, she regarded John Croxall's forthcoming departure as something of a mixed blessing. She hated to see him go, yet at the same time realised that his going might prove to be the only means by which she could keep him for herself.

Besotted though she was with the man, in her secret heart Ruth Gurnock was under no illusions as to his feelings towards her. He had a certain fondness for her, that she knew, and still desired her sexually, but basically she was only his stepping stone to be used to aid him to further his own ambitions, and when he thought the time was ripe, then he would pass on and leave her behind him. But even knowing this as she did, Ruth Gurnock was still determined to keep him with her for as long as she could possibly do so and was prepared to go to any lengths to achieve that aim.

Through the years of their relationship he had at various times shown interest in other women, but these had been passing fancies and no real threat to her. But a real threat existed now. A threat that was becoming increasingly obvious to her with each day that passed. John Croxall's feelings towards the Irish girl, Grainne Shonley, went far deeper than perhaps even he himself recognised. But Ruth Gurnock could recognise what those feelings were becoming. Her obsession with the man heightened her sense of intuition concerning all that concerned him, and she knew for a certainty that for the first time a real and immediate danger of losing him was confronting her.

She smiled bitterly, thinking how ironic it was that now she had instructions to dismiss all the servants she could not yet dismiss Grainne Shonley, whom she wished above all others to be rid of.

'If I send her packing at this time, then John will still be feeling the same way about her. And there's naught to prevent

119

him writing to her from America, is there? I have to destroy his feelings for her, before I get rid of her from this house. I have to sicken him of her. And I've already got a good notion of how I shall manage that,' she told herself with a fierce satisfaction.

John Croxall was waiting for her in her office. 'Well, what did the master have to say?' he demanded without preamble.

'That you are to go to America with him. You, and the nancyboy and the Frog. You've to leave for Liverpool this night and arrange hotel rooms there for the party.'

'America!' he grinned delightedly. 'But that's great news. I've always wanted to go to America. But I didn't dare to hope that he'd take me with him.'

Ruth Gurnock stared at his beaming face, anger stirring within her; anger provoked by his delight at leaving England, and leaving her.

'Glad to be leaving me, are you?' she questioned tartly.

He stared at her, puzzlement overlaying his delighted grin. 'Now I arn't said that, have I, Ruth?' he protested.

'You don't need to say it,' she hissed venomously. 'I can see it in your face, can't I?'

'You're talking silly.' He tried to placate her with a soft answer, but her anger and jealousy was rapidly fuelling upon itself.

'Talking silly, am I? And is that what you'll be saying to your Irish whore, when you tells her that youm leaving her and she starts whining about it?'

Exasperation replaced placation in his voice. 'Oh no! We're not going to have all this bloody rubbish again, are we?'

'We'll have whatever I decides we'll have, John Croxall!' Ruth Gurnock's control broke and the words flooded from her in a poisonous stream. 'You're forgetting your place, my buck! Shagging that Irish bitch has addled what bit o' brain you've got in that thick skull o' yourn, that's easy to see. Don't you be forgetting who is the superior here in this household. Butler you may be, and that's only thanks to me. But I'm the housekeeper, and stand in the rank of house steward. I can ruin you whenever I chooses to, you bloody whoremonger, and you'd best keep that fact well to the front of your thoughts.'

John Croxall was about to hurl a stream of invective at the woman, when suddenly a sharp visual image of Grainne

Shonley came into his mind, and realising that any continuation of this dispute could well end by harming her also, he bit on his tongue and turning away from Ruth Gurnock went out of the room.

Going to his pantry he bolted the door behind him and poured out a large tot of brandy which he swallowed in one gulp. Charles Herbertson's threat to dismiss any of his staff found to be intoxicated came into his mind, and he grimaced and made a lewd gesture with his fingers. Then he refilled the glass and took another gulp of the fiery golden liquid. The alcohol served to soothe his anger and steady his rampaging thoughts, and he considered Grainne Shonley.

'Why couldn't I have met you a couple of years from now, my little Paddy?' he murmured yearningly. 'I'd have been ready then. Ready to move to a greater household, or to leave domestic service and to go into some sort of business for myself. I only need a couple more years.'

After the episode of Amy Davis, John Croxall had admitted to himself that he was infatuated with the beautiful Irish girl. But he had exerted all his considerable reserves of self-discipline to control that infatuation and not to let it drive him into rash actions or declarations. Now, however, knowing that he would be going to America and leaving Grainne Shonley behind him, John Croxall's thoughts were very mixed.

'I can't just leave things lay as they are,' he finally decided. 'I know that she likes me. All right, that's not to say that she's in love with me at all. But perhaps if she knew how I felt about her, then she'd be prepared to wait a couple of years for me. By then she'll be well over grieving for her husband, won't she? By then she'll be ready to fall in love again, and who better than me for that? If she knows now how I feel about her, then she'll not be looking elsewhere, will she?'

Grainne was in the linen store ironing sheets when John Croxall found her. 'I'm going to America with the master and mistress, Grainne,' he told her. 'I'm sorry that you're not coming with us.'

'I've no wish to go there anymore.' She smiled sadly. 'I tried once before and found only grief.'

'Listen, Grainne, I've something that I wish to say to you.'

Bent over the table, smoothing the cloth with the hot

flatiron, Grainne kept her face averted, suspecting what it was that the man wished to say, and uncertain whether or not she cared to hear it.

'Please, Grainne, will you put that bloody iron down and look at me!'

His voice was strained, and when she did as he had asked and looked at him she saw that his expression was tense.

'Well, Mr Croxall, what is it?' she prodded, when he only remained standing staring at her in silence.

He appeared to become angry with himself and vented an impatient exclamation. Then he told her gruffly, 'I've tried to think of a pretty speech to make to you, girl, but it won't serve. So I'll speak plainly. I've come to hold you in high regard, Grainne. In fact, I think I'm in love with you.'

He held up his hands when she would have spoken.

'No! Say nothing yet, only hear me out.'

She nodded silently, and he went on.

'I know that you're still in mourning for your husband, Grainne, and if it were not for the fact that I'm going to America so soon, then I wouldn't have spoken of this matter to you. But there it is. I wanted you to know my feelings towards you. And to know also that when I return from America, I stand ready to marry you.'

'No!' she said, vehemently shaking her head. 'You should not have spoken of this to me. Not at this time. I've no wish for any man to love me, because I am not able to love him in return. I only ever wanted Con, my husband, and the way I feel now, then I doubt that I'll ever again want to marry another.'

He flinched, almost as if she had struck him physically, and Grainne experienced remorse that she should have hurt him. In a softer tone she went on, 'Listen Mr Croxall, I'm grateful to you for your friendship, and I return that friendship in full measure. But I'm not in love with you, and I don't think of you in that way at all. There's still too much yearning inside me for my husband for me to be able to think of any other man in such a way.'

He appeared to relax, and the tension visibly ebbed from his expression. He smiled at her, and said, 'I'm very pleased to hear that there is no other man in your life, Grainne. It means that perhaps one day then there will be a chance for me. In the meantime be sure that I shall always stand as a true friend towards you. Can you also continue to be my friend?'

'Of course I can. And I'm happy to have it so.'

He came towards her and took her hand in his. 'I shall write to you when I'm in America, Grainne, and I want you to write to me also. If you have need of anything while I'm over there, then you must promise me that you'll tell me of it. Will you do that? Will you give me your promise?'

She nodded. 'I will, and gladly.'

'Good!' He grinned with satisfaction, and told her, 'This must count as our goodbye, Grainne, for I'll not have another opportunity of speaking with you. The master needs me to go to Liverpool this very night to arrange hotel rooms.'

Before he could say anything more Rosy Bright came bustling into the linen store.

'I've got to give you a hand wi' the ironing, Grainne,' she beamed, then saw John Croxall was holding Grainne's hand, and eyed them both wonderingly. The man sighed, and with a gentle squeeze of his fingers released Grainne's hand and with obvious reluctance walked away.

Rosy's eyes sparkled with excitement. 'What was he telling you, Grainne?' she demanded with breathless eagerness. 'What was gooing on between you?'

Grainne experienced an unexpected sensation of disappointment that the man had left so abruptly, and was momentarily piqued with Rosy for interrupting at such an inopportune moment. Then she told herself firmly to stop acting like a silly young girl, and smilingly teased her friend, 'That's for me to know, Rosy, and for you to find out.'

Chapter Fourteen

Charles Herbertson and his wife left Millwood Hall early in the morning to travel to Birmingham in the opulent carriage. The valet and lady's maid followed in a waggon loaded high with the family's luggage.

With their departure something of a holiday atmosphere permeated through the servants, and when the gong rang at eight o'clock to summon them to their breakfast the big kitchen became the scene of an animated and convivial gathering.

Walter entered a little later than the others, wearing his cockaded top hat and outdoor coat.

'Where's you been, Walter?' Sarah Hobdon asked him.

'Mrs Gurnock rousted me out o' me bed fust thing this morning to fetch the Henley constable and his deputy back here. They'm up in her office with her now.'

'Why ever for?' Mrs Tomlinson the cook questioned.

Walter shrugged. 'I'm buggered if I knows, missus.' His protruberant eyes fastened greedily on the salvers of fried bacon sandwiches in the centre of the table, and he pushed between two of the maids on the bench and reached for the food. 'Here, let the dog see the rabbit, 'ull you. I'm bloody clemmed, so I am.'

He crammed his mouth full and began to chomp with noisy gusto when one of the row of call-bells on the walls began to jangle. Mrs Tomlinson squinted to stare at the jerking bell. 'That's Mrs Gurnock's office. You'd best get up theer sharp, Walter. Her arn't in a very sweet mood this morning from what I'se seen of her.'

'Goddamn and blast the old cow!' the footman cursed, but gulped down the mouthful of half-chewed bread and bacon and hurried away still wearing his hat and topcoat.

'There's summat up!' Mrs Tomlinson announced portentously, and stared at the faces around the big table. 'As any o' you bin doing summat you didn't ought to be doing?'

Shaking heads and vociferous denials answered her. There was an exchange of speculation about the arrival of the constables, but apart from a couple of facetious suggestions, no one could offer any valid reason.

Before long Walter reappeared in the kitchen. 'Everybody has got to come this instant to Mrs Gurnock's office.'

There was a chorus of grumbling about being taken from their breakfasts, but it was noticeable that the loudest grumblers were the first to leave the kitchen.

Ruth Gurnock was standing in the main hallway in company with Wakefield the Henley constable and his deputy, a bulky-bodied young man, wearing the same type of squared paper artisan's cap and blue smock-frock as Wakefield himself. The constable was holding his staff of office in his hand with its long thick shaft and wooden crowned top.

As the servants trooped to stand in a line outside her office door which was situated in one of the corridors leading from the entrance hall, Ruth Gurnock frowningly surveyed them. Trailed by the two constables she walked along the line, her eyes flicking from one face to another.

'Mrs Tomlinson, go back to your kitchen. Hobdon, Shonley, get on with your duties.'

The three so designated hurried away, and as they did so Sarah Hobdon whispered to Grainne, 'I reckon theer's going to be a clearout, Grainne.'

'A what?' Grainne stared at her companion with puzzled eyes.

'A clearout. They'm all going to be given their sacks.'

'What?' Grainne could not believe what she was hearing. 'All of them? But why? What have they done?'

'It'll be because of what happened last Sunday morn,' Mrs Tomlinson put in. 'I knew there'd be trouble because on it. You can't expect to make mock o' the gentry and get away wi' it can you? It stands to reason.'

'But we were all laughing,' Grainne protested. 'And you as well, Mrs Tomlinson. I heard you.'

'I never did,' the cook denied indignantly. 'I knows me place better than to do such a thing.'

By now they had reached the kitchen and they clustered close together by the cooking range, talking in excited whispers.

'That's why the constable's bin fetched up here,' Sarah Hobdon stated positively. 'In case anybody tries to kick up a ruction about being give their sack.'

'Ahr, and they'll not be give their characters, you can lay odds to that.' Mrs Tomlinson was equally positive.

'Dear Jasus!' Grainne exclaimed and thinking of the pregnant Rosy Bright wondered aloud, 'What will the poor souls do now for work?'

'Well, wi'out their characters they'll be able to do precious little,' Mrs Tomlinson sympathised. 'The poor buggers 'ull have to try and find work in Brummagem theer.'

'I 'udden't wish that on anybody,' Sarah Hobdon declared. 'It's a filthy dirty disease-ridden hole, and there's a good many girls I know that has lost their health and strength in them bloody factories.'

'But if they're being given their sacks for what happened on Sunday morn, why are we three being kept on?' Grainne wondered aloud.

'Well, we'em all good willing workers, and we knows our jobs, doon't we?' Mrs Tomlinson offered in explanation. 'Theer's none on us gets the worse for drink, does we, and we'em always early to work and late to leave off it. So, bearing that in mind, I expect Mrs Gurnock has decided that she doon't really want to lose us.'

'Bearing in mind as well, Mrs Tomlinson, that Ruth Gurnock's got to keep some servants back here with her, or face doing all the bloody work herself,' Sarah Hobdon put in cynically.

'Ahr, that's bound to be right, Sarah,' the cook agreed sullenly. 'Arter all, theer's Mr Edwin still to look arter, arn't there?'

Sarah Hobdon's handsome face wore a troubled frown. 'That's so. And who'll be directed to act as his personal servant, I wonder?'

126

'I shouldn't bother your yed about t'at for now, my girl,' Mrs Tomlinson advised. 'If I was you two I'd get cracking working instead, and keep your yeds low until the storm blows over. I'll get these breakfast things cleared and washed.'

The cook set to work, and Grainne and Sarah went to fetch their implements from the store cupboard. Sarah's face still bore its worried frown, and Grainne tried to cheer her. 'Well, Sarah, at least we've still got a place to lay our heads, haven't we?'

'That's as maybe,' the other girl snapped irritably. 'But it's wheer we might be expected to lay 'um that's bothering me.'

Grainne stared at her curiously. 'What do you mean by that, Sarah?'

'Oh, it doon't matter!' The handsome girl irritably shook her head, but Grainne was by now determined to know what secret was so visibly troubling her companion.

'Tell me, Sarah,' she persisted. 'Tell me what it is that's bothering you so much? It's bothered you before hasn't it? I can remember when I first came here what you once said to me, and then wouldn't go any further. So tell me now. Tell me, Sarah.'

For a few seconds Sarah stood silent, her expression worried and doubtful, then she drew breath sharply and as if reaching a decision asked Grainne, 'If I tells you, will you give me your solemn oath that you won't tell anybody what it is I'm agoing to tell you?'

Grainne could not help but smile fleetingly at her companion's dramatic manner.

'You must promise me, Grainne.'

Seeing how serious the other girl was, Grainne nodded.

'Very well, I give you my word. I'll not repeat anything to anyone.'

'Does you swear to it?'

'I swear.'

Sarah stared hard at her for a moment, then in hoarse whispers told her, 'When I first came into service here about five years past, I shared with a girl named Flora. Flora Kemp. She was ever so pretty, Grainne. She had lovely long blonde hair, and really white teeth. Well, she used to tell me that Mr Edwin was trying to 'tice her to go into his room with him, and to meet him outside the Hall as well. Up in the woods theer, or in the barns. She said that he'd promised to marry her, but that first she'd got to let him do things to her to prove that she loved him for himself, and not just because he was rich. You know what I mean don't you? To let him fuck her.'

Grainne frowned slightly, not knowing whether or not to give full credence to this gossip. Of course she accepted that there were many instances where the menfolk of the employers' families tried to seduce attractive servant girls. She herself had experienced such incidents when she had previously been in service. But also she knew well that many girls would relate fictitious happenings of this nature purely to gain attention from their peers.

'And what happened to this Flora?' she questioned quietly.

'Well, one night she did goo to Mr Edwin's room. She snuck there while I was sleeping. There was only me and her, and Mrs Gurnock and Mr Edwin in the house that night. The family had gone down to the London house and taken all the rest of the indoor servants with'um.

'The next morning she come back to our room, and she was crying fit to bost. It fritted me summat terrible, so it did, the way she was weeping and wailing. She told me that he'd done terrible things to her, and that she was so shamed by what he'd done that she wished she was dead and in her grave. She said that if her Dad knew what vile things Mr Edwin had done to her, and made her do to him, that her Dad 'ud kill him stone dead, and kill her as well.'

As she listened Grainne found her earlier doubts as to the veracity of the story disappearing. Sarah's voice rang with truth.

The young woman fell silent, her features mirroring the distress she herself had experienced at that time.

'Go on, Sarah, tell me what happened then?' Grainne urged gently.

'Well, Flora was so badly that in the end I run to fetch Mrs Gurnock to her. I was feared Flora might be dying you see, because there was a lot of blood coming from her private parts, and she kept on screaming out with the pain she was in.

'Mrs Gurnock come and looked at her, then sent me away, and told me that I must never tell a soul about what Flora had told me. She said that Flora was a wicked girl, who was telling terrible lies about a fine young gentleman, who hadn't got a sin on his soul.

'Anyway, I never saw Flora again. I heard later that she'd been given her sack, and no character, and Mrs Gurnock told me that it was only Mr Edwin's forbearance and good heart that had saved Flora from going to prison for the terrible lies she'd told about him.'

The handsome blonde-haired girl hesitated, her eyes deeply troubled, then asked anxiously, 'Was I wrong not to say anything to anybody else about it, Grainne? I wanted to, but I was too feared to, because Mrs Gurnock told me that if I ever repeated such terrible lies about Mr Edwin, why then I'd be sent to prison.'

She shook her head in distress.

'I was so young and innocent then, Grainne. I didn't know anything about anything, and that's the truth. But what happened to poor Flora has been troubling me all these years. You're the first one I'se ever breathed a word to about it, Grainne. But don't go telling anybody else, because it's too late now to prove the truth of what I say. And it will only get me into sad trouble.'

The two girls separated and went to work in different rooms. Grainne was stripping the sheets from Charles Herbertson's bed when Rosy Bright came into the room. She was wearing her bonnet and outdoor cloak and carried her box of belongings in her arms.

'I just come to say tarra, Grainne.'

Grainne regarded her curiously, noting that the other girl did not seem in the least upset or distressed by being dismissed in such a draconian manner.

'Will you be all right, Rosy?' she asked.

'O' course I shall,' Rosy laughed. 'I'd have bin give me sack anyway in a little while. Once Gurnock saw that I was in the pudding club, that would have bin me lot. I'm going to goo back to me Mam's and have a rest until I'se birthed this little sod.' She paused, and a fleeting regret crossed her face. 'I'm sorry that I'm parting from you though, Grainne. Still, if youm ever out Ullenhall way then come and visit me, wun't you?'

'I will,' Grainne promised, the sadness of parting from this sunny-tempered, good-natured girl now beginning to bite. 'Did any of the others play up about being sacked?'

'Only when Gurnock and the constables couldn't hear 'um. Some on 'um was as bold as bloody lions, and was promising to tear Gurnock's yed off, but when they went into the bloody office, they was as meek as lambs. They'm all gone now, except for me. Only I wanted to see you afore I went.'

'I'm glad that you did. And I'm really sorry that you've been given your sack, Rosy. I shall miss you something sore.'

A lump came into Grainne's throat as the other girl hugged and kissed her, and then left.

A feeling of utter loneliness swept over Grainne, and tears stung her eyes.

'Why is it that whenever I make a friend then they're taken from me?' she asked herself sadly.

Then she busied herself once again, immersing herself in hard work to keep depression at bay. It was an hour later when the sudden premonition struck. 'It would have been better for me to have been dismissed with the others. Even though I've no money and nowhere to go. It would have been better for me.' The thought coming unbidden into her mind had such an impact that it brought her to a standstill.

'Now what's put that into me head?' she wondered. 'Why should I think that?'

Still puzzling and troubled she turned back to her work. But try as she might to dismiss this strange sense of foreboding, during the hours that followed it only strengthened its hold upon her with an inexorable persistence.

Chapter Fifteen

When Grainne went to the kitchen for her midday meal Mrs Tomlinson informed her, 'Mrs Gurnock says youm to goo to her office, my duck.'

'What does she want of me?'

The cook shrugged. 'Her didn't say.'

Grainne hurried to the office and to her surprise Ruth Gurnock greeted her with a bleak smile. 'Ah, Shonley. You are conversant with the duties of a personal maid, are you not?'

Grainne nodded. 'Yes, ma'm. I was trained as a personal maid in Lady Dunsmore's service.'

'Are you able to clean and press gentlemen's clothing, and to serve at table?'

'Yes, ma'm.'

'Can you shave and barber?'

'I have shaved gentlemen, ma'm, and I used to dress Lady Dunsmore's hair. But it's long since that I've used a razor.'

'No matter,' Ruth Gurnock brushed that aside. 'Mr Edwin prefers to shave himself anyway.'

Grainne's sense of foreboding returned in full measure as the housekeeper told her, 'You are to be given the opportunity to better yourself, Shonley. You will act as personal maidservant to Mr Edwin. Your wages are eight pounds per annum, are they not?'

'Yes, ma'm.'

'If you give satisfaction in this new position, then your wages will be increased to sixteen pounds per annum.'

Ruth Gurnock frowned. 'You do not appear to be pleased about your good fortune, Shonley?'

131

Grainne was not pleased. She did not want to become Edwin Herbertson's personal maid. Sarah Hobdon's story about the girl Flora was too fresh in Grainne's memory.

'If you please, ma'm, I do appreciate your offering me this chance to better myself. But I'd prefer to remain as I am,' she said quietly.

The housekeeper's frown deepened. 'You do not appear to have understood me, Shonley. I have told you that you are to serve Mr Edwin as his personal maid. Your preferences may be what they will, but you will do as I bid you to do. If you choose to disobey me, then I shall have no other option but to dismiss you from this household. Do you understand me now?'

For a moment Grainne was tempted to defy the woman's threats, but she knew that she had no real choice of action. If she should be dismissed now, then she would be homeless and virtually penniless. Unhappily she accepted defeat.

'Very well, ma'm.'

'Good!' The bleak smile reappeared on Ruth Gurnock's lips. 'Now go and change into your best uniform and report to Mr Edwin in his rooms. It is his preference to inform you of the duties he expects of you.'

Edwin Herbertson was lounging in an easy chair beside the fire in his sitting room, a long cheroot in his mouth, a decanter of brandy on the small table at his elbow, and a glass of the spirit in his hand. He had been drinking steadily since his father's departure, and was now becoming aggressively intoxicated.

When Grainne knocked at his door he shouted for her to enter, then pointed to a spot opposite his chair.

'Stand there, girl.'

Grainne felt a flush of embarrassment spreading from her throat to her cheeks as Edwin Herbertson's small bloodshot eyes roamed greedily over her body, coming again and again to dwell lingeringly upon her full firm breasts.

'You're a handsome cweature, Shonley, and if you serve me well, then you'll find me a genewous master.'

'Yes, sir.' She kept her eyes downcast.

'Is the coachman still with us?' the man asked, and Grainne nodded. 'Yes sir, Parkins is still here, and the head gardener.'

'I didn't ask about the bloody gardener, Shonley,' the young man corrected her sharply.

Grainne bit her lips, and hid her fiery resentment of his attitude behind impassive features.

'Tell Parkins I shall need the cawwiage and have him hold himself in weadiness. Lay out my evening dwess and cloak. I shall be going into Birmingham this evening.'

'Will you be dining before you go, sir?' Grainne asked politely.

'Goddamn you, Shonley, don't pwesume to question me!' he shouted in sudden temper. 'Just do as you're told!'

Grainne bobbed a curtsey and went through the connecting door into Edwin Herbertson's dressing room. She took his evening suit from the wall closet and laid it ready for him to don, together with his shirt and cravat, his pumps, top hat and opera cloak, fresh underlinen and stockings. Then she returned to the other room and curtseyed.

'Will that be all, sir?'

He nodded and with a sense of relief Grainne made her escape from the room to go in search of Parkins, the coachman.

Parkins, a tall, ruddy-featured countryman, was in the stables, looking very disgruntled as he curried and combed one of the horses.

'It's a bloody disgrace, Grainne,' he grumbled bitterly. 'Sacking the grooms and all of the stable lads. Theer's too much here for me to do on me own. I've a mind to give my notice and get shut o' this bloody place.'

'Well don't do it tonight, will you?' Grainne smiled. 'Because Mr Edwin wants you to take him into Birmingham, and it'll be God help all of us if he can't get there, the mood he's in.'

'Drinking, is he?' the coachman asked with a frown.

Grainne nodded. 'Yes, and he looks to be three sheets to the wind already.'

Parkins looked disgruntled. 'Bugger me, that's all I needs to put the icing on a bloody rotten day, that is. The bastard 'ull be looking for women, and keeping me standing outside every low-life gin house in bloody Brummagem. I'll be lucky if I sees me bed afore noontime tomorrow. He'll stay the night over in Brummagem, that's for sure.'

133

Grainne was glad to hear that her master would be gone from the house all night, and wished with all her heart that he was going for good and not for just a few hours.

'Ah well,' the coachman sighed resignedly. 'I'd best get me livery on and take the carriage round to the front to wait for his lordship.'

When eventually Edwin Herbertson left the Hall, Grainne went into his rooms to tidy them. On sudden impulse she looked through the drawers of his dressing table. In one of them she found a bundle of picture cards. They were garishly coloured portrayals of perverted sexual practices, and although Grainne was a sexually hot-blooded young woman, and could enjoy Rabelaisian humour, these scenes were of such vileness that they left her feeling disgusted. In other drawers she found more pictures, and books and pamphlets, all pornographic, with detailed descriptions of acts of sadism and perverted lust.

She found herself thinking of Flora Kemp, and wondering if Edwin Herbertson had perpetrated any of these vile perversions upon the girl's body.

'If he ever tries to get hold of me I'll put a knife through him,' she told herself determinedly. 'If this sort of thing is his pleasure then he's nothing more than a wicked filthy monster.'

At suppertime she toyed with the notion of telling Mrs Tomlinson and Sarah Hobdon about what she had found, but decided against it. After all, she admitted, she could be jumping to wrong conclusions. The pictures and books and pamphlets might well have been acquired purely out of curiosity. She also admitted to herself that, despite the repulsion she felt for such things, they did have an unholy fascination for her. She had never before in her life seen anything like those pictures, and had not been able to resist staring at them.

After supper she reported to Mrs Gurnock to ask her what she should now do concerning Edwin Herbertson's return.

'Do you want me to wait up for him, Mrs Gurnock, in case he needs anything?'

The housekeeper's eyes were glazed, and the scent of cloves and gin permeated the air around her.

'No, Shonley, you can go to your bed. I will attend upon Mr

134

Edwin if needful. But I do not expect that he'll return here this night.'

'Very good, ma'm.' Grainne curtseyed, thankfully relieved by this confirmation that she would not have to face a drunken Edwin Herbertson.

During the past hours the weather had changed, bringing wild winds and heavy rain. Woken in the dark early morning by the noise of the storm, Grainne lay in bed in the tiny attic and listened to the winds howling and the rain drumming on the tiles of the roof above her head. Although when she had shared the bed with the other two girls she had often wished that she were alone, now that she was alone she missed the companionable warmth of her friends' close-huddled bodies. She shivered and drew the thin bedclothes tighter around her. The attics were bitterly cold and she thought longingly of the warmth of the kitchen and, realising that she would not now be able to go back to sleep, she rose and quickly dressed herself in her working gown. She took a lucifer match from the box she kept on the stool beside the bed and lit her candle.

She moved down the narrow staircases and through the long corridors to gain access to the lower landings. Although down here the sounds of the storm were muted, eerie noises of creaking and groaning still surrounded her, as though the very fabric of the old house was alive and struggling to give voice. The notion caused her to shiver apprehensively and long-buried superstitions roused themselves within her. Nervously she hurried on through the lower landings, her vivid imagination peopling the surrounding shadows with ghostly images, while the creaks and groans became the cries and moans of tormented souls. Then as she came to the top of the great staircase which led down into the main entrance hall there came from somewhere a terrible long-drawnout wailing scream. Grainne cried out in fright, the candlestick dropped from her suddenly nerveless hand and the wavering candle flame snuffed out, plunging her into darkness.

She crouched low and pressed against the wall, her frightened eyes peering around her into the blackness, and unconsciously she gasped out, 'Dear Christ protect me! It's the banshee!'

Again and again the unearthly wailing screams of a soul in

135

agony sounded and terror threatened to overwhelm Grainne.

'Save me! Sweet Jesus save me!'

The echoes finally died away, and Grainne remained crouched, pressing into the wall. She lost all track of time and although she tried to will herself to move, her body refused to respond to her brain's commands.

After what seemed endless hours, cold, stiff and cramped, she finally managed to force her body from that place and fumbled her way back through the darkness to the attics. In her own room she buried herself under the bedclothes and remained there shivering and afraid, until in the grey light of the dawn the voice of Sarah Hobdon roused her from the stupor she had fallen into.

'Come on now, Grainne, rouse up. If Mrs Gurnock finds out that you've been laying abed until this hour, she'll bloody well skin you.'

Grainne poked her tousled head from under the bedclothes and told the other girl with heartfelt relief, 'Jasus, but I'm glad to see you, Sarah.'

The blonde girl stared with concern at Grainne's shadowed eyes and drawn pale face. 'Whatever's the matter? Are you feeling badly?'

Grainne rose from the bed and reached out to clasp the other girl's hand, finding comfort in the feel of warm living flesh.

'This house is cursed, Sarah. It's haunted!'

'What?' Sarah exclaimed incredulously.

Grainne rapidly told her all that had occurred during the early hours of that morning. As she listened, Sarah Hobdon's features displayed a changing kaleidoscope of emotions: interest, doubt, nervousness.

'Are you sure, Grainne?' she demanded. 'Might you have not dreamed it?'

'You think I'm just a thick-headed Paddy, don't you?' Grainne burst out indignantly. 'Well let me tell you that I know I wasn't dreaming. I know what I heard last night. It sounded like the cry of the banshee, and frightened me half to death.'

'Do you know what hour it was?' Sarah asked.

Grainne shook her head. 'No, I didn't get downstairs where I could have seen a clock.'

The blonde-haired girl's teeth gnawed at her full lower lip as she stood in troubled thought. 'Look,' she said at length, 'we'll go and ask Mrs Tomlinson if she heard anything.'

They went hurrying down to the kitchen to find Mrs Tomlinson seated at the table with a fresh pot of tea before her.

'Mrs Gurnock's bin in here asking wheer you two was,' she greeted the pair, and they exchanged nervous glances.

'Oh my God!' Sarah Hobdon exclaimed in dismay. 'I never thought she'd be up so early.'

'She was up and about before I come down,' the cook told them, and her voice dropped to a hoarse whisper. 'Summat's up, I reckon. Her's been in Mr Edwin's rooms for nigh on an hour.'

'I thought he'd gone to Birmingham, and was staying there for the night,' Sarah queried.

'Well, he's back, that I do know for sure. I'se had to make him a pot o' coffee for Mrs Gurnock to take up to him.' She looked at Grainne. 'If I was you, Grainne, I'd get on up theer right away, and find out what wants doing.'

Grainne returned upstairs and as she came outside Edwin Herbertson's rooms heard the sounds of voices raised in dispute. The thick panelling of the door muffled the words, but she could make out Ruth Gurnock demanding angrily, 'And what will your father do if he finds out? Have you thought about that?'

'He'll do nothing,' Edwin Herbertson retorted scathingly. 'Because he'll not be finding out about the slut, will he? I'll not be telling him anything, and you will keep your mouth shut as you always do, won't you, so that you can continue to feather your own nest.'

The voices dropped low and after a moment or two of fruitless listening, Grainne knocked on the door.

It opened to disclose Ruth Gurnock's pale face. Her dark eyes were troubled, and her expression tense and drawn.

'If you please, ma'm, does Mr Edwin require his bath to be made ready?' Grainne asked.

'No!' The housekeeper snapped shortly, and would have closed the door again, but Grainne pressed, 'How about his clothes, ma'm, and his breakfast?'

The woman frowned angrily. 'I'll attend to Mr Edwin's

137

needs, Shonley. He is indisposed and does not wish to be disturbed today. You can work with Hobdon. Do not enter these rooms at all.'

'Very well, ma'm.' Grainne bobbed a curtsey and turned away from the closed door, then hesitated as she heard Edwin Herbertson's raised voice.

'Where is the slut now?'

'I've had to put her into my own bedroom. She's not able to walk even,' Ruth Gurnock replied, her own voice high with anger. 'Don't worry, I've dosed her with laudanum. She'll be quiet.'

'You damned fool!' Edwin Herbertson cursed furiously. 'You should have sent her packing!'

'And how was I to do that? I've just told you that she's not able to walk. Or should I have got Parkins to take her back to Birmingham in the carriage?' she asked with bitter sarcasm. 'That would be a fine thing, would it not? Letting him see the pitiful state you've reduced her to.'

'Then what do you intend doing with the slut?' Edwin Herbertson muttered sullenly.

'She'll have to stay here until I'm sure it's safe to let her go. That could take time, because I've also got to persuade her to keep her mouth shut. And I'm going to have to make sure that Parkins keeps his mouth shut as well about having brought you both back here. And then there are the rest of the servants. They're bound to suspect something is going on.'

'They'll not dare to open their mouths about anything that goes on in this house. They know that if they do it will be the worse for them,' the young man growled threateningly.

Ruth Gurnock's temper suddenly got the better of her and she berated him angrily. 'You should have learned your lesson by now. I'm becoming sick and tired of shielding you. You could have killed her, serving her the way you've done, and you'd be facing the gallows then.'

'And I am becoming sick and tired of your carping and whining, woman. What in Hell's name does it matter if a filthy little whore gets a taste of wough loving occasionally. That's what they are paid for.' The young man sounded vicious. 'You'd do well to wemember that you are only a servant in this house, and that the old man will not live for ever. Then I shall be the master here, and if you know what is good for you, you'll not allow yourself to forget that fact. Not even for a moment. Now get out and leave me in peace!'

Grainne sped silently away, her thoughts racing.

Chapter Sixteen

Throughout the morning hours Grainne was tormented by the thought of the injured woman locked in Ruth Gurnock's bedroom. She was convinced that it was this woman that she had heard venting the terrible screams of agony. Those anguished shrieks had not been vented by some supernatural being, but by a living woman suffering the torments of an earthly hell. She kept remembering what Sarah had told her about Flora Kemp, and she knew in her heart that there had been a repetition of that assault carried out again by Edwin Herbertson.

She worked mechanically, hardly aware of the tasks she did, torn by inner conflict, as if there were two separate entities within her mind – one of those entities claiming that no matter what had happened to this unknown woman, it was no concern of hers; the other entity disputing this, repeating over and over again, that it was every person's duty to aid and defend any woman who was being savagely brutalised, and that she, Grainne, should do all in her power to help this unknown woman, injured, drugged and imprisoned in this house.

Several times she was on the verge of seeking out Sarah Hobdon or Mrs Tomlinson to tell them what she had heard pass between Edwin Herbertson and Ruth Gurnock, and ask them to help her to take some action, but some instinct prevented her from doing so. Just before midday she laid aside her cleaning implements and sneaked furtively out to the stable yard in search of Parkins. She needed confirmation from him that Edwin Herbertson had brought a woman back to the house with him the previous night, so that her own nagging doubts could be put to rest. Her mind was in such a disturbed quandary that there were moments when she even wondered if she had imagined all that she had heard.

The coachman was whistling happily as he busied himself in the harness loft above the stables, and when he saw Grainne's head appear through the ladder opening in the floor he greeted her cheerily. 'Hello, Paddy. What can I do for you?'

Grainne hesitated a moment, seeking for a way to broach the subject uppermost in her mind.

'I was just wondering what time you came back last night from Birmingham, Mr Parkins?'

He stared at her curiously. 'Now why ever should you want to know that, my wench?'

'Well, I was supposed to stay up and wait for Mr Edwin to come back, but I fell asleep, and I was worried in case he said anything about me not being there to meet him,' she lied.

The man grinned and winked broadly. 'The young master warn't worried who was up to meet him, I shouldn't think, my duck. He brought company back with him.'

'Company?' Grainne affected surprise. 'What sort of company?'

'The female sort, Paddy,' the coachman chuckled lewdly. 'The sort that young gentlemen seeks out when they'm feeling their oats.' He shook his head in grudging admiration. 'He's a real gay spark, Mr Edwin, arn't he just? No sooner is his Dad out o' the way, but he's on the randy. Still, good luck to him, that's what I says. I was a bit of a gay spark meself when I was his age.'

'Did you have to take her back to Birmingham?' Grainne enquired carelessly, but there was a note in her voice which caused the coachman to look closely at her.

'Youm showing a deal of interest in Mr Edwin's affairs, arn't you?' A prurient gleam entered his eyes. 'You arn't took a fancy for him yourself, has you?'

Grainne coloured and shook her head in vigorous denial. 'No, certainly not.'

Parkins' yellow teeth showed and he cackled with laughter. 'You bloody wenches am terrible nosey, arn't you? I'll bet them others has put you up to this, arn't they, old Tomlinson and young Hobdon? It's them who's sent you to pump me,

141

arn't it? They carn't abear not knowing everything that goes on in this house.'

Grainne assumed a rueful smile, and shrugged, allowing him to believe that his surmise was accurate. He became confidential, enjoying his role of raconteur. 'Well, it was my good luck last night that I didn't lose much sleep. That makes a bloody change, I can tell you, when Mr Edwin's out on the randy. Normally we 'udden't have come back here 'til this morning, and I'd have bin standing about in all bloody weathers all through the soddin' night. But last night he picked this young fancy piece up the very fust gin palace he went into. And we was back here afore midnight.'

'What time did she go away then?' Grainne prodded.

Parkins shrugged. 'Buggered if I knows, girl. He's brought trollops back here afore, you know, when his Dad has bin away. Normally he has his bit o' fun with 'um, and then sends 'um packing. They has to make their own arrangements to get back home though. It's shanks's pony back to Brummagem for 'um. I expect this 'un was the same. I know I was up the wooden hills to Bedfordshire just as soon as I got the mare bedded down. So I couldn't tell you what time the wench left here.'

'Isn't Mr Edwin feared that you'll tell his father about what he gets up to?' Grainne enquired.

'God love you, no!' The coachman rebuffed that idea forcefully. 'Mr Edwin looks arter me well, Paddy. Theer's always a sovereign in me pocket on such occasions. And when a gentleman treats me well, why then I'm like the three wise monkeys, I am. I sees no evil, hears no evil, and speaks no evil.'

He lifted his forefinger and wagged it to emphasise his words. 'You mind what I tells you now, my wench. You take a leaf out from my book, and be like the three wise monkeys yourself. It don't pay to talk about what your betters gets up to. You can get into real bad trouble doing such. You just remember what I'm telling you now. Be like them bloody monkeys.'

She forced a smile and assured him, 'Oh I will, Mr Parkins. I surely will.'

Back in the yard her smile died to be replaced by a grimace

142

of angry repulsion. 'Edwin Herbertson is a madman, an evil murderous madman!'

In Grainne's memory she heard again those terrified, agonised screams reverberating through the darkness and a terrible anger flamed through her being.

'He has no right to serve any woman so, no matter what she is forced to do to earn her bread.'

Whore, trollop, slut, dock rat, clap bitch, drag tail, the epithets of contempt and disgust burned in Grainne's brain, and dreadful memories crowded in upon her, swamping her until she was sick and shaken, and pity for the unknown woman locked in Ruth Gurnock's bedroom swelled within her until she felt as though its intolerable pressure might stop her lungs from breathing and her heart from pumping.

'I was also called those foul names. I know what your life is like because I too was once forced into living it,' she told that unknown woman in her mind. 'I know its shame, and its suffering. Believe me I know, and I'll never ever forget what it is like. I can't forget, even though I pray to God to let me. I can't forget.'

The impulsion to go to the injured woman and help her burgeoned overpoweringly. Driven so that she was beyond caution or caring as to what repercussions it might bring down upon her own head Grainne ran back into the house and through the corridors towards Ruth Gurnock's rooms.

The bedroom door was locked, and Grainne stood undecided for a few moments. Then, remembering that the housekeeper's suite of rooms were all interconnecting, she went to try the other doors leading into them. All these were locked also. Grainne returned to the bedroom door and tapped on it, calling softly, 'Can you hear me inside there?'

She put her ear against the wooden panelling and listened hard, then fancying she heard a slight sound as if someone was stirring, she tapped again, harder this time, and called a little more loudly.

'Don't be afraid, I'm a friend. I want to help you.'

'What are you doing there, Shonley?'

Grainne gasped in shock and swung around to see Ruth Gurnock standing at the end of the corridor, staring at her with angry hostility.

'Why are you knocking at my bedroom door?'

The housekeeper came towards Grainne who could not help but feel a tremor of trepidation when she saw the menace in the other woman's features.

'Answer my question, Shonley. What are you doing?'

Grainne's shock at being discovered was rapidly lessening, and her mind began to react. She realised that to openly challenge the housekeeper concerning the unknown woman would be futile.

'If you please, ma'm, I was passing along the corridor to go and fetch some more beeswax and I thought I heard somebody calling out from your bedroom. I was just trying to find out if anybody was in there.'

The merest flicker of anxiety fleeted in Ruth Gurnock's dark eyes, and Grainne felt a thrill of certainty.

'That woman really is inside there,' she told herself.

Ruth Gurnock scowled, and snapped curtly, 'The room is empty, Shonley. Now get on about your work, and do not let me catch you acting like a fool again, or it will go hard with you.'

'Very well, ma'm.' Grainne bobbed a curtsey and obediently moved away.

Ruth Gurnock frowned worriedly as she watched the young woman until she was gone from the corridor. Then the housekeeper selected a key from the huge bunch dangling from her waist and let herself into the bedroom, re-locking the door behind her.

A small female figure, dressed in bedraggled cleap finery, was sprawled on the floor at the side of the bed. Anger flared in Ruth Gurnock as she stared down at the prone figure lying on the carpeting.

'Why in Hell's name did you have to let that bastard madman bring you back here, you bloody stupid whore?'

She gritted the words aloud as she knelt by the side of the unconscious girl, who looked pathetically young, appearing hardly more than twelve years of age.

The girl's mouth was sagging open, and her breathing was ragged and stertorous. For a moment or two Ruth Gurnock stared down at the youthful immature features, noting the fresh bruises and contusions that mottled the heavily rouged skin, greyish and grimed beneath the paint, and the cut and swollen lips crusted with dried blood. She saw the torn bodice and lifted it to disclose budding young breasts which bore the multiple lines of deep indents left by savage bites, those indents still leaking watery blood from their torn blackened depths. Then Ruth Gurnock pulled up the long crinolined skirt and drew in her breath with horror to see the caked blood on the girl's lower belly and slender thighs.

'Dear God!' she told herself fearfully. 'That bloody maniac is getting worse with each one he gets hold of. It's a miracle that this one isn't dead.'

Bitter regret assailed her that she had ever allowed herself to be drawn into shielding Edwin Herbertson, and covering up his criminal assaults on young women. But she knew that now she was too deeply enmeshed in the entrapping web of guilt and lies and subterfuge ever to be able to free herself from its coils. All she could do was to continue to shield her master in order to shield herself.

She exhaled a long ragged sigh and began to carefully examine the motionless girl, counting the pulse which was weak and thready, and feeling the chill clamminess of the bruised and torn flesh. She struck a lucifer match and pushed open the closed eyelids in turn, holding the flame close to the exposed eyeballs and breathing a sigh of heartfelt relief to see the pupils react to the light.

Ruth Gurnock sat back on her heels and considered for a while. Then she left the bedroom to return some minutes later with a jug of water, a roll of linen bandages and a box of ointment. She stripped the clothes from the girl's thin under-nourished body and bathed her ravaged flesh. Then she took the box of ointment from her gown pocket and anointed the weeping wounds and abrasions, and bandaged the worst of the injuries. She redressed the girl in fresh clothing from her own personal wardrobe, thankful that because she herself was so small and slender the gown and shift and petticoats fitted reasonably well. Then, exerting all her strength she lifted the unconscious girl bodily onto the bed and arranged her arms and legs comfortably, before covering her with a blanket. The girl's own torn and bloodied clothing she fashioned into a bundle and pushed beneath the bed.

145

Only when all these tasks were completed did Ruth Gurnock allow herself to think about Grainne Shonley, and those thoughts were savage.

'That bloody Irish bitch! First of all she tries to snare my man, and now she comes poking her nose into my affairs. She suspects something is wrong, I'm sure of it. Perhaps she heard this one squealing last night? She could well have done because the little slut made enough noise to wake the dead, that's for sure.' Fearful dread rose in Ruth Gurnock. 'Shonley could get me jailed, maybe even transported or hung if she does know what's happened here and reports it to the authorities. I'd be classed an accessory, wouldn't I?'

Virulent hatred of Grainne Shonley spasmed through her and for a while the housekeeper allowed herself to be absorbed by its violence.

Then she fought to think calmly and to plan rationally.

'I wanted what happened to this slut to happen to you, Shonley. But I can't afford to risk that now. I'll have to deal with you quickly, and get you out of the way.'

She checked that the girl was still deeply unconscious and, satisfied that she would remain so for some time, went from the bedroom, taking care to ensure that the curtains were drawn and all doors into her rooms were locked. Then she hurried upstairs to talk with Edwin Herbertson.

A short time later Ruth Gurnock came back downstairs and found Parkins in the stables. The man's stolid red face showed his surprise at seeing the fastidious housekeeper stepping daintily between the horse-droppings and urine which bestrewed the cobbles.

'Take care you doon't tread in the muck, Mrs Gurnock,' he cautioned.

She smiled at him bleakly, and holding out her hand chinked the coins she held in her palm underneath his nose.

'There's twenty sovereigns here, Parkins, are you interested in having them for your own?'

His eyes widened, then filled with greed, and he nodded his head.

Chapter Seventeen

The rest of the day passed with an agonising slowness for Grainne as she racked her brains constantly to find some solution to her dilemma. The thought of the unknown woman was a torment to her mind, but try as she might she could think of no way that she could help her. Grainne knew that if she tried to act alone, then Edwin Herbertson and Ruth Gurnock acting in concert would be too strong for her to overcome physically. She toyed with the idea of going to Henley and informing the constable there of her suspicions. But again she was forced to accept that her uncorroborated suspicions would not serve, and that no one in authority would act upon them. A maidservant's word would carry no weight against the word of a gentleman and his much respected housekeeper.

Troubled as she was, Grainne could only pick at her supper of mutton broth, and when Sarah Hobdon and Mrs Tomlinson tried to chat with her, she answered in monosyllables. At last Sarah Hobdon lost patience with Grainne's apparently sullen preoccupation and challenged, 'What's upsetting you? Youm grunting like a pig when we says anything to you.'

Grainne shook her head, and apologised. 'I'm sorry, I'm not wishing to be surly with either of you. But I've got something on my mind which is sorely troubling me.'

'Well, what is it? You can tell us, my duck,' Mrs Tomlinson invited.

Again Grainne shook her head. She wanted to confide in these two women, but was reluctant to involve them in a matter which could conceivably cause them to lose their places here in this household.

Sarah Hobdon studied Grainne for some seconds, and then

stated percipiently. 'It's to do with what happened last night, arn't it, my duck?'

Mrs Tomlinson's interest was immediately roused. 'What was that? What happened last night then?'

'Grainne heard screaming. She thought the place might be haunted,' Sarah informed the cook.

Mrs Tomlinson's dull features became wary.

'I'se never heard anything like that.' When she looked at Grainne there was a guardedness in her eyes. 'Wheer was this screaming coming from, girl? I never heard nothing, and I was laying awake most o' the bloody night because of the soddin' toothache. Are you sure you didn't dream it?'

Grainne looked at the older woman curiously. She sensed a hint of hostility emanating from her, and could not understand why that should be. She shook her head in denial.

'Oh no, Mrs Tomlinson, I wasn't dreaming. I wasn't laying in my bed when I heard it, but was on my way down to the kitchen. So I know that I was wide awake. It was no dream, more's the pity.'

'Has you told Mrs Gurnock about it?' the cook wanted to know.

'No.' Grainne hesitated, then could not keep her anxieties bottled up any longer, and the words broke from her like the waters from a breached dam. 'I haven't told Mrs Gurnock, because she already knows about the screaming. And she knows who was screaming as well, and why they were screaming. I heard her and Mr Edwin talking when I went up to his rooms this morning.' She swung round to Sarah Hobdon. 'You remember what you told me about Flora Kemp and what happened to her, don't you, Sarah? Well, it's happened to some other poor woman now. And she's still here. She's locked up in Mrs Gurnock's bedroom, and for all I know could be dying, or even dead.'

Both women stared at her aghast, eyes wide, mouths agape.

'What are you saying, girl?' Mrs Tomlinson demanded. 'Has you gone mad?'

'No, I've not gone mad!' Grainne denied vehemently. 'What I'm saying is that Mr Edwin brought a young girl home with him last night, and he's misused her, just like Sarah told me that he misused Flora Kemp!'

'You wants to be careful what youm saying, Shonley.' Mrs Tomlinson was staring at Grainne with open hostility. 'You could get yourself into serious trouble, saying such terrible things about your betters. Whatever's got into you, girl, to want to say such things? And who might this Flora Kemp be when she's about? I'se been with the family for three years, and I'se never yet heard word nor tale about her.'

'She was here before you came then.' Grainne answered, and appealed to Sarah Hobdon. 'Tell her, Sarah. Tell her about Flora Kemp and Mr Edwin.'

The other girl was staring angrily at Grainne, bright spots of colour burning in her cheeks. 'You gave me your word, that you 'udden't say anything about what I told you,' she accused hotly. 'Are you just trying to get me into trouble?'

Sudden dismay struck through Grainne as she realised that the situation was going horribly wrong.

'Listen to me, please, both of you.' She was almost pleading with them. 'There's a woman locked up in Ruth Gurnock's bedroom, who's been wickedly misused by Edwin Herbertson. And she could be dying or even dead because of what he's done to her. I need your help, so that I can help her.'

A sudden hope came to her. 'Parkins, he knows that Mr Edwin brought a young girl back with him to the house last night. He told me so this very morning. Let's go and see him, and let him tell you himself.'

The other women looked at each other doubtfully, and Grainne urged forcefully, 'Look, come with me, do. He'll be in his quarters, won't he? Just come and let him tell you the same as he told me, and then you'll know that I'm telling you the truth.'

She stared at Sarah with beseeching eyes. 'Please, Sarah.'

The blonde-haired girl shook her head in refusal, and said sulkily, 'After what you'se just done, breaking your promise and trying to get me into trouble, I 'udden't come anywhere with you, Grainne Shonley.'

The cook's curiosity got the better of her however. 'All right, my wench, I'll come with you.' She took one of the two hanging lanterns from the kitchen to light their way.

Parkins' sleeping quarters were in a small room adjoining the harness loft, and as they crossed the stable yard they saw the dim light of his candle shining through the leaded panes. They threaded their way through the hanging harnesses and horse furniture in the low-ceilinged loft, thick with the smells of leather and liniment, and hammered on the coachman's door.

He was in shirt-sleeves and breeches, a long clay pipe emitting clouds of acrid tobacco smoke in his mouth, and a flagon of beer in his hand.

'Well now, what's this?' he greeted genially, and Grainne asked him eagerly, 'Mr Parkins, will you tell Mrs Tomlinson about the young woman that Mr Edwin brought back with him from Brummagem last night?'

His stolid red face stared at her blankly.

Grainne waited a moment, then urged, 'You remember don't you, Mr Parkins? You told me this morning that Mr Edwin had brought a young woman back here with him last night. Will you tell Mrs Tomlinson now?'

He frowned at her in puzzlement. 'I told you what?'

Again Grainne repeated herself, but now a sense of apprehension was rapidly expanding in her mind. Something had happened, she sensed, which would somehow cause her harm.

This time Parkins reacted with a display of temper. 'Be you making mock o' me, Shonley?' he demanded aggressively. 'Coming here disturbing my bit o' peace with such bloody nonsense. How could I have told you about any young 'ooman coming here, when there warn't one?'

She regarded him with dismay, and protested strongly, 'But you told me that there was a young woman brought back here, Mr Parkins. Why do you deny it now?'

'Deny what?' His voice rose, and then he told her, 'Just get off out on it, 'ull you. And let me have me smoke in peace. I arn't wanting to waste any more time with your daft bloody nonsense.' He slammed the door in the women's faces.

Grainne turned to Mrs Tomlinson, shaking her head in bewilderment. 'I just can't understand why he should behave so. He told me this morning that Mr Edwin brought a young woman back here last night, and now he's denying that he said anything. Why should he do that?'

The cook scowled, and grunted shortly, 'I reckon there's summat wrong in your bloody yed, my wench.' Then she turned away and stamped off through the loft and down the ladderlike steps, leaving Grainne to fumble her own way back through the darkness.

When she reached the kitchen the two women were sitting side by side, their heads close together, and Mrs Tomlinson was talking volubly into Sarah Hobdon's ear. When Grainne would have spoken to them, they ostentatiously turned away from her, refusing even to look at her, and Grainne realised the futility of attempting any further conversation with them. She lit her candle at the range fire and went miserably to the attics.

For some considerable time she remained in her room and her thoughts were as bleak as her surroundings. Again she was beset in her mind as if two separate entities were struggling for mastery there. All her instinct for self-preservation told her that she should forget about the unknown woman and merely get on with her own life. But her stubborn sense of justice could not, and would not, accept this. She had both seen and endured far too much terrible injustice in her own personal life to be able to stand by and watch another human being suffer under injustice without raising her own voice in protest.

'But what can I do?' Anger at her own futility raged within her. 'What can I do? They're all ranged against me in this matter, I am alone here. I've no one who is prepared to stand with me.'

Then the memory of Morgan Hunter came into her mind, and she heard his words once more. 'If you have ever any need for my help, then leave a message for me with Mrs Brummage at the inn in Henley.'

Grainne pondered for a while longer, then came to a decision. 'I'll go and leave a message for him. Perhaps he really will help me.' A sad grimace crossed her features. 'It's all I can do, isn't it? There's no one else who will, that's for sure.'

She knew that she would have to wait until the household had all gone to their beds before she could risk slipping away. There was always the possibility that until the bedtime hour she would be summoned for some task or other. So she settled herself to wait patiently for the hours to pass.

Downstairs in Ruth Gurnock's office Parkins was in conversation with the housekeeper. 'Shonley brought Mrs Tomlinson with her when she come pestering me about Mr Edwin and that young 'ooman, Mrs Gurnock. O' course, I denied having any knowledge of such goings on, just like you told me to.'

Ruth Gurnock's lips pursed and her fine eyes were thoughtful.

'What about Tomlinson, and Hobdon, do they believe what Shonley is saying?'

The coachman seemed uncertain. 'Well, ma'm, it's hard to tell what them two am thinking about it. I'se just bin and had a cup o' tay with 'um, so I could find out what they thought about it. But neither on 'um was eager to talk about it.'

He paused for a moment, then realising the housekeeper's dissatisfaction with this reply, went on hesitantly. ''Tis my opinion, ma'm, that arter seeing how all the others was give their sacks, then them two am sorely feared that they might get their own sacks double quick iffen they was to venture any opinion.'

He felt a distinct sense of relief when he saw that the woman facing him accepted that explanation.

'Very well, Parkins. You have done well to tell me about this. You can rest assured that you'll not be losing your post here now that you've displayed your loyalty to me in this way.' She smiled bleakly. 'And you'll be well rewarded in due course, as you have been already, have you not?'

'Indeed I have, ma'm. And I'm very grateful for all your goodness to me,' he gushed sycophantically.

'You may go,' the woman snapped curtly and, as soon as the coachman had left, went herself up to Edwin Herbertson's rooms.

The young man was half-drunk and surly, and greeted her advent with a curse, but Ruth Gurnock was uncaring and immediately launched herself in verbal counter-attack. 'Just hold your foul tongue and try to act sensible for once, Mr Edwin. You've to listen to me very carefully, or you'll find yourself in serious difficulties. You've got to do exactly what I say.'

Her manner was such that it silenced the young man instantly, and he listened intently as she continued to speak at length.

Chapter Eighteen

The long High Street of Henley in Arden was empty and still in the moonlight as Grainne moved quickly along its length, keeping in the moon-thrown shadows of the walls, her shawl over her head. Only once was the stillness broken when a prowling cat came face to face with the young woman and hissed, arching its back, its eyes glittering with fear, tail lashing from side to side. The small inn was silent, no glint of light showing from between the cracked shutters of its windows.

Grainne hesitated a moment, her eyes scanning the surroundings, then hammered on the low front door. The noise sounded preternaturally loud in the windless night, and Grainne dreaded that the neighbouring houses would be aroused. But no light shone out from their windows, and no voices demanded explanations for the noise.

Again she hammered on the door, and above her head a window casement was flung open and a turbaned head thrust out into the night.

'Who's that down theer?'

Grainne recognised the voice as belonging to the unpleasant buxom woman she now knew as Mrs Brummage.

'I want to speak with Captain Hunter,' she called softly.

'He arn't here,' the woman stated.

Grainne's heart sank, but she remained where she was.

'If he's not here, then can you tell me where I might find him? It's very urgent that I do so.'

'I've no idea wheer he is,' the woman said.

'Then do you know when he might return here?' Grainne asked.

'No. He comes and goes as he pleases.'

A tinge of desperation touched Grainne. 'He told me that a message left here with you would always find him.'

'Did he.' The woman appeared disbelieving.

'Yes, he was most positive as to that.' Grainne was now becoming determined that she would not leave here without achieving her aim. No matter if she was forced to stay beneath this window all night.

To her surprise the woman chuckled throatily, and then told her, 'Goo round to the back door. I'll be down now.'

Grainne obeyed and made her way round to the rear yard. The door creaked open a few inches, and the woman inside whispered through the narrow opening, 'What's the message?'

'Will you tell him that Grainne Shonley needs to see him urgently. I'm up at Millwood Hall. Please tell him that it's very urgent.'

Then she appealed, 'Are you sure that you've no idea when he'll be returning here?'

'That's hard to say. The Captain comes and goes as he pleases.'

'But you will tell him, won't you?' Grainne pleaded, and the disembodied voice assured her, 'Ahr, I'll tell him.'

The door closed, and Grainne was once more alone.

She made her way back along the narrow rutted road towards Millwood Hall, and found herself wondering why an apparently wealthy gentleman such as Captain Morgan Hunter who wore such elegant clothing, and drove such a smart and expensive horse and trap should frequent such a small shabby alehouse, instead of the large and luxurious coaching inn situated further along the High Street that was patronised by the local bloods and minor gentry to which his rank gave him entrée.

'Perhaps he just prefers to lead a quiet life and keep his own company,' she concluded, and mentally shrugged and put the matter from her mind.

Chapter Nineteen

During the following day Grainne was uncomfortably aware of the coldness in her companions' manner towards her. Sarah Hobdon and Mrs Tomlinson pointedly excluded her from their conversations and Parkins ignored her completely. Ruth Gurnock merely instructed her to see to Edwin Herbertson's requirements, and then left her alone.

Edwin Herbertson made no heavy demands on her, however. After he had bathed and breakfasted he called for Parkins to bring the carriage round to the door, and was carried away in the vehicle.

While Grainne cleaned his bedroom and made the bed she found herself imagining what had happened in this room between Edwin Herbertson and the unknown girl, and she could not help but carefully search the bedding and the furnishings for any sign of bloodstains. All appeared fresh and clean, and Grainne grimaced wryly at her own actions.

'Sure now I'm behaving like an idjit. Ruth Gurnock has had all day yesterday to clean the place up.'

Several times during the course of the day Grainne managed to sneak to Ruth Gurnock's suite of rooms and each time tried to gain access, but found again that all the doors were locked. She also tried to attract the attention of the woman that she believed was imprisoned behind those locked doors, but received no answer, and heard nothing to indicate that anyone was inside the rooms.

Evening was approaching when Edwin Herbertson returned to the Hall. Shortly after his return Ruth Gurnock summoned the servants to her office. Edwin Herbertson was in that room with her when the three women and the coachman came there. Grainne could not suppress a tremor of apprehension when she saw her master's glowering expression, and the grim hard-set face of Ruth Gurnock.

'Stand at the door, Parkins,' Ruth Gurnock instructed, then scowled at the three females and gritted out, 'One of you is a thief! Possibly all three of you!'

They stared at her with consternation, and Grainne denied indignantly, 'I'm no thief!'

'Are you not?' Ruth Gurnock riposted acidly. 'We shall very soon discover the truth of that, Shonley.'

Then she asked all three women, 'Which among you have been in Mr Edwin's bedroom this day?'

'I haven't!'

'Nor me neither!'

Sarah and Mrs Tomlinson both shook their heads in denial.

Grainne flushed, mortified with herself for doing so, but answered evenly, 'You know well that I've been in Mr Edwin's rooms, Mrs Gurnock. I've been cleaning them, and making the bed.'

Ruth Gurnock's dark eyes glittered savagely, but her voice was low and controlled as she stated, 'Money and jewellery has gone missing from Mr Edwin's rooms. Against my advice Mr Edwin has very graciously decided to show mercy in this matter. If the thief will now own up and return those articles, then all that will happen is that they will be dismissed from their employment here without character. There will be no charge laid against them.' She scowled fleetingly. 'If no one of you confesses, then the constables will be sent for, and we shall make a search. I need hardly tell you, that if we have to go to such trouble to discover the culprit, then it will go very hard with whoever she might be.'

Grainne's premonition from days before returned and fore-boding flooded through her.

'This is a planned thing!' her inner voice told her with a terrible certainty. 'Ruth Gurnock has planned this!'

'Oh my Lawd!' Mrs Tomlinson's sombre features contorted and she threw her apron up over her head and began to shriek hysterically. 'I've done nothing! As God is me judge, I've ne'er touched anything! I've not stepped foot into Mr Edwin's rooms. Not stepped foot!'

Sarah Hobdon's features were blanched, and her hands trembled as she stretched them out beseechingly towards the housekeeper. 'Mrs Gurnock, please, you'se known me for years. You knows I'm an honest straight girl. Please, Mrs Gurnock, please.'

Grainne was feeling as distraught and dismayed as her two companions, but conscious of her complete innocence of any wrongdoing her fiery spirit rebelled against such accusations, and she retorted heatedly, 'You've no right to accuse any of us of being thieves! The way you're talking, it's as though you've already decided that we're guilty of taking whatever it is from Mr Edwin's rooms. How the hell can you say that we've taken his things? Maybe he's gone and pawned or sold them himself to pay for his women?'

'Hold your tongue, Shonley!' Ruth Gurnock shouted, but Grainne was by now too worked up to accept any such order.

'You accuse us of stealing, but you say nothing about what he has done to that poor girl.' Grainne flung out her arm, pointing at Edwin Herbertson's face.

The young man's complexion darkened, and his small eyes became murderous. Grainne was past fear and she thrust forward to confront him. 'Yes, let's fetch the constables up here. I'd like nothing better,' she declared vehemently. 'And when they've searched our rooms, then they can search her rooms also.' She pointed at Ruth Gurnock's face, chalk-white now as the blood drained from it. 'What will they find there, Mr Edwin?' she challenged, and, when he made no reply, went on, 'I'll tell you what they'll find there, shall I? They'll find the poor girl that you nigh on killed, won't they?'

The young man's features worked with fury, but in his eyes there were flickers of fear. He swung to Ruth Gurnock who was standing speechless and motionless as if the shock of Grainne's attack had paralysed her.

'This slut has gone mad.'

'Oh no, I'm not gone mad!' Grainne shouted angrily. 'It's you that's mad. And dangerous and perverted with it!' She gulped deep breaths into her lungs, her breasts heaving and falling with the stress of her emotion.

'You threatened us with the constables,' she told Ruth
Gurnock. 'Well they're no threat to me, because I've done
nothing wrong. So I'll go myself right now and fetch them up
here, and have this bloody madman put where he belongs.
Behind bars! And you as well, because you're just as wicked as
he is. Because you shield him, don't you? Even knowing what
evil he's done so many times, you still shield him!'

She turned away as if to go through the door, and Ruth
Gurnock started physically and shouted, 'Stop her! Stop the
bitch!'

Standing in the doorway Parkins spread his arms to block
Grainne's way, and she reacted with blind instinct, bringing
up her clogged foot in a savage kick, catching him squarely
between his legs. He vented a strangled cry, and doubled over,
clutching at his crotch.

Grainne thrust with both hands sending him reeling backwards but before she could pass through the door Edwin
Herbertson had reached her, and his fist thudded into the side
of Grainne's head. She crashed against the doorjamb, senses
reeling as his fists battered at her head and body. Ruth
Gurnock, transformed into a screaming harridan, joined in
the assault, thumping on Grainne's shoulders, tearing at the
younger woman's hair.

Grainne tried to fight back, but then Parkins recovered
enough to help her opponents, and between them the trio
managed to drag Grainne through the house and out to the
yards at the rear. They hurled her bodily into an outhouse used
for coal storage, and slammed and bolted the heavy door,
leaving her in darkness, sprawled upon the filthy dusty heap of
coals.

She heaved herself upright and launched herself furiously
against the door, kicking and battering at it, but the thick
wooden panels defied her, and at last sheer exhaustion forced
her to slump down onto the coals and drag gulps of air into her
straining lungs.

In Ruth Gurnock's office Sarah Hobdon and Mrs Tomlinson
stood facing the housekeeper. Edwin Herbertson had gone to
his own rooms, and Parkins had been sent to Henley with the
carriage to bring back the constables.

Ruth Gurnock stared silently at the two women facing her,

158

while they twitched and fiddled nervously with their fingers. At last the housekeeper broke the silence.

'You both witnessed what took place here. You both saw Shonley attempt to escape from this room, and assault Parkins, Mr Edwin and myself when we prevented her escape, did you not? I shall expect you to so testify to the constables. We are going to bring charges of assault against Shonley, as well as thievery. I am confident that she is the one who stole the money and jewellery from Mr Edwin's rooms, and when the search is made we shall then discover those articles in her room. So, you will testify as to her attempted escape and the assaults she made on us.'

The women made no immediate reply, and Ruth Gurnock frowned and pressed, 'I am waiting for you to confirm what I have asked you.' She spoke directly to Sarah Hobdon. 'Hobdon?'

The blonde-haired girl's handsome face was troubled, and she muttered jerkily. 'Well, ma'am, it all happened so quick. All I saw really was the lot of you fighting together.'

Ruth Gurnock scowled at her and turned to the cook. 'Mrs Tomlinson?'

The woman bit her lips, and kept her eyes fixed on the floor, her hands tugging and twisting at the hem of her lifted apron.

'I'm waiting for your reply, Mrs Tomlinson.' The housekeeper was losing patience.

The cook shook her head, and then appeared to summon resolve, and met Ruth Gurnock's eyes. 'If you please, ma'm, I'm not happy about it.'

The housekeeper grimaced impatiently. 'Neither am I, Tomlinson. It is always a sad matter to discover that a fellow servant is both a thief and violent. But we all have a duty to perform by giving evidence against her, so that she can be properly and justly punished for her crimes.'

Still the other woman remained patently uneasy, and a stubbornness came into her dour features.

'I'se always found Grainne Shonley to be an honest wench, ma'am. I admit that I thought she was lying when she started on about a young 'ooman being kept locked up in your rooms, but . . . ' Her voice tailed off uncertainly as her courage began to fail her.

159

Inwardly Ruth Gurnock was raging, but outwardly she remained calm. Her shrewd gaze flicked towards Sarah Hobdon.

'I should have got rid of that cow long ago,' she told herself. 'She knows what happened before when Edwin got carried away with that bloody Flora Kemp.'

Her eyes came back to the cook and she forced a bleak smile. 'I cannot really credit what I am hearing you say, Mrs Tomlinson.'

Once more the other woman was able to rally her courage and she spoke out boldly now.

'Listen, ma'm, I mean no disrespect, but if Grainne Shonley was guilty of thieving, and if she was lying about the young 'ooman, then why was she so willing to goo and fetch the constables up here herself?'

'You're talking foolish, my dear woman.' Ruth Gurnock's attitude was now one of pitying contempt.

'Shonley lied when she said that she was going to fetch the constables. That was just a ruse to get out from the Hall and so to make her escape.'

She paused, and appeared to be giving consideration to something in her mind then, as if making a decision, nodded abruptly.

'Very well, both of you shall now satisfy yourselves.' She slipped the huge bunch of keys from her waistbelt and handed them to Sarah Hobdon. 'Here, girl, take these and go through every room, every outhouse, every nook and cranny of this house, and see if you can find this mysterious young woman who is supposed to be imprisoned here. Begin with my own rooms.'

When they both stood staring at her with surprise, she badgered, 'Do it now, and I shall remain sitting here until you have done so. Go on ! Look sharp about it !'

The two women exchanged wondering looks, and obeyed.

Some considerable time elapsed before the women returned to Mrs Gurnock's office. She took back the keys and asked each of the women in turn, 'Are you satisfied now that Shonley was lying about a young woman being kept here against her will?'

Both nodded glumly.

'And can you now accept that she was merely trying a ruse when she claimed to be going to fetch the constables?'

Again, with some show of reluctance they both nodded.

'Good!' Ruth Gurnock snapped curtly, and then inexorably pressured them, 'So you are now both of you willing to give testimony that she assaulted us when we tried to prevent her escape?'

'We doon't seem to have a lot o' choice about it, does we, ma'm?' Mrs Tomlinson muttered sullenly.

'No, you do not,' the housekeeper told her sharply. 'Not if you wish to remain in service here at the Hall. I am not prepared to employ servants whose loyalty is suspect. So both of you had better make up your minds about where your own loyalties are placed, and decide now.' She paused for a moment or two, then questioned, 'What is it to be then? Are you going to testify against Shonley, or are you not?'

Unhappily both women nodded.

The three of them remained in a strained silence in the office until long after nightfall when the carriage bearing Parkins and the two constables arrived at the Hall. Then in a body they all went up to the attics where the constables began to search Grainne's room, using lighted lanterns.

Wakefield, experienced in such searches, immediately stripped the bedclothes from the straw mattress, and used his clasp knife to slit the threads of the coarse-clothed mattress cover. His big hands burrowed amongst the straw, and then a grin of triumph spread across his broad red features as he pulled out and held aloft a thick gold chain.

Ruth Gurnock looked at it by the light of her lantern, and nodded positively. 'That is Mr Edwin's watch chain. See here, there are his initials engraved upon this clasp.'

Another gold chain, a diamond stickpin, and several golden sovereigns were successively unearthed, and Wakefield told the party, 'Well, I reckon I'se catched me a thief.'

Mrs Tomlinson sighed heavily, and whispered to Sarah Hobdon, 'Poor Grainne. She's bound for Warwick jail all right.'

'She's bound for transportation if I have anything to do with the matter,' Ruth Gurnock declared forcefully, and her dark eyes gleamed with exultant triumph.

In the coalhole Grainne had lost all track of time, and she sat shivering, hands tucked beneath her armpits, her head sunk low on her chest as she tried to come to terms with this sudden dreadful reverse of fortune. Her head ached, and the bruises and abrasions inflicted on her head and body by the fists and boots of her attackers throbbed with jagged pains. She could taste the saltiness of her own blood in her mouth, leaking from a deep cut on her inner lip where Edwin Herbertson's fist had crushed the soft flesh against her sharp teeth. Yet despite all this her spirit remained undaunted and defiant, and she refused to let herself submit to any sense of despair.

'I've been through worse than this and survived it,' she told herself constantly. 'And I'll come through this as well. I'll not let these bastards beat me.'

She heard voices in the yard outside, and then the rattle of the heavy bolts being withdrawn. The door was flung open and the beams of lantern light flashed across her face, causing her to screw up her eyes against their brightness.

'Come on, girl. I'm placing you under arrest,' a man's voice told her gruffly, and Grainne knew that she had heard that same voice before, and remembered where as she rose stiffly to her feet.

William Wakefield regarded the battered, coal-grimed girl and whistled softly through his teeth.

'By the Christ, you looks as if you'se bin in the wars, my wench.'

'She came at us like a raging lunatic. We were forced to be hard with her for our own protection,' Ruth Gurnock's voice snapped defensively from behind the man's bulk.

The constable shrugged. 'It makes no odds to me, Mrs Gurnock. But I arn't so sure what the magistrates 'ull make on it.'

'The magistrates will understand that we were merely doing our duty as good citizens, Mr Wakefield.'

Grainne stumbled out from the coalhole, and drew a long breath of the cold night air. Its chill impact upon her face helped to clear her head, and she demanded angrily, 'Why am I being arrested? I've done nothing wrong. It's these others that you should be arresting.'

'Just you shut your rattle, girl!' the constable ordered

sharply. 'You'll get your chance to say your piece when youm examined by the magistrates.'

'And when will that be?'

'When they sees fit to examine you.'

'You still haven't told me why I'm being arrested,' Grainne argued stubbornly. 'I've a lawful right to be told. And I've also got the lawful right to lay complaints against the people who assaulted me, and prevented me by force from coming to fetch you.'

The constable was not a stupid man, and faint alarm bells sounded in his mind as he stared doubtfully at the defiant young woman. It was fast becoming obvious to him that she was not the normal dull-witted, unlettered domestic servant that he usually had to deal with in situations of this nature.

'Will you take this bitch to the lock-up, Mr Wakefield!' Ruth Gurnock snapped. 'And let us have done with this display of insolence.'

'Don't you becall me!' Grainne hissed at her, and Ruth Gurnock sneered openly.

'I'll becall you all I want, you dirty little thief!'

Grainne's temper snapped and she hurled herself at the other woman. Wakefield moved with surprising speed for a man of his bulk, and grabbed Grainne in a bearhug, lifting her completely off the ground. Grainne struggled to break free of his crushing grip, but his great strength easily prevailed, and he wrestled her to the ground, shouting to his assistant, 'Get them bloody irons on her, Joe!'

The other man rushed in with ankle and wrist fetters, and while Grainne howled and kicked and bit and scratched in mindless fury the two men forced the iron cuffs around her wrists and ankles and locked them shut.

Helplessly fettered, gasping harshly for breath, Grainne lay pinioned beneath the two men and heard Ruth Gurnock shrieking wildly, 'There, what did I tell you about that bitch? She's a madwoman! A raving lunatic! You can see that for yourselves, can't you? She'll do a murder if she can!'

Wakefield looked at the teethmarks Grainne had left on his arm during the fierce struggle to chain her, and scowled ominously at the helpless girl.

'Oh ahr, Mrs Gurnock. I can see what she is now all right. And I knows the very place to put her as well.'

He clambered heavily to his feet and savagely tested the chains that manacled Grainne's wrists and ankles, so that she could only crouch low and walk with foreshortened steps. Then he fastened a heavy broad iron collar around her neck.

'Gerrup, you bloody cow!'

Grabbing the long lead-chain that was bolted to the front of her throat-collar he threaded it through her wrist and ankle chains then hauled Grainne to her feet, and growled into her face, 'I'll tell you what youm being charged with, you bloody lunatic. Youm being charged with thievin', and assaulting your masters, and now with assaulting an officer of the law who was engaged in the pursuit of his duty. Youm in bad trouble, girl. Real bad trouble.'

Her temper still inflamed, Grainne spat defiantly back at him, 'I've not stolen anything, and I've only fought in self defence!'

'We'll let the magistrates decide that,' Wakefield snarled, and tugged viciously on the lead-chain, jerking her head down and forwards. 'Now come on.'

The small party travelled back to Henley in the carriage, the two constables sitting facing each other and Grainne on her knees on the floor between them.

As the carriage lurched and bucked over the rutted roadway her temper cooled, and her heart sank as she began to realise just how serious a predicament she was in. But her fierce pride would not permit her to show anything other than defiance in her face and bearing.

'Wheer am you going to put her, Will?' the assistant constable wanted to know.

'Mr Gibbs's house!' his superior grunted. 'That's the best place for the mad bitch.'

The other man chuckled wryly, and shook his head. 'It's a shame though, arn't it?'

'What is?' Wakefield challenged sourly.

'Why, to see such a pretty young wench as this 'un, locked up wi' a load o' bloody loonies.'

'The way she bit me, it's the rightful place for her to be, my lad,' William Wakefield grunted. 'Once her's in them bloody cellars with the rest on 'um, they'll all be able to chew on each other to their hearts' content.'

Grainne listened with burgeoning horror to the exchange between her captors as she realised, 'They're taking me to a loony-bin. To a madhouse!'

Aloud she protested. 'You haven't got the right to put me into a madhouse. I'll complain to the magistrates about it. It's unlawful to put a sane person in with lunatics.'

Wakefield glared at her, and brandished his clenched fist directly in front of her eyes. 'Does you see this, you cow? If you doon't keep your bloody mouth closed, then I'm going to ram it down your bloody throat.'

'Now just hold on a minute, Will.' His assistant became concerned. 'The wench has got a point, you know. I doon't want to find meself in trouble for overstepping the bounds of me authority.'

The constable snorted irascibly, 'Fuck me, Joe! This bugger is beginning to get to you, arn't her?' Again he snorted, then blustered, 'Well, for your information, I'se got the lawful rights to put her wherever is needful to secure her. She's already demonstrated that she's a violent prisoner, and is likely to do anything to escape, so I can't risk locking her up in my back shed, like I normally does with prisoners. The cellars at Gibbs's house are secure though, arn't they, and when I goes over to see Reverend Dolben tomorrow to get the committal warrant from him, I shall explain exactly why this cow has bin locked up in Gibbs's cellars. That 'ull cover us both, Joe, so you've no need to worry your yed about it. Besides, I'se used them cellars afore for dangerous prisoners, arn't I?'

'Well yes.' Joe was still troubled by doubts. 'But they was men, warn't they? Not a slip of a wench like this 'un here.'

Wakefield pulled back his coat sleeve and brandished his bitten arm beneath his assistant's nose.

'A slip of a wench, is she? Then what's this lot? Her's a bloody ravening wolf, that's what her is. And I arn't going to risk her sinking her bloody fangs into my throat. She's gooing into Gibbs's cellars, and that's that. So just shurrup about it.'

Again he glared down at Grainne. 'And that goes for you as well, you bloody mad bitch!'

The remainder of the journey passed in silence and Grainne was glad that it did so, because by now she was finding it increasingly difficult to keep her courage high, and her vivid imagination was picturing the horrors of the madhouse with rapidly escalating dread.

The carriage lurched to a halt, and Parkins' voice called, 'We're here, Mr Wakefield.'

The constable got out of the vehicle and hauled Grainne after him. Shackled as she was, her body was doubled over and her head pulled painfully down so that her vision was kept low and restricted.

The carriage rumbled away and in the darkness Grainne was led over cobbles and up a short flight of stone steps. Wakefield tugged on the bell-pull and after a short while the door was opened by a large, fat man wearing a long night-shirt, and a tasselled nightcap. He carried a lighted candle which he kept shielded from the fitful breeze with one pudgy hand.

'What's this, Will, waking me at this hour?' The fat man's voice was high-pitched and squeaky.

'Got a bit o' business for you, Mr Gibbs. This young 'ooman needs to be kept secure for a few days until the petty sessions.'

'What's she done?'

'Thievin' and assault.'

'Is she dangerous?'

'Not so long as you keeps well away from her teeth, Mr Gibbs.'

'She'll bloody soon get them knocked out if she tries to use them on me, Mr Wakefield.'

'A fact that's well known, Mr Gibbs. There's many a loony left his ivories laying on your cellar floor, arn't there?' Wakefield chuckled harshly and jerked Grainne's lead-chain.

'Has you heard that, girl? Mind you mark it well. Mr Gibbs here is not a man to be upset by anybody who likes their teeth where they are. Any nonsense from you and you'll soon find that out for youself.'

'Usual terms is it, Mr Wakefield?' the fat man enquired.

'The usual terms, Mr Gibbs,' Wakefield confirmed.

'Hand her here then.' The fat man took Grainne's lead-chain from the constable. 'Goodnight to you, gentlemen,' he said, and dragged Grainne roughly into the house and slammed the door.

The thudding impact resounded along the stone-flagged corridor and was answered by demented cries and wails seeming to come from all directions in the darkness, sending a shudder of horror and fear through Grainne. Gibbs waddled rapidly along the corridor, his candlestick held low to light his steps, and the manacles bit painfully into Grainne's flesh as she struggled to match his pace. He turned to enter a low alcove at the far end of the corridor and Grainne halted, bracing herself against the tug on the lead-chain.

The night-capped head reappeared from the alcove. 'What's the matter, girl?'

'Where are you taking me?' Grainne demanded.

'Just shurrup and come on.' The squeaky voice grated horribly on Grainne's strained nerves, provoking her to dispute.

'I'll not come anywhere, unless I'm told where it is I'm going.'

'You saucy bitch! You'll do as I bid!' the fat man shouted, and suddenly jerked on the lead-chain with all his strength, snatching Grainne's legs from under her and sending her thudding onto her back. The bruising impact knocked the breath from her body, and the fat man hauled her along the stone flags as if he were pulling in a hooked fish.

The alcove led down a steep flight of stone steps and the fat man descended, dragging Grainne feet first behind him. Her head bounced from one step to another, and by the time she reached the bottom of the flight she was half-stunned. It was only the thickness of her coiled hair which saved her skull from serious injury. She was dragged further along, and the stench of urine and faeces mingled with a peculiar acrid animal odour. Demented wailing resonated through the air, and shrieks of maniacal laughter coupled with loud cries and moans filled her hearing.

She felt herself lifted bodily and thrust back and down upon a raised platform. Metal rattled, as her collar chain was padlocked to a wall-ring, then the fat man was gone, and all was darkness.

Grainne's senses were beginning to clear as she recovered

from the pounding she had taken, and she drew back against the wall as her eyes began to distinguish pale shapes moving around her. A human hand suddenly grasped her thigh, and she screamed in terror and smashed it away from her. Loud sobbing came from her other side, and she twisted her head wildly, her eyes straining to pierce the darkness.

'Help me, God. Why don't you help me? Come to me now, and help me!' A man's cracked voice begged from opposite Grainne, and then that same voice bellowed in anger and poured out a stream of filthy invective directed against the God who had not come to aid him.

The sobbing went on and on in piteous lament, and again a hand came seeking Grainne's body. This time Grainne grasped the hand, lifted it to her mouth and bit hard upon the smelly flesh.

A scream of pain echoed and the hand was ripped away, and chains rattled as her assailant tried to escape from Grainne's proximity.

Grainne's own mind was reeling, and she fought to keep control of the terror that was threatening to overwhelm her.

'They're only people; poor sick people,' she reiterated over and over again. 'They cannot harm you if you keep in control of yourself!'

The peculiar acrid animal odour was thick around her, overlaying even the stenches of urine and excreta, and with a shudder of revulsion Grainne realised, 'It's the smell of madness!'

The noise was now lessening as the inmates began to settle down once more, and slowly the moans and cries metamorphosed into grunts and snores and snatches of gibberish sleep talk.

Grainne tried to settle herself more comfortably on the cold, wet stone platform, and although remaining tensed and nervous, gradually became calm enough to begin to think rationally.

'I can stand it,' she told herself. 'They can only keep me here for a short time, and there's no real harm can come to me, is there? After all, all those in here with me are chained as I am. They cannot reach me.'

The hand sought her again, and she vented a faint scream of

shocked fright. But now some atavistic instinct rising from the very depths of her consciousness prevented her from savaging that seeking hand. Instead she laid her own hand upon it, and gently stroked the roughened skin beneath her fingers. The hand curled and its fingers mingled with her own and then clasped them. From the darkness came a breathy exhalation of pleasure, and the hand moved slowly up and down, shaking Grainne's hand as if in friendly greeting.

'Yes, I'm a friend,' Grainne murmured, and strangely comforted and relaxed by this human contact, she remained motionless, fingers entwined, until sheer exhaustion brought her to uneasy sleep.

Chapter Twenty

'Come on my beauties, rise and shine! Rise and shine!'
    The hoarse shouts brought Grainne to bleary wakefulness, and she opened her eyes, wincing at the pain in her stiff cold limbs.

'Come on, come on, rise and shine, rise and shine!'

The owner of the loud hoarse voice was standing in the passage that the chamber opened off from. He was a diminutive middle-aged man with a dirty, pock-marked, thickly pustuled face. He wore a grimy grey smock-frock which reached to his gaitered ankles, and a battered crumpled top hat pulled down low on his head. His greasy grey hair hung down to his shoulders, and his teeth were long and gnarled, greenish-black with decay.

Grainne stared avidly about her. The chamber she was in was some fifteen feet long and six feet wide, with a low barrelled roof. At the far end an unglazed window frame barred with an iron grille, and measuring less than two feet squared, opened onto the outside world which from what Grainne could see consisted of a blank brick wall topped by a grey sky. She was seated on a stone platform, two feet high and eighteen inches wide which ran the length of the chamber and was faced with a similar platform along the opposite wall. She gazed with horrified eyes at her fellow inmates.

There were eight of them, male and female, all clad alike in long one-piece, short-sleeved, grey canvas gowns. Their wrists and ankles were fettered, and each wore a broad iron neck-collar which was chained to a thick wall ring. They were uniform in their filthy unwashed flesh, tangled shaggy hair and bare feet. At first glance they all appeared to be of a similar age, but then Grainne saw that their ages varied from early teens to advanced dotage.

'You filthy bastards!' the diminutive man bawled angrily. 'You'se bin shitting and pissing on the bleedin' floor agen, arter I warned you not to.'

His words brought Grainne to fresh awareness of the urine and faeces on the floor of the chamber and with disgust she realised that the platform she sat on was soiled likewise.

The inmates screamed and cowered, desperately trying to shield their heads and faces as the tiny man came along the length of the chamber, raining blows at them with a short length of thick rattan cane.

'Bastards! Filthy loony bastards!' He was screaming as wildly as the inmates, and Grainne thought him to be just as insane as any of his chained victims.

'Stop that!' she shouted furiously, and he appeared to notice her for the first time. His jaw dropped in shock, and he let his raised arm fall without striking the threatened blow at the woman cowering in terror at Grainne's side.

'Leave them alone.' Grainne faced him without fear, her anger at his brutality overlaying any other emotion.

'Who be you?' His red-rimmed eyes examined her wonderingly. 'When did you come in?'

'Last night. And if you raise your hand to these poor creatures once more, I'll be reporting you to your master.'

His shock at seeing her was fast wearing off, and now his pustuled features darkened with resentment at her intervention.

'Report me, 'ull you?' he challenged aggressively. 'Well then, I'll gi' you summat to report me for, you loony bastard!'

He lifted the rattan cane and brought it slashing down at Grainne's face. She raised her hands, catching the cane on her wrist fetters, and simultaneously bringing up her feet and pistoning them at his unguarded stomach.

The breath exploded from his mouth as the force of the kick sent him hurtling backwards and he cannoned against a massive-bodied inmate who roared insanely and with a single sweep of mighty arms sent him sprawling into the puddled urine and excreta on the floor. Choking and gasping, the tiny

171

man scrabbled back into the passage on his hands and knees and disappeared up the flight of stone steps.

Grainne realised that the cowering woman on her left had been the one whose hand she had held during the night, and now she examined her curiously. She saw a thin haggard young face, and a pair of timid blue eyes that expressed in quick, erratic succession fear, blankness, puzzlement, and flashes of awareness.

Grainne smiled and gently patted the young woman's cheek and, after a few moments of nervous puzzlement, the blue eyes suddenly lightened and a hesitant smile curved the cracked, bitten lips. The young woman's hands sought Grainne's, and Grainne nodded and took them in her own, and held them cradled in her lap.

Some hours passed, but Grainne was unaware of the passage of time as this strange new sub-world she inhabited enfolded and engrossed her. She found that the coming of daylight had cast out the devils that the night had been populated with. All fear of her fellow prisoners left her as she watched and listened, and made for brief instants some human contact with one or another of the people surrounding her.

She found herself moved both to tears and to laughter, and although she chided herself for what might seem the cruelty of enjoying the antics and ridiculous words and delusions of some of the inmates, yet at the same time she realised that laughter was a necessity in this grim place, otherwise its bizarre, claustrophobic confines might well drive her also across the nebulous boundaries of sanity.

Eventually an elderly hag of a woman in a ragged gown and tattered shawl, her stringy hair hanging loose and uncovered about her scrawny shoulders, came down the steps carrying a bucket, shovel and besom broom. She scraped the excreta from the stone floor and deposited it into the bucket, then swept the puddles of noisome liquids out into the passage, where there was a drain. She fetched a bucket of water down into the cellar and threw it across the floor, then swept this in turn into the drain. Grainne could hear voices and noise coming from other parts of the cellar and she asked the old hag, 'Are there more cells down there?'

The woman nodded. 'Ahr, theer's two more like this 'un

along this passage.' She studied Grainne curiously. 'Be you the one who kicked Billy Blair?'

'Is that the little man with the ugly face?' Grainne queried, and the woman's toothless gums bared in a grin.

'That's him all right, missus. But you arn't a loony, am you?'

Grainne shook her head. 'No, I'm not. The constables brought me here last night.'

'Ohh ahrr,' the hag bobbed her head. 'Youm the villain that stoled up at the Hall.'

Grainne did not bother to dispute the statement.

'Am you hungry?' the hag enquired, and to her surprise Grainne realised that in spite of the fetid atmosphere she was indeed ravenously hungry.

'I'll be bringing the skilly down shortly. It arn't very thick, and theer arn't much on it, because Gibbs likes to keep the loonies on a low diet, but I'll see if I can find a bit o' bread for you to ate with it.'

'Thank you very much.' Grainne was touched by this unasked for kindness.

The toothless mouth beamed at her. 'Youm welcome, my duck. I'm real pleased that that little bastard got his balls kicked by you. He serves me something cruel so he does.'

'Why don't you report him to Mr Gibbs for doing so?' Grainne questioned, and the old hag cackled with laughter.

'He carn't interfere between man and wife, can he, my duck? Me and Blair am wedded.'

The gruel was watery, and sour-tasting, and the piece of bread was stale and hard, but Grainne's hunger was such that she ate with eager haste, using the bread to mop up the last remnants of gruel from the tin bowl it was served in.

There were no utensils given out, except the small round bowls, and after the inmates had eaten the old hag brought round a bucket of water and served out a ladleful to each inmate to drink from.

Grainne felt the need to relieve herself and asked the old hag, 'Can I go to the privy?'

'You'll have to ask Blair to take you, my duck. I arn't got a key to unlock you. Mind you, the fright you'se give him, I doubt that the bastard 'ull come nigh you agen.'

173

'So what do I do if he doesn't come near me?' Grainne questioned, and the old hag cackled with laughter.

'You must do like the rest on 'um, my duck, and shit and piss wheer you sits.'

The idea of relieving herself on the floor in view of men and women filled Grainne with repulsion.

'I couldn't do that,' she stated vehemently. 'I'd feel like an animal.'

The hag shrugged. 'Well, my duck, that's all these pitiful creatures am by now. Bloody animals. They'll pay you no mind, no matter what you does.'

An acute despair suddenly struck through Grainne as she heard these words, and for the first time since she had woken that morning, all her courage failed her and she felt very near to tears.

Chapter Twenty-one

It was nearing two o'clock on Wednesday morning when Morgan Hunter reined in his horse at the rear of the inn.

A stubby-bodied, aproned man appeared in the doorway carrying a lighted lantern and called softly.

'Is that you, Captin?'

'Who else would it be, you bloody mawkin? Now shift your bones and see to my horse,' Morgan Hunter growled, his accent rougher than the cultured tone he used in other company.

The man, who was Alfred Brummage, husband of the inn's formidable landlady, hurried to take the horse's head.

'Make sure you rub her down well, and give her fresh oats and clean water. None of that muck you give your own poor beasts,' Morgan Hunter instructed as he dismounted from the trap, and lifted out from its well a large cloth-wrapped bundle.

'I will, Captin.' Brummage bobbed his head eagerly. 'Did you have a good trip, Captin?'

Hunter grinned and tossed a coin, which the other man caught dexterously.

'Many thanks, Captin. Many thanks.'

Hunter entered the inn and found the buxom Mrs Martha Brummage seated at the table in her kitchen with a bottle of gin and two glasses set out before her.

'I'll bet you can do with a drop o' good, carn't you Captain?' She grinned at him, disclosing her decayed, broken teeth.

He nodded, and slumped gratefully down on a wooden armchair in front of the fire of the cooking range.

The woman brought him a glass filled with gin, and he tossed it down, then expelled his breath in a noisy gasp and held the glass out so that she could refill it. He took a sip from the second drink, then placed the glass on the table, and rummaged in the pocket of his greatcoat to extract a silver cigar case.

'Do you want one, Martha?' he questioned, and she nodded eagerly.

He drew two long cheroots from the case and handed one of them to the woman, then took a taper from the holder on the table and used it to take a light from the fire.

When both of them had taken long pulls on their cheroots, and the air was wreathed with strong smelling, fragrant tobacco smoke, Hunter removed his top hat and laid it on the table. In the lamplight his hard features appeared lined and drawn, and there were purple shadows of fatigue pouched beneath his eyes.

'Anything happened while I've been away?' he asked casually.

The woman shook her mob-capped head. 'Naught that we needs worry about. But you had a visitor a couple o' nights back.'

He seemed uninterested. 'Anybody you knew?'

'It was that young wench that give me a bit o' sauce a few weeks since. The Irisher. The good-looking 'un that you took to Brummagem.'

'Oh yes,' he nodded, apparently unconcerned, but in his eyes there was instant interest.

'She asked me wheer you was, and when you'd be back, but I told her the usual. Then she said 'ud I tell you that she needed to see you urgent.'

He yawned, stretching his arms wide, before offering off-handedly. 'Still up at Millwood Hall, is she?'

'No, not her. Theer's bin bloody ructions up theer, from what Will Wakefield told me. He was in here drinking the day afore yesterday, and he give me the tale then.'

She went on to relate what the constable had told her concerning the events at Millwood Hall.

' . . . so in the death he fetched the Irish girl back here, and he's had to put her in the Stone House until he can take her up in front of the beaks. That'll be on Friday I should think. Will reckons she's sure to be committed for sessions, so the poor cow is looking at seven years transport, I reckon.'

Morgan Hunter's outward demeanour showed nothing of the turmoil of his thoughts. He drained his glass and indicated to the woman that she should again refill it.

'In the Stone House, is she?' he remarked casually. 'All among the bloody loonies.'

'Too right her is.' The buxom woman grinned cruelly. 'He's got her chained down in the bloody cellars with 'um. My old man has bin across theer a couple o' times to have a peep through the grating at her. He says she's looking very sorry for herself.'

Morgan Hunter chuckled lazily. 'I reckon any of us 'ud be feeling the same chained down there with that bloody lot, Martha.'

'Oh I dunno about that, Captain.' The buxom woman ogled him suggestively. 'I reckon if I was chained up next to you, then I'd like it well enough.' A frown of annoyance flashed briefly across her face. 'At least then I'd get to see summat of you, 'udden't I?'

'Now Martha,' he chided her jocularly. 'You know that I like to be careful about us, don't you? After all I wouldn't want Alfred to find out that you and me are so friendly. He might kick up a fuss if he did find out, and attract attention to me. And I can't be doing with that, can I?' As he spoke the last words his voice hardened perceptibly, and his eyes grew cold and threatening.

She was quick to placate him. 'No, no, Captain, I knows that. Only you know how much I cares for you.'

His jocularity instantly returned and his voice became warm and confidential as he whispered, 'I know, Martha. And someday you and me will be leaving here. Just the two of us.'

'When?' she pressed him eagerly, but all he did was to shake his head and tell her, 'Soon, Martha. Soon.'

He rose to his feet, yawning and stretching and told her, 'I'm away to me bed. I'm shagged out.'

She stared at him beseechingly. 'Shall I come to you, Captain?'

With a show of regret he shook his head. 'Not tonight,

Martha. I needs to sleep.' Then seeing her look of petulant disappointment, he winked. 'But I won't be needing to sleep tomorrow night, and I've got a delivery that I wants Alfred to make for me.' He grinned broadly. 'A delivery to Stratford. He'll have to wait there to collect something for me as well. He might be there for the rest of the week.'

She grinned delightedly, and jumping to her feet hungrily clamped her mouth to his. After a moment he pushed her gently away and whispered, 'Save that until tomorrow night, sweetheart. We'll have all the time in the world to enjoy it then, won't we?'

Upstairs in his bedroom he moved quickly to the window overlooking the main street and stared out into the darkness. The night skies were studded with fast moving banks of clouds which periodically veiled the moon, creating erratic patterns of light and dark shadowings across the old houses lining the street. At the extreme edge of his limited field of vision he could see the Stone House, an old greystone three-storeyed building standing some yards back from the road, with the remains of an ancient stone cross set before it. Morgan Hunter stood for some time, watching the play of light and shadow across its grim façade.

'Well now, Grainne Shonley,' he murmured to himself. 'Who'd have thought that you would turn out to be a flash girl. There was me thinking that butter wouldn't melt in your mouth, and here's you robbing and battering folks like a real jolly family nemmo.'

He chuckled grimly. 'I'll have to see what I can do to help you out, my honey. You're too sweet an armful to be left to get the boat. Better you should be helping me, than doing a seven out in bloody Van Diemens Land.'

He remembered not only Grainne's good looks, but also her quiet ladlylike manner, and her pleasant speaking voice.

'With the right clothes, and a bit of training you'll make an ideal canary for me, my sweet girl.'

The sounds of footsteps clumping up the stairs, and voices raised in drunken argument told him that the Brummages were retiring to their beds, and he waited to give them time to settle and fall asleep before he lifted his cloth-wrapped bundle onto the bed and undid its rope strappings. He pulled the cloth aside to disclose a medium sized rectangular leather holdall with carrying handles.

The bag contained more rag-wrapped bundles, and one by one Morgan Hunter unwound the rags and laid their contents in neat rows. His eyes studied them briefly. A brace and bit with a variety of drills and blades. A rack and pinion jack. Strong steel chisels of different lengths and thicknesses. Sets of fine-fashioned pick-locks known as Bettys. A length of rope. A small lantern designed to throw spot beams of light from its tiny aperture. 'Outsiders'; pliers with long slender jaws designed to grasp the butt end of a key in a lock. Several jemmys and hooked lengths of steel, and files, and lastly a 'petter-cutter' – a drill of the hardest steel manufactured, which could be clamped to the keyhole of a safe allowing tremendous leverage to be applied to the cutter which could bite a small opening above a safe lock through which the lock wards could then be manipulated.

Morgan Hunter's hands moved among these tools and implements, touching and caressing their cold oily lengths with the soft tenderness of a lover. His eyes gleamed with an almost sexual pleasure as he took up the petter-cutter and held it to the light of his candle.

'You little beauty,' he breathed as he fondled it. 'But I shan't need you this time. You can enjoy a well-earned rest.'

From the bag he took a small bottle of oil and soft rags, then he carefully stripped the petter-cutter into its component parts and began to clean and oil them with a loving care.

Chapter Twenty-two

The court of Petty Sessions for Henley in Arden was held in the largest ground-floor parlour of the Golden Cross inn standing at the Stratford end of the High Street, and today, Friday, had seen the usual procession of vagrants, debtors, petty thieves and non-payers of the poor rate pass before the magistrates. Now the hour was growing late and lamps had been produced to illuminate the proceedings. Only a couple of spectators remained in the makeshift courtroom when the last case was brought before the court.

The Reverend Harold Sykes sat with closed eyes as if in reverie. He had lunched well that day, and had been rendered sleepy by over-indulgence in vintage claret and roast beef. His fellow magistrate, the Reverend Charles Dolben, stared over the rims of his half-moon spectacles at the young woman standing before him, flanked by the assistant constable, her wrists and ankles fettered.

The Reverend Dolben's weather-beaten features and stocky body coupled with his unclerical broad-skirted riding jacket, leather breeches and high boots denoted a huntsman rather than a bookworm, and he was in fact a 'hunting parson', who spent his days in chasing and killing assorted animals and birds. His magisterial duties were irksome to him, taking him away from his beloved fields and coverts, and consequently he was notorious for the speed with which he adjudicated upon the cases brought before him. Apart from a fringe of white hair his head was bald and exceptionally pink and shiny, and Grainne found her eyes irresistibly drawn to the shimmering brightness of his dome-like pate beneath the overhanging lamp above the table he used as a desk.

The cleric regarded her sternly. She was dirty-faced and tousle-haired, and her dress was badly soiled and creased. Even at a distance of yards from her he could smell the stench that emanated from her body.

'What is this woman charged with?' he demanded, impatient to be gone from this stuffy room. 'Come on man, quickly, I've no time to waste.'

His clerk sitting to one side of the desk shuffled through some papers and then leaned across to whisper, 'This is the case that Mr Edwin Herbertson of Millwood Hall spoke to you about, sir. Charged with larceny from her employer, five charges of assault, one charge of resisting arrest.'

'How many witnesses?' the reverend frowned.

'Mr Herbertson himself, sir, the gentleman's housekeeper and three of his servants, and the two constables.'

'It grows very late, Mr Fardel,' Dolben grumbled soto voce. 'Do we need to listen to all those testimonies? I have an appointment to dine.'

'No, sir. I think we can cut this short.' The clerk winked slyly. 'The girl's guilt is plain enough. I shall read the charges, and take her pleas. Then you may commit her to the Warwick Sessions for trial.'

The cleric frowned doubtfully. 'Is this procedure strictly regular, Mr Fardel?'

'Oh yes, sir. Regular enough,' the clerk assured solemnly.

Reverend Sykes suddenly stirred and opened his eyes. He blinked blearily around him, and enquired loudly, 'What o'clock is it?'

'It wants a quarter to eight.' His fellow magistrate scowled, and whispered hoarsely, 'Shush now, there's a good fellow, or we'll be here all night.'

Reverend Sykes nodded owlishly, and closed his eyes once more.

'State your name to the court, young woman,' the clerk directed Grainne.

'My name is Grainne Shonley.'

'Lately employed in the service of Charles Herbertson Esquire of Millwood Hall in this parish and county?' the clerk sought confirmation.

'Yes, sir,' Grainne supplied. She was feeling sick and giddy in the fuggy, over-heated atmosphere of the room, and her tight manacles had rubbed the skin from her ankles and wrists leaving raw weeping patches which pained acidly.

'Grainne Shonley, you are charged with the following offences against the peace of Our Sovereign Lady, the Queen, in that you on or about the twelfth day of April, eighteen hundred and forty-nine, did in the parish of . . . ' The clerk gabbled on, the words tumbling from his lips so rapidly that Grainne could barely comprehend the gist of them. Periodically he would pause, and bark at her, 'How plead you?'

Each time she answered as firmly as she was able. 'Not guilty, sir.'

When the clerk had completed the long rigmarole the Reverend Dolben glanced at his fellow magistrate, who was slumped with eyes closed, breath snoring from his open mouth, and grimaced in disgust. Then he frowned at Grainne.

'Grainne Shonley, these are very serious charges and I am necessitated to deliver you before a higher court for them to be tried. Therefore I commit you to trial at the quarter sessions at Warwick County Court. You will be kept in custody at the house of correction in Warwick Town until the date of such trial. Remove the prisoner, constable.'

Will Wakefield had been standing at the rear of the room and now he moved to Grainne's other side. She shook her head, trying to clear her jumbled thoughts. Her sense of physical nausea almost overpowered her.

'Am I not to be heard?' she demanded.

The Reverend Dolben hesitated, then caught the eye of the clerk, who signalled negation with a quick shake of his head.

'I have the right to be heard,' Grainne shouted angrily, and Will Wakefield jerked his head at his assistant, and snapped curtly at the distressed and angry young woman, 'Just hold your rattle, and come out quiet!'

For a brief instant the urge to fight back surged through Grainne, but then she recognised the futility of such an action and, shoulders slumped in defeat, she allowed herself to be led out of the room by the assistant constable.

Will Wakefield went to the clerk. 'When can you let me have the warrant of committal to the house of correction, Mr Fardel?'

The clerk yawned and stretched and thought longingly of the lamb chops and port wine awaiting him at his home.

'Monday morning will be soon enough for that, Mr Wakefield. I'm sure you're not wishing to journey to Warwick before then, are you?'

'No, Mr Fardel, Saturday's a busy day for me, and I'd prefer not to make any journey on the Sabbath.'

'Just so, Mr Wakefield. She can remain in Mr Gibbs's establishment until that day.'

The two spectators who had remained sitting quietly in the shadows at the rear of the room now rose and made their way out into the street. They were a respectable looking middle aged couple clad in full mourning, the woman wearing a thick black veil which hid her features. In the dusk they made their sedate way along the unlighted street to the alehouse where Morgan Hunter lodged, and entered its low-lintelled doorway.

Morgan Hunter was sitting in the snug parlour in the front of the house with a flask of brandy on the table before him, nursing a glass of that spirit in his hand as he stared out through the leaded windowpanes that overlooked the street. The newcomers joined him at his table and he poured them both generous measures of brandy which they downed with gusto. With her veil lifted the woman displayed a handsome, olive-skinned face and bright dark eyes. Her companion was thin-featured and clean-shaven.

When the man would have spoken Morgan Hunter lifted his finger to his lips in warning and, rising, went to the parlour door. He listened for a couple of moments then snatched the door open. The passage was empty and, satisfied, he returned to his seat.

'I don't want the mot who keeps this place to hear more than what's needful for my dealings with her,' he told his companions, who nodded understanding.

'Now then, what do you think?' Hunter asked them both.

The thin-featured man shook his head dismissively. 'That Irish judy is going to get the boat. No doubt on it.'

'George is spaking the truth there, Captain,' the woman supported her man, her soft voice with its lilting Irish accent pleasing to listen to. 'Sure they wouldn't even let the poor cratur spake a word. 'Tis one o' them put-up jobs, right enough. The beak committed her to sessions without even calling a single witness.'

Hunter nodded, and sat for a few minutes in silence, his expression speculative. Then, as if reaching a decision, he told them, 'Right, now I want you to do a little job for me, and as soon as it's done, you can get on back to Brummagem.'

The woman rubbed her finger and thumb together meaningfully, and Hunter's scarred face grinned.

'Don't worry, you'll get well paid for it. Arn't I always fair to you?'

'To be sure you are.' The Irishwoman smiled and nodded assent. 'Just tell us what it is you want doing, Captain dear?'

James Gibbs was not happy to be summoned from his supper by the jangling of his front door bell. His own meanness precluded him from employing live-in servants, and his only helpers were the Blairs, who both slept in a hovel further along the village street.

'Yes, what is it you want?' he asked sourly, his fat-pouched eyes examining the sombrely dressed couple on his front doorstep.

'My name is Fleming, sir. Pastor Steven Fleming of the Methodist Central Circuit, and this lady is my wife.'

Gibbs's shrewd eyes briefly moved across the downcast, heavily veiled features, and he noted the woman's gloved hands, the fingers entwined and shaking visibly.

The thin-featured man coughed hesitantly and said, 'I would prefer that we speak with you in privacy, Mr Gibbs. I have a matter of some considerable delicacy to discuss with you.' Again he coughed, then added, 'I am most reluctant for people to see me here, and I do assure you that your co-operation will be handsomely rewarded.'

The prospect of gain caused Gibbs's eyes to glisten, but he was by nature a cautious man, and now he only invited them with a surly reluctance, 'You'd best step inside the door then.'

Once inside Steven Fleming wasted no time. 'I believe, sir, that you have a young woman here, by name of Shonley?'

Gibbs nodded. 'I do. Put in my custody by the constable. But she'll not be here after Monday. She's been committed to the house o' correction in Warwick to await trial.'

A wail of grief sounded from the veiled woman, and she burst into bitter sobbing. With obvious embarrassment Steven Fleming ordered sharply, 'Do try and control yourself, madam!' And with a helpless shrug, he informed Gibbs, 'Alas, sir, the unfortunate wretch is blood-kin to my wife.'

The madhouse keeper stared suspiciously at the other man, who grimaced apologetically and spread out his black-gloved hands in mute appeal.

'For myself I am uncaring as to what may become of the wretched girl. My ministry is not for those who are of the Romish persuasion. But my wife is possessed of a gentle heart, and she wishes to have a brief private conversation with Shonley and perhaps bring her to realise in what danger she has placed her immortal soul by her desperate crimes.'

The fat man shook his head doubtfully. 'Well, I dunno as how I can allow that. The Shonley woman is a committed prisoner.'

Steven Fleming smiled unctuously. 'I commend your sense of duty, Mr Gibbs.' To his weeping wife he said sharply, 'There now, madam, what did I tell you? We have had a wasted journey. Come now.'

He turned as if to leave, murmuring, 'I do apologise most humbly for having disturbed you, Mr Gibbs.'

The fat man glimpsed the black-gloved hand transferring what looked to be a well-filled purse from his tailcoat pocket to an inner pocket, and the fear that he might have missed the chance of making money impelled him to cast his caution aside.

'Oh now hold fast a moment, Pastor.' He smiled sympathetically at the weeping woman. 'It's not that I myself am unwilling to allow your lady wife access to the prisoner, but I'm feared of discovery. You see she is chained up in the same chamber as certain others, who are not so mad as they are cunning. And rogues they truly are. I'd have to bribe them to keep silent.'

For the first time the weeping woman spoke. 'Please, husband, give this gentleman the money to do that. Please let me speak with my unhappy kinswoman. Just a few brief words is all I ask. Just a few brief and hurried words.'

The purse was brought into view, and several gold coins were slipped into Gibbs's fat hand.

185

'Come then, Mrs Fleming, I'll take you down to your kins-woman.'

'I would prefer to remain here,' Steven Fleming said. 'I've no wish to go near the creature.'

'As you please, sir,' Gibbs agreed, and led the veiled woman down into the cellars.

'Shonley, you've got a visitor!' he announced loudly, and the veiled woman whispered to him, 'I'll speak privately with her, if you please, Mr Gibbs.'

'Very well, ma'am.' He handed her the lantern. 'Now tread careful because some of these unfortunate craturs makes the floor messy. But don't you take any alarm at their antics, because they'll none of them do you any harm. I'll wait upstairs for you.'

As soon as he had reached the top of the stone steps the veiled woman slipped to face Grainne, and hissed urgently, 'A man who is a good friend to you has sent me to help you. Say nothing, and ask nothing yet, only hear what I have to tell you.'

Grainne's wan, dirty face showed wary puzzlement in the lamplight, but she nodded in silent assent.

In the upstairs passage Steven Fleming asked Gibbs, 'Might I use your privy, sir?'

'Certainly you may. It's at the end of the kitchen scullery.'

There was a note of pride in James Gibbs's voice as he added, 'Brand new construction, Mr Fleming. Saves me going out across the yard in bad weather. Of course, it's only for my own use, and that of favoured visitors. I don't allow any of my staff or others to use it.'

After a further short space of time the veiled woman came back up from the cellars, and thanking James Gibbs profusely the couple made their goodbyes. They hurried back to the Brummage's alehouse and the woman told Morgan Hunter, 'She's agreed.'

He nodded in satisfaction, then asked a series of rapid questions, and listened very carefully to the answers the couple gave him.

'Right then, that'll do, I think,' he said eventually. 'You know where you have to be waiting on Sunday night?'

'We do,' they assured him, and then were gone back into the night.

186

In the Stone House cellar James Gibbs lifted the lantern high to cast its beams over Grainne's bowed form.

'Well now, it just goes to show doon't it, that bad apples can come from good trees!' he hectored her. 'That brother-in-law of yourn is a proper gentleman and his wife a real lady. You ought to feel shame that you'se brought such disgrace onto them by being such a wicked bad lot as you am.'

Her hands came up to cover her face and she turned away from him, and he grinned in satisfaction, then taunted her, 'It's a bit too late for tears now, my wench. You should have thought what might happen afore you started thievin' and kicking up ructions. It's your own bloody fault that youm in this pickle now, and nobody else's.'

Grainne could hear him but she felt no desire to answer back. The tears she shed now had been evoked because of kindness. Kindness shown to her by strangers when she had been buried in deepest despair. As the tears eased and she grew slowly calmer, she began to think how ironic it was that while injustice and brutality had failed to make her weep, this single act of kindness had brought the tears flowing. Now, in the chill, fetid darkness, surrounded by the grunts and snuffles of her companions, Grainne experienced a fierce gratitude towards Morgan Hunter, who had sent the woman to her with a message of hope, and promise of aid.

'It's not all up with me yet,' she whispered aloud. 'I'm not beaten yet, thanks to you, Morgan Hunter!'

Grainne was worldly enough to know that she was bound for transportation, innocent though she might be of any intentional crime. When she had been committed for trial at quarter sessions without even being allowed her legal right to speak on her own behalf, her fate had become all too plain. Impartial justice was merely a myth. Friendless, penniless, without legal representation, and with a rich and powerful gentleman, his servants and the local officers of the law all ranged against her, her situation had been truly hopeless. But now she had fresh hope, thanks to Morgan Hunter.

She summoned all her fortitude and patience to enable her to get through the intervening hours that separated her from Sunday night.

Chapter Twenty-three

'That's it, Knacker! Stir the mad buggers up!'

'Give it to 'um hot!'

'Giddy Up, loony! Giddy Up, loony!'

'Hey up, let's have a goo!'

'Come out o' the fuckin' road, Knacker, we all wants a turn!'

'Yeah, come on out on it, Knacker, youm having all the bleedin' fun!'

The crowd of youths argued and scuffled around the iron grille of the cellar at the side of the Stone House, through which one of their number was poking a long thick stick, jabbing its sharpened end into the flesh of those inmates unfortunate enough to be chained nearest to the grille. The tormented lunatics screamed and bellowed, provoked to frenzy by the merciless baiting, and the youths jeered and cat-called and laughed uproariously at the bedlam they were creating inside the cellar.

People from the neighbouring houses came out to see what was happening, angry that their Sabbath day peace should be so rudely disturbed. But nobody tried to stop the youths. They were a well-known gang of local roughs who would not hesitate to use violence against anyone who should be foolhardy enough to interfere with their brutal pleasures.

One youth pressed his hips against the grille, and unlacing the front of his breeches directed a stream of urine over the chained inmates while his friends applauded wildly, and waited to take their own turn at the sport.

'Let's see who can piss over the most on 'um!'

188

'I'll bet you a tanner that I can piss over more on 'um than you can, Benjy!'

'Youm on, matey. Piss away!'

'I'll take that bet as well!'

Grainne huddled upon the narrow platform, her back to the grille, feet drawn up beneath her, arms wrapped around her head in vain attempt to shield herself from the nightmarish tumult, and the young woman at her side burrowed her head into Grainne's lap, and shrieked piteously with fear.

One incensed neighbour ran to the front door of the Stone House and hammered upon it until James Gibbs came waddling.

'Look here, Master Gibbs, them bloody hooligans are kicking up a terrible racket tormenting the loonies!' the man spluttered. 'We canna get a bit o' peace and quiet because of 'um.'

James Gibbs, flushed with gin, shrugged carelessly.

'Lads are always having sport with the bloody loonies, Master Curry. I suspect you did exactly the same at that grille when you was a younker, so why try and spoil the lads' bit o' fun now?'

'That's as maybe.' The man was just a little abashed. 'But it is the Sabbath day, Master Gibbs. I never made mock o' the loonies on a Sabbath day. Honest folk needs to take their rest then, doon't they?' he finished self-righteously.

Gibbs belched loudly, and grunted, 'Who is it that's tormenting 'um?'

'It's that young bugger Knacker Tipping and his gang o' ruffians,' the neighbour informed.

Gibbs grimaced. 'Well then, Master Curry, you can try and chase 'um off, if you've a mind to. But you'll get no help from me. That lot am a bit too ready with their fists for my taste. I'm off back to my bed. Good day to you.'

He slammed the door in his neighbour's face, leaving the man fuming impotently on the steps.

A sizeable group had now gathered to watch the rowdy youths, some of those watchers applauding and encouraging the gang into greater excesses, others looking grim and disapproving but too timid to voice their feelings openly.

Morgan Hunter was standing among the crowd of

onlookers, but his interest was not directed towards the rowdy youths. In his mind he was turning over the information that the Flemings had garnered while they had been inside the Stone House. He took note of the grille itself, judging the angles of vision from which it could be overlooked, then dismissed it from his reckoning. His attention switched to the upstairs rooms of the building, and he saw that their windows also were guarded with thick iron grilles. His gaze moved higher to the steep-gabled roof with its moss-covered tiles and wide-stacked chimneys, and his eyes lingered upon those stacks for some time.

'I'd need a snakesman to get up to them,' he realised, and briefly regretted just such a boy who had only recently been transported for burglary. 'Shame about young Jemmy getting lagged. He would have been ideal for the job.'

When Gibbs had escorted the Fleming woman down into the cellars, Steven Fleming had quickly ascertained the numbers and positions of locks and bolts on both the front and rear doors of the building, and Morgan Hunter now considered that information.

'Top and bottom bolts and a middle lock on both doors. Might be able to make do with a centre hole, and use the long hook to draw the bolts. But that's a messy job, isn't it? Fast it might be, but it won't do for me.'

Morgan Hunter prided himself on his craftsmanship. Among a small and select fraternity he bore the reputation of being a master cracksman, and was proud of that fact. He turned and slowly walked away from the building, leaving the rowdy gathering to their pleasures. Then he thought of something else Steven Fleming had told him, and he grinned wryly.

'Brand new construction. Saves Gibbs from getting himself wet in bad weather. Leads straight into the kitchen scullery, and the seat boards are screwed, not nailed.'

His grin became one of immense satisfaction.

'They'll be wondering for the rest of their lives how this one was done, and that's a fact! And all I'll need is a few bettys and a screwdriver, and a pair of outsiders.'

Chapter Twenty-four

'Grainne? Grainne, wake up! Shhh now, not a sound!'
Grainne came dazedly from troubled sleep, with the hand gently muffling her mouth, and the man's voice whispering in her ear, 'Quiet and easy, Grainne. Quiet and easy.'

She nodded her head against the constricting fingers and they fell away from her lips. A narrow beam of light shone down upon one of her manacled ankles, and then hands moved, and metal clinked and in seconds the tight-fitting iron was eased from her raw painful sores.

By now her eyes could distinguish his dark bulk, and she whispered, 'Is it you, Captain Hunter?'

'Shhh,' he hissed in warning. 'We'll talk later. Be silent for now.'

The pencil-thin beam of light shone upon each of the other padlocked manacles in turn, and each time there followed the swift manipulation of hands and metal and then the relief from painful biting pressure.

'You're free from them,' the man breathed into her ear. 'Stand quietly and go carefully into the passage. I'll light your way.'

He shone the narrow beam onto the filthy wet floor and Grainne moved along it, avoiding the outstretched legs and feet of the twitching, moaning, grunting, snoring, gibbering sleepers.

Morgan Hunter swiftly reclamped the padlocks onto the manacles, then joined Grainne in the passage. Taking her hand he led her up the stone steps and along the corridor.

The kitchen door had its large key in its rusty lock on the

191

corridor side, and the man ushered Grainne through before him, then closed the door and used the long narrow jaws of his outsider to grasp the butt end of the key and turn it, locking the door behind them. They went through the scullery next and into the privy, where the lantern light showed the seat boards neatly piled against the wall, and the privy itself now only a great gaping black hole.

'Careful,' Morgan Hunter cautioned, and she saw his teeth gleam in the reflected light of the lantern. 'I don't want you falling into the privy barrel.'

He helped her to lower herself down into the black hole, avoiding the two large half-filled barrels whose contents emitted a vile stench. Then he stepped into the privy-hole himself, but stayed with his feet balanced on the barrel rims while he replaced and screwed down the seat boards, crouching with his arms full-stretched through the round holes to screw the final boards in position.

He stepped into the yard to join Grainne, lowering the hanging trapdoor across the barrel space and re-padlocking it. Then he led her across the yard and through the door in the wall, which in its turn he re-locked, using his bettys or pick-locks to turn the tumblers of the rusted lock.

He lifted a rolled cloak from a wall nook and gave it to her. 'Put this on, Grainne.'

She started to speak to him, to thank him, but he placed his finger across her lips, and motioned her to keep silent. Then he whispered hoarsely, 'Go quickly now along the road towards Birmingham. Keep in the shadows and take care that no one sees or hears you. About half a mile out from the village you'll come to a lane leading to the right towards Buckley Green. Hide yourself in the hedgerow on that corner and keep a look-out for a closed carriage to come from the direction of Birmingham. It will have a double lamp on its right side, and a single lamp on its left. When you see it approaching step out and hail the driver. Ask him if you're on the right road for Wotton Wawen. The woman who came to see you earlier will then look out of the window and recognise you. You're to go with her, and wait with her until I come to you. Do you understand?'

Grainne nodded. He gently touched her cheek, and warned, 'If the woman does not appear, then run back into the fields and stay hid. I'll come to check that all is well after daybreak, so you'll have nothing to fear even if for some reason or other the carriage cannot come. In that case, just stay hidden until I come myself.'

Again she nodded, and this time whispered fervently, 'God bless you for helping me, Captain Hunter. I can never repay you.'

He grinned in the darkness, and in his mind assured her, 'Oh you'll repay me, honey. Never fear about that.'

But aloud he merely instructed her, 'Go now, and remember what I've told you.'

Her heart pounding with excitement and trepidation Grainne hurried along the silent deserted street blessing the thick clouds which kept the moon veiled and the night darkly shadowed. At the turning for Buckley Green she hid in the hedgerow and settled herself to wait, her body trembling with the reaction to the heightened tension of her escape.

Eventually she heard the rumbling of iron-shod wheels and the thudding of hooves. A fleeting rift in the clouds allowed shafts of moonlight to shine on the approaching carriage, and Grainne strained anxious eyes to see its lamps.

'Two on the right, one on the left,' she counted aloud, and then stepped out from the shadowed hedgerow to call to the driver sitting muffled on the high front seat.

'Tell me, mister, is this the right road to Wotten Wawen?'

'Whoa, whoa, hotch up theer!' He brought the pair of horses to a halt, and the window of the carriage rattled down and a bonneted head appeared in the dark aperture.

'Come here, girl.'

Grainne recognised the soft Irish accents and went gladly forwards.

'Good, 'tis yourself, honey,' Bridie Fleming greeted. 'Jump in here with me now, and let's be away.'

As Grainne climbed into the cab and settled herself on the leather seat the driver swung the horses around and whipped them into a fast trot back along the road they had travelled.

'Here, honey, take a swig o' this. It'll warm your heart.'

The Irishwoman handed a small silver flask to Grainne, who took a sip from its contents, gasping as the strong brandy burned down her gullet.

'You settle back now,' her companion instructed. 'Try and sleep if you can, and I'll wake ye when we get to Brummagem.'

'Is that where I'll be staying?' Grainne queried.

'Oh yes, that's to be your home now, honey, and you'll be as safe as houses there, sure you will. Safe as houses.'

Thankfully Grainne leaned back against the cold leather padding, and let herself relax.

Chapter Twenty-five

Behind the glittering façades of the bustling prosperous commercial thoroughfares of the centre of Birmingham festered some of the worst slums in Europe: seething, pullulating cesspits of crime, vice, disease, abject poverty and degradation. It was to one of the most notorious of these slums, the Hinkleys, that Bridie Fleming brought Grainne.

The two women descended from the carriage in New Street, illuminated by hissing gas lamps and still thronged even at this hour of the morning with drunken merrymakers and those that preyed on them. Then Bridie Fleming grasped Grainne's hand and hurried her past the opulent Theatre Royal and the fine Hen and Chickens hotel, before leaving the thoroughfare to plunge into the unlit fetid alleys and passages of the Hinkleys.

Here there were few human beings abroad, and they encountered only an occasional furtive figure scurrying through the rancid darkness, or the huddled shapes of sleeping derelicts seeking shelter in doorways and entries.

Grainne marvelled aloud at how her guide could travel so unerringly through the bewildering maze of tumbledown ramshackle buildings, and Bridie Fleming laughed. 'Swate Mary mother o' God, I know this place like the back o' me hand, girl. I've lived all over it! Peck Lane, the Froggery, King Street, I know every stinking inch of the place.'

'Do you live here still?' Grainne asked, and began to experience a lessening of the euphoria she had been feeling at having regained her freedom, not relishing the prospect of remaining here in this dreadful place for any considerable length of time.

'No, thank God. But we keep a room here for when we need

195

to keep out of the way for a bit. The crushers daren't come down here unless they're in full strength and armed. So it's a safe place to hide in.'

She chuckled, and teased good-naturedly. 'You're not very taken with the Hinkleys, are you?'

Grainne felt constrained to answer truly. 'Indeed I'm not. It reminds me too much of Liverpool, when I was forced to live there.'

'I shouldn't think you'll be forced to stay here for too long, honey. But you'll have to wait for the Captain to explain matters to you. He'll be along in a couple of days or so, I shouldn't wonder.'

They passed through a few more alleys and then Bridie Fleming led Grainne down a flight of steps and through a long covered passageway, inches deep in stinking muck, from which they emerged into a narrow court bounded by tall buildings which rose like black cliffs all around them, creating a claustrophobic sense of being at the bottom of a great pit.

Bridie Fleming used a key to unlock a door which was sunk into one of the towering walls, and then through a pitch blackness led Grainne by the hand up flights of hollow-echoing, rickety wooden steps. She halted on a landing, unlocked another door and told Grainne, 'Stay there,' before she disappeared through the door.

Grainne stood in the blackness, hearing her own breathing made harsh and heavy by exertion and increasing apprehension. Doubts suddenly flooded through her as to why she had been brought here – why Morgan Hunter had risked his own neck by setting her free. Was he a pimp, or a procurer? Was he something more sinister even?

Her heartbeat raced as her fears fed upon themselves, and she was tempted to turn and flee through the darkness, even if it meant risking a fall and perhaps injury or death. Then a pale radiance of light came through the open door and Bridie Fleming was taking her arm and leading her into the room.

'Here now, it's not too bad a lodge, is it? Rough and ready, but clean enough. You'll be real comfortable here when I've brought you some grub and drink in to keep you going.'

Grainne stared about her and saw a small room, with a curtained window, a trestle bed with a heap of blankets and a pillow upon its narrow length, and a table and chairs. Bridie Fleming studied Grainne's expression, and grinned sympathetically.

'Beginning to wonder why you're here, are you, honey?' she stated perceptively. 'Well, you've nothing to worry about, I'll swear to that on me dead Mammy's grave. The Captain's not a ponce, and he's no thought of being your cash-carrier, that I can tell you truthfully. He's not expecting you to be his tail. Nor any other judy come to that.'

She slid the side of her hand across her throat. 'May bloody owld Cathcart top me outside Warwick Jail afore next Sunday morning if I'm lying to ye, honey.'

Feeling slightly reassured, but still doubtful, Grainne could not help but question, 'But why has he helped me like this? Surely he'll want something from me in return for risking his own neck.'

The other woman nodded and answered readily. 'Of course he'll be wanting something, honey. But take it from me, it's not what's between your legs. I know the Captain well, and you've nothing to fear from him, believe me. He's a gent.

'You just settle down and rest now, I've got to be leaving you for a while. I'll have to lock the door behind me, but that's not to keep you in, it's to keep the thievin' bastards round here out. I'll see you later. There's more oil for the lamp if you need it in the cupboard there, and a couple of bottles o' porter if you're thirsty.'

With that Bridie Fleming was out of the house and the door closed and locked behind her. For a few moments Grainne could only stand and stare dumbly at the closed door, then a wave of sheer exhaustion brought her slumping down upon the narrow bed.

'I'll worry about things later,' she thought dazedly, and lying back on the mattress allowed the sleep she craved for, to overwhelm her.

Chapter Twenty-six

Three days elapsed before Morgan Hunter came to the room in the Hinkleys. During that period Grainne remained in the room, leaving it only briefly to perform her personal offices. Bridie Fleming came to see her every day, bringing food and drink and staying many hours to keep Grainne company.

Although Grainne was not happy to be pent up as she was, the other woman pressed upon her the absolute necessity to stay hidden, until it could be determined whether or no a hue and cry had been raised against her. Grainne could accept this, but found that the hours passed with a mind-numbing slowness.

From the single window she had a view of the narrow cramped court in which the building stood, and found it peculiar in that the other buildings surrounding it had all their doors and windows bricked up, so that she was faced with nothing but towering, black-grimed blank walls.

'They're all workshops and storehouses,' Bridie Fleming explained. 'And there's so much thieving that the owners has had everything bricked up. The entrances are on the opposite sides now. That's why we keep this place. We can't be overlooked here, and the crushers don't even know that there's anybody who stays in here at all. They think it's just a midden.'

Grainne could understand that, because when she sat at the high window staring out at the patch of sky above her head, she would occasionally see a man, woman or child come out of the covered passage into the court below and use it as a privy, adding to the stinking piles of filth and refuse that almost filled the small confined ground area.

Whenever she tried to ask the other woman more details about Morgan Hunter, and what he did, Bridie Fleming would only grin and wave the questions away.

'I'm not able to tell you anything about anything yet, honey. But you'll come to know all that ye need to when the Captain's here to spake to you.'

Morgan Hunter came in the darkness of the night. Grainne was lying asleep on the narrow bed when the loud knocking on the door caused her to wake, her heart pounding with apprehension.

'Don't be alarmed, Grainne, it's me, Morgan Hunter.'

She sighed with relief and rose from the bed as he unlocked the door and entered the room, his bull's-eye lantern casting its thin bright beam before him.

'I hope I didn't startle you, Grainne.' He smiled at her, and she returned his smile.

'No, I'm happy to see you.'

She used the lucifer to light the table lamp and as she did so the man seated himself on one of the straight-backed chairs, and invited Grainne to take the other chair on the opposite side of the table.

'Have you just come from Henley? What happened when they found I'd escaped? Was there a hue and cry raised for me?'

Excited eager questions bubbled from her, and he laughed and held up his arms playfully as if in defence.

'Hold hard now, my dear. I'll tell you all if you'll but give me a moment to marshal my thoughts.'

She smiled ruefully. 'I'm sorry, it's just that I've been so anxious.'

'Of course you have.' He nodded understandingly, and looking at her loosely bound hair and her green eyes glowing with excitement he thought how beautiful she was, and blessed the luck that had brought her into his power.

'By Christ, you'll be worth a fortune to me, my honey-lamb,' he exulted in his mind. Then aloud, he told her, 'Yes, there was an almighty uproar when they found that you had escaped. Some of the old biddies in the village swore that it was by witchcraft.' He grinned with relish. 'Naturally Gibbs was suspected of letting you go, but the magistrates and the constables know him to be a trustworthy jailer, and too mean anyway to risk losing his regular gaoler fees. So in the death it was decided that the manservant, that ugly little cove named Blair, had done the business, and he's been committed for trial for aiding and abetting.'

Grainne could not help but feel a guilty concern. 'But that seems so unfair to put the poor man in jail like that. Is there nothing we can do to take the blame from him?'

The man chuckled harshly, and his expression hardened. 'Don't waste any sympathy on Blair, my dear. The man is an evil little bastard. His wife's been on the spree since the moment he was taken away. She's telling everybody that it's the best thing that has ever happened for her. Hanging would be too good for the evil bastard, from the tales I've been told of him about the way he treats the poor loonies and his own wife. Why, it's rumoured that he even beat his own child to death.'

Grainne remembered how the lunatics screamed when Blair had attacked them, and his wife's battered, broken features, and her sense of guilt withered.

'Perhaps you're right, Captain Hunter,' she agreed quietly. 'Perhaps Blair is where he deserves to be.'

'There's a reward been offered for you, Grainne. You're valued at twenty-five guineas.' He smiled at her. 'Personally I would value you a deal more highly, but there's no accounting for other people's opinions, is there?'

She felt a heightening of anxiety. 'Then there's a hue and cry been raised for me?'

'I wouldn't term it to be that exactly, Grainne,' Hunter soothed. 'But yes, there have been posters printed and put about with your description.' He paused and regarded her expression, then leaned across the table and patted her cheek. 'But don't you go worrying your head about that. The description doesn't really do you justice, and there's nigh on a quarter of a million people running about in Brummagem, so you'll be like the needle in the haystack. Especially if you work with me, because I'll make sure that instead of the servant girl they seek, you'll be a fine lady.'

Grainne drew a long breath as she heard his last sentence. With level eyes she asked him, 'Why have you helped me, Captain Hunter? And what is it you want from me in return?'

He regarded her keenly, and replied with a tinge of admiration in his voice. 'Yes, my dear, I read you rightly, did I not? I knew you'd prove to be plain-spoken. Well, I'll speak with an equal plainness. As you've doubtless realised by now I am numbered among those whom the respectable term the ''dangerous classes''. I earn my bread outside the law.

'You're also outside the law now, Grainne Shonley, and after escaping from custody like you've just done, you'll be transported for life if you're ever retaken. So, in all frankness I don't see that you've any other choice but to become one of us. I don't mean to prostitute yourself. That's a fool's game which only leads a woman to a premature death. No, I mean that you could work with the ''swell mobsmen'', or with a ''snoozer'' or a ''shofulman''.' He paused and grinned. 'Or if you've got the heart to risk all for the really big rewards, then you could work with a master cracksman such as me. A woman like you, with your good looks and intelligence, can always find rich pickings in the right company.'

He saw the instant distress and protest in her face, and went on quickly. 'I know that's hard for you to accept at this moment, my dear, but when you've had time to reflect upon it, you'll come to see that you've no other choice, honest woman though you may be, and innocent of any real crime. But now the world will not permit you to continue to be an honest woman.'

'But I needn't remain in this city,' Grainne objected, shocked by what he had said. 'I can go to other parts to find work.'

He smiled, and there was a hint of mocking cruelty in his eyes. 'What sort of work will you be able to find, Grainne?' he challenged scoffingly. 'You've no character now, and no one to swear to your good name. You've no money, no home, no possessions, and apart from me, no friends either. And worst of all, my dear, you're now an escaped prisoner with a life term in Van Diemens Land hanging over your head, if not the rope itself even.'

Grainne felt a dull heavy sense of oppression like a palpable presence in her breast, and her breathing shortened with her distress. She remembered Liverpool, and what had happened to her there when, penniless and desperate, she had been forced to sell her body to survive.

'I could not face that again.' She knew with absolute certainty. 'I would kill myself, mortal sin though that is, rather than sell my body to any man ever again.'

The terrible surety of the truth of Morgan Hunter's words gripped her like a life-crushing pressure. Now, there really was nothing left in this life for her but to do as he suggested. To join with those who were known as the 'dangerous classes'.

'If I want to live, then what can I do, but as he says?'

For a few wild moments she thought of doing away with herself, of casting herself through the window and falling to death and oblivion. But all her childhood conditioning, the training and indoctrination of her religion, forbade her from taking such a step.

'It's the worst sin of all. The most damning. I would lose my immortal soul,' she thought fearfully.

The man sat watching the play of emotions across her expressive features and had the good sense to allow her to battle through her own personal purgatory confident that in her, as in all creatures, the instinct for personal survival would inevitably win through. Seconds became minutes, and minutes lengthened, one following the other as the man and woman sat in silence, each locked within the recesses of their own secret thoughts. Then, finally, Grainne vented a long shuddering sigh.

Morgan Hunter smiled and said gently, 'There's no choice, is there, my dear? So, will you work with me?'

Her green eyes were wide and filled with a sad hopelessness as she slowly nodded her head in agreement.

Chapter Twenty-seven

The men's boots stamping down on the wooden floors of the drill hall created a thunderous resonance and dust rose in clouds, and was dislodged to fall from the beams and rafters of the old warehouse, once known as Beardsworth's Repository, but now in this month of April 1849 the principal station and headquarters of the First Division of the Birmingham City Police Force.

The tall, ramrod-backed, be-whiskered drill-sergeant, looking every inch the ex-guardsman that he was, screamed the words of command, and the ranks of sergeants and constables in their tight fitting blue swallow-tailed tunics, white trousers, tight neck-stocks and black oilskinned top hats, wheeled, left-turned, right-turned, about-turned, formed fours, halted, saluted to left, saluted to right, slow marched, quick-marched and double-timed until the sweat ran down their faces, and the dust that was pounded up from the floor, or dislodged from the beams and rafters above their heads mingled with that sweat to form dark sticky runnels down their heads and necks.

'Paraaaadde! Paraaade Halt!'

Boots thundered in unison and the long ranks thudded to a standstill, chests heaving, mouths gaping as they gulped the stale, over-heated air into their straining lungs.

'You there, Constable Murdoch!' the drill sergeant's voice screeched in an ear-splitting falsetto and his face purpled alarmingly. 'Stand fast and look to your front, man, or I'll have you on the flank, you thick-skulled yokel clod. By the Christ, I've seen some useless bastards in my time, but ne'er yet one as useless as you, Murdoch. Not in twenty five years in Her Majesty's Foot Guards, and ten years in this force.'

At one end of the drill hall, which was merely a bricked off section of the old warehouse, two police inspectors were standing watching the drill parade. Both wore uniform dark blue, silver-buttoned, double-breasted dress coats, black top hats and dark blue trousers.

Hearing the drill sergeant's abuse, Inspector Andrew Munro laughed jeeringly and asked his companion, 'Ain't that the man you've requested from me, Bill? It is Murdoch, ain't it? My oath, Bill, what's the detective force coming to when you're taking numbskulled oafs like that one into it? He can't drill worth a light!'

Inspector William Hall, a lanky-bodied, hatched-featured, grey whiskered man of some fifty years, regarded his fellow officer with sour resentment, and grunted, 'I'm not seeking bloody guardsmen to stand sentry outside the public office, Andrew. I'm seeking a suitable man for detective work.'

He stared at the red-faced, sweating Constable Murdoch, a clumsy, broad featured young man, who really did resemble the popular caricature of the dull-witted yokel.

'Well, all that bugger needs is a bit o' straw in his boots, and he should be able to tell which is his right foot from his left,' the other man scoffed. 'He'll make a prime Jack he will. A first class detective, I don't think.'

'That remains to be seen, Andrew,' William Hall defended. 'His dad was a fine thief-taker, and I'm betting that some of what he had has rubbed off on the son.'

While the two men had been talking the drill sergeant had ordered the distribution of basket-hilted sticks, and now he was putting the parade through the sword exercises. There were certain areas of the city that were so dangerous to patrolling policemen that cutlasses were issued for their self-defence, to supplement their twenty-inch staff, rattle, and handcuffs.

'Right flank parry! Head attack! Recover guard! Retire! Left step! Left cheek attack! Right flank attack! Thrust attack! Advance! Right flank attack! Thrust parry! Head parry! Thrust attack! Left flank parry! Recover guard!'

The sticks whirled and hummed through the air, and the lines of men moved with ragged unison, some with dexterous certainty and agile grace, others with clumsy slowness and constant error.

'Constable Murdoch! That's supposed to be a soddin' cutlass you've got in your hand. Not your bloody prick! You're supposed to kill with the bloody thing, not piss through it!'

The drill sergeant's face was deep purple, and he looked near to apoplexy as he slavered with rage.

'Murdoch, if you'd ha' bin there, we'd have lost at Waterloo. You're too bloody slow to catch a soddin' cold! Gawd in Heaven, why did your bloody mother send you here to torment me? Why couldn't she keep you down on the bloody farm with all the other soddin' sheep? Get a grip of yourself, man! A bloody crippled tailor with a bent bodkin could stick you, you stupid useless lump of shit!'

'On my life!' Munro's meaty face beamed with good-humoured contempt. 'Surely you can't find a use for that bloody mawkin, Bill, no matter how well you knew his pa. He wouldn't even serve as a bookend!'

'Can I have him then, Andrew?' Hall sought confirmation, and the other man blew out his cheeks to expel a gust of scorn.

'Have him and welcome, Bill. Have the clumsy useless bugger, and welcome! He ain't smart enough at his drills to suit me.'

'Many thanks to you, General.' Hall accepted with ironic humour.

When the drill period had finished and the parade was dismissed William Hall shouldered through the sweating men until he reached his quarry.

'Constable Murdoch, you're to come with me.'

Reuben Murdoch's pleasantly bovine face was impassive as he followed the inspector out of the police station and into Moseley Street. Once there the older man asked, 'Do you know where Crooked Lane section station is, Murdoch?'

'Yes, sir, it lies close to the town hall.'

'You're in the lodgings here, are you not?'

'Yes, sir.'

'Well move your traps over to Crooked Lane straight away, you can bunk in with my lads. There's a spare bed in their quarters. When you've done that then change into your plain clothes and report to the commissioner's office in Waterloo Street. Don't be too fancy in your dress. Look lively now.'

Hall didn't bother to return the constable's salute and

ambled away leaving the young man staring after him, a broad grin slowly spreading across his red sweaty face. Another young constable came out from the station behind Murdoch, and there was envy in his eyes.

'Has Billy Hall agreed to take you then, Reuben?'

'It looks like he has, even though he's not mentioned the application I sent to him,' Murdoch informed and suddenly crowed with joyous laughter. 'I'm going to be a Jack! A bloody prime Jack!'

'You lucky bastard,' his companion ejaculated enviously, then as if to vent his own sour grapes added spitefully, 'O' course, all that means is your chances of getting your head kicked in have just increased by one hundred. Sooner you than me, Reuben, sooner you than me.'

No amount of snide jealousy could dampen Reuben Murdoch's pleasure however, and his delighted grin merely widened.

'Just so, Tommy, sooner me than you. I'll drink to that.'

At the imposing offices of the police commissioner in Waterloo Street, William Hall was waiting for Reuben in the vestibule. The older man had also changed into civilian clothing, and with his broad brimmed hat and dark threadbare clothing resembled a schoolteacher rather than a policeman. His shrewd gaze travelled over the younger man's figure, noting with approval the depth of chest and the width of shoulders.

'You look to be a strong chap, Murdoch.'

'I am, sir. I was counted the strongest man in our half-shire, and the best runner and steeplechaser.' There was no boastfulness in the young man's voice, merely a factual statement.

He was wearing a dark green velveteen jacket, black corduroy trousers, and low-crowned peaked cap, with heavy thick-soled boots, and his hair done in twisted side curls. He resembled a bucolic dandy up in the big city for the day, and William Hall was satisfied.

For a few moments he studied the other man closely, evaluating him. Hall was a vastly experienced policeman, having been a thief-taker in the old city police before the present new police force was formed in 1839, and he was an excellent judge of human nature. He divined the acute brain and agile wits that existed behind the bovine yokel features of Reuben Murdoch; the young man's clumsiness at parade and sword drill did not bother the inspector. As he had already told Munro, he was seeking a potential detective, not a guardsman. Murdoch obviously possessed great physical strength and stamina, and that was more important than parade-ground skills.

William Hall knew already that the young man had shown strong nerve and bravery in the frequent brawls and assaults that occurred in normal police work. Whether he possessed the type of cold unemotional courage that was needed by a detective would very quickly be easily and accurately assessed. The detective inspector accepted that he could quite justly be accused of practising a form of nepotism in giving this in-experienced constable preference over so many other more experienced and longer serving members of the force who had applied to fill the vacancy in the detective branch. Now he mentally shrugged in indifference to such justified accusations. He had known and served with the young man's dead father. The older Murdoch had been his trusted partner. For that reason he was now prepared to give the son his chance also, confident that the sturdy stock he came from would prove to be potent still.

A little later both men were in the office of Chief Superinten-dent Richard A. Stephens who commanded the City of Birmingham police force.

'Remember young man, that truth is the hidden gem we all should dig for.'

Richard Stephens was very fond of using aphorisms, and he prided himself that he had one for every occasion. He leaned back in his capacious leather armchair, fingers laced across his equally capacious stomach.

'This new post is an important advancement in your career. Do not betray the trust that Inspector Hall, and myself also, are placing in you. My advice to you is to be always a friend to virtue, a stranger to vice. Remember always that pleasure is precarious, but virtue is immortal. He that neglects time, time will neglect. To hope and to strive is the way to thrive.'

He nodded abruptly in dismissal, and Reuben Murdoch

thankfully escaped. Outside once more, William Hall glanced along the thronged and bustling street.

'We'll take a stroll, Murdoch.'

The stroll turned out to be a perambulation of the city which lasted several hours, and for Reuben Murdoch it was a revelation. Before he had only known the city as a visitor, and later as a raw, countrybred young policeman. Now he was seeing it through the eyes of a man who had spent most of his life as a thief-taker and detective.

They wandered through the Bullring, the Market Hall, the jewellery and gun quarters, the churchyards of St Phillip's, St Paul's, St Martin's, the railway terminus of Curzon Street, the areas where the slums were being demolished to make space for the new railway stations of New Street and Snow Hill, the mighty town hall, the law courts of the public office, the close-packed factories and workshops, the fetid slums of the poor and the fine streets of the rich, and everywhere William Hall pointed out men and women, youths, girls, and children that he had cause to know were engaged in villainy of one sort or another, petty or serious, profitably or pitifully rewarded.

Colmore Street and Coventry Street, Moat Lane and Jamaica Row, Paradise Street and Newhall Street, High Street and Ludgate Hill. The medical enclave of Temple Row, the butcher's enclave of Smithfield. Each had their stories. Reuben listened and looked with unflagging fascination as the detective inspector related anecdotes and snippets of information, and indicated faces among the Jews in Severn Street, the Quakers in Bull Street, the Catholics in Easy Street and Shadwell Street, Congregationalists in Carrs Lane, Baptists in Cannon Street, Methodists in Cherry Street and Unitarians in their Old and New Meeting House Lanes.

And all through this long long voyage of discovery the city pulsed and throbbed and bustled around them. Forge hammers pounded. Waggons rumbled over cobbles. Men and women shouted and swore and laughed. Chimneys gushed out filthy clouds of black smoke and showered red hot sparks. Shopmen and pedlars cried their wares. Beggars pleaded and street urchins capered. Businessmen bargained and dealers chaffered. Navvies swung picks and labourers carried hods. Porters hauled loads and thieves watched and pounced. Ladies in fine gowns sauntered and shopped. Prostitutes in tawdry fineries sauntered and invited.

In an area measuring little more than six miles wide and two miles deep a quarter of a million human souls battled to survive and somehow or other to earn their daily bread.

Late that night Reuben Murdoch returned to his austere comfortless sleeping quarters in the Crooked Lane and, exhausted though he was, found that he could not sleep. He lay in his narrow cot, his mind seething with what he had seen and been told that day. Despite his weariness he grinned into the darkness, and felt utter contentment.

'This is what I was born to do,' he realised. 'I was born to be a detective.'

Chapter Twenty-eight

The week following Morgan Hunter's visit to Grainne was unlike anything she had ever experienced before. Bridie Fleming came to fetch her to stay in a large new-built villa that fronted the Pershore Turnpike Road in the pleasant suburb of Balsall Heath. Unlike the filth and stench of the Hinkleys here Grainne was surrounded by trees and open spaces, and clean fresh air.

Her days were spent in shopping for clothes, accessories, jewellery, bonnets and shoes, all of the very finest materials and latest fashion. She spent many hours being conducted around the city both on foot and by carriage in company with Bridie, with whom she was fast becoming close friends.

There were only she and Bridie staying at the house, and no living-in servants. An elderly woman came in daily to cook and clean, but for all the conversation Grainne held with her the woman might have been a deaf mute. She came, did her work, and left, without offering to exchange a single sentence, and Bridie impressed upon Grainne that she must not venture to talk with the woman.

She saw nothing either of Morgan Hunter or of Steven Fleming and wondered aloud about their absence.

Bridie winked and told her, 'In our business it's best that we're not seen together too often. Sure, you'll be seeing more than enough of them both when the time comes to go back to work.'

'When will that be?' Grainne enquired, with some trepidation. 'And what will be required of me?'

'Well now, that all depends.' Bridie's handsome face was thoughtful.

210

'Depends on what?' Grainne pressed.

'On what lay the Captain might have in his mind. You're a new face you see, and that opens up a lot of possibilities. You've got the presence and looks of a real lady, and the Captain will be able to use you anywhere.'

Although she had done her best to come to terms with the fact that she was living outside the law, Grainne was still troubled by the prospect that she was now expected to join with her new friends to rob people who had done her no harm. Grainne was basically an honest woman, and she wondered frequently whether, when the time came, she would actually be able to go through with the committing of a deliberate crime. Now she emitted a troubled sigh, and Bridie guessed what the matter was.

'You were brought up a good Catholic girl, weren't you, honey?' She smiled sympathetically. 'And it's bothering you that you're going to be a flash judy from now on, isn't it?'

Grainne nodded.

'I was the same when I first started,' Bridie told her. 'But what else am I to do? Sell me mutton? I did that, and all it got me was into the bloody lock ward. I nearly died with the shame of it. Catching the clap was mortal sin to me.' She frowned with the memory. 'You've been lucky, girl, that you've never been forced onto the game.'

A bitter grimace made her momentarily uglier and older than her years. 'Being on the fuckin' game they call it! As though it's fun to be playing it! And they call us "gay girls" that are on it!'

She spat with virulent disgust.

'When I was laying in that fuckin' lock ward, smelling the stinks of me own rotten body, seeing the poor bitches dying, and some o' them not above ten years old, I swore then that if I lived, I'd get me own back on the rich bastards who'd put me in there. The evil old bastards who'd started abusing me when I was still only a child, and God help me, an innocent child at that.'

She scowled angrily at Grainne, and gritted out, 'I'll rob from any man, and strip him without mercy, Grainne, to repay what men have done to me.'

For an instant Grainne was almost driven to tell the other

211

woman about her own experience of being forced to sell herself on the streets of Liverpool. But some deep buried instinct impelled her to stay silent, and keep that particular bitter and shameful secret to herself.

The woman stared hard at Grainne, and challenged, 'Listen Grainne, will you be able to do what we expect of you? Or when the crunch comes, will you let us down? It's best that you tell me the truth now.'

The memories that Bridie's story had brought flooding back into Grainne's mind served to steel her, and she answered evenly, 'No, I'll not let you down.'

After the initial excitements of wearing fine clothes, and travelling in carriages like a fine lady, Grainne found that she took more pleasure from the evenings spent quietly at the villa, when she and Bridie would sit at the fireside, reading, or chatting, or playing card games. Sometimes they would sing the songs of their childhood, and then when they had shared a flask of gin, they would lift their skirts and dance polkas and waltzes and jigs, singing out their own musical accompaniments at the tops of their voices, and collapsing with breathless laughter when exhausted.

One night, after just such a wild carefree dancing session, Grainne fell back into her chair gurgling with breathless laughter, and suddenly realised: 'For the first time since I lost my Con, I'm really enjoying myself.'

She experienced a momentary flash of unreasoning guilt, then reflected: 'He'd be so pleased that I can laugh again. He'd have roared himself if he'd been here with us now.'

A sadness invaded her at the memory of how she and her beloved husband had laughed together so many many times, and she wished with all her heart that he could have shared this present laughter with her. But the sadness she felt at this moment now held a strange quality of poignant sweetness, rather than the bitter rending of grief, and now for the first time Grainne knew without any doubt that the process of healing from her terrible bereavement was truly beginning to happen.

Later that same night Morgan Hunter and Steven Fleming came to the house. They brought with them a well dressed, slender-bodied young man, with pale sensitive features, and abnormally long thin hands. His hair was worn poetically long and flowing with a centre parting and his appearance was that of a delicately nurtured aesthete.

Hunter introduced the newcomer to the two women as Arthur Taunton, and the young man bowed gracefully over their hands murmuring, 'Charmed to meet you, ladies. Most charmed.'

His voice was in keeping with his physical appearance, fluting and whispery.

'Arthur's come up for the Industrial and Trades Exhibition at Bingley House,' Morgan Hunter informed them with a broad grin. 'He's a craftsman, you see, and most tremendously interested in the new machinery, ain't you, Arthur?'

'Indeed, I am. Most tremendously. Machinery is the very breath of life to me,' the young man fluted whisperingly, and sinking down onto the richly brocaded chaise longue lay languidly back against its cushions.

Bridie grinned knowingly at the other two men, and chuckled. 'I know who this cove is, boys. You can't gammon me. He's a swell mobsman. He used to work with Bristol John's gang until they got the boat. Arthur here was their prime tooler, wasn't he? He's reckoned to be the best fine wirer in the business.'

Both Morgan Hunter and Steven Fleming burst out laughing.

'You're too fly by half, my girl,' Morgan Hunter told her jovially. 'I didn't think we'd be able to put one over on you for very long. Anyways, you and Grainne are going to be working with him. You'll be his stickmen, Steve here will be the stall.'

Grainne sat listening to the exchange in bewilderment, the cant words they were using completely alien to her.

Morgan Hunter saw her expression and chuckled. 'Don't worry, my dear. Everything shall be made clear to you in a short while. But first, let's have a drink. Have you got some daffy in the house, Bridie?'

'Never without it,' she declared, and opening up the wall cupboard produced several bottles of gin.

The gathering quickly became light-hearted and convivial, and while they drank and talked and laughed Morgan Hunter explained matters to Grainne.

213

'Arthur is a very highly skilled pickpocket, Grainne. They work in gangs if they're any good, and the most successful ones are known as swell mobsmen. The stickman's job is to help distract the mark, that's the one whose pocket is to be picked, and also to take the pickings from the tooler or the fine wirer who does the actual business. The stall comes into play if the tooler is discovered. His job is to impede the pursuit and to shield the tooler's getaway.'

'But how do I distract the mark?' Grainne wanted to know. 'I've never done anything like this before.'

'That's exactly why I want you to work with Arthur.' Morgan Hunter grinned. 'Because you're a new face you'll not be known to the crushers and the local Jacks. You'll be able to work the exhibition first, and then the music halls and theatres, and perhaps do a little business in the markets and shopping streets without any danger of recognition.'

He saw the doubt still lurking in her green eyes, and re-assured her, 'There's nothing for you to worry about, or be nervous of. We'll make good and sure that you are practised enough to know what you are about before we put you to work.'

'And you?' she wanted to know. 'Will you be with us in those places?'

His smile disappeared and his eyes became harder and colder.

'It's not your place to question me, girl,' he told her curtly. 'I run this gang, and I tell you what's what. All you need do is to trust me and obey without question. I'm a man of honour, Grainne, and I don't risk my people where I wouldn't risk myself.' He indicated her fine costly gown. 'Where do you think the money comes from to buy this finery, and to keep this house, and to live as high and well as we all do?' Not waiting for her reply he went on. 'It comes from my business, girl, and I'm very good at that business.'

Made a little apprehensive by his abrupt change of mood she said mollifyingly, 'Very well, Captain Hunter. I wasn't meaning that I was mistrusting of you. I'll do as you say.'

His hard eyes remained fixed on her for a couple of seconds, and then the broad grin curved his lips once more, and his manner again became easy and jovial.

'That's a good girl. And just to show that there's no hard feelings on my part, I'll tell you that when you go out to work, I'll be close by, and if there should be any danger threatening, then I'll be ready to deal with it. So you can be sure that you'll be safe at all times.'

She nodded her acceptance, and he appeared satisfied. Then he went on to question her at great length about Millwood Hall, wanting to know every minute detail concerning its inhabitants, and its physical layout and construction. Grainne answered as best she could until he signified enough.

It was very late when the impromptu party came to an end. Morgan Hunter went away to some mysterious destination, Steven and Bridie Fleming to their bedroom and Grainne to her own, leaving Arthur Taunton stretched out snoring loudly on the chaise longue.

Grainne lay sleepless, the gin she had drunk causing her head to whirl and her thoughts to career wildly. She knew now that within two or three days at the most she would be embarking on a life of crime as a member of this gang. Faces of those she had known and in some cases had loved came through her mind's eye in succession, and disparate though they were it seemed in her fevered imaginings that each one stared accusingly at her, as if condemning her for what she was about to become. Her own sense of guilt returned to torment her, and she tossed and writhed restlessly among the disordered, rumpled bedcoverings.

'What else can I do, if I am to live?' She hurled the question at those silent accusing faces. 'You tell me? What else can I do?'

But question though she might, she received no answers from them. Until, right at the very last, Conrad Shonley appeared and smiled lovingly at her.

'What else can I do, Con?' She begged him. 'Tell me. What else can I do?'

And it seemed that she heard his voice answering faintly from a long long distance.

'Nothing else, my honey. Nothing else.'

'Then so be it,' was her last conscious thought before she fell asleep.

Chapter Twenty-nine

During the days following his appointment to the detective force Reuben Murdoch met the two other detective constables and the sergeant who together with himself and William Hall comprised the total manpower of the branch. Detective Sergeant Osbert Cooper resembled his inspector in his lanky build and hatched-faced looks. The two constables, Albert Gittings and Sidney Hay were nondescript looking men, with no remarkable physical attributes which would make them stand out in a crowd. Reuben marvelled at the fact that an hour after his initial meeting with them both, he had difficulty remembering what they looked like.

For two weeks Reuben was given no formal duties to perform. William Hall ordered him to spend all his waking hours in familiarising himself with the physical layout of the city and its immediate environs.

'When you're doing that, then dress the part,' the inspector instructed. 'Dress up in your Sunday best for the rich quarters and the quality hotels and shops. Put your second best on for the respectable areas, and look like a bloody tramper in the slums.'

William Hall from time to time would take Reuben to small quiet alehouses, and there over pewter pots of frothing porter share with the younger man the fruits of his own hard-bought experience. Reuben would listen intently, storing every scrap of esoteric lore in his mind, gaining a knowledge which would serve him well for the rest of his days.

'Always remember that the good Jack blends in with his surroundings. The good Jack never looks out of place wherever he might be. He's not there to shine in present company, he's there to keep his eyes and ears open and his mouth shut, and to learn all he can about what's what, and who's who. But he takes care that no one comes to learn who or what he is himself.'

The good Jack keeps himself trim and hard, and stays alert at all times to watch for a chiv in his back, or a neddy across his skull. A Jack can never afford to put his full trust and reliance in or on anybody, not even another Jack or Crusher. His full trust and reliance can only ever be placed in and on his own courage and capabilities.'

'A Jack needs to remember that at Stop-tap a drunken man really will be prepared to lay down his life for his drinking mate. But come six o'clock in the morning, that same drunk will not be prepared to give even a halfpenny of his own money to save the life of his drinking mate. And if his need for another drink is strong enough, he'll sell his mates, his women, his kids even, for a bloody shilling or two.'

'Remembrance is everything in our trade. The Jack needs to be able to remember faces, names, places and happenings. He needs to be able to recall what he's heard, and where he heard it. And most important of all, the good Jack needs to be able to make the connections and tie it all in together.'

'The good Jack needs knowledge, like a tree needs air, water and sunlight. Knowledge is all these and more to the Jack. So never cease from trying to gain knowledge. Read, watch, listen and ask. Learn as much as you can about everything that you can. And when I say everything, I mean just that. Because everything on this earth is inter-connected in some way or another, and the more knowledge a Jack has in his head, then the more dangerous he is to them who he's hunting. So never cease from trying to learn about things, not even when you're on your bloody deathbed.'

A rare smile curved William Hall's thin lips. 'Because even on your deathbed you might learn something that can serve even at that last minute to save your bloody life.'

Reuben Murdoch listened and absorbed all that the inspector told him and inwardly vowed that he would do just as his superior advised and spend the remainder of his life in learning all that he could.

*　　　*　　　*

Early one Monday morning William Hall came to hammer on the door of the room that served as the bachelor lodging for the three detective constables. Only Reuben was there, the other two being out on some surveillance operation.

'Come on, lad, it's time for your first show up as a Jack,' the inspector told him brusquely.

An hour later, both wearing plain clothes, they were in a room in the police station at Deritend, and even through the thick walls the din of the workshops and factories that surrounded the station could be heard.

The room they stood in was windowless with only a door set into its unpainted bare brick walls and at one end a wooden partition topped at chest height with a close-fretted grille. It was empty of furnishings, except for a battery of overhead gaslamps with their massed hissing flames casting a garish light and heating the room so that Reuben after scant minutes was already sweating heavily.

'Come behind here.' William Hall led Reuben behind the partition into the narrow space between the partition and the end wall.

'We just stand here and look through the grille,' he explained. 'We can see them, but they can't make out who we are. It's like I told you before, the less we're known, the better we can do our work.'

'Who is them?' Reuben queried.

'Our customers, Detective Murdoch.' The older man smiled bleakly. 'You just look, listen and learn now.'

There sounded a dull thumping of many pairs of boots on the floorboards of the passage outside the room, and then the door opened and a uniformed constable entered, followed by a file of men and women dressed in a variety of rigouts. More constables, and sergeants and an inspector followed the civilians through the door, and ranged themselves around the walls, leaving the space before the partition open.

The civilians were formed into a line with their backs against the wall opposite the grille. There were twelve of them, male and female, and of differing ages. Some were comparatively well dressed, others were in rags. Some looked clean and presentable, others were filthy, their hair matted, their bodies and clothes visibly verminous. Some wore hats and bonnets, some were bare-headed; some scowled defiantly, others appeared frightened and submissive. The only thing that they held in common was that all had been arrested and taken into custody during the weekend.

The portly inspector produced a small ledger and opened it, peering at the closely written pages through his round rimmed spectacles. His fat finger moved up and down the lists of names, then he cleared his throat and ordered, 'Charles Ellis, step forwards.'

A ragged youth shuffled out from the line, his head bent low, and the inspector jeeringly told him, 'Come on now, Charlie, hold that handsome head high and proud, so that we can all see and admire its perfect symmetry.'

The youth obeyed, his furtive eyes behind their veiling fringe of matted hair darting in all directions.

'Walk up and down the room, Charlie. Then stand in the centre and turn yourself slowly around.'

As the youth did so the inspector informed the assembled policemen, 'Charlie is a sneak thief, gentlemen, who specialises in pinching the milk money from tiny infants. He ain't bold enough to tackle anything else. He's usually found skulking around them courts at the back of Dale End.' He broke off his recital to shout at the youth. 'Keep turning slow, you young dog, and pull that bloody hair back from your filthy rotten mug so that we can see you clear, or I'll take a bloody stick to your stinking hide.'

The youth was permitted to rejoin the line, and the inspector called out, 'Samuel Tandy, Thomas Tandy, step forwards.'

Two burly smock-clad, ruddy-featured countrymen with widebrimmed hats on their shaggy heads slumped out, scowling sullenly, and the inspector told them jovially, 'Take them hats off. You may smile if you wish, boys. There's no law forbidding that. Now walk up and down until I tell you to stop.'

As the men did so the inspector continued: 'These two yokels are brothers, gentlemen. At least so they claim. But personally I take leave to doubt whether their mother could know who fathered which. You'll note that Samuel has got a bit of a limp and favours his left leg. That's because a few years since when he was poaching out Warwick way he got his right leg caught in a mantrap. And it's been gammy ever since. They was took up on Saturday at Smithfield, suspected of selling stolen sheep. Enquiries are continuing about the sheep's rightful owners out at Coleshill.'

His plump sweating face beamed happily. 'If found guilty, they'll be topped. And bloody good riddance as well. But knowing the stupidity, and soft-heartedness of the present day juries the buggers will probably get acquitted. That's the reason they're included in our little display today. I want them to be known to you, just in case justice fails to be done to them. There'll always be another time.'

Reuben Murdoch was concentrating hard, trying to imprint the faces and mannerisms and antecedents of each successive person upon his mind's eye.

'Fanny Caldicot, step forwards.'

The first female was called from the line-up: a buxom red-haired young woman wearing bedraggled finery, and bearing the cuts, bruises and abrasions of recent savage beatings upon her swollen unhealthily pallid face.

'Walk up and down, girl.' The inspector's tone lost some of its jeering harshness, and a fleeting expression of pity crossed his eyes.

'Fanny's a newcomer to our fair city, gentlemen. She was taken up for soliciting in St Martin's churchyard. While the morning service was in progress, no less, blasphemous sinner that she is. Claims to have been a respectable girl in gentry service until a few weeks since, and I don't doubt her story. You'll note that she's walking very awkwardly, and holding her ribs, but that's only a result of the kicking her ponce gave her a day or so past, and shouldn't prove to be a permanent affliction. She refuses to name him, and as far as I know he's not on our records at the present time. But doubtless that situation will soon be rectified.'

The show-up went on until all the prisoners had taken their turn. Then they were led out from the room.

'Well, will you know them again?' William Hall asked Reuben.

The young man considered for a moment, and then answered truthfully. 'I'll remember one or two of them, sir. But I couldn't swear to it that I'll remember them all.'

The older man nodded, and did not seem dissatisfied. 'Attend as many show-ups as you can, Murdoch. You'll find a lot of the faces will soon become as familiar to you as your own is. The show-up is one of our best tools. Every division holds them, some more regularly than others. Find out what days they are being held on and, if at all possible, attend them.'

The two detectives came out from behind the grilled partition. The portly inspector had stayed behind to speak to them, and William Hall introduced Reuben to him.

'This is Inspector Benjamin Ride, Murdoch. Whenever you want to attend at a show-up in the Third Division you'll make application to him.'

'Murdoch?' the inspector repeated curiously. 'Any relation to Tommy Murdoch?'

'He was my father, sir,' the young man affirmed.

'Was he now?' The fat man nodded. 'He was a bloody good thief-taker. If you can match him then you'll do well.'

Reuben felt a glow of pride at hearing his beloved father praised.

'I'm going to do my best to live up to him, sir,' he replied quietly.

'Anybody you've got a particular interest in today, Bill?' the inspector asked Hall.

The hatchet-features frowned reflectively, then he shook his head. 'No, Ben, nobody in particular today, I just wanted to introduce Murdoch here to you really, and get him used to the way I want things done.'

'Just so, Bill, just so,' the other man agreed. Then he told Reuben, 'I hold a show-up every Monday morning, young man. If you wish to attend then just come along. There's no need to make written application to me, not now that I know you. There's some who reckon the show-up to be a bit of a waste of time. They say that it's not possible to remember all the different faces that you'll see week after week. But speaking for myself I've always thought it a good thing. Because if a man can only recall just one face, it might come in very useful at some time or another.'

'I agree, sir.' Reuben was not being ingratiating when he said this. He truly meant it.

As he and William Hall retraced their steps up past the

spired church of St Martin's and the steep slope of the Bull-ring, threading their way through the thronging crowds and heavy wheeled and hooved traffic, the older man related some anecdotes concerning Benjamin Ride, whom he appeared to like a great deal. Then at the top of the Bullring, opposite the tall stone Doric frontage of the great market hall with its massive arched roof more than five hundred feet in length, William Hall slowed his pace and turned to look into a nearby shop window, gesturing Reuben to do likewise.

'There's two coves standing talking halfway up the steps of the market,' William Hall said in a low voice. 'I'm interested in the one wearing the dark paletot and fawn trousers. He's got a scar running down the left side of his face, from temple to jawbone. Take a peep at him.'

Reuben did as he was bidden, and risked a quick glance backwards. He spotted the two men, and noted the one described, but he was too far distant to distinguish the scar. However, knowing Hall as he did, he was prepared to take the other man's word for its existence.

'I have him,' he informed.

'Right, just mark the bugger well. He calls himself Morgan Hunter. Captain Morgan Hunter. I've had my eye on him for quite a time. Now he'll most probably go into the Swan later on, or the Hen and Chickens. He likes the swells' watering holes.'

Hall regarded Reuben's clothes momentarily. The younger man was clad in a wide skirted jacket and black corduroys with leather knee-gaiters, and a shiny peaked cap on his head.

'You can follow him in there I think, because you look respectable enough in that rig. You'll pass as a well-to-do bumpkin. Note who he talks to and where he goes. Stay with him as long as you can.' With that, William Hall turned from the window and walked away back down towards St Martin's church.

Reuben's heart was thumping with excitement at so un-expectedly receiving his first independent assignment as a detective. Striving to move and act casually he turned and leaned back against the window frame, confident that with so many people and vehicles criss-crossing the roadway between them, his quarry would not notice him, and if he did would only take him for just another lounger, of which there were many dotted around the area watching the crowds go by.

After a while the two men on the steps parted and Morgan Hunter mounted to the top and entered the market hall. Reuben hurried across the road and followed. Inside the great building the stalls were a permanent fixture and arranged in long straight rows running the full length of the hall. On each side of the central passage were newly reconstructed stalls of fruit and flower, plant, vegetable, shrub and root sellers, their wares creating a vividly coloured, wonderfully scented display In other passages were stalls offering hardware, confectionery, toys, domestic pets and many other miscellaneous goods, while on the extreme edges of the hall poulterers, butchers and fishmongers plied their trades.

Morgan Hunter was midway along the central passage, apparently studying the bunches of flowers on a stall. Reuben casually sauntered past him and, some distance further on, stopped to purchase some oranges from another stall. While waiting for his change he glanced sideways.

Although the elegantly dressed Morgan Hunter seemed relaxed and casual, Reuben's instinct told him that the man was tensed and watchful, and he was thankful that the market was crowded with shoppers to shield him from his quarry's seeking eyes. The stallman gave him his change and from the corner of his eye he saw that Morgan Hunter was now strolling in his direction. Reuben walked quickly before him, and went out of the opposite entrance of the hall into Worcester Street.

On this side of the building there were extensive demolitions of slum properties being carried out to clear space for the construction of the New Street railway station, and curious idlers and passers-by had gathered to watch the demolition gangs at their dusty wrecking.

Reuben moved to join one of these groups of onlookers and waited for his man to appear from the entrance of the market hall, praying that Morgan Hunter had not doubled back on his own tracks. For several moments Reuben remained watching surreptitiously, his anxiety rising fast, and then he breathed a sigh of relief as the elegant figure in tall hat, dark paletot and fawn trousers came from the entrance and into the street.

Again some inner instinct caused Reuben to remain standing where he was as Morgan Hunter turned south and walked down the slope and turned left into Bell Street along the side of the market hall as if to walk back towards the Bullring.

The seconds ticked by and Morgan Hunter did not reappear, but Reuben repeated inwardly over and over again, 'Trust to your instinct! Trust to your instinct! Trust to your instinct!'

Then the dark coat and fawn trousers reappeared around the corner of the hall, and the young man crowed inwardly with delight and satisfaction that he had recognised the ploy of the other man.

'You really are a fly cove, ain't you, Hunter?' he thought with a tinge of admiration. 'If I'd followed you close, then you would have had me spotted by now.'

This time, when Morgan Hunter walked up the slope towards the corner of New Street Reuben followed unobtrusively behind him. The elegant figure sauntered slowly along the full length of the bustling thoroughfare to its western termination where five roads met at the Victoria Square, dominated by its magnificent centrepiece, the massive Grecian templed structure of the new town hall. It was unfinished still, and lacking several of its mighty pilasters and columns, but there were swarms of workmen upon scaffolding making ready the various capitals, cornices and architraves necessary for the completion of the task.

Morgan Hunter came to a standstill outside the new post office building, and stopped to gaze up at the town hall. Reuben Murdoch walked some distance in an opposite direction further away from the man, and then waited, concealed in a shop doorway, and watched.

'Young man, will you kindly allow me to pass?' An elderly gentleman came from the interior of the shop behind Reuben.

'I beg your pardon, sir.' Reuben politely touched his hand to the peak of his cap and stepped out from the shop entrance to give the old man passage.

The exchange took barely seconds, but when Reuben looked across at the post office, Morgan Hunter had disappeared.

'Goddamn and blast it!' Reuben swore beneath his breath,

and again stepped out from the shop entrance, his head turning rapidly to scan the entire area. Among the numerous pedestrians he could catch no glimpse of dark coat and fawn trousers.

He hurried towards the post office, dodging past carriages and waggons and flies and drays, threading between slower walking men and women, brushing off the importuning hands of ragged street urchins begging him for pence. Hidden under one of the colonnaded arches that formed the ground floor façade of the town hall Morgan Hunter watched the young man's frantic progress, and smiled grimly to himself.

Reuben Murdoch reached the post office and halted, again staring wildly about him. Then he hurried on and in a few moments was lost to view among the traffic and pedestrians. Morgan Hunter grinned and turned away to walk slowly around to the other end of the town hall.

There were four people waiting for him there: the Flemings, Grainne Shonley and Arthur Taunton.

The two women were wearing fashionable crinolines with multi-layered flounces, and veiled, flower-decorated bonnets with elegant laced parasols opened upon their shoulders. Steven Fleming was equally elegant in his clothing, top-hatted and tail-coated. The tall slender Arthur Taunton was wearing clerical garb, with black knee-breeches and stockings, wide-skirted black frockcoat, white stock and cravat and a wide-brimmed, low-crowned beaver hat on his long flowing hair. He wore small, round, gold-rimmed spectacles and carried a black leather-bound Bible in his black-gloved hands.

'You're a bit late, Captain,' Steven Fleming observed. 'I was beginning to wonder if anything might have happened.'

'There was a new young Jack trying to tail me,' Morgan Hunter grinned. 'And he was fly with it, for a green 'un. I took my time about slipping him because I wanted to get a good look at him.'

'How did he get on to you?' Steven Fleming's thin face was concerned.

'William Hall marked me outside of the market. But what he didn't realise was that I'd got him and his new bloodhound marked while they were still coming up the Bullring.'

'What's he look like, this new Jack?' Fleming asked, and

Morgan Hunter gave them a brief description of Reuben Murdoch.

' . . . So, watch out for flash bumpkins today!' He finished with a grin. 'They might be bleedin' new Jacks.'

He looked at Grainne. 'And how are you feeling, my dear? Excited?'

Grainne was feeling differing types and shades of emotion: reluctance to actually embark on her new career and begin to steal, apprehension, tension and, she was forced to admit, a tingling of anticipatory excitement.

She forced a smile. 'I'm a bit nervous,' she admitted.

'That's all to the good, honey,' Morgan Hunter chuckled. 'Being nervous keeps you alert, and your blood high. It stops you becoming sluggish and careless. We're all nervous before we go out on a new lay, arn't we?' He appealed to the others for confirmation, which they readily gave.

'You'll be all jack a dandy when the work starts, Grainne, you'll see.'

He looked about him, and checked his gold watch. 'It's time we were getting on. We'll split here. I'll meet you back at the house tonight.'

With that the party separated, Arthur Taunton and Morgan Hunter moving away in different directions and, after a moment or two, Steven Fleming and the two women following as a group.

Bingley House was not far distant from Victoria Square. A large open-plan building, it was now the site of a 'Grand Exhibition of Trades', and it had recently been confirmed that the Prince Consort himself was to honour the exhibition with his august presence at some time in the near future.

The big hall with its iron girdered roof was crammed with the stands displaying the latest engineering marvels and products of the 'City of a Thousand Trades', and swarms of eager sightseers came from all parts of the British Isles, and indeed the world, to view the wonders of this modern age. The prospects of rich pickings also brought swarms of predators to Bingley House and its immediate environs, and the city police were hard pressed to control the crowds and to protect them.

Grainne was at first made confused and disoriented by the deafening clamour and the stifling proximity of so many people, and she felt the desperate need to fight her way clear of the crush and noise, and seek clear space around her. But then she realised that this seething human sea was her protection and she was able to merge into it and draw comfort from its concealment.

Beneath the flounces of her crinolined skirts were several cunningly hidden pockets, so artfully constructed that even if she were searched it would be difficult for the seeking fingers to find whatever they might contain in their innermost recesses.

Now, arm in arm with Bridie, she edged slowly through the crowds, Steven Fleming behind them. Arthur Taunton was moving through the crowds with an uncanny ease, and seeing him Grainne wondered fancifully if he might be a wraith, so smoothly did he slip through seemingly impenetrable barriers of flesh and bone.

After about half an hour of crawling progress Arthur Taunton brushed against Grainne's side. She felt something small and round pushed into her free hand, and automatically she slipped the object into one of her secret pockets. She felt herself blushing furiously, and was guiltily certain that everyone around her knew what had just taken place.

During the next hour the sequence was repeated several times, and Grainne found that she was able to stifle the sensation of guilty awareness more easily with each reoccurrence.

As they were passing a jewellery stand, Bridie squeezed her arm hard, and when Grainne looked at her, gave a slight nod of her bonneted head, indicating a well-dressed man standing some yards from them who wore a profusion of heavy gold chains across the front of his waistcoat. Standing at the man's side with his back to him was Arthur Taunton.

Bridie put her head close to Grainne's and whispered. 'I'm going to bump you into that flat. You be cokum now. Keep looking over there.'

Grainne's throat seemed to tighten, and her heart pounded. Striving to appear interested in the jewellery stand she allowed Bridie to pull her through the crowd while she kept her head turned towards the stand. Then Bridie pushed her hard and sideways and Grainne collided heavily with the gold-chained man.

'Damn me, take care will you!' the man exclaimed angrily.

'I do beg your pardon, sir. I wasn't looking,' Grainne flustered as Bridie pulled her on through the crowd.

The next instant Arthur Taunton appeared before her, crushing against her crinoline.

'Pray excuse me, ma'm.' He threw his arms forwards to steady himself and his hands disappeared momentarily into the flounces of her voluminous skirts.

Grainne sensed rather than felt the heavy metal chains and the objects attached to them sliding down into the recesses of the pockets.

'I've been robbed! Blast my eyes, I've been robbed!'

A voice bellowed from behind them, and an instant commotion erupted.

Steven Fleming bent his head close to the two women and hissed, 'That's it, girls. Time to go home now, I think. Move smooth and steady towards the exit gate. Nice and easy does it. Nice and easy now.'

The group went out through the Broad Street entrance of the hall, and walked sedately towards Victoria Square.

'You've done well, Grainne,' Steven Fleming congratulated, and sought confirmation from his wife. 'Didn't she, Bridie?'

Bridie Fleming readily gave that confirmation. 'I'll say she did. She's a diamond!'

Grainne's thoughts and emotions were a confusing mélange. One moment assailed by troubled conscience that she was now a thief, the next instant elated by the ease with which it had all passed. Relief that it was over, mingled with apprehensive awareness that it would soon happen again. The praises of her companions warmed her, and at the same time she felt guilty that she should be praised for having preyed upon people who had never done her any harm. But one emotion ran like a constant thread through all others, and that was a throbbing thrill of excitement.

'I could become addicted to this,' she suddenly thought with a sense of dread. 'I really could become addicted.'

Several streets away from the trio Reuben Murdoch at last accepted defeat in his frantic search for Morgan Hunter, and glumly trudged towards the police station in Crooked Lane.

When he arrived there he reported to William Hall, and admitted glumly, 'I lost him, sir. He gave me the slip at the Victoria Square.'

The older man showed no emotion, merely nodded, and replied, 'He's a fly cove. You'll just needs be flyer than him next time.'

'What's known about him, sir?' Reuben felt an intense interest in Hunter. The man had become his first personal adversary as a detective, and his first defeat also.

'Not a lot.' William Hall grinned mirthlessly. 'Not that would stand up in court as evidence, anyway. But I've heard a deal of rumour concerning him. He's purported to be a master cracksman, and a swell mobsman. He moves about the country a lot, and has contact with rogues wherever he is. Last time I spotted the bugger in this city was about three years past, and at that time there was a couple of big robberies took place. Safes were cracked and a lot of money went missing. I reckoned then that it was Morgan Hunter who'd done the business, but I couldn't get information or proof enough to nail the bugger. He's artful, and he's cool and daring. But we'll have him one day.'

'That man he was talking to at the market?' Reuben suggested reflectively. 'Is he known? And if he is, couldn't we pull him in for questioning about what Hunter's doing back here?'

William Hall chuckled harshly. 'The man Hunter was with at the market is Edward Whitfield. He's a respected and influential councillor, and a member of the watch committee, and one of the biggest rogues unhung in this bloody city. He owns a jewellery business up by St Paul's. I've known for years that he's a fence, but proving it in court is a different kettle of fish altogether. I'd like nothing better than to pull Whitfield in for questioning, but can you imagine the stink that he'd be able to raise if I ever did so?'

He paused, shaking his head in grudging admiration.

'No, that crafty bastard is too well shielded for me to have him.' He grinned at the younger man. 'But that's not to say that some day you might not be able to have him, my boy. Off you go now, and have a wander.' He winked broadly. 'You might just run into our friend, Captain Hunter, again.'

A mood of grim determination came over Reuben Murdoch as he went back out into the city streets, vowing to himself, 'If I ever do run into you again, Hunter, you'll not shake me so easily. I'll swear to that.'

Chapter Thirty

A week following Reuben Murdoch's introduction to the detective force, Chief Superintendent Richard A. Stephens left the public office in Moor Street after a most unpleasant afternoon meeting with certain influential members of the watch committee, the body which controlled the city police force. He mounted his horse and trotted through the streets to the headquarters of the Second Divison in Sandpits. As soon as he arrived there he summoned the Second Division commander, Inspector Edgar Leggat, into the office.

The fat face of the chief superintendent was puce with temper, and as soon as the other man entered the room he shouted, 'What the devil's going on at Bingley House, Edgar?'

Leggat, grey-haired and distinguished looking, became instantly wary.

'I don't know that anything's going on, sir.'

'Oh, don't you now? Well it don't surprise me to hear that you don't know what's going on there. So I'll tell you, shall I?' The fat man was scathing. 'I've just come from an emergency session of the watch committee. Alderman Bolton was there, and Alderman Hutton, and Aldermen Muntz, Stone and Thornton besides.' His tone became heavily sarcastic. 'Now perhaps you might not know either that they're all men of great influence in this city, manufacturers and men of business. It's mainly thanks to them that the present exhibition is being held at Bingley House. An exhibition that you, by virtue of Bingley House being in your divisional area, are supposed to be policing.'

231

Surly resentment crossed Leggat's aquiline features. 'And so I am policing it, sir. I've had a sergeant and three constables there every day.'

'This sergeant, and the constables, where did you recruit them from, Edgar? A bloody asylum for the blind?' Stephens roared. 'There's been pockets picked in that exhibition every day, and yesterday one of those pockets belonged to a personal friend and important business associate of Alderman Bolton.'

'There's bound to be gonophs where there are crowds the size that there's been at Bingley House. I haven't got the man-power to watch every single visitor there, have I?' Leggat was now openly resentful. 'I've asked the watch committee to increase my division's strength time and time again, and they keep telling me that the city can't afford more policemen. I do the best I can with what men I've got, sir. I can do no more.'

The chief superintendent's mood abruptly metamorphosed to weary resignation. 'I know, Edgar. I know,' he breathed out gustily, and he recalled the previous year's statistics. 'Population almost a quarter of a million. 837 public houses. 834 beer houses. During the year, 7,947 persons were arrested for offences, of which 943 were committed for indictable offences. There were 798 robberies by day, and 683 by night, 1,567 premises were found to be insecure by the police, and there were 148 fires at which policemen attended to aid the fire brigades. During the year there were an average of 102 constables filling the day beats, and 338 on night duty from 9 o'clock p.m. to 6 o'clock a.m., together with a small horse patrol during the early evening and night.

'Anyway, Edgar, what do you think to these pickpockets at Bingley House? They've got to be swell mobsmen, haven't they? The doorkeepers don't allow no roughs and scruffs in.'

Leggat was quick to agree. 'There could be more than one gang operating, sir. But I would think that they're outsiders. Our local gonophs will know that we've got men patrolling the hall, so I shouldn't think they'd risk themselves inside the place. They can be trapped too easily if they're discovered and the beef is raised against them.'

Stephens concurred with that statement, and then said, 'I'm going to go and see Billy Hall. He can loan you a couple of his Jacks for a day or so. If they can lay just one gonoph by the heels then it might serve to shut the damned watch committee up.'

'Very well, sir. And I'll put one of my sub-inspectors and another two extra constables in there from tomorrow morning.'

Good man.' The chief superintendent's temper was now much improved, and he was humming happily to himself as he made his way towards the Crooked Lane station.

Chapter Thirty-one

The gold chains, watches and jewellery glittered against the dark green of the velvet table-mantle, and Morgan Hunter nodded in satisfaction as his practised eyes estimated their worth. There were two pocket books among the haul, and the contents of these yielded several high value banknotes, as well as sovereigns and half-sovereigns.

Morgan Hunter glanced at the others seated around the table, their faces bathed in the pale glow of the hanging oil lamp, and he smiled inwardly with contempt to see the lust in their expressions as they gazed down at the heaped wealth.

'They're easy bedazzled, for all their bloody flyness,' he thought. Then his attention centred on Grainne Shonley's thin beautiful face, and he saw the awe in her green eyes, and his feelings of contempt softened into sympathy.

'Poor little cow has never seen anything like this in her life. She's well hooked.'

Grainne was indeed feeling somewhat awed by what she could see. In barely a week the gang had amassed an amount which would take her a lifetime to earn by honest labour.

'A very good pickings, mates,' Hunter observed aloud, and a murmur of agreement went around the table.

'When do we divvy up?' Arthur Taunton wanted to know. As the actual tooler he would receive a larger share than his accomplices, in recognition of his skills.

'I'll fence these yacks and chains tomorrow.' Hunter tapped his fingers on the pocket-watches, and then the jewellery. 'And the brights at the same time. The sovs we can split now.' He quickly divided the coins into the due shares.

Then he sorted through the bank notes. 'These stiffs are a bit too long-tailed to risk changing here in Brummagem. We'd do better to get rid of them down in the Smoke. Mind you, we could get a bloody good deal up here if we were to use these to buy shoful.'

He noted Grainne's puzzlement, and chuckled, telling Bridie, 'You'd best explain my meaning to Grainne. She's looking a bit confused by it all.'

There was a general laugh, and Bridie explained, 'He means that the banknotes are too high-value to risk changing them here, Grainne. There'll be notices being put out already about them, and people will be keeping an eye peeled for them. But we could use them to buy snide money. You know, false banknotes. Brummagem flimsy is reckoned the best quality stuff in the whole of the country.'

Although Morgan Hunter was the acknowledged leader of the gang, a swell mob was peculiarly interdependent and democratic, and so each member was ready to voice an opinion, and could expect that opinion to be given due consideration by the other members.

'What's the total?' Bridie asked.

'Five hundred and twenty pounds,' Morgan Hunter told her. 'But there's two two-hundred notes drawn on the Clydesdale, so we'll only get about a third face value for them, and the usual two thirds for the rest.'

'What's the rate for snide at present?' Arthur Taunton wanted to know.

'In top quality finnys, I reckon I can get two thousand's worth.'

'That's two thousand pounds value in counterfeit five pound notes,' Bridie whispered to Grainne.

Morgan Hunter allowed them a short while to think about it, and then pressed, 'What shall it be then? Snide or straight change?'

'Why don't we wait and see what we get tomorrow?' Steven Fleming suggested. 'If we get lucky we can have straight and snide both.'

Arthur Taunton nodded. 'That's fair enough.'

Morgan Hunter raised his eyebrows in silent query at the two women, and when they both nodded, stated, 'So be it.'

He replaced the banknotes into one of the pocket books, and swept the watches, chains and jewellery into a soft-cloth pouch.

'I think that we should do the market hall tomorrow, and then call it a day.' He was aware of their surprised reaction to this suggestion. 'Look, you've done the exhibition on two separate days now, plus the main shops, and both St Martin's and St Phillip's churchyards. I reckon it's time to split up now for a while, each go our own ways for a bit.'

'But the exhibition is the best pickings, Captain,' Arthur Taunton objected. 'We didn't do any good anywhere else this time, did we? One bloody cheap ticker in St Martin's, and a bit of shoddy from the shops. It arn't going to be any better in the market hall the way things are looking. I think we should stay where our luck is, and that's the exhibition.'

Both of the Flemings voiced their support for the tooler.

'I'm not happy about it,' Morgan Hunter persisted. 'The crushers must be putting extra men in there by now, after the amounts we've lifted. And there's got to be others working the hall as well as us. I think we're chancing our arms too much if we go back there again.'

'The crushers up here ain't downy enough to mark our card. And I arn't recognised any swell mobsmen yet, so if there are others working Bingley House they'll be gonophs and clyfakers only fit for buzzing billys.'

Arthur Taunton spoke with the fine scorn of a master-craftsman when he voiced his contempt for the petty thieves and unskilled pickpockets capable only of stealing handkerchiefs.

'Arthur's right, Captain,' Steven Fleming chimed in support. 'Bingley House is our best lay.'

Morgan Hunter looked keenly at the determined faces around him and realised that he would have to give way in the interests of any future combinations with his present associates.

'All right then, so be it,' he agreed with obvious reluctance. 'But if I spot anything the least bit flummut looking, then we scarper double quick.'

'That's agreed, Captain,' Steven Fleming assured him, and with that he had to rest content.

When the gathering was splitting up to go to their separate

beds, Morgan Hunter asked Grainne, 'Can you stay for a while, Grainne? I'd like to talk with you.'

Once they were alone he asked her, 'What do you intend doing after tomorrow, Grainne?'

She shook her glossy head. 'I don't know, Captain. I didn't realise that we were all going to part company so soon.'

'It's usual practice, Grainne,' he explained. 'We join together for a particular lay, and then we split up again until the next lay comes along. It makes it harder for the crushers when we keep our distances.'

He fell silent, as if he were thinking hard about something, and then almost diffidently, he told her, 'There's no need for you and I to part company though, my dear. We can stay together.'

She stared at him doubtfully, then said bluntly, 'You mean live together as man and wife, don't you?'

He nodded gravely. 'I'd treat you well, Grainne, and you would lack for nothing. I can show you a world that contains many pleasures and interests to entertain you. We could be happy together, my dear. I know that for a fact.'

Grainne did not make any immediate reply. Instead she thought hard about his offer. The prospect of once again being alone and friendless was not an appealing one, and, at this time in her life, Grainne badly needed the warmth of human companionship and friendship. But she was hesitant about entering such an intimate relationship as this one being offered to her. With a ruthless self-honesty she inwardly accepted that she was hungry for a man's loving. She was a woman with strong sexual needs, and her self-imposed celibacy at times became almost unbearable. She found Morgan Hunter physically attractive, and his strong, self-assured masculinity sexually exciting. She did not love him in any romantic sense, but she enjoyed his company and liked him a lot.

Suddenly she became angry at her own indecisiveness, and castigated herself furiously. 'Jasus Christ, girl! Why are you behaving like a silly young virgin maid? God knows you've given yourself to men other than your husband, if only in order to survive. You've accepted that Con is dead to you, and you've come to terms with that, and with your grief over losing him. This man offers you a chance to gain some happiness and pleasure. You'd enjoy sleeping with him.' A sudden doubt clamoured: 'But he's a criminal! A dangerous criminal! He could be capable of doing anything.'

Another inner voice countered. 'And what are you, if not a criminal yourself now, Grainne? You're as bad as he is, so stop being so hypocritical. And what if he is dangerous? Why can't you admit that you find him attractive? You've always admired reckless, rebellious men who dare to live life on their own terms, and are not afraid of risking their liberties and lives in order to do so.'

While the furious debate raged within her, Morgan Hunter waited silently. A hunger to possess this beautiful woman for his own had intensified during these last days. If he was capable of love, then that was what he felt for Grainne Shonley. He saw in her a fit mate for himself. A mate who possessed in full measure his own reckless courage. A mate who like him stubbornly refused to let life's tragedies beat her down and destroy her spirit. A mate who was stamped in her own individual mould, a mould that he could respect and admire wholeheartedly.

At last she sighed heavily, and regarded him with troubled eyes. 'I thank you for your offer, Captain. Can you give me a little more time to decide upon it?'

He smiled, and nodded. 'Take whatever time is needed, my dear. I would not have you come to me unless you are full certain that that is what you want.'

Chapter Thirty-two

Reuben Murdoch and Albert Gittings were the two detectives assigned to Bingley House and as they made their way there in mid-morning Albert Gittings advised Reuben, 'Now we're looking for swell mobsmen. So they'll be chaps who are fly. The only chance of actually catching one in the act is to be the flat ourselves.'

Both men were wearing tail-coats, top hats, and fancy waistcoats, with checked trousers and highly polished boots.

'You'd best be the flat, Reuben, just in case somebody might recognise my face. Come, let's get out of the way and get you looking the part.'

He led Reuben down a narrow alley and into a covered entry. There he produced a selection of gold chains, watches and jewellery from his pockets, and a thickly stuffed pocketbook. He laughed at his companion's shocked expression, and explained.

'Don't worry, this is all snide stuff. Brass and glass and folded paper.'

Reuben took the various articles and arranged them about his person. Albert Gittings examined him critically, and after making a minor adjustment or two, declared himself satisfied. 'You'll do, my buck. Any gonoph will see you as a prime flat, just ripe for plucking. You go on ahead now, and remember, you don't know me.'

Bingley House was again crowded, and Reuben wandered slowly around the various exhibits with Albert Gittings closely shadowing him. The young man felt tense and excited, but as the hours passed and nothing occurred his excitement lessened and his attention began to be diverted from the main objective. He found himself noticing the women and girls that were parading around the hall with their menfolk.

One young woman in particular attracted his attention. She was wearing a flowered bonnet, and a costly satin gown, the shimmering colours of the materials setting off her own pale complexion and startlingly green eyes, which coupled with her glossy raven ringlets created a vision of exceptional beauty.

Reuben Murdoch had a romantic streak in his nature, and when he looked at this young woman all his longings for love and romance quickened. She was in company with a well-dressed man and woman, who were older than she, and who he thought might possibly be her parents.

Reuben moved slowly through the crowds towards her. A tall slender-bodied parson in a flat-crowned, broad-brimmed hat momentarily blocked Reuben's view of the beautiful girl and then moved away from in front of her and Reuben quite unexpectedly caught her eye. He smiled, and he saw her pale complexion flush, and she dropped her head as though overcome by shyness. He was charmed by her reaction, and experienced a powerful compulsion to speak to her. He started to move more quickly towards her, his agile mind seeking for some means of obtaining an introduction. Although a homely-featured, clumsy-bodied young man, Reuben had charm and confidence and was at ease in the company of women.

Then the next moment a hard powerful body interposed itself between Reuben and the young woman, and a booted foot came crushing down upon his.

'Oh I do beg your pardon, sir. Pray forgive my clumsiness.'

Reuben's jaw momentarily dropped as he found himself looking into the scarred face of Morgan Hunter.

Again the man apologised profusely. 'Do excuse me, sir, I beg of you. I was so engrossed in the exhibit there that I didn't look to see where I was going.'

Albert Gittings materialised at Reuben's shoulder, and Morgan Hunter's hard hazel eyes gleamed as if with triumph as they flicked from one to the other of the policemen.

'I'll bid you a good day, sir.' He lifted his top hat politely, and then moved away into the crowd.

Reuben's eyes flickered wildly in all directions, seeking the beautiful young woman in the glowing satin gown, and trying at the same time to keep Morgan Hunter in sight.

Albert Gittings scowled disgustedly. 'I moved too quick there. I thought we'd hooked one.'

Reuben also scowled with disgust. He had lost Morgan Hunter and the beautiful young woman.

Then, from close at hand a woman wailed. 'My watch! My watch has gone! Someone has stolen my watch!'

Her cry triggered off other angry shouts, as almost simultaneously two men close by the woman discovered that they also had been robbed.

'God rot my bloody eyes!' Gitting cursed angrily. 'We've missed the bastards all right.'

Suddenly Reuben instinctively knew that Morgan Hunter had somehow or other been involved in the thefts. 'He was the stall!' he uttered aloud, and Albert Gittings questioned sharply, 'What's that you're saying?'

Reuben stared at him, and repeated, 'He was the stall for them. Morgan Hunter, that scar-faced cove who just trod on me. He was the stall. He must have thought I was heading for their tooler, and so he stalled me.'

Albert Gittings' nondescript features mirrored his doubt. 'I don't know this Morgan Hunter.'

'Billy Hall knows him.' Reuben was beginning to feel angry with himself. 'I'd got the fly bastard in front of me, and I was too bloody slow-witted to grab hold of him.'

The other detective shrugged dismissively. 'What could you hold him on anyway? If he was the stall he'd not be carrying anything on him, would he? And you can't arrest a man for accidentally bumping into you.'

'Come on, let's look for him,' Reuben urged eagerly, but the older man shook his head.

'Don't waste your time or your boot-leather, my buck. If that cove was one of the swell mob, then he's well gone by now, as the rest of them will be. We might as well bugger off ourselves, for all the good that we'll do here now. They've scarpered, my buck, and that's all there is to it.'

Reuben Murdoch knew that the other man was right, but anger and self-disgust continued to burn inside him.

'That's twice you've bested me, Hunter. You must think

I'm a real mawkin. But my turn will come. I'll take my oath to that. My turn will come.'

His chagrin persisted for some considerable time, but then became increasingly overlaid by the memory of the beautiful green-eyed girl, and he wondered where she had disappeared to so quickly.

'I'd love to see you again,' he told the vivid image of the girl in his mind. 'And perhaps I will. God, I hope so.'

Two hours later, in the drawing room of the select villa on the Pershore Turnpike Road a heated exchange was taking place.

'I told you that the crushers would be keeping close watch, didn't I?' Morgan Hunter stated angrily to his gang. 'That new Jack of Billy Hall's would have had you, Steven, if I hadn't stalled him.'

'Well I never spotted any Jack there,' Steven Fleming argued sullenly. 'Are you sure that he'd marked us?'

'Of course I'm bloody sure. Why else should I stall him?' Morgan Hunter retorted angrily. 'He was heading straight for you. I'd been watching him. He couldn't take his bloody peepers from you. And then, just after Arthur passed Grainne that dollymop's ticker, he headed straight for you. I reckon he'd twigged that there'd been a pass-over made, even though he hadn't marked Arthur. He's a fly bastard that new Jack is, without a doubt, for all he looks like a thick-skulled wapstraw.'

'Well, I never saw him, or that other Jack you reckon was with him,' Steven Fleming persisted doggedly.

Grainne sat silently listening as the men continued to argue and dispute. The news that the young man who had stared at her with such admiration was a detective filled her with trepidation, but she did not believe that he had suspected her of being a thief. Grainne was used to men staring admiringly or lustfully at her, and during the brief moments of eye contact she had seen nothing of suspicion in the young man's expression, only simple admiration and longing.

Sadness suddenly touched her as she realised that now she could no longer accept any man's look as being simple curiosity or admiration. Now she must regard every glance as being one of suspicion, and be forever on her guard.

'It's been a poor day's work. We ought to have stayed on

longer,' Steven Fleming grumbled at the meagre display. A small woman's watch, a cheap man's watch, and a pair of tawdry seals.

Morgan Hunter scowled at the other man. 'Stayed on longer?' he challenged. 'Stayed after the nemmo had screamed she'd been done? You must have a powerful wish to be lagged, Steven, to want to risk staying on after that.' He paused as if considering something, and then told them, 'I say it's time we divvied out and split up. This lay's gone sour.'

'It's all right for you,' Fleming accused. 'You've got plenty o' rhino stowed away. But me and Bridie went to a lot of expense to set this place up, and we looked to make a lot more profit this trip than we've made so far. We haven't got enough rhino to finish with the lay yet. What say you Arthur, Grainne?'

Arthur Taunton, lying on the chaise longue, lifted one hand in languid agreement. But Grainne could only shrug uncertainly.

Morgan Hunter's eyes were hard and his mouth a thin angry line. 'Come on, Steven, spit it out. Let me hear what you've got in mind.'

The thin features worked unhappily and then Fleming blurted, 'Me and Bridie and Arthur are going to stay on a bit longer here, Captain. We reckon there's still good pickings to be made. Don't forget that Macready's coming to play at the Theatre Royal shortly, and Prince Albert's coming up to the exhibition. There'll be rich pickings in both places when that happens. What we reckon is to take things easy until then. Just do sufficient to pay our expenses, and then after we do the business at the Theatre Royal and Prince Albert's visit, why then it'll be time to split.'

He waited for Bridie and Taunton to express their concurrence, and then continued. 'What you and Grainne do is down to yourselves, Captain. Naturally we'd like you both to stay with us. But if you feel that you can't, then there's no hard feelings on our side. We can always work together in the future, can't we?'

'Well, Grainne?' Hunter asked her. 'What do you want to do? Stay here with them, or come away with me?'

Now that the moment for decision had arrived, Grainne

found it easy to make. 'I'm not yet ready to take another man to stand as husband to me, Captain,' she told him softly, but without any hesitancy. 'I think it best that I stay with Steven and Bridie for a time. I know that I owe you a great deal. Perhaps more than I can ever repay. Without your help I'd have been transported. But if I was to live with you as your wife, in the end I would not be able to give you all that you deserve. I'm not able to do that as yet.'

To his credit, Morgan Hunter accepted her rejection of him with good grace. 'That's fair enough, Grainne, and I wish you well. As I do all of you. I'm going to split, because I think that this lay has gone sour. I've a bad feeling about it since that Jack marked you. Still, I'll not argue with custom. We're all free agents in our trade. I'll make the arrangements to get the stuff fenced, and we'll divvy up. I take it you'll be wanting the straight change for the stiffs now, and not any snide finnys.'

They all signified their agreement.

'Right then, I'll be seeing you in a few days,' he told them, and taking his hat and gloves went from the room.

In William Hall's office Reuben Murdoch was expressing his conviction that Morgan Hunter had acted as the swell mob's stall.

'You've no proof of this, have you Murdoch?' the hatchet-featured inspector objected. 'And you've admitted yourself that you hadn't marked the tooler. A stall would only intervene if you were close to grabbing his tooler or one of the stickmen.'

'One of the stickmen! One of the stickmen!' The sentence was like an explosion of revelation in Reuben Murdoch's brain, and the sequence of events flashed vividly through his mind's eye. He saw again the beautiful green-eyed girl, saw the tall slender-bodied clergyman pass in front of her, saw her eyes meet his own, saw her flush and drop her head as though overcome with shyness, saw himself start towards her, and then felt the collision of Morgan Hunter's body interposing between himself and the green-eyed girl. Then he saw the empty space where she and her companions had been, and heard once more the woman wailing that she had been robbed.

'The green-eyed girl was the stickman,' he exclaimed aloud.

'And the parson was the bloody tooler. That's what they were: the stickman and tooler. And Hunter was their stall!'

William Hall stared curiously at the younger man. 'What are you gabbling about, Murdoch?'

Reuben Murdoch's eyes were alight with excitement. 'The swell mob who've been working Bingley House, sir. I know who they are now. Not their names, but I know their faces. There's Morgan Hunter himself, and then there's the tooler, he's tall and slender built, and dresses like a parson. And the stickmen are two women and another man.'

William Hall pushed paper, pen and ink towards Reuben.

'Write it all down. Descriptions of all of them,' he ordered sharply. 'Get it down now while it's fresh in your memory.'

Reuben did as instructed and wrote out as detailed a description of each of his suspects as he could. William Hall scanned the paper, and nodded. 'Not bad, my boy. Not bad at all.' He pursed his lips and regarded the young man keenly.

'I'll tell you what's in my mind, Murdoch. I'm considering whether or no to give you a free hand on this.'

Reuben's heart thudded with excited anticipation, but he kept silent.

After a while William Hall grinned and nodded. 'You concentrate on this gang, Reuben. See if you can put the salt on their tails.'

The young man felt like crowing aloud with exultation, but instead he only answered quietly, 'I'll do that, sir. You may rely on it.'

'How are you intending to go about it?' Hall asked interestedly.

Reuben Murdoch's agile brain was already formulating a plan of action. 'Well, sir, there's not much point in my wandering about hoping to catch sight of them. That's leaving a deal too much to chance,' he spoke his thoughts aloud.

'So?' the older man pressed.

'So,' the younger man's broad red face wore a grin. 'So, sir, I'd appreciate any information you can give me concerning Mr Edward Whitfield. Such as his business address and where his house is?'

William Hall nodded appreciatively. 'I like it, Murdoch. I like it. You're thinking like a real artful Jack. I like it.'

'And there's one thing more I'd like to ask for, sir.' Reuben was emboldened by his superior's attitude. 'Can I call on Albert Gittings to help me keep Whitfield under observation?'

'All right,' Hall agreed. 'There's one thing I want to caution you about, though. If, as you hope, Morgan Hunter contacts Whitfield to fence his stuff, and then Hunter leads you to the rest of his gang, don't go in like a bull at a gate. Be patient and make sure you've got everybody bottled nicely. And then don't try to make the collar until you've got enough help to take them all.' He winked broadly. 'Always be ready to share the glory of a good collar, young man. It can pay dividends in the long run.'

'Very good, sir,' Reuben Murdoch agreed readily, and added with heartfelt feeling, 'I just hope I'm watching the right man. Or I'll end up by looking to be a real mawkin.'

Hall shrugged. 'What other leads have you got to Hunter? It's no use just wandering around hoping you'll bump into one or the other of them you suspect, is it? At least we know for certain that Hunter and Whitfield are known to each other. And we know that Hunter's got stuff to fence. It's well worth a try in my opinion, and if it comes off, why then you'll be giving me the last laugh over Andrew Munro, by proving to him that I was right in believing you to have the makings of a good Jack.'

He drew pen, paper and ink towards him and quickly scribbled some words, then handed the sheet of paper to the younger man.

'Here's Whitfield's address, and the names of his immediate family.'

He jerked his head in dismissal. 'Get off now, and start watching the bugger.'

Chapter Thirty-three

The task of keeping Edward Whitfield under observation was made much easier by virtue of him living over his business premises, in a street of tall buildings facing the cemetery of St Michael's church, in the jewellery quarter of the city. Whitfield's business was the retailing of job lots of shoddy imitation jewellery, and his office fronted the small warehouse in which he kept his stock in trade.

During the day the cemetery was the scene of funeral processions and interments, and the two detectives found it easy to mingle with the sombrely clad mourners, and hide among the parties of bannermen, mutes, bearers, and all the other assorted participants in the almost continuous succession of funerals. The coming of nightfall found one or other of them secreted among the profusion of gravestones and tombs.

They had also enlisted the aid of the local beat constables, and through these men had been enabled to find convenient stabling for the horse they had borrowed from the mounted patrol, in case their quarry should be mounted and thus be able to move faster than they could follow on foot.

Considering his various duties as councillor and watch committee man Edward Whitfield left his premises only rarely and, when he did so, Reuben found him very easy to tail. But the days followed one another with a dull monotony, and the long cold nights spent shivering among the graves began to take toll of the two men. Lack of sleep sapped their energies and powers of concentration. But both were tenacious and determined hunters, and were resolved to see the job through to a successful conclusion, even though there were many times

247

during the cold night watches when, shivering and bleary-eyed, Reuben Murdoch would begin to seriously question his choice of a career. But even as he questioned he knew that there could now never be any other work that he could be happy in – he was born to be a thief-taker.

Then early one afternoon the patience of the two detectives was rewarded as the elegantly dressed Morgan Hunter sauntered casually up to the front door of Edward Whitfield's premises.

Chapter Thirty-four

The 'divvy up' had been made and Grainne stared down at more than twenty pounds in gold and silver coins heaped on the table before her: her share after all expenses had been deducted for clothing, food, lodgings, an amount that would have taken her more than two, possibly three years to earn as a housemaid.

Bridie saw Grainne's impressed expression and laughed gaily. 'It beats slaving your guts out skivvying for a living, don't it, honey?'

Steven Fleming and Arthur Taunton were not so impressed with their shares however.

'This won't last long, will it?' the tooler grumbled, and Steven Fleming echoed him.

'That bastard Whitfield gets tighter by the fuckin' day. I don't know why you deal with the bastard, Captain.'

Morgan Hunter frowned irritably. 'Because he can be trusted to keep his mouth shut, and not blab his business when he's got drink in him. And his prices are no worse than any other bloody fence. I told you that we'd only get a third on the Clydesdale stiffs, and none of you wanted to buy snide, did you? So it's no use you moaning at me.'

'Oh, shut your arguing, will you?' Bridie snapped sharply. 'We've enough to see us through this week and longer. I fancy a night out on the spree. It'll do us all good. We've been cooped up in here for too long. It's making us all dull and doleful. What d'you say, Grainne? Shall we have a night out?'

Grainne was still troubled by how she had acquired this

money and was beginning to doubt if she could ever really adapt to a criminal life. Her conscience troubled her whenever she thought of the people she had helped to rob. But a sense of hopelessness invaded her as she remembered that in the world's eyes she was already an escaped felon.

'What else can I do?' she asked herself now, and could only answer, 'Nothing. Nothing else. I'm trapped into this life now, and there's no escape for me.'

'Grainne, I just asked you summat!' Bridie leaned over and shook her friend's arm. 'Come on, Dolly Daydream, are you game or not?'

Grainne shook her head in bewilderment. 'What was it you asked me?'

'Are you game for a night out on the spree, girl? It'll cheer us all up.'

Grainne nodded. 'Yes, that's what I need,' she told herself. 'A night out somewhere, so I can forget my troubles for a few hours.'

'And you lot, what about you?' Bridie asked the men.

Her husband and Arthur Taunton agreed readily, but Morgan Hunter shook his head. The Brummage woman was waiting for him at Henley, and lately her jealous possessiveness was becoming a worry to him. He was ready to leave her for good, but she held certain properties of his, and he needed to regain those from her before he could make that final break. Also he realised that if he goaded her too much, she might well in a fit of jealous rage, inform against him to the authorities.

'I've got to go. I've urgent affairs to attend to.'

He was inwardly torn in separate directions. Now that the time had come for him to split from the gang, he was reluctant to do so, the reason for this being Grainne Shonley. Despite her rejection of his offer, he still wanted her, and hoped that she might have a change of heart. But, at the same time all his instincts told him that it was increasingly dangerous to remain in company with the others.

When he had left Edward Whitfield's premises that afternoon and made his way back to the villa, he had had the feeling that he was being tailed. He had utilised all his skills in doubling, and trapping, and had not been able to sight anyone of whom he could justly be suspicious, but still the uncomfortable sensation of being observed had remained with him, and now he felt distinctly uneasy.

He made ready to depart, and then glanced at Grainne. The sight of her beautiful face and lucent green eyes triggered off his hunger for her with an unbearable intensity, and he could not help but delay his departure.

'Where are you thinking of going tonight?' he asked Bridie.

'The George and Dragon down Steelhouse Lane. There's some prime acts put on there, and I feel like dancing.'

This was a casino, or music hall, where there were entertainments, bands and dancing.

Morgan Hunter mentally computed. His horse and gig were at the rear of the villa, and the horse was well rested and fresh. He could reach Henley and soothe his lover, and be back here in a matter of hours.

'I'll try and meet you there later,' he told the others, and with a parting smile at Grainne left them sitting around the table.

Reuben Murdoch and Albert Gittings were sitting behind some bushes on an open space of ground some forty yards away and opposite the villa. Both men were smoking cheroots and their haltered horse was cropping the grass a little distance from them. To any casual observer they appeared to be merely a couple of men enjoying the fresh air, as other men, women and children were doing on that fine warm evening all along the Pershore Turnpike Road.

They remained in their position until Morgan Hunter had passed them in his smart gig. Reuben Murdoch's broad features became worried and uncertain. 'What do you think, Albert. Should we take him in?'

The more experienced man shook his head. 'He'd be out again within hours. We've nothing to hold him on, have we, except suspicion? And once we take him, then we'll have warned the other buggers.'

'But he could be scarpering,' Reuben objected.

His companion shrugged. 'If he is, then there's not much we can do to stop him. I'll go with him. You stay with the rest of them.' He grinned with a degree of sympathy. 'I know how you're feeling, mate. But one thing you've got to get used to in our trade, is fuckin' frustration.'

Allowing Morgan Hunter's gig to almost disappear from view, Albert Gittings mounted the horse and trotted on after his quarry. Gusting a sigh as he realised his present impotence, Reuben Murdoch grimly settled himself to continue his vigil.

Chapter Thirty-five

The sound of the band echoed along the Steelhouse Lane, and the glaring, hissing gaslights of the George and Dragon casino drew the Saturday night merrymakers as flames draw moths.

'Get your entry checks here, ladies and gentlemen. Get your checks here. No admission without your entry checks. Get your checks here!'

A sweating corpulent doorman in greasy black evening dress and grimy white linen bellowed hoarsely in the casino entrance, and even as he shouted another man bellowed in angry outrage as he was carried bodily from the building by burly stewards, likewise clad in shabby evening dress, and pitched headlong into the filthy roadway, to sprawl among the rotting refuse and animal excreta.

'There you see,' the check seller chortled happily. 'That's what happens to them who doon't get their checks. Get your checks here! Get your checks here!'

A pathetic crowd of beggars and street Arabs hovered around the entrance, but kept out of arms' reach of the burly stewards, now standing glowering at the ejected man.

'Spare a copper, lady?'

'Spare a copper, sir?'

'Do you want a nice time, ducky?'

The derelicts' entreaties mingled with the invitations of the drabs and streetwalkers standing in the shadows of the walls where the glaring lights would not reveal their raddled flesh.

'Do you want anything, darling?'

'Show you a good time and cheap, darlin'.'

'Help an old sodger, sir?'

253

'Spare a copper, sir? Spare a copper, sir?'

'How much for the checks?' Steven Fleming demanded, and the doorman told him.

'Sixpence a check for the gentlemen, my lord, and fourpence for each of the ladies.'

'Right then.' Steven Fleming bought two sixpenny brass counters and two fourpenny, and led his party into the overheated, smoky din of the casino's concert room.

Both he and Arthur Taunton wore immaculate evening dress, their persons glittering with jewellery and exuding the scents of expensive pomades.

Beneath their cloaks Grainne and Bridie were dazzling in fashionable and expensive ballgowns, cut low to show off shapely shoulders and the powdered tops of rounded breasts. They also glittered with jewels and their hair was worn long and held in elongated jewelled nets.

'Here, you.' Fleming beckoned imperiously to a steward, and handed him a golden sovereign. 'We want a decent box, and then you can see that we're well looked after. There'll be another of those for you if you do so.'

The brutal face of the huge steward creased into an ingratiating grin, and his manner metamorphosed instantly from surly truculence into servile obsequiousness.

'Certainly, your honour. Be so good as to follow me, if it pleases you, your honour.'

He bludgeoned a clear passage through the crowds with his massive shoulders, and those who resented his rudeness took one look at his face and body and swallowed their protests.

Grainne stared about her with a lively interest. The room was long and wide, and filled with rows of trestled tables flanked by benches crammed with men and women, of all ages and types, and in a multitude of different costumes, drinking, eating, smoking, flirting, laughing, gesticulating, talking and disputing.

Each side of the room was lined with elevated boxes occupied by well-dressed parties, and at the far end opposite to the entrance doors was a raised stage which jutted some distance forwards and had tables at its sides but a clear space for dancing before it. Above the entrance was a wide gallery supported by iron pillars with a bar and a promenade, where tawdry-clad, painted women offered their own wares with discreet smiles, and meaningful glances.

On the stage at this moment was a small band playing accompaniment to a red-faced male singer, straining his voice to its utmost in an ineffectual effort to make it heard above the din.

Grainne and her party took their seats in a box close to the stage, and Steven Fleming tossed their brass checks onto the table.

'What do you fancy, girls?' He was in high spirits. 'You can change these for apples, oranges, cakes, ginger ale, porter, beer or cigars.'

Bridie made a mock grimace of disgust, and her husband laughed and told the steward, 'Send a waiter to us. And don't forget to come and see me before I leave.' He winked broadly. 'That's just so long as you make sure we don't get troubled in any way.'

'Don't you worry, your honour,' the man assured him forcefully, and brandished one great scarred fist before their eyes. 'Anybody who looks twice at you 'ull soon get this in their chops. I'll see that youm well looked arter, your honour.'

His huge body blundered away in search of a waiter and Steven Fleming saw Grainne's puzzled look, and told her, 'These places can get a bit rowdy, Grainne, and there's always drunks who're ready to insult fine gentry like us. But we'll not be troubled by any of them now that I've pieced off that bruiser.'

A perspiring waiter hurried to bring the newcomers brandies and port wine, cigars for the men and small cheroots for Bridie. Then he looked at his lavish tip and bowed happily. 'I'll keep me eyes on you, sir. Anything you need just raise your finger.'

The singer disappeared from the stage to be replaced with a group of acrobats who postured and shouted and contorted their bodies in grotesque poses to the delight of the crowd.

The hours passed and Grainne became light-headed from the effects of the wine, and found herself giggling inordinately. A sense of warmth and wellbeing pervaded her and the world took on a roseate hue. It seemed that she had only to wish for something, and attentive waiters instantly produced it. If she required a favourite tune, then the band played it, their conductor bowing low towards her, and the entire band lifting the glasses of drink that she had bought them in salute to their benefactor. Grainne had never before in her life known what it felt like to be able to spend money like water without a care for the morrow, and she found it a headily intoxicating experience.

'Now you know what it's like to be a swell mobsman, my duck,' Steven Fleming grinned at her, and she smiled back at him through a haze of alcoholic happiness.

Half hidden by one of the iron pillars supporting the gallery, Reuben Murdoch sipped his glass of porter and kept his eyes on the beautiful green-eyed girl in the box. He saw her smiling and laughing, and found himself wishing that it was him she was smiling for, and his sallies that she laughed at. He was forced to remind himself repeatedly that she was in the opposing camp to his own, and that he was here to hunt down her and her companions, not to worship her from afar and indulge himself in hopeless daydreams about her.

A bitter sense of regret seared him at one point, and he almost turned away and walked out of the casino.

'Why did she have to be a flash girl and a thief? Perhaps even worse, a gonoph's mot and gay girl?'

He watched with jealous eyes as she casually leaned across to touch the tall slender young man's arm, and then laughed with head thrown back, soft white throat exposed, at some quip the man made.

Later after the stage acts had ended dancing began, and Reuben envied the tall slender man as he swirled the green-eyed girl around the floor in waltzes and polkas.

The night came to a close, and the band packed up its instruments as the casino began to empty of its horde of pleasure-seekers. Outside the crowd spilled across the roadway, and a line of carriages plied for hire, while the beggars and the street-walkers swarmed in ragged, bedraggled desperation, and hidden in the shadows other more sinister figures lurked like savage beasts of prey, seeking the solitary drunk who could be followed, bludgeoned and stripped on his homeward path.

A pair of top-hatted, greatcoated policemen stood opposite the casino entrance, and Steven Fleming grinned and jerked his head towards them as he and his party came out onto the street.

'There now, ain't it a comfort to know that we're being so carefully looked after by the crushers?'

Grainne could not help but laugh at his droll tone, and still smiling she looked casually around her at the seething noisy mass.

Across the street Reuben Murdoch turned away as the green-eyed girl's regard swept across the intervening space, and when he next looked back he saw the party was moving down the street towards the line of hire-carriages.

Grainne felt completely content as she walked along arm in arm with Bridie, the two men following behind.

'I've really enjoyed myself tonight, Bridie,' she told her friend, who chuckled and agreed.

'And me, honey. We needed a good night out. And there'll be lots more of them, you'll see.'

Reuben Murdoch remained where he was, watching the four move slowly away. Then, directly in front of them a sudden flurry and commotion erupted.

'You fuckin' useless bitch!' The tall man's lips were slack and slimed with stale grease, and his face was vicious with drunken hate.

He grabbed the streetwalker and slammed her brutally against the wall, and his fist smashed into her haggard painted face.

'No, Henry! No!' the woman screamed piteously, before the fist smashed into her face again, crushing her lips and bursting the soft flesh so that blood flew from her mouth. She fell to her knees and the man's hands wrenched at her tangled frizzed ringlets, dragging her head back so that he could smash his fist into her face yet again.

She vented a muffled shriek and he stepped back. Then while she huddled against the wall trying frantically to shield her bleeding face, his boots thudded into her.

Grainne had come to a standstill, her eyes wide with horrified recognition. 'It's Fanny! Fanny Caldicot!' she gasped, and Bridie questioned, 'Do you know her?'

'I know both of them!' Grainne uttered, shaken by the suddenness of this happening. 'His name is Henry Jenkins.'

A clustering mass of excited onlookers gathered around the

couple almost instantly, some protesting against the man's savagery, others callously applauding and cheering him on.

Jenkins staggered drunkenly, then steadied himself to kick again at the terrified, screaming woman.

'Stop him!' Grainne demanded, and Steven Fleming and Arthur Taunton stared at her in amazement.

'You don't interfere between a man and his mot, Grainne. Neither of them will ever thank you for it,' Steven Fleming declared, eyeing her as if astonished she should even suggest such a course of action.

'But he's killing her,' Grainne protested.

'We've got to think of ourselves, girl,' Arthur Taunton put in, and both of the Flemings voiced their agreement with him. 'We can't afford to draw any undue attention to ourselves. We risk our own necks if we do. Come on now, let's be off.'

Taunton attempted to grasp Grainne's arm and to pull her away from the scene, but she angrily thrust him off.

'Let me be. Something's got to be done to help her.'

'You fuckin' lazy bastard! You've earned fuck all today! I'll learn you, you stinking piece o' shit!'

Henry Jenkins spewed filthy abuse through his wet lips, and kept on kicking and stamping on the defenceless flesh of the huddled woman, whose screams had now become a half-choked howling of agony and fear.

Grainne stared in horror at Henry Jenkins, taking in his shabby dirty clothes, and his debauched, unshaven features. Behind her and across the street, Reuben Murdoch saw what was happening and went to the two uniformed policemen. Quickly identifying himself he told them, 'I can't intervene, I'm on a job. Will you take that animal in?'

They both stared at him with contemptuous grins.

'You must be a real Johnny Raw,' the elder of the two sneered. 'We got better things to do than to waste our time with scum like that.'

Reuben could hardly believe what he was hearing. 'There's a woman being beaten half to death there, and it's your duty to prevent it.'

'There's a tanner-whore being give a hammering by her bloody ponce. It happens all hours of the day and night in this city, my bucko. If we was to interfere, why then she'd be the first to turn against us and try to stick a chiv in our guts.' The man shook his head. 'Like I said afore, we got better things to do than to worry what the scum gets up to with one another. We'm here to protect the decent respectable citizens, not the shit.'

'Are you telling me that you're going to do nothing?' Reuben was becoming angry.

The elder policeman grinned sneeringly and nodded. 'You've got it in one, my chavvy.' He jerked his head towards the noisy tumult. 'If you're so worried about a bloody slum whore, then you go and stop it.'

With that, he and his partner turned on their heels and walked with ponderous dignity in the opposite direction.

Reuben's thoughts raced wildly. To intervene now in the presence of the green-eyed girl would betray his identity, and would most definitely alert the gang to their own danger. All the long weary hours of careful surveillance would have been for nothing.

From out of the commotion there sounded a raucous jeering shout.

'That was a corker, mate! Right on target! That's done her snot-box a power o' good, I don't think!'

Reuben peered across and saw the drunken man stagger and then steady himself, as if he had just lost his balance by delivering another wild kick. The young man shook his own head and then started across the street.

'I can't let it carry on!' he decided. 'No matter what that woman might be, I can't let him keep on battering her like this.'

Grainne saw the boot land squarely in the middle of Fanny Caldicot's bloodied features. She heard the terrible shriek of agony, saw the explosion of blood from the shattered nose, and could stand no more.

'Leave her be, you bastard! Leave her be!' Howling with fury she hurled herself against Henry Jenkins, tearing at his face with her nails, kicking at his legs with her daintily-slippered feet.

'Hey up, now!'

'Here's the bloody cavalry come!'

'Give it to him, girly!'

'Sic him, girl! Sic the bugger!' The onlookers bawled and applauded their delight. 'Five to one the skirt! Five to one the skirt!' a wag roared, and was immediately imitated.

'Ten to one, the judy!'

'I'll take threes she taps his claret!'

'I'll give you twos on the bloke!'

Grainne's sudden onset had taken Jenkins by surprise, and at first he fell back, but then recovering he swung his fist and the blow caught Grainne on the side of her jaw. She staggered sideways, her feet cannoned against the kerbing and she tripped and went down.

'I'll fuckin' kill you!' Jenkins bellowed, and aimed a kick at her.

Reuben Murdoch came hurtling through the onlookers. He had kept his truncheon secreted in his inner pocket and as he reached Henry Jenkins he drew it and brought it slamming down on Jenkins' shoulder. The impact forced the man back against the ring of spectators, and they howled and thrust him upright once more.

Mad drunk as he was Jenkins snarled and came back at the detective, who ducked under his opponent's wild swing, and simultaneously smashed the truncheon across Jenkins' kneecap. He yelled and crumpled, both hands clasping his damaged joint.

The ongoing tumult had brought another policeman running from his adjoining beat, and when he saw the uproar he sprang his rattle. The loud staccato clattering fell on ears well used to the sound, and voices shouted in warning:

'It's the crushers!'

'Here's the crushers!'

The peculiarly penetrating sound of the rattle alarm ricocheted down the surrounding streets, and the two policemen who had earlier declined to aid Reuben Murdoch, now looked at each other.

'That's one of our own lads, not a bloody Jack,' the elder constable declared, and springing his own rattle as he ran, led his companion back towards the uproar.

The arrival of uniformed constables sent the crowd scattering back in all directions, only to coalesce and surge forward once more to eagerly watch and hear what took place.

Reuben Murdoch was the first to gather his wits. 'Get hold of those two cabs,' he ordered one of the uniformed men, and then the four policemen quickly bundled the two women and the man into separate closed carriages, and made the drivers take them to the Crooked Lane police station.

As the carriages rumbled away Arthur Taunton and the two Flemings exchanged looks of disgust tinged with alarm.

Then Arthur Taunton grimaced. 'I don't know about you two, but I for one won't be sleeping in the Pershore Road this night.'

Steven Fleming cursed softly, and answered, 'Nor us either.' He sighed and ejaculated, 'What possessed that stupid Irish mot?'

'She knew that whore,' Bridie explained. 'That's why she jumped in.'

'Well, she's just jumped into the bloody nick, arn't she, the stupid cow!' Steven Fleming spat out disgustedly. 'And we've lost a comfortable bed for this night at least. Come on, let's get back to the house and get our gear together. I want to be well away from there before the crushers come calling.'

'Grainne won't shop us, she's a diamond,' Bridie insisted. But her husband turned on her savagely.

'How can you know that she won't shop us? You know what the bloody crushers are like. They'll threaten to charge her with causing riots and then promise to let her off if she should be able to tell 'um anything interesting. Besides, didn't the Captain swear on his life that the Jacks had already got her marked at Bingley House? That young Jack who belted that bloke might well have been tailing Grainne tonight, for all we can know about it.'

'Hadn't we best split up?' Arthur Taunton suggested.

'All right,' the other man agreed. 'Me and Bridie can stay with Taffy Davis until this blows over.'

'How about the Captain?' Bridie wanted to know. 'He'll have to be warned.'

'I'll do that,' Taunton assured her. 'Let's you and me take a cab back to the house now. Steven, you fix up some transport and follow us there. I'll need a nag.'

The other man nodded. 'Taffy can fix me and Bridie up with a gig to shift our stuff to his place. He'll be able to fix you a nag as well. Let's get going now, we've not a deal of time, I'm thinking.'

Henry Jenkins, groaning and swearing with the pain of his damaged kneecap, travelled in the leading carriage with two of the constables.

In the other carriage Grainne sat with the sobbing, moaning Fanny Caldicot cradled in her arms. On the seat opposite Reuben Murdoch and a uniformed constable stared steadily at the women.

It was Reuben Murdoch who broke the uneasy silence between them.

'That was a brave thing you did, miss, tackling that fellow.'

Grainne was very worried by her present situation, and this caused her to react sharply to the young man's words of praise.

'If what I did was a brave thing, then why have you arrested me?'

'Who says you've been arrested?' The detective was trying to play for time. He desperately needed the advice of older more experienced heads about how he should handle this new development.

'Well, what else can you call it?' Grainne's anxiety caused her to snap aggressively at him. 'I was hauled into this carriage, and there's two policemen bringing me along with them to their station. That's being arrested, isn't it?'

The uniformed constable was the grizzled veteran who had initially refused to aid Reuben, and he was feeling equally uneasy now about the possible consequences to himself of that refusal should the young detective report it to his superiors. He growled at the girl, 'Shut your mouth, young 'ooman. You've been arrested for breach of the peace, making an affray and, if that ponce in front of us chooses, he might well charge you with assault. Is that enough for you to be going on with?'

Fanny Caldicot's sobs and moans increased in tempo, and Grainne looked worriedly at her.

'Can't we get her injuries seen to before anything else?' she asked Reuben Murdoch.

'When we get to the station I'll send for a surgeon to come and look at her,' he promised.

Now that he had calmed as the excitement engendered by the fight ebbed from him, he was once more uncomfortably conscious of how powerfully this green-eyed girl affected him. He wanted desperately to be able to be alone with her, and to talk to her without constraint. At the same time the knowledge that she was a member of a gang of swell mobsmen gnawed painfully at him.

He turned to the grizzled constable and requested in a voice low enough to prevent the women from understanding him, 'I need your help, mate.'

The older man sensed that he was being presented with the opportunity to avoid censure for his earlier refusal to help, and so was quick to assent. 'Anything I can do, you've only to ask me.'

'When we get to Crooked Lane don't rush to press any charges straight away. I'm going to ask the desk sergeant just to shove this lot in cells and hold them for a while until I'm able to have a talk with Detective Inspector Hall.'

'All right,' the man nodded. 'But do I get credited with the collars when charges are pressed?'

It was Reuben Murdoch's turn to assent, which he did readily. Both men knew that the formality of taking down the particulars of the prisoners could be delayed if necessary. After all, prisoners such as the ponce and his mot would most probably only give false names and a farrago of lies anyway until such time as they could be properly identified.

At Crooked Lane the two women were hustled into one cell, and Henry Jenkins into another. A surgeon was sent for to examine the prisoners' various injuries, and Reuben Murdoch closeted himself with his superior officer. William Hall listened without comment or interruption to all that his new detective had to tell him, then sat and pondered briefly when the young man was done.

Eventually he asked, 'How sure are you in your own mind that this young woman is part of Morgan Hunter's swell mob?'

'In my own mind I'm certain of it,' the young man stated positively.

William Hall nodded as if satisfied, and then asked, 'Why did your girl jump in to help the whore, do you think?'

Reuben had not really given any great thought to this point

before. He had unconsciously assumed that it was the act of a Good Samaritan. Now he frowned, and the older man grinned knowingly.

'It would be a rare woman who intervened between a ponce and his mot in such a case, wouldn't you say, my boy? Particularly when as you tell me, that woman is dressed like a respectable lady of quality, like rich gentry. I can't help wondering if they might have had a previous acquaintanceship. Go and fetch the whore in here. And from now on I want her kept separate from our pigeon.'

Reuben stared at his superior in puzzlement, and Hall winked slyly at him, 'Just keep quiet and listen and learn, my boy.'

When the snivelling Fanny Caldicot limped into the room, her smashed nose already plastered by the surgeon, William Hall behaved towards her with all the fond tenderness of a father towards a favourite daughter, seating her in his own chair, enquiring as to her comfort, pressing a glass of gin into her hand.

'Now my dear, I just want you to answer a few simple questions, and then I'm going to see to it that you've got a comfortable bed for the night, so that when I release you tomorrow you'll be well rested.'

She stared at him with open disbelief in her eyes, and he smiled reassuringly.

'You've nothing to worry about, young lady. I've only had you fetched in here for your own protection. You'll be free tomorrow, and have money in your pocket as well.' He paused to gauge the effect of the offered carrot, and then showed the stick. 'Just so long as you tell me the truth, and don't try to gammon me. If you should try to tell me any lies, or to hold anything back from me, then matters will take a turn for the worse for you. I can promise you that.'

He urged her to drink her glass of gin. 'Get that down you, my dear, there's plenty more left in the bottle.'

Bemused, the wretched young woman drank and gasped and accepted another refill.

'Are you going to help me then, my dear?' William Hill enquired sweetly, and she nodded.

'Good. Now this won't take long. All I want to know from

you, is whether you knew that young woman who helped you before you saw her tonight?'

Fanny Caldicot nodded, and her eyes, slitted now in swollen blackened flesh, glittered with sudden hatred. 'Oh yes, I know that Irish bitch all right, sir. I knows her well.'

Hall's hatchet face showed gratification, and he urged softly, 'You start from the beginning then, my dear. And tell me everything you can about her.'

In the event it took only a short time for Fanny Caldicot to relate what she knew about Grainne Shonley. Reuben returned the young woman to her cell, and following Hall's instructions supplied her with bedding, and settled her comfortably for the night. When he returned to the office the inspector was sorting through a pile of old and new wanted notices. He grinned at Reuben and handed him one of the notices. 'I thought I'd come across that name Shonley before, my boy. She's wanted for escaping from custody, and faces charges of theft and assault.'

Reuben Murdoch scanned the crudely printed sheet with a sickening sense of dismay.

'She really is a gonoph's mot!' he thought, and his face mirrored some of what he was feeling, causing his superior to regard him doubtfully.

'Are you all right, Detective Murdoch?'

Reuben took a grip on his rampaging emotions and, assuming an impassivity he was far from feeling, answered firmly, 'Never better, sir.'

'Fetch Shonley in here and let's find out what she can tell us,' Hall ordered.

Grainne's apprehension had been deepening since her arrival at Crooked Lane, and when left alone in the dark, musty-smelling cell her courage had almost deserted her.

'It's not just because of what happened outside the casino that they're keeping me here,' she became convinced. 'They know about the other things.'

Paradoxically when Reuben Murdoch came and fetched her into William Hall's office all her stubborn courage returned in full measure. She found reality easier to confront than her own fearful imagination. William Hall gestured her to be seated on a tall three-legged stool placed in the centre of the room, and he perched on the edge of his desk to face her.

'Well now, how are you feeling, Grainne?' he asked pleasantly, and she started slightly with shock that he knew her name, then instantly realised that he had gained that information from Fanny Caldicot, and all hope deserted her. She drew a long shuddering breath and steeled herself.

'Oh yes, we know all there is to know about you, Grainne,' Hall continued, a confident smile lurking around his eyes and mouth. 'We know that you escaped from the custody of the Henley constables, and that you're facing theft and assault charges.'

'Those charges are false,' Grainne answered levelly. 'I've stolen nothing from Millwood Hall, and the assault was only me trying to defend myself.'

The smile on William Hall's features momentarily faltered, as he looked into the young woman's lucent green eyes. He was a man of vast experience in dealing with liars, and he sensed that this young woman was now speaking nothing but the truth.

'If the charges are false, then why did you escape from custody, Grainne? If they were indeed false then that fact would have been revealed at your trial.'

'Jasus Christ!' Grainne ejaculated in scathing disgust. 'I'd already been judged guilty by the magistrate who committed me to the quarter sessions! You know as well as I do that given that fact the result of any trial would have been against me.'

'So, you're saying that you are innocent of any wrongdoing, are you?' Hall's tone became hectoring.

Grainne's pale face flushed, and she hesitated noticeably, before muttering, 'I'm innocent of those charges.'

Inwardly she was mortified by her own reactions, and bitterly castigated herself, 'You can't afford conscience now, you stupid melt! It's your freedom you're losing here. Just because you've helped to steal a few purses and watches doesn't make you an evil bitch! Do whatever you must to get free.'

But no matter what degree of self-directed anger she was capable of generating, she could not hush her own tormented conscience at having helped to rob people who had done her no harm.

'Where does Morgan Hunter hide out?' Hall snapped.

Grainne's colour heightened still further, and she dropped her head.

'Come now, young woman, stop wasting my time!' the inspector suddenly shouted, causing Grainne to jump in shock. 'We know that you're a member of a swell mob. And we know that you've been cly-faking with your confederates at Bingley House. We can prove that. So for your own sake you'd best tell me where Morgan Hunter is.'

A curious sense of relief burgeoned within Grainne's mind, and she felt as if a great weight had been lifted from her. With a feeling of wonderment, she found herself almost eager to pay the price of her own misdeeds, and somehow knew that she would have no real peace of mind until she had atoned for her crimes and dispersed the cloud of self-guilt which constantly enveloped her.

She lifted her head and met the inspector's challenging eyes.

'If you can prove my guilt, then that's fair enough. But I don't know where this Morgan Hunter you speak of is. And I'll tell you nothing about anyone else.'

'Oh yes you will, young woman!' Hall grated out, and began to badger her relentlessly, shouting threats and abuse, telling her lies about the information others had laid against her, implying physical menace. But Grainne stubbornly defied him, and remained silent. The interrogation lasted for more than two hours, and then William Hall abruptly jerked his head at Reuben Murdoch.

'Take her back to her cell, then come straight back here to me.'

The young man had been an unwilling witness to the interrogation, and had been forced into the unpalatable realisation that he was indeed infatuated with this green-eyed girl. He knew how stupid and unjustified such an emotion was, but he was unable to control or diminish it.

Now he escorted Grainne back to her cell, but could not bring himself to either speak or even look directly into her face. For her part, Grainne felt unaccountably serene, and as she sat down on the bare wooden sleeping shelf that was bolted to the cell wall she marvelled at her own lack of grief or worry.

'What's to be, will be,' she told herself calmly. 'And at this moment I'm feeling able to face whatever might be in store for me.'

William Hall grinned wryly at Reuben Murdoch.

'She's a bit of a hard nut, isn't she?'

The young man nodded sullenly, and his superior looked knowingly at him, and said, not unkindly, 'If you stay in the police service, my boy, you'll be meeting a good number of pretty women in distress. You'll have to learn to harden your heart against their beauty, or you'll never be any good as a Jack.'

Reuben ruefully accepted the point his inspector was making. 'I'll try to do so, sir,' he answered stiffly.

'Trying isn't good enough,' Hall snapped curtly. 'You must do it, or I've no room for you in my department.'

After a brief pause the young man nodded. 'I will, sir. It's just that this is all very new to me.'

'Good!' the older man accepted, then went on brusquely. 'We'll get nothing out of Shonley. She's not the informing type. But with any luck Gittings will still be on Hunter's tail. Once we've got Hunter, then the rest will fall like bloody skittles.'

Disturbing thoughts had been racing through Reuben's mind as the other man was speaking, and now he ventured hesitantly, 'Sir, did you believe Shonley when she claimed to be innocent of any theft from Millwood Hall?'

Hall's shrewd eyes showed appreciation. 'You caught that too, did you, boy? She spoke with the ring of truth there, didn't she?'

'I thought she did, sir,' Reuben spoke more positively.

'Then we're in agreement.' Hall patted the younger man's shoulder as if in congratulation. 'You've got the makings of a prime Jack. You've been born with the right instincts for the job.'

'But if she is speaking the truth, sir, and she is innocent of what they've charged her with, surely we should do something to find out what the truth really is about Millwood Hall?' Reuben asked eagerly. 'Surely we can't let the woman be punished for something she hasn't done?'

The other man's hatchet features were emotionless, and he shrugged carelessly.

'Millwood Hall and Henley in Arden don't come under our care, Murdoch. So that's a matter for the local constables and beaks to settle. It's nothing to do with us.' He frowned warningly. 'We've got more work than we can handle right here in Brummagem, Murdoch, without going looking for extra out in bloody bumpkinland. So you just keep your mind on present matters. I want Morgan Hunter and his bloody swell mob, if only to shut Alderman Bolton's jawings.

'Before you go off duty you can write up the charges against that bloody ponce. We'll put the bugger inside for a while. His poor silly Judy can go tomorrow. By the looks of her she needs a bit of a holiday from him.'

Reuben Murdoch had the good sense to keep his expression and tone neutral.

'What's to be done about Shonley, sir?'

'We'll put her in front of the beak tomorrow, and get her remanded to our custody. I shan't be turning her over to Henley until I've finished with her here.'

'Very good, sir.' Reuben Murdoch turned away, but already ideas were taking shape in his mind concerning Grainne Shonley's possible future.

When he had finished the charge sheet against Henry Jenkins, Reuben went to the duty cell-keeper and asked to be let into Grainne Shonley's cell. The young woman was still awake, sitting on the wooden sleeping bench, staring at the dirty wall with its crudely scribbled graffiti.

'Mrs Shonley, I just want a few words with you.'

She regarded him calmly, and he felt again that sharp regret that she should be on the opposing side of the law to him.

'First of all I want to explain something to you.' The detective tried to keep emotion from his looks and voice, and to present an impassive façade. 'We want Morgan Hunter and his gang. If you should agree to tell us where we can find them, and to turn queen's evidence against them, then I think that you could be granted immunity from prosecution yourself.'

Grainne shook her head. 'No, I'll not turn queen's evidence.'

'Listen, we know that you're one of the gang. I was at Bingley House myself and watched you working with them. There is no way that you can avoid being sent to jail, maybe

269

even transported, unless you agree to turn queen's evidence.'

Again without hesitation Grainne told him emphatically, 'No! I'll never do that.'

Inwardly she was offended that any policeman could even suggest that she would be capable of betraying people who had befriended her.

'Very well.' The young man reluctantly accepted her refusal. Then he asked, 'What about Millwood Hall, Mrs Shonley? Why should you have been accused of stealing from your employer there?'

Grainne frowned at him curiously. There was something in his manner and tone which seemed to indicate that he himself did not believe in her guilt. Yet she felt wary that his question might be designed to trick her into somehow revealing information about her fellow gang members.

Her suspicious attitude stung Reuben Murdoch into a flash of anger.

'Look, Mrs Shonley, I'm not asking you this for any other reason but my desire to find out the truth. I'm not one of your swell mobsmen, Mrs Shonley. I'm a policeman, and I don't deal in lies and trickeries when that would entail injustice.'

He extended his forefinger towards her and as if admonishing a naughty child waggled it in front of her face, as he lectured, 'I'm quite prepared to press charges against you for what I saw happen at Bingley House, and if that means that you are sent to jail, then so be it. That is the due and rightful process of law. But I would not be happy in my own mind to see anyone convicted and punished for crimes they are innocent of committing. You told Inspector Hall that you were innocent of any wrongdoings at Millwood Hall, and both he and I thought that you spoke with the ring of truth. So tell me now your version of what occurred there, and why you were wrongfully accused by your employers. And if I believe what you tell me, then I will do my utmost endeavour to help you in the matter.'

Grainne's uncertain frown remained on her face, and inwardly she wrestled with her quandary. One part of her wanted to accept what this young man was offering, the other part of her was still wary and suspicious of his motives.

Reuben Murdoch was percipient enough to understand the

dilemma tormenting her, and he said softly, 'You may find it hard to believe, Mrs Shonley, but the truth is all that I seek from you. My offer to aid you in the matter of Millwood Hall is not dependent on anything you can give me in return.'

She stared at him with questioning eyes. 'Can you really be so idealistic about seeking for truth?'

He shrugged. 'You may call it idealistic if you will, Mrs Shonley. I only regard it as the simple duty of any policeman to seek out the truth. After all, that's what we are paid for, isn't it, to do our duty?'

The conviction that this man before her was honest and genuine suddenly flowered in Grainne's mind, driving out her previous doubts as to his motivation.

'Very well,' she said quietly. 'I shall tell you all I can about Millwood Hall. I think I'd best begin with the story that I was told by the upper housemaid, a girl named Sarah Hobdon, concerning another girl named Flora Kemp and what happened between Flora Kemp and Edwin Herbertson, the son of my employers . . . '

Grainne talked on in her soft voice, and Reuben Murdoch listened intently, occasionally interjecting a question, or asking for reiteration of certain points. When she had finished and fallen silent the young detective's broad red face was very serious. Grainne's green eyes fixed on his, and he could see the pleading in their lucent depths. He nodded slowly.

'I believe what you've told me, Mrs Shonley. And I promise you now, that no matter what may happen concerning the swell mob you've become part of, I'll do my best to bring this Edwin Herbertson to book for what he's done, and to prove your innocence of his accusations against you.'

Her grateful smile caused his heart to pound and, embarrassed that his expression must be betraying the way he felt about her, he quickly left the cell.

Chapter Thirty-six

Morgan Hunter was in a foul mood as in the early hours of the morning he guided his horse and gig around the rear of the villa on the Pershore Turnpike Road. Although the front of the house had been dark, the rear windows of the ground and first floor were showing the pale glow of gaslight.

At Henley his mistress had created a scene when he had told her that his visit was to be a brief one, and the echoes of her raucous tantrums still lingered in his mind. The quarrel had been long-drawn out and vicious.

'She really would have blurted everything out to her husband if I hadn't managed to calm her down,' he thought. 'Well, that's the last straw. Once I leave here then I'm done with the cow!' he told himself yet again as he drew his horse to a halt, and dismounted from the gig.

Before he could release the horse from the shafts the rear door of the kitchen was opened and Bridie Fleming called, 'Captain, get in here right away.'

He obeyed her urgent summons, and when he went into the house, frowned to see several trunks and carpet bags piled on the kitchen floor.

'What's this then?' he demanded.

'It's Grainne. She's been lifted by the bloody crushers.' Bridie Fleming's face was haggard with strain.

'What?' Hunter exclaimed incredulously, then drew a deep breath, and fought to stay calm. 'You'd best tell me all about it.'

The woman spoke volubly, her hands waving in agitation, and as she related her story Arthur Taunton came into the room behind her, carrying a bulging carpet bag. Morgan Hunter's expression hardened, and his mood grew murderous as he listened, but he kept himself under rigid control. When Bridie had done, and stood staring at him with wild, frightened eyes, he said through gritted teeth, 'Where's Steven?'

'He's gone to Taffy Davis to get a horse and trap for us, and another horse for Arthur. I was expecting him to be back here before now. I'm scared that the crushers might have lifted him as well, he's taking so long to get here.' The woman's voice rose to a frightened wailing as she spoke, and Morgan Hunter scowled and told her sharply, 'Don't panic, you stupid mot! That won't serve!'

'I'm not waiting for Steven any longer,' Arthur Taunton fluted nervously. 'I'm off now. I'll get the train back to the Smoke!'

Hunter turned on him savagely. 'You'll do no such thing! Just hold hard, and let me think for a minute.'

White-faced and visibly trembling with fear, the tooler stood shifting from one foot to the other, his long thin hands twisting upon the carrying-straps of his carpet bag.

Hunter's scarred face scowled contemptuously at the other man.

'Stop pissing your britches, Arthur. I'll get us all out of this.' He pondered for a few more moments then told them, 'Load all your traps onto my gig and go to Worcester. You can take rooms at the Horn and Trumpet there as man and wife. Lie low, and keep your mouths shut.'

'What about Steven?' Bridie wavered nervously.

'I'll need him to stay with me.' Morgan Hunter appeared sure and controlled. 'We'll come on to Worcester when I've made things safe here.'

'What do you mean, made things safe here?' Bridie queried doubtfully. 'We can all be safe once we're gone from Brummagem. There's no need for you and Steven to stay here at all.'

'Just do as I say,' Hunter ordered harshly.

Bridie's agile brain was working rapidly, and a fearful idea was taking shape.

'When you say you're going to make things safe, what do you mean by that, Captain?' she asked uncertainly.

273

'That's no concern of yours, woman. Now load those traps and get on your way.'

The fearful idea in Bridie's mind now crystallised into certainty.

'Look Captain, there's no fear of Grainne shopping us, you know. She's a diamond, she is.'

'I'll be the judge of that.' The man's control was perilously near to breaking, and his expression became so menacing that the woman involuntarily stepped back from him.

'Get on your fuckin' way. I'll not tell you again!' Hunter grated out, and Bridie's nerve broke, and she hastened to load her baggage into the gig with Arthur Taunton helping frantically.

Then the tooler took the reins and the gig went rattling away at a fast trot. As they swept through the darkness Bridie gasped, 'He's going to do something bad to Grainne, Arthur! I'm bloody certain of that! And there's no need because she's a diamond, so she is. She'll never shop us, I know that for sure!'

'That's her bad luck then, arn't it, if that's what the Captain intends. Sooner her get topped than me,' the man grunted unfeelingly. Then he protested, 'What can he do to her if she's locked away in the bloody crusher's hotel?'

'He'll find some way of getting to her,' Bridie stated with fearful certainty. 'He's devil enough to get at anybody he's a mind to, and you know that as well as I do.'

A sob burst from her, and she prayed fervently: 'Holy Mary mother o' God, look after that poor wee girl, I beg of you. Keep the poor wee soul from harm.'

Alone in the house, Morgan Hunter extinguished all the lights, and then left the building and crossed the roadway to where there was a stretch of open land dotted with shrubs and trees. He concealed himself in a clump of bushes, and settled to wait for Steven Fleming's return.

Some distance from him a weary but tenacious Albert Gittings also watched and waited.

The first palings of dawn were showing along the eastern horizons when Steven Fleming came trudging down the road, his fine clothing creased and muddied, his face sour and dispirited. As soon as he was satisfied that no one was following the other man, Morgan Hunter crossed to intercept him.

'It's all right, Steven, I know what's happened with Grainne. Let's walk this way.' He took the other man's arm and led him off the main highway to take a circular route back towards the city centre. 'Why haven't you got the horses and gig?'

'That fuckin' Taffy couldn't get hold of any when it came to the crunch,' Fleming complained bitterly. 'I've been waiting in his gaff all bloody night, because he swore he'd have them there first thing this morning. But nothing showed up. He reckons now it'll be this afternoon afore they come.' He shook his head. 'And pigs might fly. I wouldn't trust that Welsh bastard as far as I could throw him. Where's Bridie and Arthur?'

'I've sent them on to Worcester in my gig,' Hunter told him.

'Well, we'd best follow them directly I get changed.' Fleming stared ruefully down at his finery. 'I can't go tramping about the bloody country in this rig, can I?'

Morgan Hunter shook his head. 'We've got business to attend to here before we follow them, Steven.'

His companion stared curiously. 'What business?'

'We've got to make sure that that Irish mot can't turn queen's evidence,' Hunter said grimly.

'She wouldn't.' Fleming spoke confidently.

'Well, I can't take a chance on it.'

Fleming's thin face showed his apprehension. 'You mean to kill her, don't you Captain?' He shook his head. 'I don't want no part of that. That's a topping job, that is! Besides, if she's blabbed already then there's nothing to be gained by killing her, is there?'

'You're talking foolish, man,' Hunter scoffed contemptuously. 'She can tell the Jacks all she wants to, but unless she gets into that witness box and lays evidence against us in court, it won't do them a deal of good, will it? After all, they already suspect us, but unless they can produce a witness in court, what they suspect doesn't count as proof.'

Reluctantly the other man was forced to concede the point. 'You may be right there, Captain, but . . .'

'There's no but about it!' Hunter cut him short. 'It's either her neck or ours, Steven. And let me remind you of something that seems to have slipped your mind, my bucko. It was you

275

who insisted on staying here, when I wanted to split. It's you who's to be blamed for getting us all into this bloody mess. You should think yourself lucky that I'm ready to get us out of it.'

Fleming glumly nodded acceptance. 'All right, Captain. What's the lurk you've got in mind?'

'The crushers will have to bring her up before the beak today at the Moor Street public office. We'll be waiting for them to pass along New Street. We'll go to Taffy's gaff now and get ourselves different rigs. I've got a couple of barkers stowed away in the Hinkleys. We can collect them on our way to Taffy's.'

Again Fleming nodded in glum acceptance, and Morgan Hunter's hard face creased into a satisfied grin. In a sudden bizarre outburst of high spirits he laughed and clapped his companion on the shoulder.

'Cheer up, bucko, by this time tomorrow we'll be safe and sound in Worcester without a care in the fuckin' world.'

Albert Gittings cursed long and hard when he saw the two men leave the highway and begin to circle back towards the city centre.

With the dawn he had lost the shield of darkness, and at this hour there were very few people moving around this locality. To tail the two men without them spotting him would be an impossibility. Added to this was his consciousness of his own physical exhaustion. The past days and nights had taken a heavy toll of his strength, and he desperately needed to rest for a few hours.

'I'll head directly for Crooked Lane,' he decided. 'At least I've got this place marked, and his kennel at Henley.'

Gittings had left his horse tethered some distance further along the turnpike, and now he went to find that it had some-how broken its tether and had wandered off.

'Goddamn and blast the fucking thing!' he swore with heart-felt feeling, and wearily set out in search of the errant beast.

Chapter Thirty-seven

Grainne had spent a restless night. She had been given a threadbare, bad-smelling rug and a blanket and had tried to sleep, but the eruption into the neighbouring cells of bellowing, fighting drunks brought in by the night patrols had created an ongoing uproar which had constantly disturbed her.

When the dawn light penetrated through the small barred window of her cell she abandoned any further attempt to sleep, and began to pace up and down the cramped floor area in an effort to warm her stiff chilled body. She longed to wash herself and change her clothing, and to slake the thirst engendered by the after effects of the night's carousal. As she paced she examined her own mental state. Although depressed, she was able to accept with fatalistic resignation the certain prospect of being sent to jail.

'I helped to steal from strangers who had never harmed me, and I spent that ill-gained money for my own pleasure. It's only just that I should now face the consequences for my wrongdoing.'

The alternative of turning queen's evidence to escape punishment herself, she rejected utterly.

'It would be truly dishonourable to do such, and betray those who stood friend to me when I so sorely needed friends.'

A wry smile touched her lips. 'Here's me, a thief, talking about honour. How can a thief ever be honourable?'

She refused to indulge in self-pity. 'I called the tune, and I must now pay the piper.'

The nagging sense of shame which persisted in tormenting her, she could do nothing to dispel, except to remind herself that it was sheer desperate necessity which had forced her into theft.

The clumping of heavy boots sounded in the corridor and keys rattled in her cell doorlock. The heavy iron-studded door swung open, and the broad red face of Reuben Murdoch appeared.

'Here, Mrs Shonley. Have some breakfast.'

He offered her a piece of bread spread with salted butter, and a mug of steaming coffee.

The liquid was gritty and unsweetened, but she drank it gratefully to ease her raging thirst. The bread and butter she went to hand back to him.

'No thank you, Mr Murdoch. I'm not feeling hungry.'

'Keep it anyway.' He smiled. 'You may well feel hungry later on.'

She nodded and put it on the sleeping bench.

'Listen, Mrs Shonley, have you changed your mind about turning queen's evidence?' the young man asked.

She shook her head emphatically. 'No, I'll not do that.'

'Very well, I respect you for it, but at the same time I think that you are being very foolish to yourself.'

'That's as maybe,' she replied quietly. 'But I can only act as my conscience directs me.'

'Now, concerning your other problem.' Reuben Murdoch was pensive. 'My colleagues are much more experienced than me, and I'll need to ask their advice as to the best way of proceeding with such an enquiry. But I do give you my solemn promise, that I shall begin at the very first opportunity I have.'

'Thank you for your kindness.' Grainne was truly grateful. 'Is there anywhere I can wash myself? I'm feeling very stale.'

'I'll see if you can use the station washroom,' he promised. 'Today you'll be taken in front of the magistrate to be remanded into our custody.'

'Where will that happen?' Grainne was already anticipating the embarrassment and shame of appearing in public as an accused felon.

'At Moor Street,' he told her. 'The magistrates' courts are in the public office there.'

'Oh Jasus!' she exclaimed softly in distress. 'That means I'll be paraded through the streets, won't it?'

278

He nodded regretfully. 'I'm afraid it does, Mrs Shonley. The prisoners are taken on foot to the public office from all the stations. Fortunately, Crooked Lane isn't too far from Moor Street, so you'll not have to endure it for too great a distance.' He paused, and could not help but add, 'Of course, if you were to cooperate in the matter of giving evidence against Morgan Hunter, then other arrangements for transport could most likely be made. I'm sure that a closed carriage could be used to take you to Moor Street and back.'

She frowned and shook her head. 'I think the walk will be the lesser shame, Mr Murdoch.'

'As you wish,' he accepted, and said very sincerely, 'I truly do wish you luck, Mrs Shonley. It's a sadness to me that we had to meet under these unhappy circumstances.'

As soon as he had said this his ruddy colour deepened, and he appeared to become flustered.

'I'll speak with you later,' he muttered, and hastily vacated the cell.

Grainne considered for some moments, then a wry smile again briefly crossed her lips. 'Jasus, I think that young fella is a wee bit smitten with me.'

The irony of the situation afforded her a certain amount of grim amusement in the bleak hours that followed as she waited for her public ordeal to commence.

Chapter Thirty-eight

It was almost midday when the cell-keeper came to fetch Grainne to the wash-house. He worked the small handpump while she splashed water on her face and neck and arms, and handed her a piece of rough towelling to dry herself. Then he took her into a small enclosed yard where her fellow prisoners had been gathered for manacling. The first person she encountered there was Henry Jenkins, dirty and unshaven. His mouth spewed filthy abuse and threats at her until one of the uniformed constables present in the yard warned him sharply, 'One more peep out of you, chavvy, and I'll break your bloody head.'

A set of manacles were clamped onto Grainne's wrists, and those manacles then padlocked onto the end of a long chain which held the prisoners in a single snake-like file. She glanced at her fellows: the previous night's drunken brawlers, now sick-sober, blear-eyed, hangdog and bruised, three bedraggled young prostitutes, an elderly well-dressed man in frock coat and shiny top hat, a couple of filthy ragged derelicts, and several youths and men dressed like casual labourers, who eyed their surroundings with either depressed resignation, or cunning ferity.

To her relief, Henry Jenkins was several yards away from Grainne on the chain. A burly sergeant carrying an open ledger came into the yard, shouting, 'Give voice when you hear your name.'

He called out the names from the ledger and the prisoners responded to them. Then the sergeant warned, 'If any of you play up, or misbehave in any way while we're crossing to Moor

Street, then I personally guarantee that you'll sorely regret it. Lead off!'

The yard gate was opened and the snake-like file shuffled through it and out into the street. The sergeant led with constables on the flanks and at the rear. The appearance of the prisoners brought a howling of jeers and mockeries from the loungers and street Arabs, and shuffling at the end of the file Grainne's cheeks flamed. Never before in her life had she felt such a sense of humiliation as she experienced now, and she kept her head down and her eyes fixed on the ground.

Then, as the file passed the front of the station, Reuben Murdoch, smart in top hat and tailcoat, came hurrying down the steps to take station at Grainne's side, and help to shield her from the verbal brickbats hurled by the onlookers. A warm feeling of gratitude towards him coursed through Grainne.

'Bear up, Mrs Shonley. We've not that far to travel,' he whispered, but she was still too embarrassed and shamed even to look at him.

The small procession entered the glossy shopping area of New Street, and now it was well dressed shoppers who gazed avidly, or turned away with ostentatious displays of revulsion and disgust.

Further along the street a little distance past the Theatre Royal two men lounged in the narrow entrance of an alleyway that led to the fetid slum quarter of the Hinkleys. Both wore shapeless broad-brimmed hats pulled low on their foreheads, and kerchiefs around their necks which could be drawn up to muffle the lower parts of their faces. Their clothing was ragged and they wore similar patterned corduroy coats with wide skirts.

From his position in the alley's mouth Morgan Hunter could see almost the entire length of New Street, and now he straightened and told his companion, 'Make ready, they're coming towards us.' He peered for a few moments longer, and grinned in satisfaction. 'I've got her marked. She's right at the end of the file. That makes things easier.'

Surreptitiously he checked the priming and flint of the small pistol he held under his coat skirt, and warned the other man, 'Look to your priming and flint, Steven.'

Steven Fleming's face was pallid, and sweat ran in runnels down his cheeks. His hands were visibly shaking as he checked his pistol, and Morgan Hunter snorted with anger and contempt, 'Fuck me, man, you're shitting yourself, arn't you!'

'I'll be all right,' Steven Fleming mumbled sullenly.

'You'd better be,' Hunter growled threateningly. 'Because if you let me down, then I'm going to blow your fuckin' head off, after I've done for the Irish mot.'

Again he peered down the street, unhappy with the fact that the small procession was approaching on the opposite side of the roadway to the alley's entrance.

'Ah well, it can't be helped,' he shrugged mentally. 'We'll just have to move fast.'

He knew that he would have to break from cover and cross nearer to Grainne Shonley if he was to be sure of hitting her, because the pistols were inaccurate at any range over two or three yards. He glared at his frightened companion once more and warned, 'Wait for my word, then follow me out and do the business.' He slid his forefinger across his own throat. 'And remember what will happen to you if you let me down, Steven.'

The trembling man flinched and stuttered. 'I-I'll not l-let you d-down.'

The burly sergeant led his small procession past the alley entrance, and as the prisoners shuffled after him, Morgan Hunter jerked his kerchief up to hide his lower face.

'Now's our time!' he urged, and darted across the road directly towards Grainne.

Reuben Murdoch was positioned between Grainne and the alley, and he sensed rather than saw the oncoming man. In the middle of the roadway Hunter halted, raised his pistol, and fired. Grainne felt a thudding impact on her bare arm which half spun her. Hunter clubbed the empty pistol and hurled it at the young woman. It cartwheeled through the air and smashed into the side of her head, dropping her into a stunned heap upon the filth-strewn cobbles.

The crack of the pistol shot and Grainne's collapse caused the nearer passers-by to erupt in panicky confusion, and their shouts and screams shattered the air. Hunter turned and ran back towards the alleyway, and Reuben Murdoch went rushing after him.

Steven Fleming, unfired pistol clutched in one nerveless hand, stood transfixed, blocking the alley entrance, eyes wide and staring, mouth gaping open, face chalk white, and his entire body shaking uncontrollably.

'Clear the way, you gutless bastard!' Morgan Hunter roared, and tried to thrust the other man aside. Their bodies collided heavily, legs tangled and both went sprawling. An instant later Reuben Murdoch was on them with his truncheon flailing, to be joined in seconds by constables from the escort.

As soon as Morgan Hunter and Steven Fleming had been secured, Reuben ran back to where Grainne was lying on her side, her legs drawn up towards her stomach, blood seeping through her thick black hair and from her arm, and spreading in a widening stain across the bodice of her extravagant ball gown.

A middle-aged, white-haired man came hurrying from a nearby building, and thrust himself through the noisy excited crowd around Grainne.

'I'm a doctor. Have the girl carried into my surgery.'

Grainne was released from the long chain, and borne by willing hands into the nearby building. She was laid on a leather-covered table and while Reuben Murdoch and a constable cleared the room the doctor began his examination of her wounds. When he had finished he smiled reassuringly at the tense, worried-faced Reuben Murdoch.

'She'll live, young man. The ball passed through her arm, and lost most of its force as a consequence. See here.' He pointed to the blood-drenched side of her bodice. 'It's embedded itself between these ribs. I'll have it out in a jiffy. Her head is badly cut, but will soon heal. She's a very lucky woman.'

Reuben Murdoch grinned with relief, and asked with some degree of irony, 'What would you consider to be unlucky, sir?'

Chapter Thirty-nine

It was the following day before Grainne woke from sleep. The doctor had dosed her heavily with laudanum before he cut for the ball embedded in her ribs, and the drug coupled with the after effects of the blow on her head had ensured her remaining unconscious for many hours.

She felt she was rising from black depths up through succeeding layers of colours which shaded from deep purple to blue, to green, to yellow and opened her eyes slitting them against a blinding light. Dark blurred figures shimmered through the light and she blinked hard several times, and abruptly the figures stilled and solidified, and a white-haired man smiled down at her, with the red face of Reuben Murdoch grinning over his shoulder. Recollection flooded back, and she moved, then groaned as pain lanced through her arm and side and head.

'You must lie still, young woman, and let your wits gather at their own pace,' the white-haired man told her. Then he asked, 'Do you remember what has happened to you?'

'Yes, I do.' It was painful for her to speak, her lips and mouth were so parched.

'Drink this.' The man held a glass to her lips, and she sucked the liquid it contained, feeling an immediate easing in her throat and mouth as the drink moistened and softened the parched flesh.

Cautiously she moved her undamaged left arm and with her fingers explored the bandagings around her head, chest, and right arm. Seeing the burgeoning fear in her eyes the doctor soothed, 'Now there is nothing to worry yourself about, young

284

woman. Your injuries are not severe. Within a few weeks you will be fully recovered from them. I must leave you now for a little while.'

He spoke to Reuben Murdoch. 'You may talk with her for a short time, but do not prolong it. She needs to rest.'

When the doctor went from the room Grainne's eyes fixed on the young detective.

'Morgan Hunter? It was him who shot me, wasn't it?'

The policeman nodded. 'Yes. But he didn't get very far. We took him and Steven Fleming. They're in the cells at Crooked Lane. We expect to have all of Hunter's accomplices in custody before very long. Steven Fleming has already turned informer against Hunter. There are some people in Henley in Arden named Brummage who Fleming has incriminated as well. He's even turned in his own wife. Our lads are already on their way to Worcester to arrest Bridie Fleming and Arthur Taunton.'

Grainne sighed unhappily. The thought of her friend Bridie being put in jail distressed her. As if he could read her thoughts, Reuben Murdoch soothed her.

'I shouldn't think Bridie Fleming will get too harsh a sentence, Mrs Shonley. The law considers that a wife acts under the control of her husband, and that will be taken into account in her case.'

'And me? What is to happen to me?' Grainne asked apprehensively. 'I was not acting under a husband's control.'

His expression became pensive.

'I can't really know what exactly will happen to you at this precise moment, Mrs Shonley. However, surely now you must agree to turn queen's evidence against Morgan Hunter? He meant to murder you, and very nearly succeeded in doing so.'

Grainne hesitated, her thoughts whirling, and the young man persuaded, 'Listen, it will be a formality only. It's doubtful if you will even be called upon to give evidence against him for any other matter than his attempted murder of you. Now that Steven Fleming has turned informer it's not likely that we shall need to use you for the other charges.'

'Will I be charged also for that scuffle outside the casino?' Grainne questioned.

Reuben Murdoch shook his head.

'Inspector Hall feels as I do, that after what happened to you yesterday you've been punished enough. We know that you were only trying to help Fanny Caldicot. As for what happened in Bingley House, well, you had only been with this gang for a few days, and your role was such a minor one, that the inspector is prepared to overlook it if you will agree to aid us. So, will you give evidence against Hunter for trying to murder you, and if it is considered necessary about his leadership of the swell mob also?'

Grainne reflected briefly, and then sadly assented.

'That's the right thing to do, believe me,' Reuben Murdoch assured her.

He waited for a couple of moments to allow Grainne to come to terms with what she had agreed to do, and then smiled at her.

'I went to Henley in Arden last night, to bring in the Brummages for questioning. Morgan Hunter used their inn as his hiding hole. My colleague Albert Gittings had discovered that fact even before Fleming told us about them.'

'I've met with Mrs Brummage once.' Grainne grimaced ruefully. 'But it wasn't a pleasant meeting.' She sighed unhappily. 'When am I to be returned to the Henley constable?'

The young man shook his head. 'Perhaps never.'

She stared in shock.

'Listen very carefully, and say nothing to anyone else about what I am going to tell you,' the young man whispered conspiratorially. 'My inspector is cock-a-hoop because we've laid Hunter and his gang by the heels,' the young man preened himself unconsciously. 'And he has highly commended me for the part I played in it. To reward me, he has agreed to let me investigate fully your allegations concerning Edwin Herbertson's assaults on young girls.'

Burgeoning hope flooded through Grainne, and tears of gratitude filled her eyes.

'Because you are needed to materially aid me in that investigation, you are to be released into my custody on bail. I am standing surety for you.'

Grainne could hardly credit what she was hearing, and could only shake her head, as tears fell down her cheeks.

'I have some further good news for you.' Reuben Murdoch's

broad red features beamed delightedly. 'Because you were in our custody when you were wounded, the department has settled terms with the doctor for you to remain here in his house and under his care until such time as you are sufficiently recovered from your injuries, to be able to care for yourself.'

'Here, use this.' He handed Grainne a large white handkerchief, and as she wiped her eyes and blew her nose, he looked down at her with a loving tenderness glowing in his eyes.

'All will be well, Mrs Shonley. Trust me! I'll bring Edwin Herbertson and the Gurnock woman to book. Just trust me!'

She smiled through her tears at his homely features, and told him with absolute honesty, 'I do trust you, Mr Murdoch. I would trust you with my life.'

'I could hope that maybe one day, you might even be willing to share that life with me, Mrs Shonley,' he said gravely, and with an equal gravity she met his gaze and answered, 'I hope that someday that might be so, Mr Murdoch. I truly do so hope.'